CW00860407

555

WILLIAM ROBERTS

ATHENA PRESS
LONDON

555

Copyright © William Roberts 2009

All Rights Reserved

No part of this book may be reproduced in any form
by photocopying or by any electronic or mechanical means,
including information storage or retrieval systems,
without permission in writing from both the copyright
owner and the publisher of this book.

ISBN 978 1 84748 453 6

First published 2009 by
ATHENA PRESS
Queen's House, 2 Holly Road
Twickenham TW1 4EG
United Kingdom

Printed for Athena Press

For

Christine, Robert and Helen

who kept the faith

One

He lay awake for a long time before the alarm went off. When it finally broke the pre-dawn silence, he threw the bedclothes to one side, sat up and moved so that he could place his feet on the floor. The temperature was just above freezing in the small bedroom and the man shivered. In winter he always slept in his clothes and he only had to pull on his boots before making his way to the arctic wastes of the bathroom. The moonlight limping palely through the small frosted window was adequate for his purposes – he never shaved in winter. On returning to the bedroom he found his overcoat, hat, scarf and gloves that had been draped over the chair and got ready for his journey.

He made his way through the kitchen and opened the back door. The wind was icy and he stamped his feet on the step to get the circulation in his body going. He didn't bother to lock the door – he had nothing that was worth stealing – and crossed the backyard to where his bike and trailer rested against the side wall. A smile came to his lips. Many years before, when he and his wife were thinking of buying the house, they had laughed when the estate agent had described this part of the property as a 'rear patio'. It was a long time since he had smiled. It was a long time since he had seen his wife. The 'rear patio' was now piled high with junk and bits of household rubbish.

He blew on his hands before pulling on his gloves. The wind continued to blow and he was already chilled to the bone. He thought back to the days when he had sat in front of the fire with a cup of coffee before going out in weather like this. Those days seemed part of ancient history now. He collected his bike and disturbed a rat, which scuttled away out of the yard. The back gate had been stolen long ago and so he pushed the bike and trailer out into the passageway that ran along the back of the row of old terraced houses. Only the sound of the wind and his own breathing disturbed the quiet. At the end of the alley, he mounted the bike and crossed the now disused car park. When he reached the street he turned left and made his way slowly to the main road. He passed buildings, most of which were empty and derelict, that gave no protection against the cruel wind and he shivered again.

The main road, now renamed England Avenue, was the only road in the town that boasted street lighting and the man blinked as he reached the well-lit thoroughfare. He couldn't understand why the authorities wanted to light this street – if anything, it was in a worse state than the dark side streets that fed off it. It was full of shops. He had counted them one morning the previous summer.

Eighty-four retail units made up this shopper's paradise. The only problem was that there were only five shops that opened on any regular basis. All the others stood empty and derelict as monuments to a bygone age.

He was nearing the guard post at the end of the Avenue and he slowed, coming to rest by the red-and-white-striped barrier that blocked the road. No one was about but a light was on in the small hut and after a few moments the door opened and a guard made his way slowly towards the barrier.

'Good morning. How are you today?'

The man on the bike nodded, reached into his coat pocket for his papers and handed them to the guard.

'I'm all right, thank you. Are there any problems today?'

'Problems? No – none that we've heard of anyway. Could you do me a favour when you get to the Border?'

'I'll try.'

'Tell them we could do with some milk. I haven't had a cup of tea since last night.'

The guard moved to the side and lifted the barrier. He walked back to the cyclist and handed him his papers.

'Thank you. I'll tell them about the milk.'

The man carefully returned the papers to his pocket, re-mounted his bike and rode on. Behind him he heard the barrier being pushed back to the horizontal position and then the sound of the hut door closing. The silence of the February morning once again blanketed the Suffolk coastal town.

He turned left at the roundabout and pedalled hard for about two miles. Eventually he came upon the floodlit area that was the first sign of the Border. He reached the first barrier and stopped. There was no hut here for the guards, since they were expected to be on full alert at all times. The young guard shouldered his automatic rifle and raised the barrier.

'Come on through. Jesus, it's cold. I think my bollocks have dropped off. I've got to get a transfer soon. I can't stand any more of this.'

The man with the bike gave a bleak smile.

'The guard at the end of the Avenue asked me to ask you for some milk so that he can have a cup of tea.'

'Well he can piss off! Cheeky bastard, sitting in his little hut all night. He can do without his bloody cup of tea. Let's have a look at your papers – you might be a terrorist.'

The man reached into his pocket again and offered the precious documents for inspection. The guard glanced at them and quickly handed them back, then led the way and the man followed behind, wheeling his bike. They walked towards the gun emplacement, which was about thirty yards to the right of the barrier. Another guard was in the trench manning the gun. He gave no greeting to the man or his colleague. The tall floodlights picked out every detail of the barren wasteland that formed the border area. Dominating the scene were the two enormous fences, with the hundred yards of no-man's-land in between, which marked the actual border between the town and the rest of the world. The Border was built across the main trunk road that used to be the busiest road in East Anglia. No lorries came to the town now. Nobody in the town had any idea of what went on beyond the Border. The world finished at the Border.

The man unhitched the trailer from his bike and walked up to the gate in the fence with the guard. The guard took out the keys from his pocket and unlocked the padlock.

The man had been making this journey every day for three years and, although the guards were changed regularly, most of them knew him by sight. But in all that time he had never been allowed to ride his bike across no-man's-land. He had never been allowed to get this near to the Border without his papers being checked twice. He knew why. The guards were afraid. They were terrified that he would inform someone they were getting slipshod. He had no one to inform but he didn't tell the guards that. Let them have their fear, he thought. Everyone else was afraid, why not them?

His breath showed up starkly in the bright light and he looked around him, marvelling at the peace of the morning. Some stars shone down on the eerie scene. He wondered if God was looking down. He wondered if God was up there at all. He doubted it.

'OK. You can take the trailer through,' barked the guard.

The man went through the open gate and began his slow lonely walk across no-man's-land to the other fence. He heard the gate clang shut behind him. Although the distance between the fences was only one hundred yards, the gates were not directly opposite each other and the diagonal route between them was nearly double that distance. By the time the man reached the other side, he was sweating. He waited in front of the gate and felt very exposed. After a few minutes a face appeared from the darkness at the far side of the fence. Another minute elapsed before the electronic gate opened with a loud click. The man on the far side of the fence pushed it open and walked through pulling a trailer behind him. The gate clicked shut behind him leaving the two men together in no-man's-land.

The newcomer was old and dirty. His clothes, which seemed to have many layers, were in tatters. When he spoke, it was with a broad Suffolk accent.

'Mornin'.'

He reached out and the two men shook hands.

'Hello, Amos. How's things? Cold enough for you?'

'We don't need a freezer back at the farm anyway.' The old man laughed and rubbed his hands together. The two men were not friends – they had only ever met under these surreal circumstances – but there was a comradeship evident in their meetings. The man looked forward to their meetings but could not have explained why. Perhaps it was the absurdity of it all. A shopkeeper meeting his only supplier at five o'clock in the morning between two electrified fences with only a machine gun as witness. Perhaps it was the privilege of being able to talk to someone, however briefly, from outside the fence.

The two men began to transfer the goods from one trailer to the other. There was no need to talk. The shopkeeper was forbidden to buy goods from anyone else and he had never heard Amos admit that he had any other customers. He bought everything that Amos could grow but it was never enough. There was never anything left in the shop at the end of the day. The man handed over the money, the same amount every day, and Amos nodded. Two sacks of potatoes were the last items to be loaded and then the two men shook hands again. Amos raised his arm above his head and the gate opened. The darkness enveloped him as soon as he stepped through and the shopkeeper was alone again. He waited for the gate to close and then began to haul the trailer back to the inner fence. It was much harder work with a full load and he was sweating again by the time he reached the gate. The guard let him through and then watched whilst he hitched the trailer back on to his bike. They never helped. The man remounted his bike and set off back towards England Avenue.

The guard came out of his hut and raised the barrier.

'Did you get my milk?'

'No, sorry. Your mate said you can piss off because you've got the hut.'

'Charming! See you tomorrow.' The guard watched the shopkeeper begin to pedal to the town and then went back inside the hut.

The return journey took a lot longer with the loaded trailer and the man was nearly exhausted when he reached the shop, which was situated halfway along the still-deserted England Avenue. He unlocked the door, pushed it open and wheeled the bike and trailer inside. He switched on the one electric light that barely lit the whole shop. He began to unload the farm produce and stack it on the shelves. Thin carrots, limp beans and small, half-rotten cabbages made up today's uninteresting load. Only the potatoes looked fresh and worthy of sale. But it would all be sold. The man's customers had no choice. This was the only food shop in the town.

He went into the small back room that served as office,

stockroom and kitchen. There was no paperwork and no stock, but there was a kettle and the man began the preparations for his first cup of tea of the day. He always filled the kettle before going home at the end of the day in case the water was cut off at night. He found the box of matches and lit the battered old paraffin stove that was his most prized possession. He found the powdered milk and picked up a new tea bag, which would last him the whole day. He heard the sound of a car and, as it passed, he heard a dull thud as something hit the front door. He remembered when he had a newsagent's shop and his supplies had consisted of ten parcels of all the national newspapers with lots more of various magazines. Now all he got was one small parcel of the free paper, which was printed at the Town Hall. Four pages of crap. Everybody was supposed to read it but nobody did. He brought the bundle of papers into the shop and untied it. He looked at the headline on the front page – ANNIVERSARY OF 555. This incredible news had no effect on him whatsoever and he put the papers on the shelf without another thought. The kettle began to whistle and he returned to the kitchen. The stove had taken some of the chill off the room and, after making his tea, he sat down on one of the two rickety chairs. He pulled the chair nearer to the stove and took off his gloves. The tea warmed his whole body as he sipped it from the chipped mug.

This was his private time, his time for private memories and thoughts when no one – not even 555 – was permitted to disturb him.

Eventually, after about ten minutes, his thoughts were disturbed by the sound of the shop door being opened. He put the kettle back on the stove and began to make two fresh cups of tea. When he looked up, his shop assistant was standing in the doorway.

'Hello, boss. Where's my bloody tea? Christ, it's cold. I've got three pairs of tights on and I'm still fucking frozen.'

Her 'boss' smiled and handed her the tea. The man remembered Shirley Tate when she had been one of the best-looking women in the town. A proud, beautiful woman who had been admired by all the women and lusted after by all the men, she had probably been the happiest woman the man had ever met. She had lived with her husband and her twin daughters in one of the best houses in the old town. Now in her late thirties, she looked as if she lived on the streets. Her blonde hair was cut short, which only seemed to emphasise the lines on her face. Her daughters had been killed in the Chaos and her husband had disappeared. She never spoke about this time in her life but the man knew that it had left an indelible mark on her. At times, he was convinced she only survived on pure hate. Her attitude to the present state of things seemed outwardly to be one of indifference but she invited trouble with some of her comments to those in authority. Her clothes hung loosely about her still-firm body and she moved closer to the stove whilst drinking her tea.

'Everything go all right at the Border this morning?' she asked.

'Of course – why shouldn't it? It's always the same down there.'

'I worry that one day you'll have a problem and won't be here when I arrive. I don't know what I'd do if that ever happened. Don't you worry about it sometimes?'

'Not really. I tend not to worry about things I can't do anything about. If it happens, it happens – it's no use worrying about it. What could happen anyway? It all runs like clockwork.'

'I don't know. Perhaps the guards could all get AIDS or something equally pleasant.'

'Nice thought but you know as well as I do that there is no such thing as AIDS anymore – it's been banned.'

'Everything's been fucking banned except breathing. That doesn't mean it doesn't exist anymore.' She stood up and went to the door that led to the shop. Turning, she smiled and went over and put her hands on her boss's shoulders.

'Listen to us: what a pair of miserable old sods we are! Tell me a joke. Make me laugh.'

'I don't know any jokes,' the man said quietly.

'Liar! When you ran the shop in the old days you were always telling jokes and laughing with the customers.'

'That was a long time ago, Shirley, or it seems like a long time. There doesn't seem to be much to laugh about now.'

Their conversation stopped and both were left to their own thoughts. Shirley looked at the man and saw a shadow of the man she used to know. In her previous life, if she had considered being unfaithful to her husband, he would have been at the top of the list of possibles. Now neither of them looked at the other with any such thoughts. They were just two sad people, old before their time, living in a nightmare.

'Do you have to report today?' asked Shirley after a few minutes.

'Yes. I'll go early and get it over with, then you can get off at lunchtime. The queue seems to have been getting worse lately. Last month, if you remember, I had to wait for four hours. I'll open the shop and go, see if I can beat the rush.'

'I don't know why they bother. Same old questions, same old answers. I think I'll send a recorded message next time. I doubt if that old cow Emily Fairfax would even notice.'

'Now, Shirley, be careful what you say about our judge advocate. She used to be a friend of yours – a very good friend, if I remember correctly.'

'She stopped being a friend of mine when I went to see her after Geoff disappeared. Do you know what that bitch said to me?'

'No,' replied the man, 'but I have a feeling you're going to tell me. Stop it, Shirley – you're getting upset.'

He saw the tears forming in her eyes.

'Upset? No, I'm not upset. I'm fucking furious. Our glorious judge advocate said, "Ours is not to reason why, Shirley – 555 knows best." I'll never forget those words as long as I live. Fifteen years we were married and my husband is taken away to God knows where and all I get when I ask my best friend what has happened is "Ours is not to reason why". The bitch!'

She looked down at the bare floorboards. A tear fell by her foot. The man went over to her, put his arms around her and held her close. Despite the several layers of clothing they were both wearing, he could feel her body as it became engulfed with her tears. They stood in this embrace for a long time. Neither moved or said a word. The man felt her pain but could do nothing to lessen it. It was Shirley's pain and only she could suffer it. It was not transferable. Eventually she pulled herself away and looked at the man.

'Do you think he's dead?'

The man hesitated. What possible answer could there be to that question?

'Fuck knows – I certainly don't. I try not to think about things like that. Where are my lovely Rosie and the kids? If you start to try and unravel this mess we're in, you'll go mad. We have 555, the rules, Mrs Fairfax and the Border. End of story. Dry your eyes and let's have another cup of tea.'

'You sound as if you've given up,' said Shirley.

'I gave up ages ago,' said the man and walked into the shop. He looked at the shelves. They seemed to echo his life – empty and lifeless, old and dusty, no use to anyone.

It had grown light outside but the morning looked miserable and cold. Shirley brought the tea and the pair of them stood at the window, staring at the still-deserted street. She slipped her hand into the man's but he didn't seem to notice. After a while, he put his cup down, straightened his hat and without another word walked out. He turned right and slowly began to walk down England Avenue towards the sea.

Two

The morning was grey and the icy wind coming off the sea made the man hug his coat tighter around his still-cold body. There were a few people about now, making their way to work. Most of these were cleaners who worked at the various official and military offices that were dotted around the town. It was too early for the important people to be seen. They only began work at nine. The man quickened his pace and nodded greetings to the few people he recognised.

He reached the crossroads and stopped to ensure that no traffic was coming. This road, which ran parallel to the sea, was a favourite route for military vehicles and they were not noted for their observance of the now nearly forgotten Highway Code. Three people had been killed since summer while they had been trying to cross at this particular spot.

As he waited for an armoured car to pass, he looked up and considered the two buildings that faced each other on opposite corners of the junction. They had been branches of two of the big high-street banks and it had always seemed to the man that they had been like two boxers, waiting for the bell to sound so that they could start the fight to manage people's money. They were empty now and blackened from the fires that had engulfed them during the Chaos. They no longer fought for people's money. People no longer had any money – certainly not enough to warrant the use of a bank account – but the buildings still stood proud, dominating this part of the town.

His reverie was interrupted when a man came and stood beside him. George Fenton had been a friend for a long time. He was older than the man by a good twenty years but from the first time they had met they had found an affinity, which had developed into a deep and lasting friendship. In the old days they had played snooker and had a few pints together and George and his wife Cissy had often been round to the man's house for dinner. Now the two men hardly ever saw each other.

George Fenton was a fisherman; one of the very few left in the town. Once the proud owner of a seventy-foot trawler, he now plied his trade with a small rowing boat, using an array of old nets and lobster pots to catch whatever he could during daylight hours – the only time he was allowed to fish. In addition, he was not allowed outside the one-mile limit that was marked by the ever-present gunboats. It was a miracle he caught anything at all. He surrendered all the best fish to the authorities and sold the remainder from one of the few beach huts now slowly rotting on the pebbled shore.

He was a jolly, fat man who had retained his big stomach, which spoke volumes about the benefits of a fish diet. Small and round, he had not lost his sense of humour despite all the problems and the man always felt better after speaking to him on the few occasions when they met now. They turned to face each other and made a comic pair: George hardly reached up to the man's shoulder and the taller man had to stoop to hold a conversation with his little fat friend.

'On your way to give your report, are you, young fella?' asked George, clapping his gloved hands together in a vain effort to keep warm.

'Yes, I thought I'd try and get there early to avoid the crowds. How are you and Cissy these days?'

'Struggling along like everyone else, I suppose. Don't forget to tell them about all the sex you've had in the last month. Christ, chance would be a fine thing! Last time I went and they asked me about meeting any strangers I told them I'd met a German fisherman called Octo Puss. The stupid cow wrote it down and I never heard anything more about it. They're dafter than us. How are you anyway? Any news of Rosie and the kids?'

'Nothing. No one seems to know anything or if they do they're not saying. You be careful what you say – I wouldn't want to see you getting into trouble.'

'Ah, bollocks! They make me bloody mad with all their stupid bloody questions. You know when you're getting towards the end of your time and they let the next person into the room to speed things up?'

The man nodded.

'Well, three months ago, I went in and the man in front of me answered every question as polite as you like and then farted. Nobody took a blind bit of notice. I was nearly on the floor laughing. "Have you contravened Section 39?"; "No" – Varumph. "Have you had sexual relations with anyone in the last month?"; "No" – Varumph. Every question came and went with a "No" and a fart. Nobody said a word and that daft, old cow just kept writing down the answers. Talk about smell – it was fucking terrible.'

The man was laughing now. George was a good person to have around when you needed cheering up.

'Why do you think he did it?' he asked.

'I suppose it was his way of showing what he thought of the whole bloody farce. Nothing happened to him – I've seen him since. I think I'll try it next month. Have you got twenty tins of baked beans in that supermarket of yours?'

'I haven't seen a tin of baked beans for over a year. You be careful. I must admit, though, it would be good to see what would happen if we all did something like that. But what's the purpose of the report if nothing happens when people treat it like that?'

'No bloody purpose at all, my friend. None that makes any sense anyway – except it reminds us every month of our place in the scheme of things. I don't see why they ask us our name, address, age and all that other fucking rubbish because she's got it all written down in front of her. I suppose it gives the stuck-up bitch something to do but I can't see any other reason.'

'Did you know our judge advocate, Emily Fairfax – God bless her soul and keep her safe – in the old days?'

'Do you mean in the biblical sense of that word or just know her in the normal way?'

The man looked down at his old friend and saw him smiling.

'Don't tell me… Oh no! I can tell by the smirk on your face, you dirty old sod. How? When? I don't believe it – actually, yes, I do. Serious, was it?'

'No, don't be bloody stupid – it was crazy, really. I used to deliver fish to her house. She was one of those rich people who thought it was beneath them to come down to the hut to buy. She used to ring me up whenever she was having a dinner party and I'd deliver the fish up to the house. I didn't mind – I charged them double price and they thought they were getting the stuff fresher than anyone else. One day I went there and she was on her own and she invited me into the kitchen. Then she made it very plain that she was prepared to pay for the fresh sea trout in any way I wanted. She was a lovely-looking woman in those days – still is, come to think of it – and I had her on the kitchen table. Bloody good she was, as well. Neither of us has spoken of it since.'

'Did you ever tell Cissy?'

'No – why should I? It wasn't that important. It was more a question of being in the right place at the right time than anything else. The only problem was that she must have stopped eating fish because she never rang me up again. I lost a good customer but I'm not complaining.'

'Well, you learn something new every day,' said the man who now looked at his friend with renewed respect.

'Don't mention it this morning when she's taking your report – she might not like to be reminded of her past. Well, I've got to be going. Take care of yourself – I'll pop into the shop one day and we can have a good old chinwag. Cheerio.'

With that, the two men parted with a handshake and George set out towards what was left of the town centre.

The man crossed the road and continued on his way towards the sea. The road dropped steeply from the crossroads until it reached sea level after about two hundred yards. The flat part of the coast, along which the man now walked, had been cleared of all buildings and its monotony was only broken by the numerous gun emplacements that peppered its surface. It was a desolate scene and the man avoided it unless he had to cross it to reach the Town Hall, which still stood proudly at its southern corner. In days gone by, this part of the town had boasted amusement arcades and a funfair but these were long gone and nothing remained to confirm that they had ever existed. He reached the wire fence that encircled the Report Centre and showed his papers to the guard. He was admitted and crossed the fifty yards that separated the fence from the building. The old Town Hall –

displaying its plaque that announced that it had been built in 1897 – had lost none of its grandeur and stood as one of the few untouched monuments to a bygone age.

The man mounted the eight steps, pushed open the heavy oak door and walked inside.

The entrance hall was completely deserted and the man was able to stand and admire the wonderful architecture of the building. The black-and-white, marble-tiled floor caught the eye first. Laid out in a series of concentric circles, the tiles looked too much like a work of art to be actually walked on but even after a hundred years of almost constant use there was not a mark on them. The man looked up and let his eyes wander over the oak-panelled walls before gazing at the high vaulted ceiling. Stucco angels and seraphs hung suspended, peering down on the tranquil scene. It was perhaps the only building in the town where time had stood still. Its splendour belonged to another age and it seemed totally out of place when compared to the surrounding devastation.

The man walked to the wide staircase, which was on the side wall, and made his way to the old magistrate's court that now served as the Report Centre. The first floor was nowhere near as grand as the entrance hall downstairs. There was no oak panelling here – only pale walls covered with innumerable coats of ivory-coloured emulsion. There were two doors in the corridor – one of which had a sign which said 'No Admittance' and another, which bore no sign. At this unmarked door a small queue had formed. The man joined the queue and noticed there were four people ahead of him. He knew from past experience that within half an hour or less this snaking line of miserable people would stretch along the corridor, down the stairs and out into the freezing morning air. He knew no one in the queue and nobody spoke. The man had no watch and there were no clocks in the corridor but he reckoned that they only had a few minutes to wait before the whole procedure began. More people joined the queue behind him and soon the corridor was full.

After a short while, the door was opened, the first person entered and the queue shuffled up. Half an hour elapsed before the man was first in line and, when the door opened with a loud click, he stepped inside.

The old magistrate's court – now the Report Centre – had not been changed in any way. The same furniture was there with places for lawyers and the accused and, dominating the room was the bench where the magistrates used to sit in their glory. Only one of their high-backed thrones was occupied now. In the middle sat the judge advocate for the coastal region of south Suffolk: Mrs Emily Mary Fairfax.

Only two other people were in the room – the woman who had been in front of him in the queue was giving the last of her answers in her report and the questions were being asked by the recorder whilst the judge advocate wrote down the answers. The recorder was a tall pale-faced man who sat at a large table below the bench. The man didn't know his name or where he lived – he had never seen him about the town. The woman had finished her report and sidled out of the door marked 'Exit'. The man made his way to the dock where the accused used to stand and waited. The recorder, already sounding bored, shuffled through the papers in front of him and handed a sheaf of them to the judge advocate above him.

Although she never spoke, there was never any doubt who held the power in this room.

Emily Fairfax was a striking woman who looked much younger than her fifty-five years. Her perfectly oval face bore no blemish and was meticulously made up. Her wide, full mouth spoke of a beauty when she was younger and her wide forehead gave hints of a woman happy with the power she wielded. Her jet-black hair was tied tightly in a bun at the back of her head. She wore a plain lawyer's gown over a scarlet suit and presented a dominating and severe picture to the world as the recorder turned to face the man and began the interrogation.

'Name?'

'Philip Edward King.'

'Address?'

'108 Victoria Way.'

'Age?'

'Forty.'

'Occupation?'

'Shopkeeper – general groceries at 42 England Avenue.'

'Marital status?

'Married – wife Rosamund, son Robin and daughter Deborah – whereabouts of all three unknown. Disappearance of all three notified to the authorities on 14 November 2015.'

'Since your last report, have you seen, met or spoken to any person or persons who could be classified under the Aliens Act of 2015 as a stranger?'

'No.'

'Since your last report have you engaged in any activity that could be construed as being injurious to the present government?'

'No.'

'Since your last report have you committed any crime?'

'No.'

'Have you any information about any other person who may have committed a crime?'

'No.'

'Are you a homosexual?'

'No.'

'Have you any information about any other person who is a homosexual or a lesbian?'

'No.'

'Do you own a weapon?'

'No.'

'Since your last report, have you broken any curfew laws and/or their ancillary regulations?'

'No.'

And so it went on and on and on. Phil King became bored but the recorder droned on. After a few more questions, the recorder pressed a button on his table, the entry door opened and the next person in the queue took their place at the back of the room, ready for their turn. The questions continued without further interruption.

'Do you own a motorised vehicle?'

'No.'

'Do you own any sort of vehicle?'

'Yes – a bicycle and a small trailer.'

'Please state the reasons for your ownership of these items and quote the relevant "vehicle ownership" document number.'

'Transport of produce for shop from the Border – VO345897/32.'

'Do you know the three principles of 555?'

'Yes.'

'Recite them.'

'Loyalty, truth and obedience.'

'Do you know the twenty-five rules of 555?'

'Yes.'

'Recite rule number fifteen.'

'No person, at any time, shall by thought, word or deed seek to undermine the authority of the administration as defined in the 555 Government Act of 2015.'

'Are you between the ages of eighteen and thirty-five and thereby eligible for military service?'

'No.'

'Are you over the age of sixty-five and thereby eligible for voluntary euthanasia?'

'No.'

'Have you ever had treatment for a mental illness?'

'No.'

Phil King now went on to autopilot. In his case, all the remaining answers were 'No' and he began to think of other things. In particular, he mused about what his customers would like to buy more than anything else if he could get hold of it. Surprisingly, it wasn't fillet steak, or grapes, or strawberries, or stilton cheese, or any other long-forgotten luxury. The item that was most requested was tinned rice pudding. It had now become a joke in the shop. The customers asked for it, Phil said he was waiting for it on his next order and the conversation would move on. Unfortunately, he was still thinking about this curious fact when the recorder asked his penultimate question.

'Have any of your answers in this Report been untruthful?'

'Tinned rice pudding.'

Nobody made any acknowledgement of this answer. The judge advocate continued to write and the recorder moved on to the final question. Perhaps George had been right.

'Is there anything you wish to report to the judge advocate that has not been covered by these questions?'

'No.'

Phil relaxed and prepared to make his exit, but for the first time ever to his knowledge, the judge advocate spoke.

'Five minutes' recess,' she announced, her loud voice startling the other three people in the room. 'I wish to speak to Mr King in private for a moment.'

The recorder bowed and Philip King went weak at the knees. He looked around him in panic. What the hell could this mean? What had he done wrong? He suddenly became very afraid.

Emily Fairfax rose and made her way to one of the doors behind the bench. She motioned Phil to follow, which he did with a deliberately slow pace. She led him into a small room which was empty apart from a desk and two chairs. The judge advocate sat down in the chair which was positioned behind the desk and signalled for the now very frightened Phil King to sit in the other one facing her. He sat and was slightly relieved to see a smile appear on the face of the most powerful woman in the town, or the world as he knew it.

'How are you, Phil? We haven't spoken for ages.' The voice was softer now than in the Report Centre. She sat back in her chair and smiled again.

'We move in different circles.'

'Yes. Yes, I know. I've been very busy for the last few years but we used to be friends.'

'Not friends – we knew each other.'

'Don't be tetchy, Phil. I'm trying to be pleasant.'

'Why?'

'My, my, this is going to be hard work.'

'I'm sorry, Mrs Fairfax, but what do you expect? For three years I've been living the life of a sewer rat and you've been swanning around – you haven't spoken to me or even acknowledged my existence and now you want to talk to me. Why?'

'I want to invite you to dinner.'

Phil King sat back in the chair, looked at her in amazement and started to laugh.

'You've got to be joking. Dinner? Me? Why?'

'We have some important guests coming and they requested that I invite some different people. I saw that it was your report day and decided to ask you. Black tie.'

'I can't come to dinner. I haven't even got a decent pair of trousers, never mind a jacket and a tie. Good God, what kind of world do you people live in? Black tie? When I have dinner, I have a black plate because there's never enough hot water to wash the bloody thing. No, thank you – thanks for asking but I must decline your kind invitation. You'll have to do without my witty after-dinner conversation. Can I go now?'

He got up and went towards the door.

'I don't think I made myself clear, Mr King.' The softness in the voice had disappeared and the judge advocate rose from her chair. 'I was trying to be polite by inviting you to dinner. I'm very sorry but you will attend at my house tonight at seven thirty so that you will be in good time to join us for dinner at eight.' She reached into the pocket of her gown and extracted some sheets of paper. She quickly glanced at them before handing them to the dumbstruck Philip King, who by now had returned to his seat. 'Those are a voucher for Archer's so that you can hire a dinner suit and a pass to get you to my house. A car will call for you at seven fifteen so there is no excuse for your being late. If it's any consolation for you, we will not be having tinned rice pudding.'

With these last words she swept out of the room leaving Phil alone. He sat for a long time without moving. He didn't understand what was happening but whatever it was he knew he didn't want any part of it. He put the voucher and the pass into his pocket and went out of the other door, which did not lead back to the Report Centre, and found himself back in the corridor. He made his way down the stairs and out into the open air. The queue now stretched to the fence and beyond. Nobody looked at him but if they had, they would have seen a man with only one thought on his mind – what the hell was going on?

Three

Archer's was an anachronism. Founded in 1897 by a Henry Archer as a small haberdashery, it had prospered and between the two European wars of the twentieth century had expanded into a high-class gentleman's outfitters. This had been its main business up to the time of the Chaos after which it had managed to stay alive by executing a subtle change in its strategy. The shop still had suits and overcoats on display but it now dealt mainly in military uniforms and all the trappings that went with them. Phil King had never shopped there, even in the old days, since it had always seemed, even then, to be a shop clinging desperately to the past and charging high prices for old-fashioned clothes.

It stood in the centre of England Avenue on the opposite side to Phil's shop but was similarly surrounded by empty, derelict and decaying buildings. If it had appeared incongruous in the past, it seemed so out of place now that anyone passing would probably have thought it had been put there by mistake. One window showed its usual wares – hats, suits, trousers, jackets, ties and shoes. The other window was completely given over to the military side of its business and in its centre was a notice that read, 'Forms AT7 and PH4593 MUST be produced at the time of ordering any of these items.'

Phil King studied his reflection in the window, smiled, straightened his smelly twenty-year-old overcoat, pushed open the door and stepped inside.

The first sensation that hit him was the smell. The shop had managed to preserve the warm, fresh aroma of new clothes. Phil marvelled at this because his own shop smelled mainly of smelly people – perhaps Archer's had a better clientele, or at least they had a bath more often. There were racks of suits and along the right-hand wall was a display of shirts of every size and colour, looking immaculate in their cellophane wrappers. Nobody else appeared to be in the shop and Phil went over to one of the racks of suits and began to browse. He had never had a real interest in clothes – if it fitted, he bought it – but because he hadn't bought anything for so many years, he felt like a kid in a toy shop. He took off his gloves and began to feel the various cloths. He couldn't imagine when he would ever be able to buy clothes of this quality again. He moved around and noticed that all the left side and back of the shop were given over to the uniform business. A sign pointing to the stairs informed him that the Hire Department was on the first floor and he followed the arrow and began to climb. He only reached the second step before hearing a voice.

'Where do you think you're going?'

Phil stopped and turned. The voice belonged to a man who had appeared from nowhere. He was smartly dressed in an immaculately cut suit of blue serge with a white shirt and dark red tie. He was about Phil's age, his thin, bony face contorted into a sneer as if he was speaking to someone beneath him. On any other day, Phil King would have apologised to the man and explained his purpose in a polite way but he had always had an aversion to rudeness and, remembering the papers in his pocket, he found himself getting annoyed.

'What the fuck's it got to do with you?' he shouted at the man who stepped back, visibly stunned. He soon recovered his composure.

'I am the manager of this shop and I would ask you kindly to refrain from using such appalling language in here. I asked you were you thought you were going as I cannot believe that someone like you could possibly have any lawful business in a shop such as this. Do you wish to leave now or should I call the military police?'

Phil felt the anger rising within him. He walked slowly over to the man, who tried to back away but was hemmed in by a stand displaying military caps. Phil put his hand in his pocket and drew out the voucher that Emily Fairfax had given him. He held it near the man's face and the man began to read it.

'After you've read that, bollock brain, I would be grateful to hear your definition of your phrase "someone like you".'

The manager's face crumpled. He looked at the voucher and

then at Phil and back again at the piece of paper. He swallowed hard.

'Yes – I see. Well, everyone can make a mistake. I do apologise, sir. I obviously didn't realise that you were here with a voucher from the judge advocate. If you'll kindly follow me, sir, I'm sure we can more than satisfy your requirements.'

Phil King could not believe that one little piece of paper could change a person's attitude so quickly. From an arrogant sod to a fawning slave in five seconds – he must remember to ask Emily Fairfax for more pieces of paper with such power. He followed the manager up the stairs and found himself in a room filled with racks of eveningwear. He remained silent whilst the man measured him in all the right places and then began to fill an oversize leather briefcase with items of clothing from the various racks.

When the man had finished, he closed the bag and handed it to his customer.

'There you are, sir. Bring it back any time this week or whenever it's convenient for your good self.'

'You can pick it up tomorrow from my shop – number forty-two – and we'll try and give you the same warm welcome you just gave me.'

'Certainly, sir. Let me apologise again, sir. If you could see your way to forgetting the first few moments of our meeting I would be most grateful – perhaps we could see about supplying you with a new winter coat, sir?'

'Oh, shut up,' said Phil, wearily. 'I've no intention of telling the judge advocate what a rude bastard you were and my old coat is all right, thank you very much.'

With this, Phil walked down the stairs and out of the shop. He was already tired of the game where you talked to someone as though they were pig shit and put them in fear of their life. He turned left and headed for his own shop. It was a different man making the return journey from the one who had set out earlier that morning. The fear that had ruled his life for so long had disappeared during the last few hours, although it had not been replaced by any sort of bravery. After talking to George Fenton and the episode of the tinned rice pudding, he had acquired the simple attitude of 'who gives a shit?'. Thus, it was a different man, one more like his old self, and a happier man, who re-entered the best grocery shop in the town. Shirley was alone and sitting behind the counter.

'Where the hell have you been? I was getting worried about you! Jesus, are you all right? What's the matter? Don't just stand there fucking smiling at me – what's wrong? Are you ill? What's in the briefcase?'

'My dinner suit.'

'Don't take the piss, Phil. What the fuck would you want with a dinner suit?'

'I am not, as you so politely put it, extracting the urine. What would anyone want with a dinner suit? I have been invited out to dinner.'

'Now I know you're taking the piss. You've been into one those illegal drinking cellars and had some of that home-made hooch, haven't you? You daft bastard. It's gone straight to your head because you're not used to it – come into the back and I'll make you a cup of tea.'

'No alcoholic liquor has passed my lips.' Phil King smiled. 'Our very own judge advocate, no less, has invited me for dinner at her house tonight and gave me a voucher to hire a dinner suit for the occasion from Archer's.'

Shirley Tate stopped and turned to face her boss. She gave him a long hard look and saw the difference in him. This was not the man who had gone to give his report earlier that morning. He was holding himself more erect and his face bore a look of self-confidence that she had not seen for a very long time. He looked a different man.

'Why?'

'What do you mean, "Why?"?'

'Why you?'

'She obviously wants the benefit of my quick wit and repartee to entertain the other guests around her dinner table.'

'Yes, I can understand that – but why?'

'She has important guests coming and, I quote, "They requested that I invite some different people". Good God, Shirley, I don't know why she's invited me – I wish I did. When it was just an invitation I said no but then she left me with no choice and so I am going out to dinner tonight.'

'I don't like the sound of it. She's become a devious bitch. Do you know her well?'

'Not as well as George Fenton but we used to speak in the old shop when she came in to pay her paper bill. We passed the time of day, that sort of thing, but I wouldn't say I "knew" her. I know her husband, though – Gerald Fairfax was our solicitor when we bought our house and made our wills, so Rosie and I got to know him quite well. He seemed a good sort of bloke and if he ever saw me in the town he'd come over and say hello and sometimes we'd have a pint together. Perhaps his wife has just realised that she wants me as a toyboy.'

Shirley looked at Phil again. She began to seriously worry. Phil's new attitude could spell danger if he said the wrong thing at the wrong time in the wrong place.

'You will be careful, won't you? Don't say anything tonight.'

'Shirley, stop it. Don't start worrying yourself. I'm worried enough for the both of us – I promise I'll be careful. Come on, cheer up. We'll have that cup of tea and then you can get off home. I'm going to close early today so I can have time to make myself look beautiful for tonight.'

'I can't help worrying – you're about the only friend I've got left. I don't want to lose you as well.'

They walked together into the stockroom and Shirley put the kettle on to the little stove. The afternoon was now nearly gone and it was already quite dark with the winter gloom. For a while they stood in silence but, after the kettle had boiled and she had made the tea, Shirley spoke again.

'What do you think it's all about, Phil? I don't mean the dinner invite but the whole fucking mess we're in. What's going on and why?'

'You mean why are we living in abject poverty under quasi-military rule without access to radio, newspapers, television, telephones, the internet or any other form of communication? Why are we living in a town that five years ago had 35,000 inhabitants and now has less than 3,000? Why people disappear for no reason and are never seen again? I've told you before, I have no fucking idea whatsoever. Perhaps tonight might provide some answers.'

Phil rose from his chair and went over to Shirley. She had been watching him all through his little speech and now managed a faint smile.

'You take care. This thing tonight worries me.'

'I promise to be on my best behaviour. You go home and don't worry.' Phil kissed his shop assistant on the forehead and went into the shop, at which point the door opened and somebody entered. Shirley followed him and greeted the customer.

'Hello, Margaret – how are you?'

The customer was, or appeared to be, a bundle of rags. Phil wondered how Shirley had recognised her or even worked out that she was female – if he hadn't seen the bundle moving he wouldn't have been able to tell that it contained a human. The bundle stopped by the counter and unwound the tattered scarf that covered its head. A face of indeterminate age appeared – two eyes were the only relief in a sea of sagging flesh. But the eyes were bright and the mouth which now opened showed an extraordinary full set of white teeth.

'What's the matter with you two? What are you smiling for? Been having a shag in the back have you? Dirty buggers!'

'Of course we have,' answered Shirley. 'Not much else to do in the afternoon in here. Are you jealous?'

'No thanks – I've finished with all that. Anyway, you could have picked somebody better than him. He's a miserable tosser if ever there was one.'

'Oh, thank you very much for your kind words,' said Phil with a smile. 'They're very much appreciated. I do value your opinion on such matters.'

'Don't take that tone with me, you cheeky sod. You're not too old to have your arse spanked! Got any milk left?'

It was at this point that Phil recognised his customer. Margaret Hills had been the senior English teacher at the local comprehensive school for more than thirty years – she had taught both Phil and Shirley – trying to force the beauty of the English language and its literature into disbelieving young minds. He thought, How the mighty have fallen. She was a pale shadow of her former self but her fighting spirit was obviously still there in abundance. Shirley took the container that Margaret had extricated from her pocket and began to fill it with milk from one of the large containers on the shelf that were delivered by the military every day.

'Here you are, Margaret – that'll be ten pence, please,' said Shirley.

'Fucking robbery! I'll open my own shop and then we'll see where you'll be – in the shit.' The former admirer of the English language paid over the money and walked straight out of the shop.

'My God,' said Phil, 'I can't believe that's the same woman who used to take us to Stratford-upon-Avon to see the plays. Look at her now: a foul-mouthed old woman seeing the worst in everyone.'

'She's lost her way. I don't think she can believe what's happened to us all, but I like her.'

'Come on, let's lock up and get out of here.'

There wasn't much to do and within a couple of minutes they were standing outside after having turned the light off and locked the door. The evening was cold but clear and they walked down England Avenue and turned into Elizabeth Road, leaving the street lights behind them.

Nobody lived in Elizabeth Road now – all the houses had been flattened to make way for a huge fenced area which housed a vast array of large vehicles. Bulldozers, tractors and lorries stood quietly in the early-evening gloom, awaiting their opportunity to demolish the next street of half-derelict houses. It was quiet and menacing and Phil was glad when it was time to turn into Victoria Way. They stood for a moment, not knowing how to say goodbye, and then Shirley spoke.

'I meant it when I told you to take care. I don't know why, but I don't like the sound of this invite.'

'I promise to take care. Stop worrying – I'll be all right. I'll see you tomorrow at the shop and tell you all about it. OK?'

He made to go towards his house but Shirley grabbed him and hugged him. She kissed him quickly on the lips before running away down Elizabeth Road towards her own home. Phil was surprised. She'd never done that before. He hadn't found the kiss unpleasant – just surprising.

108 Victoria Way was cold, lifeless and unwelcoming. He put the kettle on in the kitchen, went into the bedroom and after opening the briefcase proceeded to lay out his clothes for the evening on the bed. A dinner suit, a white dress shirt, black bow tie, two gold cufflinks, purple cummerbund, a pair of black patent-leather shoes, a pair of black socks and two white cotton handkerchiefs made up the ensemble. He turned and looked at himself in the mirror, still wearing his normal clothes. The transformation about to be attempted would be startling, he decided. The kettle began to whistle and he went and made himself a cup of tea. He sat down to have a rest and promptly fell asleep.

He was woken by the sound of the six o'clock siren, which boomed across the town and signalled the end of all work for the day. Two hours later the siren would go again to signal the start of Curfew, when everyone had to be in their own houses except those people, for one night only, who had a pass from the judge advocate and an invite to a dinner party!

Phil undressed and shivered his way to the bathroom. He had decided to keep his beard but proposed to give it a monumental trim. He picked up the scissors and began the task. For the first time in many months he began to whistle. There was no hot water so he chose not to have a bath and made do with a quick splash. He rummaged through the debris of the bathroom cabinet and found an old bottle of aftershave curiously named Boomerang. A liberal sprinkling of the pungent lotion made him feel refreshed and smell like a perfume counter in one of the old department stores. Retracing his steps into the bedroom, he began to dress for his big night out. Before he could even pick up the shirt, there was a knock at the front door, and heaving himself into his old overcoat, he went to see who it was.

He opened the door and saw a young black man standing on the front step. He was tall and muscular with a scar running down the right side of his face. The man smiled and his teeth shone in the darkness.

'Mr King?' The voice was courteous and gentle.

'Yes. I'm Phil King. Who the fuck are you and what do you want?'

'My name's Leroy Preston – I've been sent here because my flat has been demolished and the man said you might have a spare room.'

'Which man?'

'The sergeant who was in charge of the demolition. He had a list and he gave me your name and address. Obviously nobody's told you anything about it – I'm sorry.'

'I have got a spare room,' said Phil, 'but I didn't want to let it out to anyone. Isn't there anywhere else you can go?'

'He didn't give me any other names – he just told me to come here and fix it up tonight so I could move in tomorrow.'

'Oh God – you'd better come in and we can have a talk. I can't leave you out there all night. Come in, Leroy.'

The visitor followed Phil into the kitchen, closing the front door behind him, and gazed around him.

'I'm sorry I appeared so rude when I opened the door. I've got used to the lonely life and I don't get many visitors, but if the authorities have sent you I suppose we'll have to try and work something out. Do you want to sleep here tonight?'

'No – I've got a bed at the hostel but I'd like to move in tomorrow if that's all right with you.'

'I don't see any problem but I've only got the one key to the front door so you'll have to come and collect it from my shop in England Avenue. Do you know it?'

'Yes, I've just come from there because I thought you'd still be open.'

'Normally I would have been but I closed early today because I have to go out in a minute.'

'Oh,' said Leroy. He had never heard of people going out at night and looked puzzled.

'Impressed, are you? You will be when I tell you that I'm dining with the judge advocate and her guests. Anyway, let's get back to the other thing. Move in tomorrow, like we said. I sleep down here on the ground floor so you can have your pick of the rooms upstairs. There's a bathroom up there as well but we'll only have this kitchen between us. I can't see any problem there and we'll work something out. Now I really must get ready.'

Phil went back into the hall but his visitor stayed where he was, looking intently at the floor.

'Come on, Leroy – I've said you can have a room. What's wrong?'

The young man looked up and turned to face his new landlord.

'I'm sorry – you've been more than generous already but I said I'd ask if there was a chance. There were three of us in the block of flats – could my two mates come as well?'

Phil paused.

'Are they in the hostel as well? What's it like? I've heard some terrible stories.'

'Yes, we're all there for tonight. If you're dining with the judge advocate, I suppose I shouldn't say this but from what I've seen after one quick visit to drop my stuff off, it's a rat-infested shit hole. I think we'll be lucky to survive even one night in there.'

'Said with feeling, Leroy. I could tell you meant that. OK – I'll take all three of you – but no more or we'll have to sleep three to a bed. Now, piss off – I need to get ready and don't worry about my dining with the judge advocate. It's a surprise to me as well!'

'Thanks, Mr King. We'll be round tomorrow.'

Phil noticed that his visitor had smiled for the first time since he had entered the house. They shook hands as Phil pushed him out of the front door.

He returned to the bedroom and began to dress again. Socks first, then trousers, shirt, cufflinks, cummerbund, tie and jacket. He looked in the mirror and laughed. There was another knock at the front door and he went to answer it looking like a very smart butler.

On the step stood Shirley, a red carnation in her hand.

'I grow these in the garden and I wondered whether you needed a buttonhole and... I can't stop because of the Curfew and I'm talking rubbish and... I only came so that I could see you in your dinner suit and – Christ, you look absolutely bloody marvellous – and I must go...'

She held out the carnation but Phil grabbed her and pulled her into the hallway.

'The least you can do is to put the flower in its place. Do I look that good?'

'Better! Distinguished and dashing and handsome.'

She adjusted the flower to fit the buttonhole and placed her hands on his shoulders. Phil's arms went round her back and he pulled her closer.

'You took me by surprise earlier – now I'm ready.'

Shirley extricated herself from his embrace and went back to the front door.

'If I let you kiss me when you're dressed like that, I doubt whether you'd make it to the dinner party. I'm off – have a good time.'

With that she was off into the night. Phil stared after her and scratched his head. He went to pick up his coat from the bedroom and returned to the hall to see a black Jaguar standing at the kerb. A man in military uniform emerged from the driver's seat and came to the front door.

'The judge advocate's compliments, sir.'

'I'll be right with you.'

He turned off the light and closed the front door behind him. The man opened the rear door of the sleek car and Phil slid in and settled himself in the luxurious leather seat.

It had been an eventful day: George Fenton, his Report, 'tinned rice pudding', the invite, Archer's, Margaret Hills, Shirley, Leroy Preston and Shirley again.

Philip Edward King, Esq., in his chauffeur-driven limousine, wondered what the evening would bring.

Four

At the roundabout where Phil normally turned left on his bike to go to the Border, the car turned right into the tree-lined avenue that was now called Churchill Crescent. The road was dark but Phil could make out the silhouettes that lined both sides of the wide curving thoroughfare. A guard post and a barrier emerged out of the blackness and the driver slowed to a stop. A guard appeared at the car window, which the driver opened. No words were exchanged but, after examining the driver's papers and looking in at the rear seat, the guard stepped back, raised the barrier and the car swept on effortlessly along the road. There were fewer houses now and none of them showed any light or any other sign of life. The only sound was the purring of the three-litre engine as the car continued towards its destination.

Phil could remember when this was *the* place to live in the town. In that respect, he supposed, nothing much had changed. He hadn't been up here since the Chaos but in the old days he had come every last Friday of the month to collect the outstanding newspaper bills. He'd never met the owners of the houses – he'd dealt with the au-pairs or the cleaners, and even a butler in one case. The people who had lived here had existed in a world of their own, with little or no contact with the rest of the town. Most of them had not even shopped there, preferring to have their goods delivered from the nearby city or even London. They had always seemed immune from any sort of economic recession and, even in the worst days of a financial crash, gardeners could always be seen working in the well-kept flower beds. Now it looked as if all these people were gone. No lights shone in any of the properties they passed and the gardens were overgrown. Nature had reclaimed the once immaculately mown lawns and weeds had made a successful takeover bid for their borders.

Perhaps it was not *the* place to live any more.

Suddenly, the driver slowed and turned carefully through a pair of high metal gates on to a gravelled drive. The drive was narrow, with tall trees on either side. After about three hundred yards, the trees disappeared and the drive widened. Phil could see grassland at the sides but not much else. The car drove on but it had slowed dramatically. They inched forward and then stopped. After a wait of about ten seconds all was revealed. The whole area around the car was bathed in a harsh white light and Phil had to shield his eyes momentarily. The car moved forward again and came to a halt at the front of a large house, which stood at the eastern boundary of the lighted area. The driver got out and came to the rear of the car. He opened the door and Phil stepped out on to the rough gravel. The driver closed the door, resumed his seat and drove off towards the side of the house and out of sight.

Now, alone in the oppressive bright light, Phil King felt exposed and vulnerable. It was not unlike the feeling he had in the morning at the Border when he was waiting for Amos to appear. He turned to look at the garden. It was magnificent, with lawns, flowers, shrubs, trees, fountains and even a stream – obviously the judge advocate had kept her gardener. He was jolted out of his horticultural appreciation by the sound of the front door of the house being opened. He walked towards it and tried to get some sort of idea of the size of the building but, just at that moment, the floodlights went off and he was left in absolute darkness apart from the small chink of light emanating from behind the open door. He climbed four small steps, pushed open the door and stepped inside the house.

He found himself in a reception hall whose only apt description was 'grand'. About the size of half a tennis court, it was rectangular and painted, both walls and ceiling, in a brilliant white. The walls were adorned with oil paintings but Phil was no art expert and therefore couldn't decide whether they were priceless originals or cheap copies. On closer inspection of a couple of them, he tended to favour the first option but, whatever they were, they looked right. The room was carpeted in a lush red Axminster, which did nothing to dispel the notion that this was a rich person's house. There was a wide staircase, which disappeared towards the first floor at the far end, and six doors, three on each side, but they were all closed. Phil waited, uncertain of his next move. He heard a noise behind him and turned to see a young woman in a maid's uniform closing the front door. She must have been behind the door since he had come in – indeed hers was probably the hand that had opened it so promptly on his arrival.

'May I take your coat, sir?' She spoke quietly and looked nervous as she approached.

'Yes... Yes... Of course. I'm sorry – I'm not used to this.'

Phil took off his old overcoat, handed it to the maid and felt embarrassed. The maid took the coat, folded it neatly and laid it over the back of a chair that was standing against the right-hand wall. She began to walk towards the staircase.

'If you'll follow me, sir, I'll take you to the library where they're all having drinks.'

'Am I the last to arrive? Am I late?' asked Phil as he followed his guide down the hallway to the farthest door on the left.

'I think that your arrival completes the party, sir, but by my reckoning you're right on time. Here we are, sir. Please go straight in.' With this polite request, she left him and walked back in the direction of the front door, leaving Phil King staring at the door to the library.

He ran his hands through his hair, patted his beard, straightened his jacket, wiped his shoes on the back of his trousers, took his courage in both hands, opened the door and walked in.

He found himself in a large room in which three walls were covered from floor to ceiling with bookcases full of books. Two black leather sofas faced each other either side of a log fire, which burned brightly in a large, ornate Victorian fireplace that dominated the other wall. Four black leather armchairs were also dotted around the room, which seemed warm and welcoming.

Emily Fairfax rose from one of the sofas and came over to her new guest. Six pairs of eyes followed her and began to inspect the new arrival.

'Good evening, Phil. I'm so glad you could make it. Come and meet our other guests. I think you already know my husband, Gerald.'

Phil followed her across the room and shook hands with the

former solicitor who was seated in a wheelchair, looking very smart in a white dinner jacket.

'This is Corporal Robson and his wife Doreen.' Phil smiled politely and shook hands with a very serious-looking young man and his nervous, pretty wife.

'This is Miss Jeffers, one of our guests from out of town.' Phil bowed and shook hands with a very beautiful woman. About his own age, or a few years younger, she was stunning. Her facial features were without blemish and framed by a cascade of luxurious jet-black hair that swept down to her equally alluring shoulders. She was dressed in a figure-hugging black satin creation that whispered 'I cost a lot of money' in a very seductive way. Phil mumbled something like 'Good evening' and moved on, but not before noticing her ample breasts, which were highlighted by her low-cut dress and the diamond choker at her throat, which sparkled in the light of the two chandeliers that lit the room.

'This is Mr Stanton – another of our out-of-town guests.'

'Call me Harry. I hate the formality when we're at a dinner party like this.'

'Right… OK… Good evening, Harry. Phil – that's my name. Phil.'

They moved on and, for some reason, Phil was feeling less relaxed as he met each new person. Although the smiles and the words of welcome from his fellow guests were friendly enough, there seemed to be a stiffness about the occasion which did not augur well for the rest of the evening. Eventually, Emily steered him towards the fireplace and the last guest.

He was standing with his right elbow leaning on the mantlepiece. A tall, distinguished-looking man with luxurious white hair brushed back from his face, he was dressed in a uniform similar to that worn by Corporal Robson. The difference was that his uniform boasted two red epaulettes, five gold stars on each lapel and three rows of medal ribbons on the left-hand pocket. His proud patrician face, eyes wide apart, large nose, full lips – the upper one covered with a thick moustache, the same colour as his hair – looked down benignly at Phil.

'And this is our guest of honour – General Turner,' said

Emily. 'This is Philip King, General.' The general offered his hand and Phil took it. A vice-like grip nearly made him wince but he managed a smile. 'Would you like a drink, Phil?' asked Emily. 'Whisky all right?'

'Yes... thanks... whisky would be fine.' Phil hadn't tasted whisky for over three years and wondered how he would react but he hoped one wouldn't be a problem. Emily moved away and the other guests began to talk amongst themselves. The general spoke and his voice matched his face and bearing – deep, resonant and accentless.

'Nice to meet you, Philip. I suppose this is a bit of a surprise for you – a small reminder, though, of what we used to call civilised society. I've always thought that the success of a dinner party is dependent on one thing and one thing alone. You can forget the food and the wines – they can be good or bad – it doesn't matter. A dinner party can only be judged on the quality of the people who attend.' The general paused and looked round the room. 'I'm glad you've come or we might have had problems this evening.'

'How do you know I'll be a quality guest?' asked Phil.

'Emily has told me all about you – or all that she knows – so I have high hopes. Talk of the devil, here she comes with your drink.'

The judge advocate arrived at Phil's side and handed over the drink – a large measure of whisky in one of those cut-glass, heavy-bottomed tumblers that made even cheap whisky taste good. Phil sipped the whisky and decided it wasn't cheap. The single malt melted down his throat and slowly warmed the rest of his body. He took another sip.

'Take it easy, Philip – don't rush it. We have all evening and spirits tend to do funny things to the system if you're not used to them.' The general had said this in a friendly way and Phil decided to take his advice. He didn't fancy having to face Shirley the next day if he had to report that he had passed out before the meal had begun.

Harry Stanton came over and, ignoring Phil, began to talk to the general. Phil turned and saw that Doreen Robson was standing alone by one of the bookcases so he went and joined her.

'Do you read much, Mrs Robson?' he asked whilst eyeing the books. This section was obviously given over to reference titles and contained numerous dictionaries and thesauri. None of them looked as though they were used much.

'No,' answered the diminutive wife of the corporal.

'I used to,' said Phil trying his hardest to keep the conversation alive, 'but I don't now. The main reason for that being that I haven't got any books any more. I don't know what happened to them – they just seemed to disappear. I wouldn't mind spending a few weeks in this room – how about you?'

'I don't know.' Doreen Robson had not even glanced in Phil's direction during this brief exchange but had kept her eyes firmly on the floor. She looked up at him now. 'I'm sorry, Mr King – I didn't mean to appear rude but I'm not very good at this. To tell you the truth, I don't know what I'm doing here. I'm only here because my husband was invited and I've never been to one of these things before. I don't know what I'm supposed to say or do.'

'You and me both! I think I'm going to get drunk and forget everything else for one night. If you want my advice, you should do the same.'

Doreen Robson smiled and for a brief moment an inner warmth showed in her face.

'I wish I could but I don't think my husband would be too impressed. He says that I have to be on my best behaviour. He says it might be important for his career. I don't know anyone else here and he won't talk to me because he wants to "circulate". "Circulate" – that's his word for arse-licking, I think.' Doreen Robson stopped and put her hand on Phil's arm. 'Oh God, don't tell him I said that, will you?'

Phil laughed and patted her hand.

'My lips are sealed, madam. I wonder why they invited us. I suppose it gives them a chance to see how the other half lives.'

'I can't see why they have to invite us to a dinner party for that. They know how we live. They decide how we live.'

It was at this point, just as the conversation was getting interesting, that Doreen's husband came over and grabbed her by the arm.

'Come on, Doreen, Mr Stanton wants to meet you.' He led

her away towards the centre of the room and, for the second time that night, Phil was ignored. Finding himself alone, he began to examine the books again. He felt a hand on his shoulder and turned to find himself looking at the delicious Miss Jeffers. Her eyes smiled at him and he felt his knees begin to buckle. This woman was sex on legs and Phil doubted whether he had lusted after anyone so much in all his life.

'I'm pleased to meet you, Phil. I've heard a lot about you from our hostess.'

Phil just stood with his mouth open, unable to speak.

'Perhaps after you've stopped looking at my tits you could get me another drink. Gin and tonic, please – lots of ice.'

'I'm sorry… I'm not used to this.'

'Not used to what? Acting in a civilised manner for a few hours? It doesn't usually have the effect of making men speechless.'

'I'm sorry.'

'If you apologise again, I think I shall knee you in the balls. Right, can I have my drink now?'

None of this was said in anger but in a soft voice with more than a hint of humour and Phil was getting more confused as each minute passed. He walked over to the drinks cabinet, mixed a stiff gin and tonic with lots of ice and returned to this mysterious lady.

'All right, Miss Jeffers – no more apologies. I don't know what I'm doing here but if this is some sort of game, then I'll play along. I was looking at your tits – as you so politely put it – but that's presumably why you wore that dress and, if I may say so, very beautiful they are, too.'

'That's much better. This is no game – it's a dinner party. Relax, talk to me.'

'What about?'

'Oh, for God's sake, come on! Talk about anything, everything: sex, politics, sport, books, the weather – all the usual things people talk about at dinner parties.'

Phil paused for a few moments. He knew what he wanted to say but didn't know whether this was the right time or the right place and he certainly didn't know whether he was talking to the right person. Eventually, he remembered his new motto was 'who gives a shit?' and began to speak.

'Now, that's where my difficulty lies, Miss Jeffers. I don't know anything about everything. I know nothing – zilch, zero – about anything. I haven't had sex since my wife disappeared three years ago. Politics have been banned and there is no sport. I used to own a lot of books and my great hobby was reading but my books have all disappeared – I either sold them to buy food or they were stolen by someone even more desperate than me. As for the weather, it's bloody cold. So, there you are – there's nothing to talk about. However, I would find it a great honour if we could both stand here in silence and, with your permission, I will examine your gorgeous tits in minute detail.'

'Well, well. There's a rebel behind that bloody awful beard.'

'No, absolutely not. You misunderstood me. I'm not a rebel. I'm confused – confused and just a little frightened. I still can't work out what this evening is all about but every time I take a sip of this excellent whisky, I find myself caring a little less as to whether it's about anything at all.'

'Could you not just accept the evening at face value? A meeting of people, wining and dining together?'

'No, I can't.'

'Why?'

'I can't because of what preceded it and what's going to follow it. Have you any idea of the kind of life I lead? I live in absolute poverty – a prisoner in the town where I was born, with no hope of an early release. Nobody will tell me what's happened to my wife and kids. This so-called dinner party is obscene in the context of the rest of my life. There, I've said it and bollocks to the lot of you.'

Phil stopped. He knew he'd said too much. He looked around the room and noticed that everyone was looking at him – his voice must have risen in volume as he warmed to his subject. He looked back at Miss Jeffers, who was staring at him with her piercing blue eyes. Suddenly, she threw her head back and let out a long, throaty laugh. The others in the room resumed their separate conversations and Miss Jeffers spoke again.

'I like you Mr King – I shall call you Philip. Play the game.

We'll talk later but there is one small error in your last passionate speech. It is untrue to say that you have no hope of an early release.'

With this cryptic comment she left him and went to talk to General Turner, who was still standing by the fireplace. Phil went to look at some of the other books, noting that none of them showed any evidence of having been read. No doubt, he thought, the lovely Miss Jeffers was relating his verbal bravado to the general, but what the hell? Who cared? Gerald Fairfax was making his way towards him, pushing himself in his wheelchair. Phil sat down in one of the fine leather chairs so that they would be at the same level.

The two men, old acquaintances if not friends, sat in silence for a few moments.

'It wasn't my idea to invite you, Phil – the general wanted to meet you. I heard the last part of your conversation with the lady. I'm sorry but when the general asks, we have to jump.'

'Don't worry about it, Gerald. There's no problem with it as far as you and Emily are concerned – forget it. How are you, anyway? I heard you'd had a couple of heart attacks.'

'They slowed me down a bit – as you can see – but I'm still alive, which is more than can be said for a lot of others. Have you had any word about Rosie and the kids?'

'Not a thing – you haven't heard about them, have you?'

'No, but your being here has reminded me about them. I'll have a poke about and ask Emily, although don't get your hopes up too high. She hardly tells me anything and I can't get about much in this bloody thing.' Gerald looked sad but with a shake of his head he resumed his usual jovial nature of old and looked around the room. 'I saw you talking to our Miss Jeffers – Christ, she's a fine-looking woman! If I was twenty years younger I'd give you a run for your money, you dirty sod!'

'Who is she, Gerald? What does she do? Where does she come from?'

'I've no idea – she came with the general, as did that buffoon Harry Stanton. He told us he was bringing two guests but he hasn't told us who they are or what they do. Stanton, I think, is some sort of politician but that's only a guess based on the fact that he talks a lot of bollocks. He's the most boring man I've met for a long, long time. The delectable Miss Jeffers is something of a mystery. At first I thought she must be the mistress of one or both of them but that's not true. She's a very intelligent lady and she's here in her own right but what she does I don't know.'

'Have you seen her before?' asked Phil.

'Never, and neither has Emily, who was a bit put out when she arrived.'

'Why?'

'You know what women are like – when Emily gives a dinner party for someone like the general, she likes to be the centre of attention and doesn't take too kindly to a beautiful woman like that turning up and hogging all the limelight. But the woman herself has been pleasant enough and Emily has been won over by the fact that she is obviously a very important person.'

'Doesn't hold back with the language, does she?'

'That's why she's so desirable, Phil. A woman with a classic beauty who gives off sexual signals every time she moves, has a wonderful sense of style and a mouth like a fish porter – what a combination! If you want my advice – which you don't – I'd stay well clear of that dangerous lady. Ah… here's the interesting Mr Stanton coming to join us. God help us.'

Harry Stanton stood in front of them. He was a small man with very pointed facial features. Phil didn't actually know what a weasel looked like but he thought Mr Stanton might have fitted the description of one if he did.

'I saw you two having a little tête-à-tête and I thought I'd join you. Is this where the dirty jokes are being aired?'

'No,' replied Gerald. 'Phil and I were just wondering what the wonderful Miss Jeffers did for a living. Do you know?'

'I'm afraid not – she didn't speak at all during the car journey down here. Why do you want to know?'

'We were hoping she was the strippergram hired for the evening.' As Gerald said this, he slapped Phil on the knee and they both burst out laughing.

'I'm sure she's nothing like that,' said Harry Stanton and walked away.

'I told you he was a boring old fart, didn't I? God the man

can't even take a joke. Come on, Phil – I can see Emily gesturing to us. I think she wants us to go in for dinner. Can you give me a push?'

Phil put down his drink and stood up. Across the room, Emily Fairfax was going from group to group and people were moving in the direction of an open door on the left-hand side of the fireplace. He went behind the wheelchair and pushed it slowly across the room. Emily met them halfway.

'Thank you, Phil. Are you all right, Gerald?'

'Never better, my love. How are things at your end? Is the general happy?'

'Seems to be – let's hope it continues. Come on, you two – dinner awaits.'

Emily led the way and Phil pushed the chair after her. The door to the dining room was held open by the young maid who had greeted him at the front door. She closed the door from the library behind him and he pushed the wheelchair to the near end of the table, where a space had been left for it. If the library had been a pleasant surprise to Phil, the dining room was a different world and he could only stand in open-mouthed astonishment at the scene that was laid out before him.

Five

The dining room was spectacular. The table dominated the room. Rectangular and easily capable of seating the eight guests who were there, its dark mahogany top shone like glass. The only light in the room came from three tall silver candelabras that stood to attention down the centre of the table. Each of the eight settings was made up with numerous items of silver cutlery and boasted four wine glasses of different shapes and sizes. Everything sparkled in the candlelight, including the jewellery of the ladies, who were now seated. The room itself was decorated with a pale, cream wallpaper and small bureaux and tables were dotted around the walls. Deep red, velvet curtains covered one wall and, presumably, a large window that looked out over the rear garden.

Emily Fairfax was at the head of the table, at the opposite end to her husband. The general stood by the chair to her left and Doreen Robson and Harry Stanton completed that side of the table. Corporal Robson was to Gerald's left. Miss Jeffers sat in the middle and thus the empty place between her and Emily Fairfax had been left vacant for Phil. Before going to his place, he bent down and spoke to Gerald.

'Is that all right, Gerald?

'Yes, that's fine. Thanks for your help,' answered Gerald, who then lowered his voice to a whisper. 'Christ, you won the star prize. I'm going to be bored bloody stiff!'

Phil made his way to his place at the other end of the table and like the other male members of the gathering, except for Gerald, stood behind his high-backed chair. Emily Fairfax spoke.

'Please be seated, gentlemen. Dinner is served. Let's enjoy ourselves – oh, and since we have a distinct shortage of staff, Gerald and I would be grateful if we could all help ourselves to the wine. Now, you were saying, General…'

The gentlemen sat and there was a general hubbub whilst people picked up their red linen napkins and placed them on their laps. In between the candelabra were small displays of red roses, the colour of which perfectly matched the napkins. Everything was perfect and exuded luxury, apart from the lack of a wine waiter! Phil started to think how different this scene was to his normal eating arrangements – if he was lucky and had managed to scrounge a tin of sardines, he would sit in his overcoat and eat them straight from the tin!

The guests began to talk to each other quietly but Emily Fairfax and Miss Jeffers were talking to their other neighbours so Phil reached out for the bottle of white wine that was near his right hand. He poured some of the chilled Chablis into the smallest glass of the four ranged in front of him. He went to put the bottle back into its silver holder when he felt a tap on his left arm and found Emily smiling at him and pointing to her own glass. He filled that and replaced the bottle.

'I'll serve myself with the wine, shall I?' It was the honeyed tones of Miss Jeffers.

'Sorry,' said Phil. She glared at him.

'I thought we agreed, Philip – no more apologies.'

'You're right – we did. Would you like some wine, Miss Jeffers?'

'That's most kind of you, Philip – thank you.' She winked at him in a flirty kind of way and then returned to the conversation she was having with Corporal Robson.

The young maid entered the room from somewhere behind Phil, and was followed by two older ladies dressed in the same uniform. They carried trays, stood behind the ladies at the table and began to serve the first course of the dinner.

The magnificent feast lasted for two hours. Chilled vichyssoise was followed by fresh salmon. The main course was pheasant cooked in a green apple sauce and the dessert was a choice between soufflé oranges and crème brûlée. The cheese board of seven different cheeses came and went with the precision of all the other courses. The Chablis was succeeded by a magnificent Mouton Rothschild 1983 and the coffee accompanied by a gloriously smooth Armagnac.

Phil had barely spoken a word. Emily Fairfax had been speaking to the general most of the time and Miss Jeffers had totally ignored him. But he had done better than Doreen Robson who, to his certain knowledge, had not uttered a single word during the whole meal. The guests started to move their chairs back to gain some extra comfort when Emily Fairfax stood up.

'Shall we continue back in the library? Bring your drinks with you if you wish.'

The general was the only person who answered.

'Emily, I hope I'm speaking for us all when I say that was a wonderful meal. You and Gerald should be congratulated.'

The other guests murmured in agreement and Harry Stanton shouted 'Hear, hear'.

'But I'll join you in a few moments in the library if I may. I just want to have a private word with Mr King.'

Emily nodded and led the other guests back into the library, with Corporal Robson pushing Gerald. The waitresses had long since disappeared and Phil was left alone with the general and Miss Jeffers, who had pointedly not followed the other guests.

The general leant back in his chair and took a pull on the enormous cigar he had just lit. His now ruddy face glowed in the candlelight.

It was at this point in the evening that Phil realised he was in danger. He wasn't worried at all about what the general wanted to say or even the sarcastic comments that Miss Jeffers might wish to insert into the forthcoming conversation. The danger was that he had drunk far too much – the Mouton Rothschild 1983 had turned out to be too big a temptation for someone in his circumstances. 'Drunk' would not have described his condition accurately, but it would have been nearer than the word 'sober'.

Obviously the preliminaries were over and the real reason for his being invited tonight was about to be revealed. The three of them sat in silence and Phil helped himself to some more coffee, hoping it would clear his head a little. Eventually, the general spoke.

'You've been quiet tonight, Philip. I've been watching you out of the corner of my eye and, apart from thanking someone for passing the salt or wine, you've hardly said a word. I'm disappointed – I came here tonight to talk to you and Emily and the corporal and his wife to find out what you were thinking. Talk to me – why won't you speak?'

'I haven't anything to say,' replied Phil trying hard to keep a lid on his temper. He took another drink of his coffee and waited.

'Come on, loosen up. We've had an excellent meal – now's the time to tell me what you think of the way things are going. This conversation will be strictly off the record – neither I nor Miss Jeffers will relate anything that is said in this room to anyone. You have my word on that.' The general appeared more exasperated than angry – he genuinely seemed to want Phil to talk but his listener remained suspicious. It was Miss Jeffers who spoke next.

'Perhaps Mr King is quite happy with his lot, General, and is not inclined, anyway, to believe your promise of confidentiality.'

Phil looked sharply at his neighbour – the smile was still there but a sneering had crept into her voice during her little speech that had not been there before. Philip Edward King was becoming tired and bored. He decided to take the bull by the horns and finish this charade once and for all. He took a deep breath, sat back in his chair and began to tell the general what he was thinking.

'Listen – I'm tired and weary of all this crap and it doesn't matter to me whether this conversation is confidential or not. Also, I don't tell anyone what I think of my "lot" and that includes you two. I want to go home and so if you've got something to say – which I presume is the reason why I was invited to this fucking stupid event – spit it out. Don't give me anymore of this spurious "what do you think, Phil?" –let's just get to the nitty-gritty and then we can all go home.'

'Good, a reaction at last,' said the general. 'All right, if that's the way you want it – you're quite right, you were invited tonight for a reason. We want you to do us a favour.'

'Who's we?'

'The authorities – the elected government of Great Britain.'

'What's the favour?'

'Do you know a young man called Leroy Preston?'

'I don't "know" him – I met him this afternoon when he was sent round to see whether he could have a room in my house. I said OK because there didn't seem to be much of a choice for either of us. He's coming round tomorrow to move in – he seemed a nice lad.'

'Is he bringing anybody with him?'

'He asked if he could bring two mates and I said yes. What's the problem?'

The general thought for a moment before answering.

'Mr Leroy Preston is the problem. In times like these, it would be naïve to think that some people were not going to mount some sort of resistance against the regime. We understand that and of course we monitor it pretty closely. We know who the members of the resistance in the town are and what they get up to and so there's not much of a problem there. But Mr Preston and some of his friends have formed a very small group on which we have no information.'

'This is all news to me,' said Phil. 'I've never heard of any resistance in the town or seen any results of their handiwork. Are you sure you're not making all this up?'

'I can assure that things are as I say. The "official" resistance puts sugar in the petrol tanks of military vehicles or tears down executive posters – that sort of thing. Nothing serious.'

'Good for them,' said Phil. 'Where can I join?'

'As far as I know, you don't join – you are invited. Anyway, that's not the point at issue here. We know all we need to know about them and they present no difficulties. However, Mr Preston is something else.'

'What's he supposed to have done? He seemed quite a pleasant lad to me.'

'He hasn't done anything yet – he and his friends resigned from the resistance three weeks ago. We want to know what, if anything, he has planned for the future. We thought you might like to help us with that small task. You're his new landlord – who could be better placed to find out what his intentions are?'

Phil looked at the general and then at Miss Jeffers. Both of them appeared to be deadly serious.

'Is that the favour? You want me to spy on my new lodgers and report my findings to you. You must be bloody insane. The answer is no. Now you've told me all that, if I find out that they're planning something to give you lot a bloody good kicking I'll be the first in line to join them. Spy for you? Fuck off! Help you? If I saw you were on fire I wouldn't piss on you!'

'It's not exactly a favour, Philip – it's an order,' said Miss Jeffers. 'We've gone to an awful lot of trouble to set this up. We demolished Preston's block of flats and got him quartered with you in order that this could proceed. I must admit it would be a big bonus if his two friends were the same two who resigned from the resistance with him, but we've been working on the Preston angle for three solid weeks. This operation will go ahead.'

'Why me?'

'You're clean, by which I mean you have no affiliations to either side – the resistance or us. Nobody will suspect you, certainly not Preston. Just be yourself – a miserable bastard of a shopkeeper – and everything will be fine.'

'Everything won't be fine, Miss Jeffers, because I'm not bloody doing it.'

Silence descended on the room for a moment or two. Miss Jeffers looked at the general, who gave a little nod. She leaned forward to Phil before she spoke in a quiet voice.

'Don't you want to see your wife and children again, Philip?'

He sat motionless, unable to breathe. So this is what it had come to – the elected government of Great Britain blackmailing a man with his wife and children. How could these people sleep at night? He felt his anger rising within him like the bile when you're going to be sick. For a second or two he knew he could have killed both of the bastards opposite him. But, almost immediately, the anger subsided to be replaced by a terrible, terrible sadness. The tears began to roll down his face as pictures of Rosie, his beloved Rosie, and Robin and Debbie appeared in his mind's eye. He recalled the life they had enjoyed together before the Chaos – the laughter, the tears, the arguments, the bedtime stories, the holidays, the parties and the dull normalities of a normal family life. Did he want to see them all again? There could only be one answer to that question. Yes, yes and yes a million times more!

The tears stopped and Phil King looked at the general.

'Have I your word that if I help you with this, I will see my wife and children again?'

'You have my word.'

'Then I'll do it. How do I report back to you?'

'Miss Jeffers is in charge of the operation so she'll work out the details. Glad to have you aboard, Philip – I'm sure you won't regret it.' The general stood and offered his hand, which Phil ignored.

'There's just one thing you should know, General,' said Phil who also stood up and, leaning forward a little, placed both of his clenched fists on the table.

'What's that, young man?'

'I need to say this because I don't want there to be any ambiguity between us. If for any reason you break your word to me on this matter, because of the way you've done it and because of what this blackmailing bitch to my left has just said, if you break your word I'll fucking kill you both. I've never been a violent man – I've always hated violence – and I don't know how I'll do it, but I will do it. Now I'm going home. I have an early start in the morning. No, don't see me out or wish me any pleasantries. I might throw up at the fucking hypocrisy of the pair of you.'

He turned and walked towards the door to the library, passing Miss Jeffers on the way.

'I'll be in touch,' she said, still with a smile on her face.

'No doubt,' said Phil. 'But let me give you a piece of advice. When you do get in touch, don't be wearing that fucking smile. I don't know what your job entails but if this is a typical example of the way you work, you shouldn't be smiling. Also, if or when we meet, cover your tits up – they're too big to be out in the open on their own.'

With this he marched out of the dining room and into the library where the other guests were still gathered. He said a quick goodbye to Gerald Fairfax, went into the hallway, retrieved his overcoat and left by the front door, slamming it behind him. He walked home taking his chances with the Curfew and met no one. The walk was good for him because it gave him time to think and he knew that, in the new reality of his situation, this was what he needed to do most. He had just a few hours to decide what to do but as he reached the house there was a noticeable spring in his step. He had worked out a plan that might, just might, allow him to see his family again and also live with his conscience for the rest of his life.

Six

The reality of Phil's situation hit him like two sledgehammers the next morning. The first blow came as he tried to open his eyes when the alarm went off. His head felt as though it was made of jelly and his whole body ached. He had a hangover of gigantic proportions and, when he tried to swing his legs off the bed to find his boots, he noticed that his right leg didn't seem to know where his left one was. He fell off the bed and lay on the floor for a couple of minutes to get his bearings. Eventually he made it to the bathroom and had a pee. The noise inside his head seemed to be saying, 'This is what you get if you drink as much as you did last night, after three years on the wagon'. He told the noise to piss off and went back to the bedroom to look for his boots. He found them and noticed that he was still wearing his clothes from the previous evening. Bollocks, he thought, let that little shit from Archer's clean the dirt off it, and he put his overcoat on. As on every other morning, he collected his bike and trailer from the backyard and set off on his journey to the Border.

As he was cycling along England Avenue, the second sledge-hammer blow hit him. He started to remember the events of the previous evening. His mind began to function and the promises made aligned with the threats started to become a lucid picture. By the time he had reached the guard post at the end of the Avenue, he remembered his plan and knew that he only had one thing to do that day. He had to talk to Leroy Preston.

The journey was uneventful, as usual, but physically it nearly killed him. However, he eventually arrived back at the shop only an hour later than normal. He put the key in the lock but just as he was about to open the door, he heard a noise behind him. He turned and saw someone hovering in the shadows.

'Hello, who's that?' he shouted. There was never anybody about at this time of the morning. The figure moved towards him. He felt the sweat pouring down his back. The figure emerged into the light and spoke.

'Where the fucking hell have you been? I've been stood here for at least an hour waiting for you.'

He relaxed – it was Shirley

'Bloody hell, Shirley, you gave me the fright of my life. What are you doing here?'

'Waiting to see you and ask how last night went. Christ, I haven't slept a wink all fucking night, worrying about you. How did it go? You obviously got home safely. What happened?'

Phil opened the door, pushed the bike and trailer into the shop and turned on the light. He started to unload the goods and put them on the shelves. Shirley Tate was not happy with his failure to respond to her questions.

'Well?'

'Well what?'

'Fucking hell, Phil! How did it go last night? Have you gone fucking deaf or something this morning?'

Phil looked at his shop assistant, legs apart, hands on hips and steam coming out of her ears.

'May I say something, Shirley? Dear, sweet Shirley.'

'I wish you fucking would.'

'Your language deteriorates with each passing day. I'm not complaining – I find it quite sexy – but have you heard yourself lately?'

'Is it that bad? I never used to swear at all, what with the girls and Geoff, but in those days we didn't swear because it was bad manners. Now who gives a fuck about manners, good or bad?'

Phil was laughing now because he realised that Shirley had got into the habit of swearing and it would take a return to the old days to get her out of it. Her effing and blinding was just a symptom of the hate that consumed her.

'I think you have excellent manners, madam, which combined with the odd sexy phrase makes you a very desirable woman. However, I have work to do so go and put the fucking kettle on and over a cup of your wonderful tea I will reveal all. Can you wait for ten minutes to hear all the salacious details of the orgy up at the judge advocate's house?'

'Orgy? With Emily? I can't wait ten minutes to hear about that. I'll give you five – and if you're not in the kitchen by then there'll be fucking trouble. Oh Christ, there I go again.'

Phil was still laughing as she marched away to make the tea and he continued with his work. He had purposely had this conversation with Shirley because he wanted her in a good mood before he told her of the previous night's events. He had never found that lying came easily to him – at school, to his family, to his bosses or even his shop customers – and he was now going to lie to Shirley Tate. This was not because he didn't trust her – he did, implicitly – but he had decided to tell no one of his conversation with the general and Miss Jeffers. By sticking to this rule, then if news of it got out, only one of two people could be responsible – the general or Miss Jeffers. He would have to confide in Leroy to a certain extent but he had no intention of telling him the whole story. There was a shout from the kitchen.

'Time's up! Tea's ready, and I'm ready, willing and waiting for you to reveal all. Get in here, you bastard, or else.'

'Or else what?'

'You wouldn't want to know! Come on, Phil – you're being a fucking tease now.'

Phil went obediently to have his tea and reveal all. In the end, the lying was easy. This was mainly because Shirley was more interested in other things rather than the after-dinner conversations. Phil had to supply full details of the house – curtains, carpets, furniture, rooms, lighting and wallpaper. They spent a good five minutes on the flower arrangements in each room and whether the flowers used were plastic or real. Next came questions about the meal. Was the pheasant properly cooked and was the soufflé all right? How many wine glasses were provided, was there a carafe of water, how many forks did each person have? Phil was on his second cup of tea by the time they got to Shirley's most important questions: what were the ladies wearing? What colour, style, with pleats, low-cut, long-hemmed? Phil kept telling her he couldn't remember but she quizzed him so expertly that eventually he gave her the information she wanted. When he couldn't remember, he lied – which was good practice for what lay ahead.

'What did you talk about?' Shirley asked at last.

Here we go, thought Phil.

'I didn't talk much – there was a lot of small talk about the food and wine but it was mostly people introducing themselves because none of us had met before.'

'So what did they all do for a living – this Harry Stanton, for instance?'

'I think he was some kind of politician but I didn't talk to him much – at dinner he was deep in conversation with Gerald.'

'How is the old bugger?'

'In a wheelchair after his heart problems but he's still good for a laugh and I enjoyed meeting him again.'

'And the general – the guest of honour – what was he like?'

'Again, I didn't speak much to him but he seemed an amiable sort of chap. No one got much of a chance to talk to him really. Our judge advocate took him under her wing from the start and tended to monopolise his brief time with us.'

'Now, there's a fucking surprise. I suppose the old cow thought she might get a promotion out of it.'

'Now, now, Shirley – I've told you before about being bitchy when talking about the lovely Emily.'

'Well… The woman makes my blood boil. How she ever got Gerald to stay with her all these years, God knows.'

'Mrs Robson, the Corporal's wife, was a pleasant woman but she was very nervous about the whole thing, just like me. We stuck by each other for protection. Anyway, the whole thing was pleasant enough but it's over now and it's back to reality with a vengeance. It was nice while it lasted, though – I enjoyed the food.'

'What was the point of it? Did you find that out?'

'No. I don't think there was any point to it except they needed some people to make up the numbers for the general's visit.'

'Are they going to have another one?'

'I don't fucking know, Shirley – why?'

'Perhaps they'll invite me next time.'

'God I hope not,' said Phil with genuine alarm, which Shirley noticed.

'Why not? You cheeky sod! I suppose I'm not good enough for your new snobby friends. Just remember, I used to be Emily's best friend.'

'I do remember, but times have changed and now you can't say her name without using an expletive. I would genuinely fear for your safety if you went to the next dinner party, if there ever is one. I can just see it now – candlelight, polite conversation as the main course is served and Emily Fairfax asks her old friend Shirley Tate to pass the salt. I can hear the silence descend on the room as her ex-best friend replies in her loudest voice, "You lost the use of your fucking arms, fish-face? Get it yourself, fucking lazy cow."'

They were both laughing.

'I can be polite when I want to be.'

'I know you can, but not around Emily in those kind of circumstances. If you had a couple of drinks before the meal, it probably wouldn't get to the main course – you'd have killed her with your cheese knife!'

'Perhaps you're right, but it would be nice to see the house. It's no use asking you – you don't look at curtains like women do. Do you want me to open the shop? It's time.'

'Yes,' said Phil, grateful that the grilling was over. He was convinced that he had got away with his white lies. He was wrong. Shirley popped her head round the kitchen door.

'You forgot one – what about that other woman? The mysterious Miss Jeffers, what was she like?'

Phil realised that he had been celebrating too early – this was going to be tricky.

'She was a mystery. Gerald and I wondered if she was the general's mistress but Gerald said that she was there in her own right, so God knows what she does. She was pleasant enough but she ignored me most of the time and talked to the corporal.'

'Did you talk to anybody? Everyone seems to have been talking to someone else.'

'Well... that's just how it worked out. I must admit I tried to stay out of it – you told me to be careful so I was.'

'You're a good boy – do you always do what you're told?'

'All the time – it's safer that way.'

'Mmm,' said Shirley, 'I wonder. Anyway, let's get on – the customers will be pouring in soon. Come and help.'

They both went into the shop and began to serve the few

customers who were already arriving. They dealt with the complaints, the moans, the protests and the groans from everyone – there was never anything else due to the poor quality of the goods and the relatively high prices they had to charge by law.

It was a little after nine o'clock when Leroy Preston walked into the shop and asked Shirley if he could speak to Mr King. She looked him up and down before replying.

'Why?'

'He asked me to call here for the key this morning.'

'What key?'

'The key to his house.'

'What do you want with the key to his house?'

'I'm his new lodger. I saw him last night and he agreed that we could move in today.'

'We?'

'Me and my two friends.'

'It's the first I've heard of it – are you sure it was Phil King?'

'108 Victoria Way?'

'That's his address. You said you agreed this last night – were you at the dinner party?'

'Pardon?'

'Never mind – where did you see him last night?'

'At his house – listen, lady, are you Mrs King or something, because I'm getting a bit tired of all these questions. Is the man here?'

'He's in the back and, for the record, I'm neither Mrs King nor his "something". I'm his first line of defence and protector so don't be so fucking cheeky.'

'Then he's a very lucky man – how about protecting me as well?'

'Against what?'

'Everything and everybody.'

'You're being cheeky again – what's your name?'

'Leroy Preston – what's yours?'

'Mrs Tate and don't you forget it.'

'I wouldn't dare.'

Shirley walked to the back of the shop with Leroy watching her all the way. She reached the kitchen and shouted, making sure that Mr Preston could hear her, 'Phil?'

'Yes?'

'There's somebody here who wants to see you.'

'Who is it?'

'Calls himself Leroy. He's a big, cheeky bastard but he seems all right – shall I send him through?'

'Christ – yes, I didn't think he'd be so early. Send him in.'

Shirley turned to shout to Leroy but found that he was right behind her.

'Back off, Mr Preston – I'm spoken for. Mr King will see you now.'

'Thank you, Mrs Tate, you have been most kind,' said Leroy and walked into the kitchen.

Shirley wandered back down the shop and wondered about two things: why had Phil taken in lodgers? And who had she been talking about when she said she was 'spoken for'?

Meanwhile, Phil and Leroy decided to have a cup of tea together before going round to the house.

'So, what was the hostel like?' asked Phil.

'Let me put it this way, Mr King—'

'Phil. Call me Phil – I'll call you Leroy, if you don't mind. If we're going to share the house, we might as well be on first-name terms.'

'That's fine by me, Phil. My two mates are Davie and Karen. You'll meet them in a minute – I told them to go straight round to the house. I didn't think you'd mind.'

Phil shook his head.

'You were asking about the hostel – well, let me put it like this: if the authorities offer you a choice someday between an hour in the hostel and death, I would seriously advise you to opt for the latter. The place is fucking appalling.'

'I'd heard. Anyway, you're out of there – let's get you over to the house and settled in. Is that all your stuff?' asked Phil, pointing to the pack on Leroy's back.

'Yes, that's it. I travel light.'

They walked into the shop and Phil waited until Shirley had finished serving a customer – he couldn't forget all the old customs – before speaking.

'I'm just taking Leroy round to the house, Shirley. Hold the fort until I get back – I shouldn't be too long. OK?'

'No problem, boss. Make sure you've locked the silver away.'

'You've met Shirley Tate, my assistant, Leroy. Take no notice of her. It's nothing personal – she hates everybody.'

'I think she's lovely,' said Leroy. 'If she wasn't "spoken for" I'd make a play.'

'Fuck off, the pair of you,' replied Shirley.

The two men left the shop, turned left along England Avenue on their way to the house and Shirley found herself alone.

She sat down behind the counter and began to think. Too much had happened in the last twenty-four hours or so. Phil had changed beyond all recognition. The previous day, when he had gone to give his Report, he had been exactly the same as he had been for the previous three years – beaten, morose, sad, pessimistic and an all-round miserable bastard. He had changed – taking in lodgers, flirting with her, laughing with the customers – and become almost his old self again. What had caused this change? Perhaps he had seen the light and realised that it was no good being depressed for the rest of his life. Whatever it was that had brought about the change, it was something that had occurred since he went to give his Report and that could only mean one thing. There was only one event which had been out of the ordinary – the dinner party. Something must have happened at the house of that cow Emily Fairfax that had brought about the revolution in her boss's behaviour. Something had been said or done up there which had caused him to join the human race again. She was worried and pleased at the same time. Worried because she had become very fond of Phil and didn't want anything to happen to him, but pleased because he was more like his old self. Her thoughts wandered to what she should do. The first thing, she realised, was to find out what had really gone on at the dinner party.

She stood, her decision made – she would go and see her ex-best friend Emily Fairfax and ask her politely for a summary of the night's events. If that didn't work – well, there was always the cheese knife!

Seven

Phil let them both into the house – there was no sign of Leroy's friends – and they went into the kitchen. Phil showed Leroy the cupboards that the lodgers could use and they talked for a few minutes about a share of tea and sugar. They seemed to be getting on well together and Leroy realised he had got a good deal after the demolition of his flat.

'OK,' said Phil, 'come upstairs and I'll show you the rooms. There are four bedrooms and an attic so you shouldn't be too cramped.'

They went up the first flight of stairs and Phil motioned to where the upstairs bathroom was situated but he then ignored the three bedrooms on the first floor and ascended the next flight of stairs to the top of the house. Nobody had been up here for years – he and Rosie had never used this floor – and the dust rose from their footsteps as evidence of this. Leroy struggled with the large pack on his back but eventually they were both standing in the unused small fourth bedroom. Phil turned to face his new lodger.

'All right, put the pack on the bed and take all your clothes off.'

Leroy stared at him.

'What did you say?'

'Put the pack on the bed and take all your clothes off.'

'Fuck off, man – I don't know what you thought but this ain't part of the deal. I'm not queer and I don't propose to join today.'

'Leroy, I'm not a homosexual either and I don't want your body. I want to make sure that you're not carrying any recording devices. I want to talk to you about something in private and I just want to make sure that it is in private. If it makes it any easier, I'll get undressed as well.'

'No thanks, that wouldn't make it any easier at all – a damn sight worse in fact. You keep your clothes on. Recording devices? Why would I want to record you? Who for?'

'The authorities.'

'Jesus, I've heard it all now. Are you on tablets for this? The doctors may be able to cure you before it's too late.'

'Humour me, Leroy, please. I need to be sure. It's very important.'

'OK, but you stand over by that wall.'

Leroy began to undress. When he was naked and shivering, Phil spoke again.

'Right, get dressed again – I'm satisfied. I'll start going through your pack – is that all right with you?'

'Sure, man – be my guest. Christ, I only want to rent a room. I hate to think what the interview would be like if I was asking for a job at the shop.' Leroy started to laugh. 'Hey, is that it? How did the lovely Mrs Tate get the job? Did you bring her up here as well? You dirty bugger!'

'No, I didn't. You are a special case. OK, I've checked your pack as well and I can't find anything. I'm sorry about all this, Leroy, but I had to be sure – double-dog, absolutely one hundred per cent sure – before I take you into my confidence.'

'Man, forget it – this obviously means a lot to you. OK, let's start again. You've got my full attention.'

'Do you agree that this will be strictly between us?'

'Yes – but... if this affects Davie and Karen then I'll have to tell them. We've been friends for a long time now and we keep no secrets from each other. But, I agree that I won't say a word to anyone without telling you first. Is that OK with you?'

'That's fine.'

'Right, fire away. What's the problem?'

Phil smiled and looked at Leroy. Could he trust this man whom he had only just met? He had to – he had no choice.

'I asked that question of someone last night – "what's the problem?"'

'What was the answer?'

'You, Leroy Preston – you're the problem.'

'You must have been talking to my mum, that's what she used to say.'

'It wasn't your mum, it was a General Turner. Last night, if you remember, I kicked you out of here because I was going to a dinner party at the house of the judge advocate. I didn't know why I was invited but I found out at the end of the meal. This General Turner and a woman called Miss Jeffers cornered me at the end of the meal and said they wanted to speak to me in private. They talked a lot of shit about what I thought about my life but eventually we got to what they wanted to really talk about – you.'

'I know General Turner – I've never met him but I know of him. He's a stupid bastard who'll believe anything that enables him to hold on to his status. I've never heard of a Miss Jeffers – describe her.'

Phil did this and soon the light dawned on Leroy's face.

'Arabella Corcoran – that's who she is. Is this room safe?'

'To my knowledge nobody's been up here for ten years – since Rosie and I bought the house. Why?'

Leroy didn't reply. He got up from the bed where he had been sitting and went over to his backpack. He opened it and extracted a pad and a pen. He wrote something and then showed it to Phil. Phil read what Leroy had written and nodded. They both rose, went downstairs to the front door and out into Victoria Way. Leroy led the way, turning right towards the sea. When they reached the cliff top, Leroy stopped and faced his landlord.

'What did they say about me?'

'They intimated that you were some kind of subversive or terrorist.'

Leroy nodded. He thought for a moment.

'Jesus, what a fuck-up. What did they want you to do?'

'Spy on you, find out what your plans were.'

'Jesus, the bastards! Why are you telling me all this?

'I want us to come to some sort of arrangement.'

'Arrangement? With bastards like those two? You're out of your fucking mind. Phil, I'm sorry you got involved in all this but the best thing would be if we all buggered off. Tell them we didn't like the rooms or something equally stupid. We'll go back to the hostel and find somewhere else to stay. There's no sense in your getting involved. Come on, let's go back to the house and I'll pick up Davie and Karen. You're out of your depth with those two shitbags and us. Come on.'

Phil hadn't moved. Leroy looked at him for a while and then spoke.

'Shit! They promised you something if you did what they said, didn't they? What did they promise? A quick shag with Arabella? No, that wouldn't be enough. I know – safe passage for you and Shirley Tate to a better life. No? Oh, Christ, you're married, aren't you? With kids? Do you know where they are?'

'No, they disappeared during the Chaos.'

'The fucking bastards. I bet they promised that you would see them again if you helped them by spying on me. Is that it?'

'Yes, I wasn't going to tell you that bit but that's what they said.'

There were tears in Phil's eyes as he spoke. Leroy gripped the railings they were leaning on and looked out to sea. The morning was cold but clear – you could see the gunboats on patrol.

'I have a question, Phil. Why are you telling me all this? Why didn't you just spy on me and collect your reward?'

Phil thought for a moment before replying.

'I thought about it. I really did. But I couldn't, in the end, reconcile my conscience with working for these bastards, even if it meant not seeing my wife and kids again. My plan was to come to a compromise with you – it sounds a lot of bollocks now but at the time I thought it might work. It won't, will it?'

'Never in a month of fucking Sundays, Phil. Let's go back to the house. Don't say a word to anybody about this conversation. Fucking hell, what a mess! Come on, we'll work something out.'

'Are you a terrorist, Leroy?'

'I don't know what that word means any more. I always thought it meant someone who tried to overthrow a lawful government without using a ballot box. Someone who used terror and violence instead of his vote to change the status quo. In the present circumstances, I don't see how anyone who wants to change this bloody mess could be accused of being a terrorist.'

'Last night the general said he represented the "elected government of Great Britain".'

'And you believed that load of old bollocks, did you?'

'I didn't see how I could argue with what he said. I've not seen a newspaper or any kind of news broadcast for more than three years.'

'Listen, Phil, we've got other problems at the moment so this is not the time to go into the history of all this. We don't know the whole story, but we know bits of it, and if those bits are right – and I think they are – your general and the bitch who goes by the name of Miss Jeffers are as much the representatives of an "elected government" as my arse is representative of a map of Europe!'

They had reached the house and outside were a young man and a girl. Phil opened the door and they all followed him inside. They went into the kitchen and, while Phil busied himself making a pot of tea, he took the chance to cast an eye over his three new lodgers.

Leroy was a tall, young man but he wasn't thin or fat. He looked as if he was the perfect weight for his height and age. He looked fit and Phil wondered how he kept in such good trim with the awful food they all had to eat. His skin was dark brown rather than black and Phil guessed there was some Caribbean blood in him somewhere. The scar down his face was the first thing you noticed about him. Stretching from his ear lobe to his right nostril, it looked old but it gave him a menacing look when he wasn't smiling. In a fight, Phil thought, he would rather have Leroy on his side than against him. His hair was short, black and curly. His eyes were deep pools of indeterminate colour. Phil wondered if he was trustworthy. He hoped so – he had just trusted him with his life.

Davie Lennox was the complete opposite to his mate. Small and wiry, with a marked Glaswegian accent, he was scruffy and looked as if he needed a bath. His brown hair was long and hung down to his shoulders and could certainly have done with a wash. His little round face was covered in spots and he wore thin, metal-framed glasses. Phil wondered how these two opposites had ever become friends – what did they have in common? But Davie seemed pleasant enough, although the accent took some getting used to. When he was thanking Phil for letting him stay, the latter had to ask him to repeat what he had said before he could understand.

Karen Markham was the second mystery woman to enter Phil's life in the last twenty-four hours. She was very young – no more than sixteen, Phil guessed – and she hadn't said a word since she had arrived. She was dressed, like the other two, in layers of old clothing. She had straight black hair and a pretty face but her dark green eyes continuously darted back and forth around the room as though she was looking for something. Phil found it disconcerting at first but then got used to it and after a few minutes didn't notice it at all.

The three men sat down around the kitchen table to drink their tea but Karen stood in the far corner, refusing the chair that Phil offered her. Phil went through all the stuff again about the shared kitchen and the rooms upstairs for the benefit of the two newcomers and then Leroy spoke.

'Right – let's get down to the main item on the agenda. Our good friend, Phil, has a problem and before we go any further we have to see if there is a solution.'

Davie leaned forward and started to speak but Leroy butted in.

'This may not be the time and the place, Davie. Can we use the room upstairs where I had my interview, Phil?'

'Yeah, sure. Do whatever you think is best. Are you going to tell them everything?'

'I have to – it involves them. Don't worry – Davie and I have been best friends for years and he's never let me down. As for Karen, well, she's been with us for about six months. We found her in the street and she just tagged along. I don't think she's got any other family apart from us two but she's a good girl and she won't say a word to anyone. She hasn't spoken a word since we met her. Davie reckons it's a reaction to something she's seen but I don't know – perhaps one day she'll be able to tell us what it's all about.'

'Are these two the ones who resigned from the official resistance with you?'

'Ah, they told you that as well, did they? Cheeky sods! Is that why they want you to—'

'Yes. They knew all about the other lot. Names, membership and their plans. There was no problem when you were in with them; now… well.'

'Right. Good. Now I have the full picture. Come on, you two – let's go and sort out our rooms.' Leroy winked at Phil.

'I'm going back to the shop. I'm sorry about all this – but I couldn't see what else I could do.'

'Perfect. Listen, Phil, if we're not here when you get back, you'll know we couldn't find a way to help. We'll disappear and you'll never see us again. Nobody will know about our little conversations. Is that OK with you?'

'That seems fine to me. I hope I see you all later. Cheerio and thanks again.'

Phil left them to it and walked slowly back to the shop. He realised his life and his future rested in the hands of the three people back at the house, but what else could he have done? His life was becoming an unholy mess but it had been that way for three years. At least now there might be a chance of seeing the light at the end of the tunnel. Ah, what the hell. 'Who gives a shit?' – that was his new motto. Let's see what this new roll of the dice brings, he concluded. It didn't take him long to find out.

He turned into England Avenue and found himself in a queue for one of the regular checks that the guards mounted to verify people's papers. Nobody seemed to mind – the people had got used to them. Everybody stood patiently in the queue until it was their turn. It took ten minutes for Phil to reach the guards and the man in front of him was frogmarched off to an empty shop where they had established their temporary office. He handed over his papers and waited. The guard examined them in fine detail but didn't give them back.

'You'll have to come with me. There's a problem with your documents – follow me.' The guard set off in the direction of the office and Phil followed. This had happened to him once before over a technicality of the dates on the papers and he was not unduly worried. However, his state of mind soon turned to panic as he went into the shop. The guard went past the table where a sergeant was going through the other man's documents and carried on towards a door at the back.

'You – in here.' He opened the door a fraction and walked away.

Phil pushed open the door and entered a small room. There was a desk with two straight backed chairs. In one of the chairs sat Miss Jeffers – no ballgown this time – wearing a military uniform like those of the guards. She was smoking a cigarette and smiling.

'Good morning, Philip. I told you I'd be in touch. How are you today?'

Phil stared at her in disbelief. Was this what working for these people was going to be like? Everyone stopped at the checkpoint would know within five minutes that he had been given special treatment.

'You are one hell of a stupid bitch. What the fuck do you think you're doing? How do I explain this to all those people outside?'

'Don't worry, Philip – one in every three people stopped this morning has been brought in here. Our secret is safe. Would you like a cup of coffee?'

Phil put his head in his hands and didn't know whether to laugh or cry. What had he got himself into? Eventually he recovered enough to sit up and look at her. She looked no less desirable than she had the previous evening, despite the fact that the uniform disguised the voluptuous curves that had been in evidence when she had worn the black dress. But he couldn't forgive the smile that she still wore after what she had said then. Somehow he realised that he needed to find a way to gain the upper hand in this relationship – if that was what it was. But how? In the end he decided to try politeness.

'Coffee would be lovely – two sugars, please. How nice to see you again so soon after our last meeting. I was beginning to wonder whether you'd ever get in touch. Are you free for lunch by any chance?'

She leant on the desk and looked directly at him.

'Fuck off, Philip. Let's get down to work.'

Perhaps, he thought, politeness was not the answer. Maybe rudeness would bring about a reversal of the balance of power between the two of them.

'No, you fuck off and I'll go back to the shop.' He stood up and made to leave.

'Sit down, now. As I said, we have work to do.'

He sat down. Politeness and rudeness hadn't worked. Perhaps he'd have to think of something else.

Eight

The coffee arrived on a silver tray as if by magic and the two of them got down to work.

'Has the devious Mr Preston been in touch yet to see about his room?'

'Is there something personal in this between you and Leroy?'

'No, why?'

'I just wondered. Yes, Mr Preston has arrived with his mates and they are assessing whether the accommodation is suitable. I left them at the house – if they are there when I get back, then they are staying and if not… well, they'll have moved on to somewhere else.'

Miss Jeffers looked up and studied Phil intently.

'That wasn't part of the deal – we want them at your house where we can keep an eye on them.'

Phil sighed and took a sip of his coffee.

'Look, Miss Jeffers – what's your first name by the way?'

'It doesn't matter. Go on.'

'Look, I've never done this sort of thing before and so you'll probably know all the right methods, but I would have thought that the best way to find out anything about Leroy and his plans would be to make him feel relaxed and safe. I can't see that it would help our cause if he became suspicious of me and the house. We don't want him thinking that the authorities want him to stay with me, do we?'

'I just hope, for your sake, that they like the rooms. What are the names of his two mates?'

'Davie Lennox and Karen Markham.'

'I see. That's good.'

'Are they the "bonus" you wanted? Are they the other two who resigned from the official resistance?'

'No, I've never heard of Karen Markham. It was another man who was with Preston and Lennox on the committee. His name is

Charles Corcoran – so I wonder where that bastard has gone.'

Phil's face betrayed nothing but the name registered inside his head. He remembered what Leroy had said after he had described Miss Jeffers to him: 'Arabella Corcoran – that's who she is.' It wasn't a common surname by any stretch of the imagination – were they related? Husband? Brother? Father? Phil came to the conclusion that it was all becoming too complicated and he should concentrate on one thing at a time. He had enough problems with this interrogation.

'Shall I let you know if he turns up?' asked Phil.

'Yes, and get me some information on this Karen woman.'

'She's not a woman, she's just a girl – a very frightened one by the looks of it.'

'Fancy her, do you, Philip? I suppose you want to help her overcome her fear. Be careful – these are all dangerous people.'

'You are something else, Miss Jeffers, do you know that? How do you sleep at night when you're such a cruel bitch during the day?'

'My sleeping arrangements are not your concern. Come on, let's fix up our next meeting.'

'Let's not – this is getting ridiculous. Why all the fucking rush? Why don't we take it easy and see how things develop?'

'We may not have the time. These people have been out of our sight for three whole weeks. Something may have already been planned – we need to know what they're up to and we need to know fast.'

'Why don't you just take them in for questioning, like you did with my wife and kids? You could find out what you want and then they could "disappear".'

'That course of action was considered and discounted. There may be other people involved – we think it's better, for the time being, to keep an eye on them.'

She consulted a diary that was on the desk.

'Will Friday be OK? I could come to the shop to see you.'

'Jesus, I'm not getting through to you, am I? I knew at the dinner party that you lot lived in some sort of time warp compared to the rest of us. Now listen to me for a couple of minutes. Please, I don't want to end up dead. It's in your interests as well – my being dead wouldn't push the operation much further forward, would it?'

'Go on.'

'Firstly, you've convinced me that this is a dangerous game but if these people, like Leroy, are still alive after three years then they can't be stupid. I can't just barge in and ask what they are planning – I'll need to gain their confidence and their trust. In that way, they might let something slip or, better still for your purposes, they might even take me into their confidence. Whichever, I can't see that happening overnight – you've got to give me some time.'

'Right, I'll give you a week – no longer. You said "firstly" – what were the other points?'

'Secondly, when the fuck is Friday? It may have escaped your attention but we have no calendars here. I hardly know what month it is. We have to attend to give our Report every twenty-eight days. We all keep a chart on the wall – marking off the days. So let's just say we'll meet seven days from now. OK?'

'Anything else?'

'Yes, whatever you do, don't come anywhere near my shop.'

'Why?'

'You wouldn't fit in with the surroundings or the clientele. I serve regulars in my shop who come in every day. They – no, that should be "we" – all smell! Your visit would be all round the town within half an hour and I don't think I could handle the questions. Plus the fact that my shop assistant guards me like a hawk – she'd probably tear your eyes out after just one look at you.

'Send a summons with one of the guards for me to report somewhere because you want to have another look at my papers because there was a problem today that hadn't been resolved. One of my customers had one of those a few weeks ago so it won't look too suspicious. How does that sound?'

Phil felt quite pleased with himself at coming up with this idea. At least it would keep this woman away from the shop and out of Shirley's claws. There was only one nagging doubt in his mind about his plan – the customer who had received the summons had never been seen again!

'That sounds fine – I'll fix it.' Miss Jeffers got up and handed

Phil his papers. 'You'd better go. Good hunting. Remember the prize at the end.'

There she goes again, thought Phil. He stalked out of the room and through the makeshift guard post to the street. Hardly anyone was waiting now – as soon as these controls were set up, word got around and people took a different route to wherever they were going. This was not because they had anything to hide – they were just fed up with the inconvenience of it all. Life was hard enough without extra problems like a document check. It was mid-afternoon when Phil returned to the shop. Shirley was serving someone with the last of the potatoes that he had brought that morning and he went straight through to the back. He thought he deserved a cup of tea after the day he'd had! He knew the onslaught would come – he reckoned in about thirty seconds' time – but he had just enough time to put the kettle on before it arrived.

'"Hold the fort", you said. "I won't be long", you said. Where the fuck have you been?'

Phil looked at her. God, what a woman. He knew that she was genuinely fond of him – he just hoped that this fondness wasn't turning into something else on her part. It would make life vastly more complicated than it already was. When Geoff, her husband, had disappeared, he had tried to help find out what had happened to him and he knew that Shirley had found great comfort in that. She, in turn, had been at his side in his search for Rosie and the kids. They hadn't uncovered any news and they never really talked about their missing loved ones but this uncertainty about their marital positions had somehow formed a bond between them. They were a team and that's how Phil wanted it to stay.

'You know, Shirley, you took me back to the old days for a few minutes with your warm welcome. Man goes out to work, wife stays at home, man gets home a little bit late, man greeted fondly by his wife who is grateful that he is home safely even though he is late. She greets him at the door with a welcoming smile and a hug and then says the immortal phrase, "Where the fuck have you been?" I'm glad I wasn't married to you! I'm sorry – I was delayed. I had to show Leroy the house, meet the other two lodgers and then I got stopped at the document checkpoint and then I rushed here so that you wouldn't be worried.'

Shirley looked at him for a long time before she answered.

'Sorry. Phil, can I ask you a question?'

'As long as it's not couched in the same terms as the last one, go ahead.'

'What's happened? You've changed. Are you all right?'

'I'm fine, stop worrying about me. I just got fed up with being a miserable, boring bastard of a shopkeeper. I came to the conclusion, "who gives a shit?" Nobody else does, so why should I?'

'If you say so, but the question still stands. Where have you been? I know you've not been with Leroy and his friends because they came round here and dropped the key off.'

Phil felt his heart flutter – so that was the end of that, he thought. Well, he'd tried, although he was not sure Miss Jeffers would see it that way.

'Did Leroy say anything?'

'No. That Karen is a funny-looking girl isn't she?'

'Yes. Did they have their bags with them?'

'I didn't notice. So, where have you been?'

'At the checkpoint – they weren't satisfied with my papers when they looked at them in the street so they took me into that little shop that they've commandeered and I had to go into the back room and have them properly checked. I was there about half an hour but she said I could go in the end.'

'She? A woman guard checked your papers?'

Here we go again, thought Phil, more lies.

'Yes – a big, fat woman with acne. She went through my papers with a fine toothcomb. God knows what she was hoping to find, but in the end she told me to bugger off and here I am.'

'She must have arrived afterwards.'

Phil looked up sharply.

'Afterwards?' he asked.

'After I stopped looking out of the shop window. I saw them erecting the checkpoint and they were all men. Perhaps she was a specialist and came on later. Anyway, you're here now and safe. Why did you want to take in lodgers?'

'I didn't – I was given no choice. Their block of flats had been demolished and they were pointed in my direction by the sergeant in charge. I suppose they keep a list of empty rooms in the town from the answers we give them at the Report. They seem a decent enough lot though, so I'm not expecting any problems.'

'That Leroy is a flirt – dirty bugger! And I still think that Karen is a funny one.'

'She's dumb – don't be too hard on her. Anyway, if they dropped the key off, they might have had a change of mind and found somewhere else or better.'

'Where would they find somewhere better around here? They can't go to an estate agent and ask to see his list, can they?'

'No, I suppose not. But never mind – let's tidy up and go home.'

'You can't – not yet, anyway. Margaret Hills wants to see you. She came in earlier and demanded to see you.'

'What about?'

'I don't fucking know. She wouldn't tell me.'

'Another complaint about the prices, I suppose. OK, you finish off in the shop and I'll wait for her.'

They busied themselves for half an hour and then Shirley left. Phil was left on his own. He looked at his bike and decided to give it a clean. It was just before six o'clock that the door opened and Margaret Hills entered. She shut the door behind her as the siren went off. She turned and locked the door. Phil looked on puzzled. The former schoolteacher began to search the shop and went into the kitchen. There was the sound of cupboards being opened and shut. Eventually, she came back into the shop and stood in front of the bemused shopkeeper. She motioned with her hand for him to follow her back to the kitchen. She sat on one of the chairs and began to unravel the scarf that was wound around her neck and face. Phil sat down and looked at her. He had been wrong about her the day before. This wasn't a woman who was a pale shadow of her former self – this was a woman who had disguised her former self and disguised herself very well indeed. Without the scarf and with no onlookers, apart from Phil, she was easily recognisable as the formidable Miss Hills from his school days. Yes, she was older, but Phil realised now that she hadn't changed all that much.

She eventually spoke in those clipped tones that he remembered so well from Class 3b.

'How are you, young Philip – still having trouble with your intransitive verbs? I had high hopes for you once but you fell in love and became a newsagent – what a waste!'

'I can't believe you ever had high hopes for me but it's nice of you to remember me. I used to enjoy your lessons – you taught me that education could be fun. We used to write and perform those little playlets in class. It was good! But I enjoyed the visits to Stratford-on-Avon best. They were a bit of magic in the overall shite of the national curriculum.'

'Yes, they were happy days – have you ever thought about whether you could do something to get them back?'

'The only thing I want back is my family.'

'Aren't they the same thing? You want to return to a time when you were a happily married man, whereas I would like to teach the glories of Shakespeare to your children.'

'I suppose you're right if you look at it that way, but what can I do to get them back?'

'Fight. Fight, Philip King, until there's no fight left in you. Have you given up? Have you accepted the fucking terrible mess that we live in now? Throughout the ages, men have fought against the tyranny that other men have sought to impose upon them. Those men left a legacy to us all – we must accept the torch that they lit.'

'Fight? What can I fight with?'

'Not "what?", Philip, "whom?" – whom can you fight with?'

'The answer to that is easy: nobody – because nobody is fighting. We've all given up and gone home.'

'Not everyone has gone home, Philip – some of us are fighting. We may not be great in number and, at the moment, are not very effective but we keep that torch alight and hope alive.'

'What are you trying to say?'

'There is a resistance group in the town of which I'm proud to be a member. We'd like you to join us. We've lost some members in the last few weeks and we need some new blood. At our last meeting, I suggested you and the members agreed. I was deputed to sound you out and invite you to our next meeting. So, what do you think?'

Phil needed time to think. Was this a coincidence? Was it someone's idea of a joke? He stood and walked around the room. He looked at Margaret and then down at the floor. He needed time.

'Can I think this over and let you know tomorrow? It's come as something of a shock. Until now I hadn't realised that there was any sort of resistance in the town. I need to weigh up the pros and cons. Is that all right?'

'Perfectly all right, young Philip. Let me know your decision tomorrow when I come in to buy your overpriced stock.'

Margaret Hills stood up, smiled and began to rewind her dirty, smelly scarf round her neck and head. When she spoke again she had reverted to her role as the horrible old woman whom nobody would suspect of being involved in any sort of resistance. The change was instantaneous and, to Phil's eyes, startling.

'Well, I'll fuck off, then. I'll get home so that you can go and have a shag with that Shirley Tate.'

'Margaret, I can assure you that there is nothing like that going on between me and Shirley.'

'More fool you, then, and it's Mrs Hills to you. See you tomorrow. We need some new ideas and a sprinkling of youth or, in your case, a shower of middle age. Think about the offer but don't talk it over with young Shirley – or anyone else, for that matter. This is strictly between the two of us. Is that clear?'

'Understood, Mrs Hills. I promise to think about it. I'll let you out of the front door.'

They walked back into the shop and Phil collected his bike and trailer. He locked the door after them and they went their separate ways along England Avenue. Only a few people were about, hurrying home before the Curfew sounded, and none of them took any notice of the two people exiting the shop.

But someone did notice the parting of the shopkeeper and the old tramp. At the back of the document checkpoint stood a woman guard – not a big, fat woman with acne as Phil had described her, but a rather beautiful young woman even in her guard's uniform. She had watched the scene with interest, made a note in the diary she was holding and stubbed out her cigarette. She made no comment except to call for her driver. She also was going home.

Nine

Phil King entered the backyard of 108 Victoria Way and deposited the bike and trailer against the side wall. The house was in darkness. He found the back door locked and so went down the side passage to the front door, which he unlocked, and entered the hall. There was no sound and he went to the kitchen and switched on the light. Nothing seemed to be missing and there was no evidence to suggest that Leroy and his mates had used anything. He put the kettle on and found a packet of soup and a pan. It was still cold and he pulled his coat tighter around him. He sat down and wondered what he was going to do about his old schoolteacher's offer.

Life was becoming very complicated! The authorities wanted him to spy on the unofficial resistance, who had obviously taken fright and cleared out. He would have to tell Miss Jeffers that her wonderful plan had gone all to cock after only a few hours of being put into practice but that would have to wait until the seven days were up and he met her again. Gone were his chances of seeing Rosie and the kids again, but he hadn't been too hopeful of that outcome anyway.

Then there was the invitation from Margaret Hills to join the official resistance. The authorities said they knew who the members of that organisation were and no doubt they would soon find out if Phil accepted the invitation. He surmised that there must be an informer in the little group and then went on to wonder if that person was Miss Hills. But joining would give him entry into the secret (or half-secret) world of resistance in the town and might, just might, help him to find some information on the whereabouts of his family. On balance, he thought, what had he got to lose by joining? Life couldn't get much worse than it already was and at least he would go down fighting. Did they award the Victoria Cross to activists who put sugar in the petrol tanks of military vehicles?

Having made his decision – to accept and take one day at a time – he had his meal. The food was not as good as that of the previous evening but the company was immeasurably superior! He washed up the few dishes he had used and went into the front room. It had remained exactly the way it was the day Rosie and the kids disappeared. When they were all here, it was in this room that they laughed and joked and told each other about their respective day's events. It was here they planned their holidays with maps and brochures spread all over the floor. The room was still and lifeless now.

Phil flopped down on the sofa, causing a huge cloud of dust to rise towards the ceiling. He looked across the room at the television set, which had been inactive for three years. He began to imagine that he was watching a rerun of *The Weakest Link* and promptly fell asleep.

He woke about two hours later when someone started to shake his arm. The room was dark and he saw shadowy figures moving around. He was only half-awake but he knew they had come for him. This is how it happened – darkness and disappearance. He sat upright and tried to focus his eyes properly. The man who had been shaking him spoke.

'Wake up, you lazy bastard – we need to talk.'

Phil relaxed – it was Leroy's voice.

'Jesus, you startled me!' cried Phil. 'How did you lot get in?'

'We know a man who cuts keys in his garden shed so we had two copies made of the one for your front door. I hope that was OK.'

'Are you planning on staying, then? I thought you'd buggered off when you handed the key in at the shop.'

'Why, have you changed your mind?' asked Davie Lennox anxiously.

'No, not at all. I'm glad you're staying. What made you think it would be a good idea? Remember they engineered all this so they'll be watching you.'

'Yes,' said Leroy, 'we know they're watching us here but they don't know we are aware of that, unless you've told them already. Therefore, I reckon we're winning one-nil at the moment. We had a long talk about it and that's what we decided so if there's no change of heart on your part, you've got three new lodgers.'

'I haven't told them anything but I was collared by that bitch Jeffers today.'

'Already? Fucking hell – she's keen! She must be worried about us.'

'She's worried about the three weeks after you left the resistance group because I don't think they had a clue what you were doing during that time. She wanted me to report back to her in a couple of days' time but I got it postponed for seven days.'

'Good man. That should give us time to sort out our plans.'

'What plans are these?' asked Phil.

Leroy looked across at Davie, who took over the dialogue.

'We have a plan to really hit these bastards where it hurts and if it works it'll send this town into uproar. But we need time and a bit of breathing space to put it into action. That's where you come in. You need to report back to Miss Fancy-knickers with details of what we're up to. Those details must be believable – you're not going to get away with a load of old bullshit. Therefore, we thought we would draw up two separate big-scale plans: one fact, the other fiction. We would work on the factual one and you would hand over the details of the fiction to Jeffers. That way, we win, you win and Miss Jeffers gets a bollocking from her bosses for lousing it up. What do you think? Do you think it will work?'

'It'll work all right but it won't help me. She said that you literally had to get caught in the act for her to keep her part of the bargain. I can't see how they're going catch you carrying out a fictitious plan when you're off somewhere doing something completely different.'

'Keep the faith, comrade. If our plan works, it won't matter where we are when the balloon goes up. On the night it happens, Miss Jeffers won't know her arse from her elbow and she'll be checking whether she has one of the first and two of the latter and not the other way about.'

Phil leaned back on the sofa and sighed.

'There's another problem,' he said.

'Christ, what now?' enquired Leroy.

'I've been invited to join the resistance group.'

Leroy and Davie looked at each other and then Davie looked at Phil before asking his question.

'Who invited you to join?'

'Margaret Hills – she used to teach me English at school. She came into the shop today and asked me to join. I asked for time to think it over and she's coming back tomorrow for my answer. The thing is, before you two say anything, I've decided to say yes. I don't believe a word of what Miss Jeffers and the general told me about them helping to find my family – I think it was a load of blackmailing bullshit. They just want me to spy on you and after that they'll just tell me to fuck off. But I want to help. I'm sick and fucking tired of my life as it is now and I want to do something to stop these bastards. You lot are into a different ball game and I can understand that. Your plans probably involve violence, which I don't think I could handle, but I can disable military vehicles as well as the next man. So, no arguments – I'm going to accept and join the group.'

Davie and Leroy began to laugh and even Karen, who had been standing in the bay window the entire time, managed a smile. Phil looked at his lodgers and wondered what he had said that had been so funny. Leroy came over to him and sat on the arm of the sofa.

'Phil King, welcome to the real world. There was a condition, which you had to agree to, before we would accept the lodgings here. If you hadn't agreed to it we were going to leave tomorrow. The condition was that you would somehow manage an invite to join the resistance group. When the time comes to put our plan into action, we could do with their help but they're fucking useless whilst there's a traitor in there. We need to find out who it is and we thought you were just the man to do it. We can help – but it'll be mainly down to you. The one thing we can tell you is that, as far as we are concerned, Margaret Hills is the only one not under suspicion. All the others are fair game and it's got to be one of them who's telling Miss Jeffers and her mates every little detail. So, we agree with your decision to join.

'As for the other thing – about your wife and kids – my experience tells me that you're right to think that way. Don't get me wrong – I'm not saying you should give up hope – but don't expect any help from the authorities. Look at the evidence: anyone who could force people to live like we do is not going to give a monkey's fuck about reneging on a blackmail promise.'

'I suppose you're right,' said Phil, sounding and feeling sad.

It was at this point that Karen came over to him and sat beside him on the sofa. There were tears in her eyes. She put her arms around Phil and began to sob.

'I think she's trying to say that she feels your pain. God knows what that girl has been through,' said Leroy.

Phil held the young frightened girl. Perhaps she too had lost a family member, or even her whole family. After a while, her sobbing stopped and she went back to stand in the bay window. Phil looked at her and then spoke.

'Karen, I can't take your suffering away from you but I can feel it. I hate to think what's caused it but, whilst you're here, if a hug helps you, then come to me and you can have a hug. All right?'

Karen nodded and Phil turned back to face Leroy.

'I hope to God you're not going to tell me any details of your real plan. I don't want to get it all mixed up and tell the wrong story.'

'No, that's what we were going to suggest. We'll keep that just between the three of us and you won't know a thing. There's something else you should know as well: we never write anything down about our activities. Davie is blessed with a photographic memory so we never commit anything to paper. I just thought I'd tell you in case you thought we were swanning round doing nothing. There is also another reason for this, apart from the secrecy aspect; if the bastards come round to search the house, they won't find anything and Miss bloody Jeffers won't be able to disprove what you're telling her. Right, is everybody clear now on what's to be done?'

Davie and Karen nodded but Phil raised his hand.

'I'm clear in my mind now about the whole thing – I pretend to spy on you and report back to Jeffers with a load of old bullshit. At the same time, I join the resistance group and see if I can spot the double agent. That's fine but there's a loose end in all this and I need some answers to a couple of questions before we go any further.'

'Fire away, buddy,' said Leroy. 'Let's clear up all the problems and loose ends now. What is it that's worrying you?'

'When you asked me to describe Miss Jeffers at the dinner party, you immediately said that she was Arabella Corcoran. This morning when the aforementioned Miss Jeffers was asking me about the two people who had come here with you I gave the names of Davie and Karen. She was disappointed because she'd never heard of Karen and so there was still one person missing from the trio who left the resistance group. She wondered where he had gone and what he was doing. But the thing that struck me was the name she gave me: Charles Corcoran. Now, Corcoran is not a very common surname so my questions are: where is Charles Corcoran? What is he doing? And what relation is he to his namesake "Arabella"?'

'Did you let on to that bitch Jeffers you'd heard the name before?'

'No.'

'Good. I don't want to make this into a big thing but you're entitled to some sort of explanation. Firstly, Charles is one of us and is out and about collecting information for the plan.'

'You mean he's in the town?'

'He could be. I don't know and I don't want to know. Secondly, he didn't start out on our side. He defected, if you like, after seeing what the enemy were capable of. Thirdly, Davie, Karen and I have no doubt about where his loyalties lie now – no fucking doubt at all. Fourthly, one day I hope you'll meet him and he can tell you the story of his life. Lastly, he and Arabella are brother and sister.'

'Fucking hell!' shouted Phil. 'Brother and sister? You've got to be taking the piss. He's on our side whilst his sister is trying to kick the shit out of us? This is fucking ludicrous! Now I know what the phrase "keep it in the family" means.'

Phil was dancing round the room like a demented dervish, kicking the furniture. Karen hid behind one of the curtains.

'Calm down, Phil,' shouted Leroy. 'What's the problem?'

'The problem is, how sure are you of your friend Charles?'

'Totally. I'd trust him with my life – in fact, I do.'

'Well I'm a bit loathe to trust him with my fucking life since

I've never met him but know the family because I have met his sister. If he's inherited any of her family traits he must be a right arsehole!'

'Phil, you'll have to take my word on this. Charles is a good man – one of the best – and nothing like his sister. Your life is safe with him.'

'I only hope to God you're right. It seems strange that brother and sister are involved on the front line but on opposing sides.'

'It's not so strange when you consider that their father, Sir Reginald Corcoran, was the principal architect of the way this town has been run for the last three years.'

Phil sat down again and didn't know whether to laugh or cry. A brother and sister trying to kill each other in a situation that was invented by their father. The whole scenario was becoming a circus, a complete farce of gigantic proportions.

'Are you telling me that this fucking mess was invented by Sir Reginald so that his kids could play bloody paintball games with each other?'

'Of course not – Sir Reginald was and is deadly serious about what is happening in this town. He wanted his children to agree with his views – Arabella did, Charles didn't and got out as quickly as he could. This is not a game, Phil, as well you know. Look around you! There's you, there's Karen, Margaret Hills and thousands of others living in untold misery because of Corcoran and his friends. Have a look at yourself. Do you think it's a game? I don't fucking think so! But, that's enough for tonight. We should all get to bed. One day I'll try and explain it all to you but now is not the time and it would probably be better coming from Charles since he knows the whole story – from both sides.'

'I want to know what it's all about – I need to know! Christ, I've lost my wife and kids – what the fuck is going on?'

Leroy walked over to the useless electric fire.

'I promise you, Phil, that we'll tell you all we know before the plan goes ahead. But let's all go to bed – we're all knackered and the story is a long time in its telling.'

'All right, agreed, but I want to know before anything goes ahead.'

It was Davie who spoke next.

'I'd like to sit in on that, Leroy, because I don't think I know all the whys and wherefores of this fucking English mess.'

'Jesus, that's all I need – a Scottish nationalist's fucking viewpoint on all this! Trust me,' said Leroy in exasperation. 'OK, it's a promise – sometime this week I'll tell you all what I know and, if we're lucky enough to have Charles back by then, he can fill in the blanks.'

The three men shook hands with each other over this agreement and prepared to go to bed. They wished each other goodnight and then stopped. Karen came towards them, holding out her right hand. She shook the hand of each of the men in turn. It was apparent to Phil and the other two that this gesture meant that she wanted to know what was going on as well.

Phil went to his bedroom and lay on the bed. He heard the others pottering about upstairs but the noise didn't disturb his thoughts, although they were more worries than thoughts. He wondered what he had got himself into when he heard a noise at the door which was pushed slowly open. Karen stood there. She was fully dressed, dragging a mattress behind her. She laid the mattress on the floor at the foot of the bed. She smiled at Phil, who smiled back, and then she lay down. Phil didn't know whether she had come to guard him or whether she felt safer being near him. Philip Edward King didn't care which of these two explanations was correct. He was comforted by her gesture and soon drifted into an untroubled sleep.

Ten

Phil woke before the alarm, as usual, and as soon as it went off reached for his boots. It was pitch black in the bedroom and as he went to the bathroom he tripped over something, banged his head as he fell and uttered a stream of curses. His eyes adjusted to the darkness, saw the extra mattress on the floor and remembered Karen. She was awake and stood up. She held out her hand and he took it. She led him to the bathroom and sat on the edge of the bath. He didn't know what to do. He needed a pee and motioned towards the toilet. She obviously understood and turned her head to the wall. Phil thought, What the hell if you're going to have a guardian angel, you might as well have her with you all the time, and had a pee. He had a quick wash and dried his hands on the towel, which Karen handed him. She followed him into the kitchen. Phil turned to face her and explained that he was going to the Border and that she couldn't come with him because of the restrictions. Her face dissolved.

'But,' he said, 'if you like, I'll pick you up on the way back and you can come to the shop with me. Is that all right? Leave a note for Leroy to tell him where you've gone.'

Karen's face beamed with gratitude. She kissed him on the cheek and shook his hand.

Phil went out of the back door and got his bike and trailer. As he rode along England Avenue, he wondered what Shirley would think of the new arrangement!

The trip to the Border was uneventful and Phil kept his promise and called at the house on the way back for Karen. She was sitting on the front step. As soon as she saw him pedalling hard along Victoria Way, she ran towards him. He came to a halt. She pushed him off the bike and got on. Expertly, she turned the bike and trailer around and set off towards the shop. Phil tried to keep up but was laughing so much that he soon ran out of breath. She was waiting for him at the door. They hauled the bike and trailer inside and she helped him stack the shelves with the day's bountiful harvest. They had tea together in the kitchen and then Phil opened the shop.

Karen watched him for a few minutes and then came behind the counter and, tentatively, began to serve one or two customers herself. It was difficult at first because of her lack of speech but Phil helped out when needed and soon both she and the customers had worked each other out. There was only one cloud on the horizon – Shirley's arrival was approaching!

But Shirley's arrival time came and went without any sign of Mrs Tate, and so did the rest of the morning. By lunchtime, Phil was worried – Shirley had never missed work in three years. He left Karen in the shop and went round to Shirley's house but got no answer. This was becoming serious. As the afternoon turned into early evening and darkness began to descend, Margaret Hills came into the shop. She looked at Karen.

'I see you you've traded the old shag-bag in for a younger model. Bloody disgusting, that's what it is!'

Karen looked at Phil and seemed ready to burst into tears.

'Fuck off, Margaret – that's not worthy of you. Karen is dumb or she would answer you. She is helping me out. Apologise or get out!'

'I apologise, Karen, but take my advice – don't believe a word this bugger says.'

Phil was seething with anger.

'What do you want?'

'Well I don't want to buy anything – I came for an answer.'

'Yes.'

'Good. Come to 89 Wellington Street tonight at seven.'

Mrs Hills marched out of the shop and Karen looked at Phil. If she had been able to speak she would have said, 'What the hell was all that about?' Phil shrugged his shoulders. It was just before six o'clock and Karen went into the kitchen to make them both a cup of tea when the door of the shop opened. Shirley came in, looked around and took notice of the fact that everything was neat and tidy.

'Christ, you don't need me. I thought the place would be in chaos.'

'I had help – nobody's indispensable. By the way, to coin one of your famous phrases, "Where the fuck have you been?" I was worried about you.'

Shirley stared at him.

'What do you mean "you had help"? Who from?'

'That young girl, Karen – she seems to have attached herself to me. She's in the back at the moment making the tea.'

'Well, get rid of her. I want to talk to you. I've got a friend coming and I think it would be better if the three of us were alone.'

'Just hang on a minute,' said Phil, 'who gives the orders around here? This is my shop and I decide who goes and who stays. Karen is a poor, harmless kid who, for some reason, likes to stay close to me and I like that – it's good to feel wanted again. Anyway, she can't speak so whatever needs to be private will stay private with her. Now, an answer to my question, please: where the fuck have you been all day?'

'I went to see an old friend.'

Karen came into the shop with two mugs of tea and froze.

'It's all right, Karen,' said Phil, 'this is Shirley Tate – my normal shop assistant. Well, when I say "normal" – she's about as normal as you can get round here.'

Karen didn't move and her fear showed in her eyes. It was at precisely this point in the conversation that Shirley Tate remembered that she had once been a mother. She saw and recognised the young girl's fear. She felt ashamed of what she had become – an unfeeling, selfish cow. How could she have turned into the person she was now? In the old days, with her twin daughters, she could sense their fear before they could. It was as if she had become blind to other people's feelings. In front of her stood a lost soul. Tears began to form in Shirley's eyes as she approached the still-terrified young girl. Karen was shaking. Shirley took the mugs from her and put them on the counter. She put her arms around her and held her tightly.

'Come here, you poor defenceless little sod. Forgive me – forgive me, please. I'm sorry, I'm an uncaring bitch. You stay close to Phil for as long as you want, he's a good man.'

They held their embrace for a long time before separating and holding hands. The fear had evaporated from Karen – she knew she had found another friend.

Shirley pointed at Phil.

'He needs looking after – we can do it together. Is that all right with you?'

Karen nodded and smiled. She went to the counter and picked up one of the teas and handed it to Shirley, who bit her lip to stop herself bursting into tears. Phil had watched the whole scene with interest. Perhaps human kindness was too strong to be destroyed completely by any sort of regime.

'Good – I'm glad that's been settled amicably. Now, Shirley…' His announcement tailed off in mid-sentence because he saw that Shirley was talking to Karen, who was now laughing. There was no sound from her mouth but there was no doubt that she was laughing. 'Excuse me, could someone let me in on the joke, please?'

The girls held hands and looked like mother and daughter.

'There's no joke – I was just telling Karen that if she ever had any trouble with you she should tell me and I would cut your balls off. All right?'

'Fair enough,' said Phil, who was in no doubt that Shirley had meant what she said. 'Now, about this other thing, who's the friend and what does he want?'

'It's a "she" and she wants to talk to us.'

Phil thought for a moment. A woman – a friend of Shirley's? Well it couldn't be Emily Fairfax because she wouldn't dare to come to the shop. It must be someone else who Shirley knew from the past because she'd said she'd been to see an old friend. Phil's heart froze. Oh shit! No! Oh please God no! He wouldn't be able to cope with all the intricacies of his life if Shirley Tate had known Arabella Corcoran at school, university or some other place where old friends meet. If Miss Jeffers, or whatever her name was, was 'the friend', he had decided what he would do. He would kiss Shirley goodbye, take Karen's hand and walk with her down England Avenue into the sea. Drowning was preferable to staying and sorting out any more complications in his life.

In the event, both he and Karen stayed alive and dry. A few moments later the shop door opened and in walked Shirley Tate's old friend. She hurried straight through to the kitchen at the back and sat down. Shirley locked the shop door and followed with Karen.

Phil remained in the shop for a moment on his own and then spoke to himself.

'Fucking hell – I don't deserve this! Why me?'

He walked to the kitchen and for the third time in three days said hello to the judge advocate for the coastal region of south Suffolk: Mrs Emily Mary Fairfax.

'Good evening, Philip. How are you today?'

'Shit scared, if you must know.'

'Why?'

'For three miserable years I've lived in this pigsty of a town without any problems except finding enough food to keep me alive. It was a boring life but it went along smoothly enough. In the last three days it's all gone arse over tit and you've been involved at every stage. Now you've turned up at my shop, after dark, and so I think I have every right to be extremely worried about what this clandestine meeting is all about.'

'Phil, Emily has come to help you if she can. Give her a chance,' said Shirley.

'I don't want her help. What have you been saying to her?'

'I went to see her because you've changed since the dinner party and I wanted to know what had gone on there.'

'Nothing went on there. I told you all about it. Why don't you keep your fucking nose out of my business?'

'You didn't tell me everything. You didn't tell me that you had a private conversation with a general and a woman and then stormed out of the house.'

'Look,' said Phil angrily, 'I went to this fucking dinner party under protest and I left under protest. I went because I was ordered to go and that pissed me off because I remembered that years ago when you got an invitation you were free to either accept or decline it. I left under protest because I was expected to have a debate with some old gasbag and his floozy about what I thought about my life.'

Shirley held on to Karen.

'I'm sorry Phil, I didn't mean to interfere – I was worried about you.'

'You're always worried about me – just leave me alone and don't bring any more of your friends here. Jesus, Shirley, what are people going to think if they see the judge advocate visiting the shop? Did anybody see you, Emily?'

The judge advocate had been listening to this exchange with interest. She now stood up and prepared to leave.

'Nobody witnessed my arrival, I'm sure, and I will be careful when I leave. Phil, Shirley came to me because, as she says, she was worried about you. I think you should first acknowledge that she put herself in considerable danger to do that. I am glad she came for two reasons. Firstly, we are old friends and I have been less than sympathetic to her during the last few years. That is between us two and Shirley has accepted the reasons for that. But, I am going to do all in my power to find out about Geoff's whereabouts. We have made our peace with each other – an uneasy peace, perhaps – but we have made a start. Secondly, I'm glad she came because if she hadn't I would have had to come to you anyway. I know what everyone thinks of me – a snobby cow who takes the Reports and then goes home to her mansion whilst you lot live the lives of pigs. Perhaps it's true. I don't know who is the real me these days – so many things have changed over the last three years. But one thing hasn't changed and never will. What I'm going to say now is very cruel because of the situations that you and Shirley find yourself in. I apologise unreservedly for the cruelty but I must say it. The one unchanging aspect of my life is my love for my husband. I'm lucky, I know, because he's still with me, whereas you and Shirley...'

The judge advocate brushed a tear from her eyes and then continued.

'Young people tend to think that love diminishes with age but they're wrong. I love Gerald more and more each day and hopefully it's the same for him. The point I'm trying to make is that when you stormed out the other night I didn't take much notice until all the other guests had departed. There were just Gerald and me sitting in the library, finishing off the coffee. We talked for a few minutes about how the evening had gone and which guests we had liked or disliked. I suggested that we both go to bed when Gerald called me over to his wheelchair and motioned me to sit down on the sofa by him. He put down his coffee cup and grabbed both my arms. He then said something to me that I will never forget – I can remember it word for word. At this point let me say that I have never liked bad language but Shirley proved to me today that in the present circumstances it probably doesn't matter.'

Phil smiled.

'I can believe that of the foul-mouthed Mrs Tate. What did Gerald say?'

Emily Fairfax paused as though she was picturing the words.

'He gripped my arms even tighter and said, and these were his exact words, "Listen, Emily, I like Phil King and I don't like what went on tonight. I don't trust that general and I certainly don't trust that fucking Miss Jeffers. You get word to Phil that he shouldn't believe a word that either of them said. Do you hear me?"

"Whatever power you've got in this godforsaken town, use it to warn Phil – those two are full of shit." That's what he said and then we went to bed. I know of no direct evidence by which my husband came to his conclusion regarding our two special guests but I promised him that I would deliver his message and that I have done. I'll go now and leave you to finish off – don't forget Curfew begins at eight. I'll be careful on my way out.'

She left and Phil heard the door close after her. He, Shirley and Karen followed her shortly after.

It was Shirley who spoke.

'So, what do you think of what Emily said, Phil?'

'Not a lot! I've no doubt that everyone round here is telling lies of one sort or another and I didn't need Gerald to tell me that the general and Miss Jeffers were full of shit – it was self-evident. Anyway, who cares – let's go home. One thing, though: I'm glad about you and Karen. She's the one we should be thinking about. Let's forget the general, Miss Jeffers and Emily Fairfax and concentrate on her welfare.'

Shirley nodded and smiled as the subject of their thoughts manhandled the transport out of the door. Karen rode the bike and Phil and Shirley shared the trailer. There was no moon and the night was black as pitch. Karen seemed to be a natural on the bike and didn't appear to have any problems with the darkness.

They saw no one, although Phil thought he saw a red glow, like the end of a cigarette, at the rear of the document checkpoint, but he dismissed it – the rest of the place was closed and in total darkness. Perhaps it was a reflection from the street lights.

Eleven

Karen wanted to drive Shirley home but they stopped at the end of Victoria Way and she walked the rest of the way by herself, waving to the two of them as she went. They stored the bike and trailer in the yard and went into the house. There was nobody there and Phil got tea ready – tinned pilchards for them both – while he explained that he had to go out soon and that she couldn't come with him. She showed her disappointment but cheered up when he said he'd be back as soon as possible. Phil was beginning to learn that if someone couldn't speak then they showed all their feelings in their facial expressions, which became substitutes for words. He told her not to wait on the step for him like she had done that morning, kissed her lightly on the forehead and went out of the front door heading for 89 Wellington Street and his first meeting as a member of a resistance group.

Wellington Street ran parallel to Victoria Way and therefore its eastern end finished at the sea. Phil had no idea where number 89 was but he liked the sea and so he turned right out of the house and at the end of Victoria Way turned left along the cliff top road. The night air smelt sweet and fresh as he passed Drake Crescent, Raleigh Avenue and Powell Close. The next turning would be Wellington Street but he paused for a few moments before he reached the corner. Below him was the burned-out shell of the theatre where he and Rosie used to take the kids to the pantomime. Phil had an awful feeling that he had enjoyed the show more than the children but they had laughed in all the right places and liked the ice creams at the interval. He wondered where they were and what they were doing now. He hoped they were looking out to sea and thinking of him. Perhaps they were dead. Perhaps…

The razed theatre was now part of an enormous military base, which stretched for a mile or so northwards. Tanks, jeeps, armoured cars, lorries, personnel carriers and various other vehicles that Phil couldn't recognise were lined up ready for battle. Only the cold winter wind off the sea disturbed the eerie silence. Phil turned away and headed into Wellington Street to see if he could find number 89.

The street was no different from the others in this part of the town. Most of the houses were derelict and empty but here and there a light showed through ill-matched curtains to prove that someone was alive and well and living in Wellington Street. He looked at the numbers as he walked and eventually reached number 91. The upper floors were non-existent and the ground floor didn't show any sign of life. He walked on a little and found number 87. This house seemed to be intact but there were no lights to be seen anywhere in its dark outline. He retraced his steps and stood between the two derelict buildings. Before him was an open space that presumably had once been number 89. There was no evidence that a building had ever stood there and the plot, for that was what it had become, was overgrown with weeds and strewn with household rubbish.

He realised that he must have misheard Margaret Hills in the shop earlier. He had been angry with her comments about Karen and probably wasn't concentrating when she gave the address. At least, he thought, I'll be home before Curfew and started to walk back towards Victoria Way. As he passed number 91 he heard a noise and looked up. The front door was slightly open and a light showed. He was sure that this hadn't been the case when he had last looked at the house and he approached the door with trepidation. He pushed it open a little further and went in. He found himself in a dimly lit hallway and then recognised the noise that he had heard in the road. Frank Sinatra was singing 'That's life' and he knew he was in one of the illegal drinking dens that had sprung up since the days of the Chaos. The pubs and the hotels in the town had all been closed but people who wanted to drink had ensured that this kind of place had flourished. It was anybody's guess what they served as hard liquor but they satisfied a need and the authorities seemed to turn a blind eye as long as they knew where they were. Phil had never been in one and when he opened the first door on his right to enter the den he was shocked by what he saw.

The scene before him resembled a Hogarth print. People in various states of undress were all over each other – male and female, male and male, female and female, and all equations in between. Phil was broadminded but the scene was too much even for him. Everyone seemed to be drunk or high or both. He had no idea what they were smoking but he felt a little queasy just breathing in the air. Candles provided the dim light and it was difficult to see the other side of the room. Perhaps this was the resistance group having their annual party – if so, the authorities could sleep easily in their beds tonight! He stepped back into the hall and went to close the door behind him when he heard his name called.

'Phil King, you lovely man – I knew you'd come. Have a drink now that you're here. Patrick, give this man a drink! He's a friend of mine.'

Phil turned round and saw Margaret Hills lurching towards him. Was this another disguise? She was neither the schoolteacher of old or the tramp she pretended to be in the shop. Now, she was dressed in a tight-fitting pink dress that showed every bulge in her ageing body. She was wearing a bright red wig and gaudy lipstick of a similar colour. She grabbed Phil by the neck and led him to a table in the corner of the room. He sat down and Margaret brought two drinks from the bar. She declined the chair that he held out for her and sat on his knee.

'Take your coat off, you stuffy old thing – we're all friends here.' As she said this, Margaret stood up and began to help Phil relieve himself of his outer clothing. The whole thing was becoming too surreal for Phil but just as he was beginning to think that the night was some sort of horrendous dream, his old English teacher leant across him and began to whisper in his ear.

'Trust me, don't let me down. In a minute we're getting out of here – follow my lead.'

Phil King wondered what the hell was happening in his life. 'Follow my lead'? Looking around him he couldn't even contemplate what that might be! He took a sip of his drink and nearly threw up – whatever it was, it wasn't Mouton Rothschild! After a few moments, Margaret stood up and grabbed his hand.

'My friend Philip and I are going upstairs for a shag. Anyone who wants to join in is welcome, but give us a couple of hours to ourselves first, OK?'

It was at this point in the evening that the penny finally dropped for Phil King – at last, he realised that this was all part of the game. He decided to play!

He grabbed Margaret's right buttock and left breast as he followed her – very closely – out of the room. He leered at the others in the room, who all began to clap, cheer and shout rude words of encouragement. When they were in the hallway his former teacher wriggled free from his grasp and turned to face him.

'That's enough now, young Philip. You played your part very well but that's what it was – a part. Those people make me squirm but they provide good cover for our group – I'll just get my coat and we can go.' Margaret Hills walked towards the rear of the hallway and Phil stood by the staircase.

'Upstairs?' he said with a smile in his voice.

'Don't be silly, you stupid boy! Come here – we're going downstairs.'

Phil followed her to the back of the hall where he found that she had opened a trapdoor in the floor. A staircase led down into what Phil thought was probably the cellar or basement of the house. It was very dark until Margaret switched on a light which revealed a metal spiral staircase. Margaret led the way and Phil followed, closing the trapdoor behind him. At the bottom of the stairs there was a corridor that led off to the right. After a walk of about ten yards they came to a door. Margaret took a key from her pocket and inserted it into the lock, which turned easily. She switched off the lights in the corridor and pushed open the door. They emerged into a brightly lit room painted entirely – floor, walls and ceiling – in a garish yellow.

'Sorry about the décor,' said Margaret, closing and locking the door behind them. 'It was the only paint we could find. I see we are the first to arrive. Make yourself comfortable – the others will be here in a minute.'

The only furniture in the room was a large rickety table and six or seven hard-backed chairs of various designs and age. Phil sat in one and waited. It would be interesting to meet his fellow conspirators, especially since one of them was supposedly a traitor. There was another door in the room apart from the one Phil and Margaret had used and Phil wondered where that led. Margaret must have read his thoughts.

'That's another entrance – there's a manhole cover on the plot that used to be number 89. It's always good to have an escape route.' As she said this, the door under discussion was opened and the first of the night's surprises walked in. Phil didn't recognise her at first, although he had only seen her a couple of nights before. Admittedly, the surroundings had been somewhat different and the new arrival had been dressed differently then. Gone was the maid's uniform that the young girl had worn at the dinner party to be replaced by the normal wear of people in the town – layers of old clothes which didn't fit the owner. Margaret greeted her and introduced her to Phil.

'On time as usual, Mandy. Phil King – Mandy Stewart. I think you two met at the Fairfaxes the other night.'

Mandy Stewart held out her hand and Phil took it.

'Nice to meet you again, Mr King – I missed your exit the other night but I heard about it from Gladys Jones, one of the other maids who lives in, earlier today. It caused quite a stir, I'm told.'

'I always aim to please,' said Phil. 'And call me Phil – "Mr King" makes me sound old and decrepit.'

'Compared to Mandy, you *are* old and decrepit, Philip! Come on, Mandy, take your coat off and let me have the latest gossip from the seat of power.' Margaret helped the young girl with her big overcoat and they sat down at the opposite corner to where Phil had sat.

Mandy Stewart could not have been much more than eighteen years old but she had a poise about her that made her seem at least five years older. She was not beautiful in the conventional sense but she had a prettiness that would have caused young men to look twice in the old days. Her short black hair framed a face that bore no signs of any make-up and as she spoke to Margaret the contrast between the two women could not have been more marked. A young pretty girl talking to an old tart!

When they had finished their conversation, Mandy got up and came over to Phil.

'I'm glad you're joining us, Phil – we need some new ideas and at least a couple more bodies. It's so hard to get people – no one wants to get involved. Anyway, welcome. I'm not strictly a member – I'm here by proxy to report back to my master about what's going on. Gerald Fairfax started this group and then he had his heart problem and his lack of mobility means that he needs someone to be his messenger. I am she.'

'Good old Gerald. Does his wife know what you and he are doing?'

'Christ, I hope not! She's a funny woman and I wouldn't put it past her to report her husband if she found out. Gerald said if she got suspicious he'd say that we were having an affair but I don't think that would help – she would report us both, then! It's probably illegal under Rule 36, Section 3A.'

They both laughed and Phil thought this resistance lark might be fun if all the members were like Mandy Stewart. He would soon find out that this would not be the case. The door through which he and Margaret had entered suddenly opened and the second surprise visitor came into the room.

The man who came in was dressed in a pale green stretch Lycra suit and was in full make-up: eyeliner, lipstick – the lot. Phil presumed that he had used the group upstairs as cover – at least he hoped so! It was only when the man started to speak that Phil recognised him.

'Bloody hell, Margaret! We've got to find another way in to this place. I can't run the gauntlet of that lot up there many more times – talk about Sodom and Gomorrah! Oh, good evening, Mr King – good to see that you're joining us.'

It was the manager from Archer's and he held out his hand, which Phil shook. He then proceeded to wipe his face clean.

'I'm sorry about our meeting the other day but I act like a snobby prick in the shop so that no one will suspect that I'm into all this. I hope you'll forgive me.'

'The shop manner is a good disguise,' said Phil, 'but not as good as the one you're wearing tonight.'

'I know – God, it's awful, isn't it? Make sure that you come via the manhole cover for our meetings or Margaret will have you dressed like this. Have you seen up there?'

'I passed through and was glad I didn't have to stay too long.'

'I have doubts about my involvement in this group every time I see those people. I hate what's happening in this town but I don't see the point of mounting a resistance for them.'

'I suppose we all cope with our problems in different ways – they've chosen oblivion. Sometimes I wonder whether they're right. Anyway, how did you get involved in all this?'

'Gerald Fairfax invited me to join – we used to make his suits and we got friendly a few years ago. You know how it is – men talk to their tailors like they talk to their barbers. Or they used to when there were tailors and barbers. Gerald mentioned the group in a roundabout way one day and I told him I was interested and here I am although I don't know what good it does. Look around you – we're not the fittest fighting force in the world, are we? Anyway, perhaps you'll change all that. My name is Peter Jackson – call me Peter.'

Phil looked at the man, who had now removed all the ridiculous make-up from his face, and saw someone different from the man he had met in the shop. He was a realist – a man who knew that this resistance group was a waste of time and effort but felt he had to do something in these awful times.

Only two other people turned up at the meeting but Phil had never met either of them before – they were father and son. Edward Houghton was in his late fifties and a huge mountain of a man who had owned a small garage on the cliff road. He had lost everything in the Chaos and, from what he said to Phil later, he regarded the group as a way to get his garage back. His son, Billy, was in his twenties and looked nothing like his father – thin and gangly, he spent most of the meeting ogling Mandy Stewart and agreeing with his father.

Phil looked at the people in the room and realised why Leroy and Davie had resigned and also why the authorities didn't worry too much about this lot: a retired schoolmistress, a young girl who was a messenger for an invalid in a wheelchair, a shop manager, an old mechanic bent on commercial revenge, his love-struck son and a middle-aged former newsagent. Margaret Hills called the meeting to order and this motley group of six people sat down to consider their campaign of civil disobedience and war against the authorities.

Margaret welcomed Phil and then gave a recap of their 'actions' since their last meeting. The list was pathetic – Peter Jackson had mixed up the deliveries for some military uniforms and so for two days a colonel had to wear a corporal's uniform; Edward and Billy had put a jeep out of action for six hours after altering the electrics when the driver was away for a few moments; Margaret had caused consternation at the Report Centre by giving the wrong name to the Recorder; and last, but not least, Mandy and Gerald had changed four road signs when she had pushed him out on one of his morning walks. The other five seemed well satisfied with this list of heroic deeds but Phil was sad and silent. Eventually Margaret turned to him.

'You don't appear overly enthusiastic about our achievements, Philip. Would you have done something different?'

'It's not really my place to comment, is it? I've only just joined and perhaps I need a couple of weeks to see how things go before I pass any judgment.'

The other people in the room were silent. Phil realised that they must have been expecting a ringing endorsement of their exploits and were a bit disappointed to hear his comments, which bore less than wholehearted praise. He tried again.

'What I mean to say is that... Christ, I don't know what I mean to say or what you expect to hear. I'm just a bit disappointed, that's all. That list of the things you've done is not going to strike fear into the hearts of the authorities, is it? It's not going to make them change their minds about anything, is it? Surely, if we want to change things in this town we've got to hit them hard and often? We've got to make them sit up and take notice and wonder what's hit them, haven't we? I didn't accept the invitation to join you to inconvenience these bastards now and again. I want to fuck up their organisation and how! Look, perhaps I want to run before I can walk but let's take Edward and Billy here. From what I can gather, these two are experts when it comes to motor vehicles – any kind of vehicles. It's no use them wasting their time putting one jeep out of action for six hours – we need to put their skills to better use. As an example, why don't they teach Peter and me to disable vehicles quickly as well, and then there would be four of us who could get amongst that enormous car park at the bottom of this road and do some real fucking damage. If they came down one morning and found that they couldn't use a hundred or so trucks and jeeps, or even tanks, then they might know that we mean business. That's just the kind of thing I thought we would be doing – but as I said, I'm the new boy here. Perhaps I need to lower my sights until I've got my feet under the table.' Phil finished his long speech and waited for the objections. It was Edward Houghton who spoke first.

'Would you be willing to have a go at something like that, Phil?'

'Yes, I would, but you and Billy would have to show me what to do.'

'There are guards in the military compound,' said Billy, 'and we'd need cutters to get through the wire.'

'I can make us some cutters in my old workshop,' said his dad, 'but the guards are something else. You see, Phil, I like your idea, or example, or whatever it is, but I don't want it to be our first and last effort at a big sabotage attempt. We've somehow got to get away with it and then do something else. You said we had to hit them hard and often and I agree with that and if we go ahead with something like this we've got to have a plan with alibis and an escape route. Now, Billy and I can bastardise the vehicles but we'll have to have help with the rest of it. Do you understand what I'm trying to say?'

'I understand perfectly, Edward – you want this to be the start of a campaign and not the final act. OK, I'm willing to have a think about the rest of it. I'm sorry, Margaret – I seem to have dominated the meeting.

'No, no, that's why we invited you – to get some new ideas. What do the rest of you think of Philip's plan?'

Peter Jackson spoke first.

'Count me in. I, personally, can't see that it will be any more dangerous than spending half an hour with that lot up there.' He motioned with his eyes towards the ceiling. 'Considerably safer in fact!'

'All right,' said Phil, 'I'll have a look and see if there is any way it can be done. I'll be responsible for getting us in and out and Edward and Billy can teach Peter all he needs to know about fucking up a military vehicle. We can report back at the next meeting to see if we've made any progress and, if we all agree to have a go, we can set a date.'

The people round the table murmured agreement. They talked of other things for a few minutes and then set the date for the next meeting – seven days' time, same time, same place. Margaret and Peter got ready to go back out through the drinking den but Phil was allowed to join the others and leave via the other exit. Margaret warned them all to be careful as it was now after Curfew and they said their goodbyes in the room before either of the doors was opened. Outside it would be too dangerous to speak.

Phil walked home alone but felt quite buoyant until he reached the corner of Victoria Way. It was here that he remembered that there was a traitor in the group and he had just outlined his one and only plan in front of them all! Oh, to hell with it, he thought, who gives a shit? and he carried on walking. He stopped and listened. He heard the sound of the armoured car moments before he dived over the nearest wall and landed in one of his neighbours' front gardens. He landed on something soft and lay there not daring to breathe. The vehicle carried on past and he waited for a good two minutes before getting to his feet and wiping the soil and shit off his coat. He made his way slowly to his house and found the door ajar. Inside the hall sat Karen, who stood up as he went inside. The young girl closed the door silently behind him, took him by the hand and led him to the kitchen. She opened the door on to a crowded scene. Leroy, Davie and another man were sitting round the table. They looked up at their slightly dishevelled and out of breath landlord.

'Welcome home, Phil,' said Leroy. 'May I introduce a friend of ours – Charles Corcoran? I've said he can share my room – is that all right?'

Twelve

It took Phil a little time to get used to the light and then he studied his new guest. It took him a few moments to get over the shock. Charles Corcoran was physically the total opposite to his sister. Whereas she had a patrician figure and a beauty to match, her brother was pudgy, if not to say fat, with a little boy's face with dimples. He had blonde curly hair and must have been in his mid-twenties but he looked about sixteen. He wore a three-piece dark grey suit, which hadn't been pressed for a considerable amount of time, and Phil couldn't get over the difference in appearance between the two siblings. You wouldn't think they were from the same country, never mind the product of one family. Phil accepted the cup of tea that Karen had made for him and sat down.

'I know what you're thinking Mr King – how could someone as handsome as me have such an ugly sister as Arabella? Don't worry – everyone is astonished at the contrast. The problem is that I got all the beauty and she got all the brains, but since she secretes them up her arse we don't need to worry too much.' The accent was posh to Phil's ears and the voice was surprisingly deep. Charles Corcoran held out his hand to Phil. 'I'm pleased to meet you at last – I've heard a lot about you from these two degenerates. I hope it's OK for me to stay here.'

'Yes, no problem,' said Phil. 'Make yourself at home – I'm sure there's enough room for us all.'

'That's very good of you. Thank you, kind sir. I won't get in the way – in fact I'll probably be out most of the time. Now, Leroy, you wanted to say something to our landlord?'

'Yes. Phil, we've nearly worked out what you can tell Miss Jeffers – Arabella – and it's pretty good, although I say so myself. But before we go any further, how did it go tonight?'

Phil recounted the night's events at the resistance group and they all listened attentively.

'Any idea yet about who could be the problem?' asked Davie.

'Christ, give me a chance! I've only met them all for a couple of hours. I don't know how long you lot were with them but you didn't seem to have a clue when you left so you'll just have to be patient.'

Charles spoke next.

'Our man has a good point, Davie – perhaps we're trying to rush things. Let's see how things proceed. Now, Phil, my friend Leroy here made you a rash promise the other day when he said I would tell you all about what was happening in this town before we blew up the fucking place. I am speaking figuratively, of course – I think! I want to keep that promise and, if you're not too tired, I believe I should begin telling you the story now. Is that all right? This may take some time but a promise is a promise.'

Phil nodded.

'Tell me all – I want to know what this fucking mess is all about.'

'Right, are you all sitting comfortably? Then I'll begin. "Fucking mess" is a pretty good description of what we're in but the story should be told in two halves. Phil, I want you to tell me first what happened to you on a personal level. Forget the big picture – I'll tell you all about that a little later. This town has been under military rule for three years – how did it happen? How did a law-abiding newsagent become a member of a crackpot resistance group? How the fuck did a thriving port and Suffolk town become this pile of shit? Come on, cast your mind back to those days just before the Chaos started.'

Phil sat in silence for a moment. Karen came over to him, sat at his feet and took his hand. She knew that he was hurting. The memories were personal and he didn't know whether he wanted to share them. He looked at the faces around the table and saw sympathy there. Perhaps it would help to talk about it, and he was just about to start when Charles Corcoran spoke again.

'I have a feeling that you think this doesn't matter and the overall picture is what we should be finding out about. That's not true – the two things are symmetrical. The little stories are just as important as the big one. Trust me; before the night is out you'll understand everything. Now, we're all friends here – let's hear it.

Karen, hold on tight to him – he may need it.'

And so Phil King began to talk about what had happened to him and his family. There were no interruptions, no questions, no asides and Karen held on tight!

'It was all so normal, really. That's the thing I remember most – the complete normality of the situation, of everything. No one talked about anything unusual – it was literally "business as usual". I owned the newsagent's shop and, although we weren't rich by any stretch of the imagination, we were certainly comfortable. Rosie, my wife, helped in the shop and did a little bit of charity work – serving in the Red Cross shop a couple of times a week, that sort of thing – and we were very happy. We had the occasional row like most married couples but nothing of any great importance and we always made up before we went to sleep at night. Rosie had this thing that if you let an argument fester overnight it made it twice as hard to make up the next morning.

'We had two great kids – Robin was eleven and just about to start secondary school and Deborah was eight and, like all daughters, was the apple of her dad's eye. Rosie and I met when we were teenagers but we didn't become an item until we were in our mid-twenties. I worked at the shop then for old Mr Gregory and Rosie used to come in to buy magazines and we started chatting. The romance grew from that small beginning and we became lovers. When Mr Gregory was coming up for retirement he offered me the shop at a knock-down price as a reward for all the work I'd done for him and I went to the bank and somehow managed to buy the place. Rosie and I decided to get married to celebrate getting the shop. I'm an only child and my mum and dad died when I was twenty so it wasn't a big wedding but a few of Rosie's relatives came from somewhere down in Wiltshire and we had a great day.

'After that it was mostly work, work, and more work for the two of us because in the early days it was difficult with the bank loan and trying to buy a house – this house. But we managed it and things got easier so we decided to have a family and along came Robin and then Deborah. They were great days! The business boomed so we took on more staff and we spent as much time as we could with the children. One or both of us used to take them or pick them up from school. We had holidays in Cornwall and France and a glorious fortnight on the Norfolk Broads where the sun shone every day and Robin and I caught fish and Rosie and Deborah went on long walks to pick wild flowers.

'I don't know why I'm telling you all this but I'm trying to emphasise how normal we and our lives were. We were a normal family with hopes and dreams – mostly to do with winning the National Lottery – and had no inkling about what was to come.

'I remember it was the week of the general election and we were very busy in the shop because, although a lot of people said they didn't, most people got their ideas of how to vote at an election from the newspapers. But apart from that it was a normal week. I gave up thinking about politics many years before and hardly ever voted – I spent my energies on my family and the business – but I used to read the headlines of the papers when I was unpacking them in the morning and noticed that the opinion polls showed Labour and Conservative were neck and neck, with the Lib Dems just behind. There was also some talk about a new party called the Right Alliance but they were way behind in the polls and were hardly ever mentioned in the same breath as the other three parties. All that changed on the Monday morning of Election Week when The *Herald* came out and urged its readers to vote for this new party. Since The *Herald* was the biggest-selling newspaper in Britain – it had double the circulation of its nearest rival – this caused an explosion in the party's support but nobody could tell how far they had moved because the opinion polls had stopped giving their predictions of the likely result. We had an argument in the shop on the Tuesday with a few of the regulars and the consensus was that even if every *Herald* reader voted for the Alliance, it still wouldn't be able to challenge the two big parties.

'On the Thursday night I watched the election results on the television for a couple of hours and the Alliance seemed to be doing quite well, but these were early days and so I went to bed, knowing that I had to be up early on the Friday. Friday's papers were printed too early for them to contain any results so it was not until I got home for lunch that I found out from the news that the Alliance had scored a notable victory and was preparing to take over the government of the country. I asked Rosie if she knew what their policies were but she said she didn't – she took less of an interest in politics than I did. We'd bought Robin a computer a few months before so I went on the internet and looked at their website.

'I was shocked – I couldn't believe what I was reading: forced repatriation of anyone who was not born in this country; banning of all religions except Christianity; the death penalty restored for all kinds of crime, including robbery with violence, and a lot of other fascist crap that I can't remember now. I wondered how it had happened that this crazy bunch of bollock-brains had seized power in my country – and then I felt ashamed. I knew it was partly my fault for not taking more of an interest in the democratic process – me and millions like me! Wasn't it Burke who said, "All that is necessary for the triumph of evil is that good men do nothing"? Well, I'd always thought of myself as a good man and I had done bugger all.

'On the Saturday morning I went to work as usual but no papers arrived. They were usually there at the latest by six o'clock so when it got to seven I started to really worry. I tried to phone the wholesalers but couldn't get through. By this time the kids had started to arrive for their delivery rounds but I had to tell them that they'd have to wait. I went off to see Johnny Ward, who ran the nearest newsagents further along the road, to see if he knew what was happening. His shop was all closed up – I knocked but there was no reply. When I got back to my shop all the kids had gone except one, who said that the mums and dads of the others had turned up in their cars and taken them home. I let him go as well and tried the phone again. This time there wasn't a sound from it. I locked up and went home – the roads were clogged with cars, full of people, all heading out of the town. I just didn't know what the fuck was going on! I shouted to a few people in the cars who I knew but they all had their windows closed and, if they saw me, they all ignored me.

'When I got here, the whole street was in chaos. Neighbours were shouting and fighting with each other. I separated two men I knew to ask them what the hell was happening and they both turned on me. They punched and kicked me until I was only semi-conscious. I lay in the gutter for I don't know how long and when I woke up the place had quietened down a bit – only a few people were left and they soon moved off. I made it to the house, unlocked the door and came in.

'The next part is easy to remember because I'll never forget it for as long as I live. There wasn't a sound – I called out and got no answer. I knew Rosie and the kids used to sleep in on a Saturday morning but they couldn't have slept through all the commotion outside in the street. I raced around every room in the house. I was screaming at the top of my voice, "Rosie! Robin! Deborah!" I was like a madman and my screams got louder as I reached the bedrooms. There was no one there. I ran out into the street and into the backyard. I was losing my voice. My family had gone, disappeared into thin air, and I haven't seen any of them since.

'I went into the lounge and switched on the television. There were no programmes, just a plain white screen with black writing on it. We had satellite TV with 974 channels – all of them shite but the kids watched some of it – and I switched the set over to that but there was nothing: no signal, nothing. I switched back to the notice. I can't remember the exact words but it was about our town and said that sixteen cases of a highly infectious disease had been found and that the town was to be sealed off from the rest of the country at nine o'clock that morning and remain in quarantine until further notice. It gave a Latin name for the disease but I didn't recognise it. I looked at the clock and it said 8.57 a.m.

'I sat back in the chair knowing I was trapped but just grateful that Rosie had got the kids out in time. I did a funny thing then but I suppose I wanted to see what I was going to die of. I went and got a dictionary and looked up the Latin name that was on the TV screen and saw that it meant "bubonic plague". It didn't register with me for a few moments that this was the Black Death of the Middle Ages but when it did I remember applauding the government for its quick thinking. I tried the phone here and found that was dead as well but both Deborah and Robin had mobile phones and I went to see if they'd left them in the rush to get away. There was no sign of them and I came in here to make myself a cup of tea but while the kettle was boiling I changed my mind and thought, If I'm going to die from the plague I might as well enjoy my last few hours, and went and got the bottle of whisky that we always bought for Christmas and poured myself a double. I think I had another couple of drinks and fell asleep for a time. When I awoke, it was gone eleven o'clock. I tried the phone again to no avail and decided to go back to the shop.

'There were a few cars coming back into the town. I suppose they were the people who hadn't made it out in time. The main shopping street was crowded but they weren't shopping because nowhere was open. I spoke to some people and had a rather deep discussion about rats and their fleas. There was no panic. Everyone just stood around to see what would happen next. I saw Shirley Tate and her husband with their twin daughters and they said they had been to the police station to get some news but it was all locked up. The whole of the Saturday was a bit of an anticlimax because nothing did happen and eventually people drifted off home. I opened the shop for a few hours but by the middle of the afternoon there was no one about and I went home myself.

'Everything was as I had left it in the morning – the phone didn't work and the TV only showed its dire warning. I had some tea and I think I sat down and read a book. I went to bed thinking that, at least, in the morning we would probably get some news of our families and what precautions we should take to avoid catching the disease.

'I woke up very early, as per usual, and got ready to open the shop because I thought that everything, or at least some things, might be back to normal. When I walked out of the front door I noticed that it was quieter than usual but it was never noisy at half past four in the morning so I didn't think much about it. As I approached the corner of England Avenue, however, I started to hear noises – engine noises and shouts and running feet. When I turned towards the shop I saw what was causing this din: the whole street was full of tanks and other military vehicles with soldiers everywhere. I noticed that the soldiers weren't wearing British Army uniforms but the nondescript tunics that the guards wear now. I didn't get the chance to look at this scene for long because two of the men grabbed me and threw me, face first, against the nearest wall.

'I suppose this was the start of the time we now refer to as "the Chaos". But that's not strictly true because it was the start of the clampdown that preceded the Chaos. Even that's not true because in those fucking appalling days we didn't refer to it as something so clinical as "the Chaos". Looking back on it, that word doesn't come anywhere near describing what we endured and we certainly didn't use that word. Fucking murder, bloody mayhem, fucking civil war – those were the phrases bandied about. But I'm getting ahead of myself – I was up against the wall, wasn't I?

'After searching me, the two guards spun me round and asked me where I was going and why. I told them I was going to open the shop and they not-very-politely told me to fuck off because there were going to be no shops or anything else opening that day. They pushed me back towards the house and when I protested one of them gave me a boot up the arse so I decided to follow their advice. You must remember that at this time, I didn't think that they were my enemy – I thought the government was making sure that the plague didn't spread and I was in agreement with that course of action. I went home and just sat in front of the television, waiting for the warning to change but it never did. I went round to Shirley Tate's and they were all in a terrible state. They had a few neighbours in and the problem was that nobody knew what was going on. I told them what I had seen in England Avenue but nobody would believe me so one of Shirley's neighbours – a man called Frank Gilmore – said he'd go and have a look. He never came back and to my knowledge hasn't been seen since.

'Let me paint a picture for you at this point because I think that there was something crucial in this stage of the proceedings that had a great bearing on what came next. My generation had been brought up in the age of information: telephones, fax machines, mobile phones, computers, laptops, the internet, twenty-four-hour TV news, satellite TV – they were all part of our lives and we couldn't believe that we couldn't get access to any of them. For the most part we took these information tools for granted but when they were taken away from us we panicked!

'We marched from Shirley's house up to England Avenue, determined to find out what was going on. I suppose there were about twenty of us in total – women, kids and old-age pensioners included. Twenty, that's all! When we reached England Avenue we found that it had been cordoned off with barbed wire and there were guards there. They told us to disperse. I remember the words they used: "Keep your distance and disperse back to your homes." We were twenty unarmed people in our own country searching for information as to what was going on! Geoff Tate – Shirley's husband – walked forward and asked to speak to the officer in charge. One of the guards told him to stay where he was or he would be arrested. Geoff carried on and asked for the man's superior officer. At this point the guards grabbed him, pulled him over the barbed-wire barrier and marched him off somewhere. Shirley went fucking berserk and ran towards the guards screaming that she wanted her husband back and then it happened. The guards opened fire on us with a fucking machine gun! People were diving everywhere, trying to avoid the bullets. God knows how Shirley survived because she was the nearest, but she did and grabbed her twins and ran home. I helped some of the wounded back to here but there was nothing we could do for them. It was no use trying to call an ambulance because we had no phones. As the day wore on they began to die and I suppose that was when people started to get really angry – plague or no fucking plague, this was fucking criminal!

'But who could we turn to for help? We were cut off from all the normal lines of communication and we had no one to turn to. As the day turned into late afternoon and early evening, some people went off to find relatives who lived across the other side of town but they never came back. I remember one man from down the road who said that his son worked in the council offices in the town-planning department and he went to see him to demand an explanation. As he closed the front door, he said that he was going to tell him that he was going to cancel the direct debit for his council tax until all this business was sorted out. We never saw him again. Those of us who were left then settled into a kind of stupor.

'Later, Shirley came round and asked if she could stay with the twins. She was in a terrible state. I thought I was lucky because Rosie had got our kids out. Other neighbours turned up and there was quite a crowd of us in the end. The kids played together while the adults drank my booze and speculated over what had happened. People went back home eventually and we all agreed that we would have to wait to see what the next day would bring. But it was obvious to me that some were hanging on to their sanity by a very, very short string. It was the not knowing that was the problem.

'When Monday came and nobody could find out any more about what was going on – this was when the Chaos started. I don't blame the people who went on the rampage – they were scared, frightened, terrified. I don't know whether it's fair to blame the guards any more – perhaps they were frightened as well and no doubt they were acting under orders. Was anyone to blame? What is absolutely certain is that once it started it took four days for it to run its course.

'As I said, people were scared and they wanted answers. The only people who seemed to have any of those answers were the guards so the people decided to ask them what the fuck was going on. The guards weren't talking so the people got angry and the town went up in flames. Literally! The people set fire to shops and public buildings and the guards responded with guns and tanks. I have no idea how many people died in those four days – the authorities were still taking the bodies away in trucks two weeks later. One of the houses that was blown to bits by a tank shell was Shirley Tate's. Shirley was at a neighbour's house at the time, trying to nurse the woman's wounded husband but her two gorgeous twins were in the house. I found her standing in the middle of the road. I'd never seen someone in such deep shock before and I never want to see it again. Jesus, what do you say to a woman who had just seen her husband arrested and then her kids burnt to death? I had no words – I just brought her back here and put her to bed. She stayed there for the rest of the Chaos.

'I stayed in the house with her and liked to kid myself that I was looking after her but that's a load of old bollocks. I know now that I was practising my own religion of devout cowardice! I was shit-scared of what was happening outside. The views from the windows of this place were bad enough – I didn't fancy seeing the rest of the town. The whole of Victoria Way seemed to be on fire at times and people got badly burned and injured. I did what I could for some of them but it wasn't much! I didn't see one ambulance while all this was going on and I didn't see one guard help anybody except if another guard had been injured. It was absolute fucking mayhem – cold-blooded murder.

'After these first four or five days, the violence died down and the streets began to be patrolled by military vehicles. I suppose you could say that order was restored but it was at a hell of a cost. I went out – I think it was the Friday after it all started on the Sunday – and went round to the shop. It was still in one piece but it was totally empty. I don't know to this day who did the looting – whether it was my fellow citizens or the guards – but at the time it didn't seem to matter much. I walked down England Avenue to the sea and stood on the cliff road. The whole of the promenade had been bulldozed away and a kind of no-man's-land created with barbed wire and fences. When I looked back at the town, I couldn't believe my eyes. At least half of the place was gone – whole streets reduced to rubble with a few fires still smouldering – and hardly a human being to be seen. Nowadays, after three years, I tend not to notice it too much – I take the devastation for granted – but that first time it knocked me sideways and I started to cry. The scene was like the towns in the Second World War in France or Belgium after the Germans, or we, had bombed the shit out of them. I walked slowly back here and saw a couple of people but we didn't speak – I don't think we'd have known what to say!

'You see, the point I'm trying to get over is that we still had no idea what was going on. We had been told absolutely fuck all about the situation and the business about the plague was beginning to wear a bit thin. Where were the medics and the ambulances ferrying us all to the hospital so that we could be immunised? Where were all the rats? So, like good boys and girls, we waited to be told what was going on and that happened on the Monday.

'An armoured car toured the streets with a loudspeaker and said the town was now under martial law and anyone found looting, congregating in groups of more than two, abusing the military and a hundred other so-called crimes would be shot. We had to stay in our houses and we would be given instructions later in the day. Late in the afternoon, two guards turned up at the door and took down all our personal details and handed us two pieces of paper and said that they were our temporary passes. Shirley, by this time, had come out of her shock phase and gone into fighting mode. I had a hard time getting her to give the right answers to the questions – when they asked where her husband was, she nearly hit them and when the bastards asked whether she had any children she came out with such a mouthful of abuse that I was sure they were going to arrest her as well. However, they must have heard it all before during these interviews because they just ignored her and went on their merry way.

'From then on it was a slow, downward spiral into the limbo we live in today. For the first few weeks we existed on any food we had in our houses or what we could appropriate from abandoned ones. We were issued with our new passes and I was told to open the shop again to sell whatever the authorities supplied and then I was ordered to go to the Border every day to pick up the fine array of fresh produce that would be on offer there. The first time I went there was a bloody shock as well – electrified fences, no-man's-land and machine guns. When I came back and told people in the shop half of them didn't believe me and the other half couldn't have cared less. That brought home to me how great our defeat had been. We were a beaten people and I suppose we just accepted the status quo.

'So, there you have it – my story. I'm not proud of some of the things I did or didn't do. I just fell into line like everyone else. Perhaps I'll get the chance now with the resistance group or you lot to make up for the three years I've wasted and sat on my arse. But my question still stands – what is it all about? Is there a big picture and if so what is it? So, come on, Charles bleeding Corcoran, I've told you my personal tale. You said there were two halves to the story – let's all hear yours.'

After he had finished, Phil sat back in the chair and looked around. Everyone seemed to be lost in their own thoughts and no one spoke for a few moments. Karen was still holding his hand. He looked at her and wondered if her story was as horrendous as his. Perhaps it was worse – he hadn't been struck dumb. They smiled at each other and the girl tried to speak but no sound came from her mouth. At last, Charles Corcoran stood up and began to speak.

'Follow that, as they say. Firstly, Phil, you have nothing to be ashamed of. When you hear my story you'll know that there are far worse people than you on God's fair earth. Secondly, thank you for telling the story with such candour – I've heard a lot of stories like it in the past but none have been so vivid. Thirdly, I would like to ask a favour: when you've heard my part, please don't take your anger out on me. And I shall warn you now: you will be angry – fucking furious in fact – but that anger needs to be channelled against the authorities and not the messenger. Agreed?'

Phil nodded.

'Right then, I shall begin, and the beginning is in the form of a question to which any of you may answer: what were you doing at half past nine on the evening of Monday, 20 November 1995?'

Thirteen

The four other people in the room looked at each other in amazement. Charles had gone mad – how could anyone remember that far back? Davie Lennox was the one who answered.

'Piss off, Charles – I can only just remember what I was doing yesterday at half past nine.' The others nodded in agreement.

'Bear with me,' said Charles. 'That is literally the start of this whole sordid affair. I'll tell you what you were doing on the night in question – if you were old enough and allowed to stay up until that time. You, like the vast majority of the country, were watching television – BBC One to be precise – where you would have seen an interview on *Panorama* with the Princess of Wales. It was greeted by the public as a bit of a let-down because most of what she said was public knowledge thanks to our wonderful tabloid press. However, they found it interesting because here at last was the truth about her sham of a marriage straight from the horse's mouth. But let's forget about the content for a moment and concentrate on the interview itself. The fact that a member of the Royal Family had gone on national television and spoken like she had caused consternation in the corridors of power in this country. Some politicians in particular began to talk in earnest about having a republic because it was obvious that the members of the first family in the land were at war with each other. Now, don't let me give you the impression that this was more than a ripple of discontent because it wasn't and on the surface everything went along as smoothly as before. The whole thing ran out of steam after a few weeks and the country went back to normal.

'But there were certain men – and they were all men – who were deeply disturbed at these ripples of discontent and began to talk about what they could do in the event of a ripple turning into a full-blown wave. At first, it was done in their clubs and after dinner at their homes, and because of the presence of alcohol at these times it was only a ragbag of half-baked ideas that were totally impractical. But slowly and surely they began to get their heads together and talk seriously of their plans to ensure that the monarchy of this country lasted for another thousand years.

'The reason for this was that the power in this country does not rest with any elected government – it never has done! It is in the hands of a select few who manipulate the rest of us into thinking we live in a democracy when we actually don't. These few never stand for election but are always in the background and they ensure that the system rules our lives. The one overriding principle of their thinking, which comes before all others, is that they retain the power. Now, of whom am I speaking here? I can't give you a detailed list with names and addresses but, if I could, it would include top civil servants, businessmen, bankers, chief constables and press barons. It would also include my father, Sir Reginald, who, at the time of the *Panorama* interview, was the Lord Lieutenant of Suffolk. I'll speak more of him in a moment but I hope you're getting the picture of who these people are.

'These men are not extremists – or weren't when they started – but when the talk began to get serious they came up with some pretty extreme ideas. I need to stress again that they wanted to hold on to their power and continue to run the country as they had done for many years. They eventually realised that they would have to get elected to give some legitimacy to their cause and thus have the best of both worlds. They would run things as before and they wouldn't have any interference from the politicians because they would be the politicians. They decided to form a new political party and they called it the Right Alliance.

'At first, they made sure that the whole thing was low-key and did not attract too much attention from the media or the other political parties but they were encouraged by the results in local by-elections and the like, and things started to move along quite nicely. The British National Party joined them and that gave them a big boost in membership but compared to the other parties they were still extremely small fry. They concentrated their policies on immigration and the death penalty and they began to get a reasonable following. The one advantage that they had over the other parties was money. Labour and Conservative were both deeply in debt and the Lib Dems have never had any money but the Right Alliance had so much fucking money that it was embarrassing. Millions and millions were pledged to it from its rich patrons and they had a hard time making sure nobody knew about their wealth. The breakthrough in the party's fortunes and progress came about, I am sorry to say, because of a visit my father made to America. He was on holiday in California and he met a couple of people and got talking. The three of them found they had a lot in common, politically speaking, and when he came back to England they kept in touch by e-mail and the telephone. He passed their ideas on to other leaders of the party and before long the two gentlemen in question were invited over here for "discussions". The two men's names were Virgil Bandaker and Clarence Clayton and they were the president and vice-president of an organisation called 555.

'555 is a society that is hard to describe in English terms. It is certainly right-wing and it propounds a lot of cranky ideas but it has no political aims, so it says, and has very few members. It likes to think of itself as a think tank of social, political and economic policies but none of these so-called policies come anywhere near being socialist or even liberal. The society advocates a return to the times when rulers ruled and the rest of the population served. My father and his chums liked what they heard from their two American guests and began to incorporate some of their ideas into the policy of the Right Alliance. However, these 555 ideas were never published in the party's manifesto or even mentioned at the run-of-the-mill local party's meetings. They were known only to a few of the top people, but since they were the men with the power and the money, plans were laid in great secrecy to implement these policies if the party ever gained full political power. As we now know, that happened three years ago and these secret plans were put into action immediately.

'I shall digress here from the main story to make two points. First, I can categorically confirm that the endorsement of the party by The *Herald* was the prime reason for the party's surprise victory. Secondly, I need to enlighten you as to how I know all this and in order to do that I shall have to explain my background and that of my family.

'My family is "old money". The Corcorans have been in Suffolk for more than four centuries – I think we were given the land and house by a grateful monarch in the dim and distant past and since then the family has served the Crown faithfully. We have served the kings and queens of this country with unfailing loyalty and have been well rewarded for this patriotism. It's a fallacy to think that the landed gentry of this country is poverty-stricken and always asking for handouts – my family has never had any such problems and still doesn't. My father inherited a considerable fortune from his father and we lived in comparative luxury for all my boyhood years. Arabella and I both went to fee-paying private schools and then on to university with parental financial backing. My father is a man of contrasts – there is no doubt that he is a political shit but as a father he was both generous and open. He taught both my sister and I, from an early age, the bases of his political beliefs. They were full of outrageous fascist crap and it was only when I was at university that I recognised them for what they were. After all, if your father tells you something is right when you are only twelve-years-old then you tend to believe him. Unfortunately, Arabella has continued to this day to believe his poisonous shite so don't underestimate her – she actually believes in what she is doing. I listened to him still, but have known for a few years that he deserves a slow death over a hot fire.

'Now the reason I have talked so much about my father is that he is the one who is solely responsible for the fucking mess that this town is in.

'One of the secret policies that 555 put forward was that four experiments should be established in various parts of the country to find out what the people were willing to endure. It said that it must be a legitimate duty of a government to see how far they could go before the people rebelled – in just the same way that a government should put up taxes until people refused to pay them. The Right Alliance took this on board and made their plans. Experiment One was established outside Carlisle two days after the election. The outward appearance was something like an open prison with people able to lead a nearly normal life but with no access to the telephone and the internet. It soon fell apart because of the lack of control and in three months it was abandoned as a waste of time. Experiment Two was set up in Cornwall in a small market town and lasted for a year. Here, the inhabitants had no access to the outside world, like the people in Experiment One, and they were also denied television and radio but there was no military presence and the place soon deteriorated into a kind of crime free-for-all with gang battles, murders and rapes. Normal law-abiding citizens began to get the taste for blood and it deteriorated into near-civil war. Eventually the military went in and, after moving everybody to different parts of the country, they torched the whole town and only the ruins remain to remind anyone who's interested that this was once a quiet Cornwall market town.

'Experiment Three was in the Midlands, just outside Coventry, and was conducted in a small village that contained only about one thousand inhabitants. High hopes were held for this one because of its size and because it was miles from the next village. The authorities built fences and patrolled them. The villagers had no access to anything or anybody outside their prison. No one told them anything about what was going on and they were deprived of food deliveries or anything else from outside the fences. The problem for the authorities was that nobody in the village took a blind bit of fucking notice to all this. They switched the electricity off and the villagers used candles and when the gas was cut off they cooked on their open fires. Every house had a vegetable patch in their garden and Mrs Brown could bake bread and Mr Sawbridge kept goats for their milk and village life went on.

'To bring matters to a head the authorities kidnapped a married couple and whisked them away to God knows where but that had no effect either. The couple were old and the rest of the villagers just thought that they had died! Eventually, after about two years, the fences were taken down and all the services restored but the villagers didn't seem to notice any difference and life resumed its normal placid existence. I suppose that village was a proper community and the authorities had no answer to it.

'And so, we come to Experiment Four – here, this town, this jewel on the Suffolk coast. My father was the one who proposed that this should be used as the guinea pig for the most drastic and fucking evil experiment of the lot – because that's what this is: an experiment to see how far government can go before we lie down and die.'

Charles sat down and waited for the reaction to his last statement. None was forthcoming immediately – the other four people in the room sat and stared at him for quite a while and, although Phil wanted to speak, it was Davie Lennox who asked the first question.

'What about the rest of the country, Charles – are you telling us that the people who live there are living normal lives?'

'Absolutely – they live exactly as you did until the experiment started. They have telephones, radio, TV, the internet and life goes on pretty much as it always has. They have less press freedom but the vast majority never wanted that in the first place. So-called investigative reporting has disappeared completely but most people are happy with their lot.'

'Don't they ever ask what happened to this town?'

'No, they couldn't give a shit – they spend their lives, as before, struggling to pay the mortgage, holidaying in Ibiza and watching *Who Wants To Be A Millionaire?*'

It was Phil who asked the next question.

'How did the authorities explain the experiments to the rest of the country and the world?'

'They didn't need to give an explanation. The rest of the country, as I've said, couldn't have cared less and soon forgot about the whole thing. Now and again someone makes a personal enquiry about a member of their family but there's a special government department set up to ensure that the enquiry is soon buried in red tape for months or even years. "Please provide your birth certificate, the missing person's original birth certificate, a copy of the police report listing this person as missing, a detailed report, witnessed by a magistrate, of when you last saw the missing person, and a photograph of the missing person taken in the last three months showing right profile, left profile and full face" – that sort of thing. The rest of the world has got its own problems and hasn't registered any interest at all. There was a French journalist, who had a relative living in the Cornish town in Experiment Two, who made an effort to find out what the hell was going on down there but he died in a car accident while he was filing his story and the matter was forgotten by his newspaper.'

'Was it an accident?' asked Davie.

'Christ knows – I doubt it.'

'How do you know all this?' enquired Phil. 'And why haven't you and your fucking friends here done something about it?'

'I knew you'd be angry and I knew you'd direct that anger at me.'

'Anger doesn't come anywhere near describing what I'm feeling now, Mr Corcoran – answer the questions.'

'I know the history of the whole thing because I used to be part of it. My father wanted both my sister and I to help with all the planning and the day to day running of the experiment. He said that it would be better for security if we "kept it in the family" and that's what happened. Arabella is still involved, as you know, but I came to see that I was supporting the wrong side and came and joined Leroy and Davie.'

'"Supporting the wrong side?" You make it sound like a fucking football match. So why haven't you done something about it?'

'Like what?'

'Like cutting your father's balls off and stringing your sister up by her fingernails.'

'Do you think that would help? There would be others who would continue with the work.'

'It would be a start,' said Phil, who was becoming more and more exasperated as the conversation continued.

'We need to have a plan of action,' said Charles, 'so we can beat them at their own game.'

'You're full of shit, Charles!' shouted Phil as he stood up and kicked his chair against the wall. 'You're so full of it I'm surprised you're not choking and if you're not out of my house in thirty seconds I'll kill you. Now fuck off back to your dad and sister, who I've no doubt you still work for, and tell them that when I see them they really will see a social experiment.'

'Now hang on a minute, Phil.' It was Leroy, trying to keep the peace. 'Charles is a mate – there's no suggestion that he isn't completely on our side. He's done some pretty dangerous things lately and was lucky to get out alive.'

'You've lost the plot, Leroy!' said Phil. 'This bugger is a plant and is still working for the authorities – you've been conned by his posh accent and his "little boy lost" face.'

'You've no evidence of any of this, Phil – you're just angry because you now know that the rest of the country doesn't live like we do. Calm down and we'll talk this through.'

'No evidence? How much evidence do you want? When you three were in the resistance group the authorities weren't worried because they knew they were a bunch of no-hopers and this bastard was keeping them informed of every move they made. Their problems started when you lot left the group, which I bet was your idea, Leroy, or Davie's, because you thought you weren't going to be able to achieve much there. I suppose Charles disappeared for a bit to find out what Daddy thought he should do and then the flats were demolished and I was told to keep an eye on you as well. I like you, Leroy, but you're a young man and I can't believe that after three years of this shit you're still "planning" something. Three years is a long time when you're your age – so just answer me one question. During those three years when you got so frustrated that you wanted to have a go at these bastards, did someone always tend towards caution and a wait-for-the-right-time approach?'

'He's right you know, Leroy,' said Davie. 'Remember that time we wanted to burn down the Report Centre? Charles said that it was a bad move because when this was all over we would need the records they kept in there so that we could bring the criminals to justice.'

Leroy nodded and then he spoke.

'Yes, and when we thought of having a go at the guards at the Border and trying to escape you said it was too risky, Charles. Why was that? We didn't even want you to come with us – we said we'd go on our own – but you persuaded us not to try. Why?'

'This is bloody ridiculous!' said Charles, who was now looking slightly uncomfortable and beginning to sweat. 'I stopped you doing those fucking stupid things because this mess is not going to be sorted out with some futile acts of James Bond heroics. We will need the records for any criminal trial and the Border is impregnable – you'd have been dead before you got anywhere near the fences. I want to end all this and I'll need people like you to help me. Don't listen to Phil – he's just pissed off with finding out that this is an experiment.'

'Yes, you're right – I am pissed off about that, but I'm also right about you, Charlie-boy. All the time you've been talking I've been having a think about this "experiment" thing. The only reason for having an experiment is so that you can monitor the results. It's no good letting the guards have clipboards and making notes on what they observe because they don't get near enough to the people to make any meaningful observations and the monthly Report is about as much use as a wet lettuce so the progress or otherwise of the experiment can only be monitored from the inside. Your father said "keep it in the family" and that's what he has done – Arabella on the outside looking in and you, you bastard, on the inside giving the inside story.'

Leroy looked dejected as if he had come upon some great truth and it was Davie Lennox who took up the battle.

'You upper-class English bastard! He's right, isn't he? He's fucking right and we've been too stupid to see it. Leroy, what are we going to do with him? He's full of piss and sweat – look at him.'

Leroy looked and saw a man on the verge of collapse. Charles was clearly frightened. His eyes darted from one of his accusers to the next, eventually settling on Karen.

'Karen, help me – they've all gone fucking mad. Say something, you stupid bitch, and tell them that they've got it all wrong. I'm on your side, guys – I swear to you that I'm on your side. Karen, tell them.'

The silence was deafening in the small kitchen. Leroy looked at Charles, who was now a crumpled wreck. He eventually stood up straight and shouted.

'All right, my father made me do it but I wanted to help you as well. But you've got no chance of winning – they'll kill you all when the experiment is over. Look, I'll go back and tell him that there is no resistance and that the experiment has been a success and we can all go back to a normal life. Arabella wants that as well.'

Leroy again looked at his former friend with contempt.

'You're going no fucking place, Charles. No fucking place at all. Jesus – what a stupid twat I've been. Thanks, Phil – we needed someone like you to make us see the bleeding obvious. Come on, Davie, let's take this bastard outside and deal with him.'

'Hang on a minute,' said Phil. 'If you're going to do what I think you're going to do, I've no objection, but I don't want the results to be found anywhere near this house. Agreed?'

Leroy and Davie both nodded.

'OK, that's settled then. We'll leave you to it. I'll take Karen round to Shirley's house – I want to see her anyway. It's been nice knowing you, Charles – keep your chin up, old boy. Don't cry. I thought this is what they prepared you for at your public schools.'

Phil stood up and went towards the door. Karen made no move to go with him and sat motionless on the floor. She had her head buried in her knees. She began to rock from side to side until her head came up and she stared at the ceiling. This went on for some time before she let out an ear-piercing scream. When this stopped, she walked over to Leroy and said, almost in a whisper, 'Let me kill him.'

Fourteen

Davie Lennox reacted first and grabbed Karen. He pulled her away from Leroy and held her close in an embrace. Phil reached her seconds later. Charles Corcoran sensed that this was his chance to escape and made a lunge for the door – he would have made it if Leroy hadn't been on his guard. He caught Charles around the neck and punched him hard in the kidneys. It was no contest and Charles slumped to the floor, hitting his head on the wall in the process. Leroy left him there while he helped the other two men guide Karen to a chair. She sat and began to cry. Whether they were tears of joy because she had regained her speech or tears of sadness for what she had heard that night none of the others knew and they just let her weep.

After a short while Karen's tears stopped and she smiled weakly at the three men around her. Phil went and brought her a mug of water which she gulped down.

'I'm sorry,' she whispered. 'It was what he said about all this being an experiment – some sort of game – I couldn't help thinking about Joey.' She began to cough and Phil gave her some more water.

'Take it easy, Karen – your voice probably needs a bit of time to adjust. Try not to talk too much in the next couple of hours – it might help.' Phil wondered how he had suddenly acquired this new medical skill to enable people to recover after they had been struck dumb by shock but the advice seemed logical to him. 'I'll take you round to Shirley's, away from this place – that might help, too.'

'What do you suggest we do now, Phil?' asked Leroy.

'After we've dealt with that piece of shit in the corner – that's the number one priority,' said Davie.

'One point about Mr Corcoran,' said Phil. 'I think it would be better if the authorities didn't know about what went on here tonight for as long as possible – say, a week or so. If anybody asks where he is, we can say he's disappeared again but we don't know where.'

'He was always off on one of his little trips – the only difference this time is that he won't be going to see Daddy,' said Leroy. 'So that's no problem. You didn't say what you think we should do now.'

'I can't tell you two what you should do now – it's up to you, Leroy. You and Davie have to do what you think is best. I don't want to say too much because I want to get Karen round to Shirley's and I'm worried that the walls around here have ears. But, for what it's worth here's what I think. You said you had two plans – a real one and one full of bullshit for me to feed to Jeffers. Did Charles know about both of these?'

'No,' said Leroy. 'He knew about the real one, of course, because he was involved in the planning but he didn't know the details of the bullshit one – it wasn't necessary.'

'He knew that it was bullshit, though,' interrupted Davie, 'and he knew we were going to feed it to his bloody sister.'

'That doesn't matter,' answered Phil, 'as long as he didn't know what the plan was. Don't worry about feeding anything to Jeffers – I'm not going back. Make the bullshit plan the real one and go for it but don't wait too long because I'm putting my plans into action tonight. After what I've heard earlier, the time for planning is over – we've got to fight and bring these bastards down now! I don't want to know what you are up to and I'm not going to tell you my target but I'm not going to sit on my arse any longer. Fucking experiment! I can't believe that a human being could do this to another. I don't expect I'll see you two again – good luck and for God's sake hit these bastards hard.'

Phil embraced both men and reached out for Karen's hand. She took it and followed him to the door.

'Good luck to you, mate, as well,' said Leroy. 'We'll see you in the Savoy when we're celebrating our victory. There is one point, though, before you go – because I wouldn't want us to go after the same fucking target. That really would be sod's law in action. Will you be having a go at either the Report Centre or the Border?'

'No,' answered Phil. 'You have my permission to blow both

the fucking things into the middle of next week. Good luck again.'

Karen went over to Leroy and Davie and kissed them both.

'Thank you for taking care of me – I need to go with Phil, now I can take care of him,' she whispered.

'I understand,' said Leroy, 'and you take care of her, Phil – she's a great girl. One thing before you go, Karen – who's Joey?'

Karen nearly started to cry again but didn't. She went over and stood by Phil and gripped his hand tightly. Her voice was no more than a whisper.

'Joey was my little nine-year-old brother. The guards shot him in the head for throwing stones at a tank. He died in my arms in the gutter right outside our house.'

'Come on, Karen,' said Phil. 'Let's get out of here and leave these two with their unconscious friend.'

With that they left the kitchen but not before Karen, having been reminded of his presence, kicked Charles Corcoran hard in the ribs. Phil thought that was probably for Joey.

It was now early morning and the Curfew was in force but they met no one on the short journey to Shirley's house a couple of streets away.

Shirley Tate lived, like everyone else, in a street of empty and half-derelict houses. After the short stay at Phil's during the Chaos, she had claimed squatter's rights on a small Victorian cottage. She had told Phil that she needed time to herself and he had reluctantly agreed to help her scrounge around for the few bits of furniture that she would need and helped her move in. Although they saw each other every day, their lives were totally separate and Phil didn't know what to expect when or if Shirley opened the door. They knocked and waited. Phil knocked harder and there was still no sign of life from inside the house. He retraced his steps to the pavement and looked up at the house – it was in total darkness. Karen bent down and peered in through the letterbox. Her eyes met only blackness and she joined Phil on the pavement.

'Has she got a back door?' she asked.

'Yes, but I doubt if I could find it in the dark. We'd have to go back to the end of the street and work our way along the alley. It would be bloody difficult to make sure we had the right house with no torch or any thing. She can't be out at this time of the morning – come on, let's try the front door again.'

They walked back up the short front path and Phil hammered on the door. Eventually they saw a dim light appear in the hallway through the frosted glass of the front door. The light flickered and Phil decided it must be someone with a candle approaching the front door. The light stopped.

'Open the door, Shirley, it's Phil – and Karen is with me. For Christ's sake let us in.'

A gruff man's voice answered.

'Whoever you are, fuck off! It's still Curfew. Get away from my house or I'll come out there and batter you.'

'We're looking for Shirley Tate.'

'That snooty old tart lives next door – fuck off.'

'I'm sorry,' said Phil. 'We're gone – sorry to have bothered you.'

Phil and Karen ran to the road and the light disappeared. Phil checked the numbers on the adjoining houses and realised where he had made his mistake – he had forgotten that nobody likes to live in a house with the number thirteen and so in most roads it is usually missed out. In the dark Phil had counted along from the first house and ended up at Shirley's rude neighbour's. He and Karen went to the next house along the road, knocked and waited. A pale light appeared in the hallway and this time there was no mistaking that they had the right house. A familiar voice sounded from within.

'Who the fuck is that at this time in the morning?'

'Phil and Karen – open the door please, Shirley.'

The door opened a little and Shirley Tate surveyed her visitors.

'Do you know what time it is? What the hell's going on?

'We'll explain inside – can we come in?'

Shirley opened the door wider and Phil and Karen pushed past her into the hallway.

'The kitchen is the second on your left. I'll put the kettle on,' said Shirley, closing the front door. 'I'm sorry I haven't got any cocoa ready but a lady is not used to being disturbed at this hour.'

'Your next-door neighbour thinks you're a snooty old tart, not a lady.'

'Jesus, you didn't wake Terry by mistake, did you?'

Phil nodded.

'Sorry – I got the numbers mixed up. Why does he think you're a snooty old tart? I can understand the "old" and the "tart" bits but I would never have said you were snooty.'

Shirley took a long hard look at her boss. The bastard had changed again. He turns up on her doorstep at two o'clock in the morning and is making jokes with sexual connotations. What had happened now to bring on this new persona? Whatever it was, Shirley hoped it was something permanent. She was getting to the stage when she needed a man – it had been so long since Geoff. She wished now that she had been sleeping in one of her nightdresses and had come down to greet him in that instead of her outside clothes that he saw every day but then she remembered Karen and put the thought to the back of her mind. Phil, for his part, was keenly aware that he felt safe here and wondered whether it had anything to do with the woman who lived here rather than the house itself.

'You're a cheeky bastard, Philip King. He calls me a "snooty old tart" because I won't let him get inside my knickers, which has been the sole purpose in his life since I moved here. All right?'

'If you say so,' said Phil with an enormous grin on his face. 'And I have a surprise for you before we go any further – haven't we, Karen?'

Karen looked at Shirley and paused before speaking.

'Hello, Shirley – we only came because we knew you would let us in and help us.'

Shirley gathered the child in her arms and they both started to cry. Phil looked on thinking that this one scene might show to the world and the authorities that the human race was basically a force for good in the world if only it was allowed to express its real feelings. They all went into the kitchen and Shirley made the tea. They sat down with Karen and Shirley opposite each other holding hands. They didn't seem to want to let each other go. It was Phil who broke the spell.

'Right – a lot has happened tonight, Shirley, and I haven't got time to explain it all now because I'll have to go and do the border run but Karen has heard it all and by the look of her she wants to tell you all about it. Be gentle with her because I'm worried about her voice but with plenty of drinks she should be all right. But there is one thing I need to say before I go – when you hear all the shit that Karen is going to tell you you're going to be as angry as I was and still am. Don't go off the deep end – I want you to help me. Not in a week's time but tonight. I'm so fucking angry that I'm going to do something about this mess tonight and I will need your help – Karen's, too, if she wants to join us.'

'When I've told her everything, I know that Shirley will want to help and she's not going anywhere without me. I lost one mum and I don't propose to lose another. Will you be my new mum, Shirley?'

'I don't know about that – mums are special and I don't think I want to try and replace yours. How about sisters? I never had a sister – I'd like a sister. Sisters against the world – how does that sound?'

'Bloody marvellous,' said Karen.

'OK,' said Phil. 'I'll go back and collect the bike and do my duty at the Border. You two sisters have a chat and I'll see you at the shop at the usual time. Don't do anything out of the ordinary – we'll need the bastards half-asleep, thinking there's nothing wrong, if we're going to pull this off.'

He went into the hall and Shirley followed him. Halfway to the front door she grabbed him and pushed him against the wall.

'I'm not snooty but very choosy. I'm not old but I can't wait for ever. As for the "tart" bit – you decide what you want me to be. But this is the important point – if this thing tonight is dangerous for either or both of us, I want you sometime today. Do you understand me, Phil? The old rules don't apply any more – if they ever did. Do you understand?'

Phil kissed her full on the lips for a long time.

'I understand. There are no rules from now on – I'll see you later.'

She saw him go and wondered whether he did understand – men were so stupid at times! She went back into the kitchen and started to listen to her new sister's account of the night's events.

At first she was only half-listening to the story and thinking of Phil at the same time but when Karen started talking about the experiments she gave the young girl her full attention. And Phil had been right – she was angry!

Phil didn't go straight home for the bike and trailer – he turned left out of the house and walked towards the cliff road and the sea.

The wind on the top of the cliff cut into him like a knife and he stooped down to gain some protection from it and also to avoid being seen. The military complex below him was enormous. Lines and lines of tanks, lorries, armoured cars and other military vehicles stretched hundreds of yards northwards to where the cliffs entered the sea. There was only one entrance, which was situated at the southern end of the compound. Phil supposed that with cliffs all along the west side and the north end and with the sea making up the eastern border, the authorities took the view that the southern end was the only part that needed defending and it was here that the one and only guard post was situated. The entrance consisted of metal gates and a movable barrier. There were two guard huts, one on either side of the gates. The one on the right had lights showing, but the other was in darkness and it was impossible for Phil to see how many men were down there. There was just one man outside the huts – a lone sentry who patrolled just inside the gates.

It was no use thinking of entering the compound that way because they would have no weapons and they wanted to get in, have some time to do their work and, hopefully, get out again without being seen. Phil crawled along the cliff top for about twenty yards and began to look down. After a minute or so, he saw what he was looking for – another way in.

When the theatre had been built in the 1930s and had attracted the top names in the variety world, a set of steps had been cut into the cliffs which led from the stage door to the cliff road. This enabled the likes of Max Miller, Sophie Tucker, Gracie Fields and Tommy Trinder to make a quick getaway to their cars or their hotel without having to walk the full length of the promenade. Eventually the steps had been used by a few members of the public from this side of the town as a short cut to and from the theatre. The steps were steep and it had been an energetic climb back but Phil had used them when visiting the theatre or even the beach. He inched his way along until he found the top step and looked around to ensure that nobody was about or watching him.

The steps were overgrown with weeds and heather from the cliffs but Phil could just make out their outline and he began his descent. He knew that there were fifty steps in groups of ten because he and the children had counted them one day in the dim and distant past. After climbing and sliding down forty steps, he encountered his first problem. Barbed wire had been stretched all along the cliff face at this point and no exception had been made for the path because, presumably, the authorities hadn't known it was there. The wire barrier was about three feet wide but stretched over one of the level parts of the path between the sets of steps and Phil was able to push it down and, with a big stride, climb over it. He was thankful that he had his thick winter gloves on. But the big stride had taken him to the very top of the final set of steps and he lost his footing. He fell over, bounced and slipped down the remainder of the path, coming to rest at the bottom, wedged firmly against another fence. This was a more substantial barrier and Phil picked himself up and looked at it.

This was the perimeter fence, which went right round the compound and was at least fifteen feet high. Because there was an overhang on the cliffs, it was impossible to see this fence from the cliff road. Phil couldn't see any outward signs of electrification but he was not an expert and if there was such a device then it could only be at the top because he had crashed into the bottom and he was still alive and no alarms had gone off as far as he could hear. He began the climb back up the path, taking more care this time when negotiating the barbed wire. He reached the cliff road and lay down on his back, exhausted. His bloody awful diet and a lack of exercise in the last three years had done nothing for his fitness levels!

He was brought back to reality by the sound of shouting. He raised himself up on his elbow and saw that it was coming from the guard huts. Three guards had come out of the hut on the right of the gate and were talking and shouting at the lone sentry. It looked like a light-hearted exchange of views to Phil and there was a bit of backslapping but he couldn't hear any of the words spoken. After a few moments the sentry went back to the hut with two of the men who had come out, leaving the other to guard the gate. It was a changing of the guard, thought Phil, and it would have been good to know how often it happened and when but they would just have to take pot luck. There was no time to do a detailed reconnaissance if they were going to act tonight – and they were going to act tonight!

The scene resumed its quiet serenity apart from one sound that Phil hadn't noticed before. There was one sound carried on the morning air – the lapping of the waves on the shore. At least that hadn't changed over these last three years but perhaps that was only a question of time. No doubt the authorities were organising an experiment to deal with the sound of the sea.

Phil left the cliffs and went home. There were no lights on at the back of the house and he didn't go in – he was half-afraid of what he might find there! He took the bike and trailer and set off for the Border.

It was going to be quite a day, he mused as he rode up England Avenue, not least because of what Mrs Tate had said to him – 'I want you sometime today'. He understood exactly what she had meant and he was more than looking forward to the encounter, if that is what it could be called. As he saw it there was only one problem – how the hell was he going to fit it into his busy schedule for the day? He'd had worse problems in his life and this was definitely one to which he was going to find a solution!

Fifteen

There was a slight hiccup on the border run. Phil had a puncture in the front tyre of his bike on the way there and he wondered if this was an omen – a bad one – for the rest of the day. When he looked back at his forty years, he hadn't seemed to have achieved much compared to some other people. He'd never climbed the Himalayas, or bungee jumped or seen the Taj Mahal – he'd not done much at all with his life. He was one of the many millions of ordinary human beings who lived ordinary lives and sat back and marvelled at the achievements of those others who always seemed to be in the right place at the right time.

Perhaps today he was in the right place and his time had come!

First, though, he had work to do and he unloaded Amos's miserable load of produce on to the shelves in the shop. It was imperative, he told himself, that things remained as normal as possible throughout the day. He didn't want to arouse suspicion from the authorities, or anybody else for that matter, and he busied himself in the shop in his normal, everyday way. He made his tea and sat down in the little kitchen. He knew he had one out-of-the-ordinary visit to make in the day but he reckoned if he went early enough he might just get away with it – before most people were out and about. He would go as soon as Shirley and Karen arrived to take over in the shop. As if on cue, he heard the front door of the shop open and he went out to greet the 'sisters'. He stood and looked at them in disbelief.

'Bloody hellfire!' he exclaimed. 'I thought I told you two not to do anything out of the ordinary.'

'What's wrong?' asked Shirley, failing to keep the anger out of her voice.

'Look at the pair of you. Christ – I don't know what the authorities will think of you but you frighten me to death.'

The sisters had obviously raided Shirley's wardrobe and Karen's bag to dress in what they thought was appropriate for guerilla warfare. Karen was wearing big over-the-ankle trainers and combat, camouflage trousers tied just above them. She had a denim top that just about covered three roll-necked sweaters and on her head wore a leather helmet with straps that were tied under her chin. Shirley Tate – now here was a woman who was dressed for a fight! Knee-length black leather boots encased tight black leather trousers and she had cut her old black winter coat down to three-quarter size, buttoned it completely up to the neck, and found a black leather belt to secure it tightly around her waist. Her headgear consisted of a black ski hat. The pair of them looked as though they were ready for any sort of opposition the authorities might have in store.

'We didn't know what you wanted us to do,' said Karen, 'but we thought this type of thing might be appropriate. Have we done wrong? Nobody saw us on the way here.'

'It's fine,' said Phil. 'I was a bit shocked, that's all – I thought you'd come to rob me.'

'We bloody well will if you don't tell us how good we look,' said Shirley.

'Sorry. You both look great – but you, Shirley, will need some minor adjustments to your costume.'

'Like what?' said Shirley. 'I thought all men were turned on by black leather.'

'They are. I am. The bottom half of you is fine. More than fine – bloody marvellous, in fact. It's the top half we need to work on.' Phil blushed and Karen laughed.

'I told you he understood what you said to him this morning, Shirley.'

Shirley smiled as well.

'Don't look so embarrassed, Phil. I told you that the old rules don't apply anymore and after hearing Corcoran's story from Karen, I'm not so sure they'll ever apply again in this town. I've told Karen all about our agreement this morning. It was an agreement, wasn't it?'

Phil blushed again and the sisters smiled.

'It was and I want to make sure that I keep to my part of it. Now listen – I've got to go out and see somebody. I'll try not to be too long but I'm leaving you two to look after the shop – and for God's sake try to act normally in front of the customers. Shirley, take your trousers out of your boots and Karen take that bloody stupid helmet off.'

The sisters did as they were told but both were giggling and Phil despaired of his shop staff. The girls removed their coats and went behind the counter, still laughing.

'Is that all right, Mr King?' asked Shirley.

'Mr King' went out of the shop so that his 'staff' wouldn't see that he was laughing as well. He turned right out of the shop and walked towards the sea. He noticed that the document check office was open but because it was behind him he didn't give it another thought. He walked slowly because he was trying to remember where Shakespeare Gardens was. It was on the other side of the town from where he lived and he had not made many visits up to that area. At last he found Chaucer Crescent and turned left. This part of the town had been completely demolished and there were hardly any buildings still standing. Nobody seemed to live here anymore and Phil wondered what had happened here in the Chaos – there was almost no evidence left of human habitation. But in the middle of the devastation sat two buildings which were nearly untouched. One portrayed itself as a Chinese restaurant but it had been a long time since anyone had eaten chicken-fried rice in there. The other building was a garage. The sign above read 'E. Houghton & Son'. Phil King went up to the double doors and noticed that they were unlocked – he pulled open one of the doors and went in.

Edward was working on an ancient Peugeot 106 and Billy was trying to get the rust off the roof of a Morris Minor. The garage was filthy and the two men weren't much cleaner. Phil shook hands with both of them and they walked to the back of the workshop. It took Phil twenty minutes to recount what he had learned from Charles Corcoran and to outline his plan for that night. The plan obtained complete agreement from the two men with certain modifications – it was Edward who spoke for them both.

'We – Billy and I – have decided that we don't need to teach anybody anything about buggering up the vehicles. Billy and I can do enough of those ourselves and we can ensure that the ones we do get to blow up will be write-offs – but Billy came up with the idea of petrol. How many will you have to help you?'

'One – a young girl,' answered Phil.

'OK,' said Edward. 'More would be better but if that's all you can muster, fair enough. Now, what Billy has suggested is that you and your young girl empty the tanks of the other vehicles in the compound and let it run all over the place. It won't matter whether it runs and forms a pond or even a lake in the middle of the place or whether it makes it to the other vehicles, because as soon as the stuff catches light it will destroy everything in there. We've prepared some bits of tubing that can be used for that but I warn you – petrol and diesel aren't like best bitter and you should be prepared for a bit of an aftertaste.'

'That's perfect,' said Phil, 'and you agree we tell no one else what we're going to do and when?'

'We agree.' It was the first time that Phil had heard Billy speak. 'We will meet you on the cliff road tonight and we will tell no one. If my father speaks to anyone today of this I will kill him! Is that good enough for you?'

'More than good enough,' said Phil who slowly began to realise how angry this 'experiment' made people'.

It was Edward who spoke next.

'What about these wire cutters – any idea of the thickness that we will need to cut?'

'The barbed wire is literally barbed wire and is not very thick, although it's painful if you sit on it like I did. The wire at the bottom, I don't know – I'm no expert – but it looked and felt like heavy-duty stuff to me.'

'We will sort it out,' said Edward holding out his hand to Phil. 'At last we are doing something. We will see you tonight.'

Phil took his hand and nodded to both of them. He took the bits of tubing from Billy and walked out of the garage. There was nobody about and he made his way back to England Avenue. He was about to enter the shop when he heard shouts calling his name. Four guards surrounded him and he was escorted to the document check office where he was thrown into the back room. He got up off the floor and sat in one of the chairs. There was no one else in the room and he waited.

It wasn't long before Miss Jeffers entered, dressed in a black business suit with her hair tied at the back of her neck.

'Good morning, Philip,' she said, as if this was an interview to discuss a bank loan he had requested. She had a red-coloured file in her hand, which she placed on the desk and opened. Phil noticed that his picture was pinned to the inside front cover. He said nothing.

'I'm sorry to ask you here before the time that we arranged but things are moving fast. Have you seen this Charles Corcoran person yet? We don't seem to be able to locate him anywhere.'

'Oh dear,' said Phil. 'What things?'

'I beg your pardon.'

'You said "things are moving fast" – I was just enquiring what things had increased their velocity of late?'

'Are you trying to be funny, Mr King?' asked the stern Miss Jeffers.

'Yes, I was,' said Phil who quickly decided to forget the humorous approach with this woman. 'Sorry, what was your question again?'

'Have you seen this man, Charles Corcoran?'

'No, I haven't. What's he supposed to have done?'

'He hasn't "done" anything as yet; it's what he's planning to do that worries us.'

Phil thought for a moment – he would have loved to have an argument with this bloody infuriating woman but what would be the point? He decided to forgo the pleasure of telling her that Mr Corcoran would probably not be planning anything ever again.

'What's he planning to do?'

'We don't know – that's what we want to find out. Has he not made contact with his friends Leroy Preston and Davie Lennox?'

'Not to my knowledge. I haven't seen much of them either – they always seem to be out and about somewhere.' Phil felt his eyes closing – he realised he hadn't had much sleep in the last few days.

'Am I keeping you up, Philip?'

'No, sorry. I didn't sleep too well last night. I think I'll go home when I get out of here. What did you want me for anyway?'

'What business did the judge advocate have at your shop the other day?'

'Have you been spying on me?'

'Don't take it personally. I spy on everyone – it's my job. Well, what was she doing there?'

'She was delivering a message from her husband. He told her to come and tell me that he was pleased to see me at the dinner party and that I could go up to the house whenever I wanted for a chat – I think he's lonely.'

'Is that all?'

'Yes.'

It occurred to Phil at this point that in a situation like the one that they were in, everybody spied on everybody else.

'I hear you've joined the resistance group.'

'Who did you hear that from?'

'That's not important – is it true?'

'Yes, I thought it would be good cover. Isn't that what they say in spy novels?'

'Cover for what?'

'God knows – you tell me. I was invited so I said yes. They don't seem to do anything so I wouldn't worry too much about them.'

'I don't. Is that what that old bag Margaret Hills was doing at the shop – inviting you to join the resistance?'

The lights at the back of the document check office were now explained! Phil would have to be extra careful from now on.

'Yes. Can I go now?'

'When will you have some information for me about the plans of Preston and Lennox?'

'When will you have some information for me about my family?'

'Touché, Philip. Yes, you can go – take care.'

'You too,' said Philip, trying to keep his face straight. He got up, walked out of the room without looking back and left the document check office before the bloody woman could change her mind. He made it to the shop without hearing his name called again and went inside. Karen was serving a customer but there was no sign of Shirley. He went into the kitchen but she was not

142

there either. He put the kettle on and shouted to Karen to ask if she wanted a cup of tea as well. She came in from the shop.

'No thanks and you haven't got time for one. Shirley's gone home and is waiting for you – she told me to send you over there as soon as you got back. She thought it would be better if you didn't leave together – not because of what people might say but just in case the authorities were watching.'

'They are,' said Phil.

'Who, the authorities?'

'Yes, they've been watching me for a couple of days from across the road. There's no problem – I'm only the means to an end. Well, I'd better go then and claim the star prize.'

Phil hesitated and Karen laughed – it was a good sound to hear after the days of silence in her presence.

'Go on with you – clear off. You both deserve each other, if you understand my meaning. What time shall I meet you tonight and where?'

'Meet me at Shirley's at about seven – take the bike and trailer back to Victoria Way on your way. I'll see you then. Cheerio.'

He left and Karen laughed again. Bloody adults – they were so stuffy about things like sex.

Phil walked quickly to meet his destiny and arrived outside Shirley's house in record time. The front door was slightly open and he walked straight in, closing it behind him. He went into the first room on the left which Shirley used as a lounge and found her there sitting on the old sofa that he had helped her drag here when she had moved into the house.

She had made an effort to look attractive for him. Her short blonde hair had been carefully combed and for the first time in three years she was wearing lipstick and mascara, which she had obviously preserved from the old days. She still wore the boots and trousers that she had worn at the shop but the coat had been discarded to reveal a figure-hugging white blouse, which left little to the imagination as regards her full and firm breasts. Phil gazed in wonder at the creature before him who now stood up and came over to him.

'I wanted you to want me – have I gone too far?'

'I've always wanted you, Shirley, and if you were dressed in a sack I'd still want you but this is something else – you look absolutely gorgeous. I feel ashamed. Look at me, in my old work clothes – you deserve something better.'

'I don't "deserve" anything and I want you, work clothes or no work clothes. The latter preferably.'

She reached up and took his coat off and threw it on the sofa. As she did, the rubber tubing that Billy had given him earlier fell on the floor.

'Bloody hell – what are you proposing to use that for? I've never had kinky sex before.'

Phil grabbed her and held her close. They kissed.

'That's for tonight's job – nothing to do with you. Unless…'

She grabbed his hand and led him up the stairs to the front bedroom, which contained only a big double bed.

They were awkward together – neither knew what the other liked to do and for the first few minutes they kissed. It was Shirley who recognised the need to progress.

'I like my men completely naked – how do you like your women?'

'Just like you – but I suppose the trousers will have to come off, unfortunately, and the blouse as well. Let's start with that and see how we go.'

They undressed and with Phil naked and Shirley in bra, panties and boots they lay on the bed together. Their nervousness with each other continued but was soon drowned in their passion. It had been a long period of abstinence for both of them and their first try at lovemaking was a series of mistakes and mistimed climaxes for both of them. They tried again a little later and their feelings for each other took them to another plane. It perhaps wasn't love – that might come later – but it certainly wasn't pure lust. It was more a kind of need and longing that they both felt they had to alleviate before their relationship went any further.

Afterwards, they lay side by side, each with their own thoughts. Shirley realised that she had been right to take the initiative with this lovely man beside her. His lovemaking had been gentle and kind and with a bit of practice she had high hopes for the two of them. She felt no shame, only a kind of contentment.

Phil lay there with the same sort of feelings, lost in a world of his own, overflowing with satisfaction. He had dreamt of this day for a long time and had not been disappointed when it had finally arrived. The woman beside him was someone to be cherished and he vowed to do just that in the future.

It was Shirley who broke the spell.

'Can I ask a favour, Mr King?' she said, snuggling up close to him.

'Ask away, Mrs Tate – your wish is my command.'

'Can I take these bloody boots off now and give my feet a rest?'

The bed rocked with their laughter. Phil took the boots off for her because he said there was something sensual about the unzipping of a lady's boot – Shirley was just grateful to be able to lie naked in the warmth of the bed. They didn't talk again for a long time and this time it was Phil who began the conversation.

'I think it's about time I got up. I've got things to do.' He jumped out of the bed and stood naked in the middle of the room. There was no embarrassment or awkwardness for either of them now – they had lost all those feelings in the last few hours. Shirley got up as well and began to get dressed.

'What did you mean earlier about the top half of my costume needing adjustment for tonight? What the hell do you want me to do?' she asked.

'I want you to act like a drunken tart,' he said matter-of-factly.

'Like I have been this afternoon, you mean?'

He looked at her and smiled. He crossed the room and put his arms around her.

'There was nothing drunken or tartish about you this afternoon – I also hope it wasn't an act, so we'll have no more talk like that. No, I want you to distract someone with your charms tonight while the rest of us get on with the business of kicking this criminal regime up the arse.'

'Anyone I know, this person I'm supposed to charm?'

'I very much doubt it – you'll have to start from square one. Like you did with me.'

Phil King ducked quickly as a black leather boot flew past his left ear.

'Sorry, didn't mean it – just a joke! Here's the plan: two friends of mine who I met at the resistance group, Karen and I are going to break into the military vehicle compound at the bottom of the cliffs and blow the whole fucking thing sky-high. If we succeed then the authorities won't know what's hit them and they also won't be able to move any of the guards about. I'm hoping the rest of the people held in this prison come to their senses and start fighting back. If they do, all well and good, and we – you, me and Karen – will head for the Border and see if we can find someway out of this hellhole.'

'And what happens if the rest of them don't come to their senses but sit on their arses like they – and we – have done for the last three years?'

'Then we carry on with our so-called normal lives until I can think of something else to hit. I can't do nothing, Shirley. When I think of what we've all lost because some daft bastard wanted to have a political experiment I refuse to sit on my arse any longer. I'd like to have you help me but if you think it's futile or too dangerous then tell me now.'

'I think it's a total waste of time because I don't think anyone else is going to join in and help. They don't give a shit any more. They've got used to this crazy system and probably don't want any more upheavals in their sad, boring, little lives. It's also stupidly dangerous – we've no weapons, no expertise, no intelligence and, I don't know about you, but I'm certainly lacking in the bravery stakes. The whole thing is fucking mad, Philip – you are out of your mind if you think this will work.'

Phil sat on the edge of the bed and realised that he agreed with every word Shirley had said. What did he hope to achieve with this ridiculous show of bravado? Of course he was angry at the way his life had been manipulated and misused. Of course, he wanted to fight back – but was this the best way? Was there another, better way? As far as he could see, there was only one other way – he could sit out the rest of the experiment and hope everyone would live happily ever after when they were told it was all over. He knew he couldn't do that! He had to do something positive to try and change things. Yes, the plan was stupid and would probably end in disaster but the alternative was not an option he could live with.

'I know you're right, Shirley, but I've made up my mind. I'm going ahead with it – I don't know how it will turn out but at least I'll know I tried.'

Shirley turned to face him.

'Good – that's settled, then. I'm glad you said that because I've just put my right boot back on and if you'd have come out with some crap about cancelling tonight, I would have kicked you in the balls. Come on, let's blow the bastards to hell and back. We'll worry about tomorrow when it comes. Now, who do you want me to seduce?'

'God, I don't want you to seduce him! Just keep his attention away from the rest of us while we're in there. There's just one sentry on duty at any one time outside the huts but I don't know how many other men are inside the huts. You'll just have to play it by ear.'

'Right, so you want me to have a gang bang with the guards while you play James Bond?'

'I'm not sure you're taking this seriously enough, Mrs Tate.'

'I don't think I could do it if I started thinking seriously about it. OK, you want me to act like one of those whores who leave the drinking clubs and then tease the guards for fun or money and make sure they're looking my way and not yours. Not a problem, Mr King – I hereby solemnly promise that you will have no trouble from the guards tonight. Hic!'

Shirley stumbled to emphasise her mock-drunken state and fell against Phil.

'All right, the audition is over – you've got the job.'

'Pretty good, eh? How long have I got to keep the act going for?'

'An hour should be plenty.'

'An hour? Bloody hell – I'll have to write a script!'

'No you won't. Take it as it comes and do the best you can. I'm sure you'll be great.'

'Suppose I get into difficulty and the guards want more than I'm willing to offer. Will you come along on your white charger and rescue me?'

'No – just shout "Phil" and I'll be there in three seconds in a tank with all guns blazing.'

'Do you know how to drive a tank?'

'No, but I'm a quick learner.'

'You'll need to be if you're going to be there in three seconds.'

They went downstairs and made tea – sardines and potatoes. They laughed and joked with each other but the humour was a thin disguise over their fears for the night that lay ahead. Shirley found a half-full bottle of gin in a cupboard which had been left by the previous occupiers of the house. They didn't drink it – Shirley said that she needed it later as a prop for her act. It was agreed that she should begin her great production number at half past ten; the time when the others were hoping to gain entry into the compound.

Phil decided to go home and change – he knew that petrol and diesel permeated your clothes and if he had to turn up for work the next day then he wanted to be in his normal clothes without them smelling of fumes. He kissed Shirley goodbye and they wished each other luck. He remembered just in time that he had agreed to meet Karen at Shirley's at seven and asked her to send her round to Victoria Way whenever she was ready. Shirley closed the door behind him and went round the house searching for an article of clothing that she had never worn before. She found it in a cardboard box in the cellar.

Two years before a woman had walked into the shop and given her a hard-luck story about having nowhere to stay and Shirley had invited her to have a room in her house. The arrangement hadn't worked out – the woman was the kind of person that Shirley was going to impersonate that night – and she had left after a week. But she had asked Shirley to keep a box of her clothes and she would pick them up later. She had never come back. Shirley remembered the blouse because the first time she had seen the woman wearing it she had laughed out loud. It was see-through to the point of being invisible and made from the smallest piece of material ever to see a sewing machine

It wouldn't cover any of the important parts of Shirley Tate and as such would be perfect for the night ahead.

Sixteen

As soon as Phil reached his house he knew that something was wrong. The front door was wide open and there was a lot of shouting that seemed to be coming from inside. He retraced his steps and went down the alley, which led him to the backyard. The back door was open as well and most of his furniture seemed to have been thrown against the wall where he usually parked his bike and trailer. He went round to the front again and entered through the front door. The chaotic scene which greeted him was something that made his anger level rise to explosion point.

'Who the fuck is in charge here?' he asked the first guard he saw. He was directed towards the kitchen and for the second time that day came face to face with Miss Jeffers. She was sitting at the kitchen table, smoking a cigarette and looking very placid in the midst of all the mayhem that was going on in the house. Guards were shouting at each other and throwing things about. Phil took a deep breath and sat opposite the calm lady.

'I was told that you were in charge – perhaps you could enlighten me as to what you think you're doing. I've not got much in this world but your men seem to be systematically destroying it piece by piece. Is there a purpose to all this?'

'They're looking for evidence,' said Miss Jeffers.

'Evidence of what?'

'Murder, Mr King.'

'Whose murder?'

'Charles Corcoran – the man you said you'd never met. We found his body tonight by the Border. He had been stabbed and then nailed to one of the fence posts. We think he was here last night and was taken from here and killed.'

'He wasn't here last night.'

'My intelligence tells me otherwise.'

'Well, your fucking intelligence is wrong for once – he wasn't here. But if he was, which I deny, why are you interested? I thought you were looking for him because he was a threat – you've found him and he won't be a threat anymore by the sound of it. What's the problem?'

'There is no problem. We would just like to tie up any loose ends.'

'We've had 30,000 "loose ends" in this town in the last three years – what's so fucking special about Charles Corcoran?'

Miss Jeffers stubbed out her cigarette and looked straight at Phil King who returned her stare. He was beginning to like this – was the tide actually turning at last?

'Mr Corcoran was a brave man who was working for the authorities. I want to find out what happened to him.'

'Let me get this straight: Corcoran infiltrated the resistance in the town and reported everything back to you. I see. So you think he was killed by someone who found out that he was a traitorous bastard and decided to do something about it.'

'Charles Corcoran was not a traitor – he was a hero.'

She's on the edge, thought Phil, one more push and she'll tell the whole story – just keep nagging away.

'That's a subjective view, Miss Jeffers. It depends which side you're on as to whether you think he's a hero or a traitor.'

Phil could see that his final push hadn't worked. Miss Jeffers had regained her composure and the conversation came to an abrupt end.

'My men will keep looking, Mr King – if they find anything to link you to Corcoran's death… even I will not be able to save you.'

'They won't find anything to link me to anything.'

Miss Jeffers rose and went out of the kitchen. Phil King couldn't resist the opportunity to have the last word.

'Perhaps you could send me a form that I can fill in to claim some compensation for the loss of my priceless possessions after your men have finished.'

She didn't hear him, or if she did she gave no hint of it as she swept out of the room. The men continued for another half-hour or so and then left without a word of apology or salutation. The house looked like a bombsite. Phil didn't bother to clear up – tomorrow it might not matter. He went into the bedroom and got changed into even older and scruffier clothes than the ones he was wearing. He heard a noise in the kitchen and went to investigate. It was Karen.

'Did you know you've got a puncture?'

'Yes. Any problems at the shop?'

'No. Any problems at Shirley's?'

'No. What are you smiling at?'

'I was just hoping that you stayed round there because if you were here, by the look of this place, it must have been a hell of a romp!'

'You're getting to be a cheeky young lady, Karen. I liked you better when you couldn't speak.'

Karen's eyes clouded over and Phil knew he had said the wrong thing.

'I'm sorry, you know I didn't mean that. Come here – give me a hug and we can talk about what we're going to do tonight.'

Karen did as she was told. She had been through a lot in the last three years – at last she had found two people she thought she could trust. One thing was certain – it wasn't going to be her who let Phil and Shirley down tonight!

Phil got the tubing and explained to Karen, as best he could because he didn't really have a clue, how they were going to suck fuel out of the vehicles and let the pipe and gravity do the rest. He told her that it didn't matter where the fuel went – down the drains, under another vehicle or into a huge lake in the centre of the compound – the whole thing would blow eventually. They would have two tubes each – one to leave on one vehicle which would, hopefully, be churning out its black gold and the other enabling them to start on the next one. Karen listened intently and asked intelligent questions at various times.

'Do you want to do this, Karen? If it all goes wrong we could be in a hell of a mess and even if it goes right, I'm not sure we'll be that far further forward.'

'I want to do it. I need to do it. Let's do it for Joey.'

Phil grabbed her again.

'That's a deal – this one's for Joey!'

They used the rest of the time checking each other's clothing. This was Karen's idea – she said that the fuel could be ignited by anything causing a spark and she spent twenty minutes cutting the numerous zips off her combat trousers and making sure that Phil's zips and shoelaces were either well hidden or devoid of metal tips. When they were ready, they left 108 Victoria Way and made their way towards the cliff road. There was no moon and they welcomed the black sky. At the top of the cliffs they settled down to wait for Edward and Billy.

They noticed that the compound was lit but not with the bright floodlights that had been erected at the Border – the authorities had relied on the street lights that had been used to light the old promenade. As long as nobody was watching them from the cliffs, Phil felt pretty confident that they would be able to move around the compound without being seen as long as Shirley kept her part of the bargain and occupied the guard at the gate.

Edward and Billy arrived exactly on time. Now all four of them were lying prone on the grass above the path. After the introductions to Karen, it was Edward who spoke.

'Listen, you two. After you'd gone this morning, Phil, Billy came down here to have a closer look at the place and he found something very interesting. Do you see to the left there on the sea side of the compound two bloody great vehicles that look like tankers?'

Phil and Karen nodded after focusing their eyes on two structures which seemed larger than the vehicles around them.

'Well, Billy reckons that they're not tankers or vehicles – he thinks they're the tanks where they keep the spare fuel. If you two could open one or both of them, we could be talking about the biggest fucking blaze that Suffolk has ever seen. I've brought you a crowbar in case you need it to open the valves on those two bastards. Right, are we all ready? We might as well get down to that fence and start the cutting as soon as possible. Sorry, Phil – I sound as if I'm taking over.'

'You carry on, Edward – it's nice to find someone in this operation who sounds as though they know what they're doing.'

The four of them made their way slowly down the path until they reached the barbed-wire barrier. At this point Billy moved to the front and made short work of cutting a hole in it with some secateurs from his pocket. They traversed the last ten steps and crouched in front of the final fence. Edward Houghton stood up and surveyed the barrier in front of them. After a while he knelt down and whispered to the other three.

'This is going to be a problem. This is heavy-duty stuff and it's electrified at the top. With the tools Billy and I have been able to make we'll need to make a hole at the bottom big enough for us all to get through and that's going to take us a bit of time. How long have we got? It's a quarter past ten now.'

'The guard should be looking the other way in fifteen minutes,' said Phil.

'That'll be time enough,' said Edward. He and Billy then started to unload numerous tools from their pockets and have a discussion as to how best to get through the barrier.

Phil and Karen sat back and waited. Karen thought of her little brother, Joey. He had never done any harm to anyone – why had he been a victim of this stupid mess? Phil thought of Shirley and hoped she wouldn't be a victim of his stupid plan! He also wondered what the hell she was doing at 10.25 p.m.

In fact, Shirley Tate – at that precise moment – was standing some five hundred yards south of Phil King on top of the cliff road. She was wedged in the doorway of the old Grand Hotel, from where she could see the gate to the compound. She had been watching for about ten minutes and in that time had only seen a solitary guard who came to check the gate and look up and down the road. He did this every five minutes or so. Shirley supposed he was bored because there was nobody else about. Curfew didn't seem to be patrolled by the authorities any longer – nobody went out when it was in force and thus it policed itself.

Shirley got ready. She unbuttoned her coat to reveal her blouse and everything else that was there to be seen. Taking the bottle of gin from her pocket, she washed her mouth out with the foul-tasting stuff and nearly choked. She spat most of it into the gutter but swallowed some and felt a belch rising from her stomach. She closed her mouth tight and it went away. I'll save that for later, she thought. She took another small sip of the gin and set off, meandering across the road and down the hill to the compound. As she neared the gate, the guard approached and Shirley saw that he was armed with a sub-machine gun, which was aimed directly at her.

She felt her knees go weak and the bile rising in her throat. She stood absolutely still and looked at the guard – her confidence had vanished and she knew she couldn't go through with her part in the plan. She was about to turn and leave when a picture came into her mind – a picture of two, small twin girls burning to death in a blazing house. She went up to the gate and leaned on it.

She belched, smiled and spoke to the guard.

'I've not seen one that big pointing at me before, darling. My name's Pinky. What's yours? Do you want a little drinky with Pinky?'

Edward climbed through the hole in the fence first, followed by Phil, Karen and Billy. They split up: Billy and his dad going to the right and Phil and Karen to the left. Each knew what they were supposed to do and the Houghtons immediately got to work on two lorries that were nearby. Phil and Karen made their way across to the seaside of the compound and began to look at the vehicles there. They came across an immediate problem – all the militarised vehicles, tanks, armoured cars and the like had locks on their fuel tanks and there was no way that Phil and Karen had the time or the expertise to do anything about them. Phil made a quick decision and sent Karen along the lines of vehicles to empty the fuel tanks of the cars, vans and lorries that were not locked while Phil would go and have a look at the two storage tanks that Billy had identified earlier. As he walked towards the first enormous structure he heard a cough and presumed that Karen had started her revenge for Joey.

The storage tanks – if that's what they were – were far larger than Phil had first thought. Easily the height of two double-decker buses, they were at least thirty yards long and ten yards wide. He moved around the first one until he came upon what appeared to be a series of valves and taps situated at waist level. There were safety notices plastered all over the tank at this point and he thought that, as he had to start somewhere, this place might as well be it. He began to turn the valves and taps one by one. Nothing happened – no fuel came out and there was no sign that his efforts had disturbed the tank in any way. He had one faint hope: there was one large red-painted tap that he had been unable to move when he had first tried it. He took the crowbar from his pocket, placed it between the handles of the tap and pushed down with all his strength. It was probably the concentration and the effort he was putting into the task that ensured he didn't hear someone come up behind him and put their hand on his shoulder.

'Fucking Jesus!' he cried, looking round, only to find Karen standing there with her finger to her lips, urging him to be quiet.

'I've done twenty-odd vehicles down this side,' she whispered. 'I'm going back towards the cliffs to do the rest of the unlocked ones – I'll meet you at the hole in the fence when we've finished. Any luck?' she asked, looking at the storage tank.

'Not yet. Sorry about the language – you startled me.'

'Apology not necessary – just get this fucking thing emptied, for Joey.'

With that she was gone, back into the gloom of the compound. Twenty vehicles? Not bad, thought Phil who was still trying to open his first. He put all his weight on the crowbar and felt the tap give a little. He tried again and this time managed to turn it thirty degrees. The turning became easier and he put the crowbar back in his pocket as he was able to use just his hands. Eventually, the tap became loose and he was able to spin it with one hand but there was no sign of any escaping fuel. He spun the tap until it wouldn't turn any further and still he noticed no escaping fuel. He scratched his head but he couldn't see what else he could do. As a last resort, he began to turn one of the valves that he had loosened earlier without much trouble. He heard a gurgling sound at first and continued to turn the valve. The gurgling became like the noise of a stream falling over rapids and suddenly he was soaked in petrol. He jumped back to avoid the torrent that was now pouring out of the tank and then went back and opened the valve a little more. He didn't stay to appreciate his success but moved swiftly to the next tank and set to work on the red-painted tap on that one.

When Phil got back to the hole in the fence, the other three were already waiting for him. Karen reported that she had let the fuel out of forty-four vehicles and would have done more but all the others had locks on them. Billy said that he had immobilised twelve tanks and set up two jeeps to explode when the ignition was turned on. Edward said that he had concentrated on the vehicles near the gates so that when they exploded the authorities wouldn't be able to move the others even if they survived the fire. He had primed three cars and a lorry – the three cars would explode if they were turned on but the lorry would go up as soon as someone sat in the driver's seat.

'Wasn't that bloody dangerous, Edward – working near the gate?' asked Phil. 'What about the sentry?'

'What sentry? There was no bloody sentry – I think they're having a night off. I heard lots of noise from one of the huts – laughing and singing – they've probably got one of them tarts in there from the drinking dens. They come down and have a gang bang with the guards in the hope of a lift home. One of the guards will oblige in the morning. I take my hat off to her – she kept the bastards away from us. Let's just hope she doesn't get a lift in one of those cars that I've fucked about with.'

'Oh my God!' said Phil. 'I'll have to go and warn her.'

'Warn her? Warn who?' asked Edward, grabbing him by the arm.

'The woman in there was part of the plan – she's a friend. I'll have to go and get her out.'

'You can't, Phil,' said Edward. 'It's too risky – you'll both end up dead and that won't help anyone. She'll just have to take her chances, like we've all done. How long did you tell her to stay there?'

'An hour.'

'Well, she should be all right then – the tarts usually stay until morning when the night shift ends and that's when they get a lift from one of the bastards. If she only stays an hour, she'll be OK. Come on, we've got to climb this bloody cliff before we're safe. By the way, how did you get on with the storage tanks – did you get them both open?'

'Yes, eventually – it's like a river down there now. I'm not going back up the cliff. I'm going to see what's happening at the guard post.'

'You're bloody not,' said Edward firmly. 'You're coming with us. You can't help your friend and there's us three to think of as well. If you go and bugger it all up now and get arrested – you know who we are. Get through that bloody hole in the fence and me and Billy will try and repair it so they won't know how we got in.'

Phil knew that Edward was right. Shirley was on her own. As he climbed the path up the cliff with Karen at his side, he found himself praying silently for the first time in many, many years.

Seventeen

The guard at the gate had looked at Shirley with interest after she had approached him. 'Pinky' – that was a new name. At least, he'd never heard of it before and he didn't remember having seen the woman either. He went to have a closer look and was surprised by what he saw. This woman was a different class to the normal slags that they got down there. She stank of gin and her hair and make-up could do with a bit of attention but apart from that he was quite impressed. She was leaning on the gate and the view was stunning. He shouldered his rifle and walked towards her.

'What do you want, Pinky?'

'I want somebody to have a drink with me. All my friends have pissed off somewhere and Pinky is feeling ever so lonely. This fucking Curfew has made a right bloody mess of my social life. What's your name? I know what it is – your name is "Hunky". That's what I'll call you, anyway. Pinky and Hunky – sounds good, doesn't it?' Shirley swayed a little and belched again. 'Ooops, windies. Sorry, Hunky. Come on, Hunky – open the bloody gate and we can have a drink and I can find out if you are a hunk or a punk.'

Hunky was a young man of twenty-one and, like all young men of that age, he fantasised about older women – not too old but those around Pinky's age, which he guessed was a very well-preserved forty. His real name was Terry Spencer and he was a very long way from home. His problem was that, if he let Pinky into the compound, the other guards would almost certainly want a piece of the action and the more he looked at Pinky the more he came to the conclusion that he would like her all for himself.

'Hunky, I can't stand here all night. I've got my reputation to think of.'

'What reputation is that, Pinky?'

'Wouldn't you like to know, Hunky? Open the fucking gate and I'll show you.'

Hunky opened the gate and Pinky staggered through. She looked at him for a few seconds and then grabbed him round the back of the neck. She kissed him as she had never kissed anyone before – all tongue and gin. Hunky responded and put his hands round her and stroked her leather-coated bum. Pinky realised that she was taking things too far too soon and pulled away from him.

'Pinky thinks you're a dirty little sod, Hunky. You need to slow down – now, let's go and have a drink and get warm while Pinky decides whether you deserve a reward for opening the gate.'

'What kind of reward, Pinky?'

'I haven't decided yet,' purred Pinky as she kissed his nose. 'You'll have to wait and see, Hunky – but I promise you that if Pinky does let you have a reward you won't be disappointed.'

Pinky took a swig of the gin and handed the bottle to Hunky, who accepted it and took a small sip. Good, she thought, we might be getting somewhere at last, and rubbed her hands together to show that she was cold.

'Which hut would you like to go in?' asked Hunky, who knew he wouldn't be able to keep this secret from his colleagues for much longer – all the guards had ears like satellite dishes when something like this was going on.

Pinky looked at the two huts. One was in complete darkness whilst the other was lit. She reckoned she'd be safer in the light but she didn't want to upset Hunky now that he was half on her side.

'Which do you suggest, Hunky?'

'I'd like to take you into the hut without any lights but the other guards would soon find out what was going on – so I suppose we'd better go into the other one.'

'A party? Pinky loves parties! How many other hunks like you are there?'

'Two, plus a corporal who's in charge of us. He's a bit of a shit but it's so boring down here he won't mind you coming in to warm up and have a drink.'

'Three hunks, a shit of a corporal and Pinky – now that's what I call the basis of a bloody good party – and Pinky loves parties! Let's go, but just remember this, Hunky – Pinky always leaves a party with the same bastard who takes her there. It's one of

Pinky's rules and Pinky never breaks her own rules.' She kissed Hunky again and rubbed herself against him. She felt him respond and pulled back again. She wanted him to know that he was on a promise – albeit a false one – and not a sure thing!

'Lead on, Hunky. Pinky needs to party – and after the party perhaps Hunky will let Pinky play with his big gun.'

Hunky laughed and led Pinky to the hut with the lights showing. He opened the door and took her into a large well-lit room containing three beds, four filing cabinets, a table, four chairs and two men. They were introduced as Mack and Fred and Pinky sat down at the table with the bottle of gin. Hunky explained how she had been at the gate and wanted to warm up. The other two guards made the usual sexist comments that men make in these kinds of situations and complimented Hunky on his good luck because Pinky looked far better than their normal female visitors. Mack handed Pinky a mug for her gin and in return she handed the bottle around the table where they were all now sitting. Pinky took a sip of her gin and for the first time that night thought she might have a chance of pulling this off. These three young lads didn't have a clue what the world was all about. They were innocents. Perhaps they got a quick shag from one of the real tarts that came in here but she didn't think they'd be any match for her when it came right down to it. There was only one unknown and that was their corporal. She decided to face the matter head-on and find out whether she would have a problem.

'So, where's this shit of a corporal, then? Doesn't he want to come to Pinky's party?' she asked in a loud voice.

'Keep your voice down, Pinky,' said Hunky. 'He's probably having a kip – leave him be.'

Pinky got up and went and sat on Hunky's lap. She snuggled up to him and then said in a loud whisper, making sure that the other two men could hear, 'You know what I said outside about Pinky's rules, darling – well there's another one. Nobody is allowed to be a shit when Pinky's having a party.'

A door opened at the end of the room and the three men shot up and stood to attention, including Hunky, who in doing so dumped Pinky on the floor. She was spreadeagled on her back with the gin spilled all over her blouse.

'Hunky, what the fuck do you think you're doing, you daft bastard? I'm going to report you to your shit of a corporal for ill treatment of a lady. Look at me – covered in gin and my ti—'

Pinky stopped in mid-sentence and looked up. Above her was the shit of a corporal who had come out of his private room on hearing the commotion. He held out his hand and helped her up.

'My name is Corporal Robson. I trust my men have been treating you courteously. I'm sure Guard Spencer didn't mean you any harm when he dropped you on the floor – military discipline is such that when an officer of senior rank enters the room the men stand to attention.'

Pinky felt a chill run down her spine. This is what she had feared. This was no innocent young boy – this was a career man who, as such, was far more dangerous than the other three in the room. Again she decided to tackle the problem head-on.

'My name's Pinky and you're not an officer of any rank – you're a shit of a corporal. My friend Hunky told me that. Do you think he's a hunk? I think he's gorgeous.' She put her arm around Corporal Robson. 'Don't you think he's gorgeous, Corporal Shit?'

Pinky found the corporal accepting her embrace and thought that she might have a real problem here – did this slimeball actually fancy her. The corporal pulled away from the embrace and took hold of her hand.

'I think we'll continue our conversation in my room. All right, men, back to work – we'll take the gin. Spencer, if you're going to stay in here talking to these other two reprobates about tonight's events, keep the noise down.'

Corporal Robson led Pinky into a small room that had a desk, two chairs and a single bed. He put the gin on the desk and brought two glasses from a cupboard on the wall. He poured out two drinks and sat down in the one comfortable chair behind the desk. Pinky seated herself on the other chair and knew she was in trouble – she reckoned that this suave, oily, arse-licking thirty-year-old had worked out that she was a fraud. Again she decided to adopt the full-frontal approach like she had done with any problem that she had encountered that night.

'That wasn't very nice, Corporal – we were all set to have a party in there. We were just waiting for you to join us. Why have you brought me in here? I hope you're not going to try and have your wicked way with poor little Pinky.'

'I'm interested in you, Pinky – you're a lot different from the other women we normally get down here. Where do you live?'

'Wouldn't you like to know? That's no use anyway because my flatmate is there and it's her turn to have a visitor tonight – we take it in turns. That's why I came down here so I could get warm.'

'I'm sure we can keep you warm, Pinky. Pass the gin – we can have our own party in here.'

'We can't have a party with just two of us. Pinky likes big parties – let's go back next door.' Pinky took a drink from the bottle and passed it over to Corporal Robson.

The corporal settled back in his chair and took a drink.

'No, I think we'll stay where we are. Take your coat off, Pinky and make yourself at home. It's not often I get the chance to talk to a woman like you.'

Pinky did as she was told and sat opposite the corporal in her leather boots and trousers, and her all-revealing blouse. Corporal Robson smiled and for the first time that night Pinky felt a little afraid. There was something about this man that she didn't trust and somehow she had to find a way back into the other room and the comparative safety of the company of Hunky, Mack and Fred. She wondered how she could regain the initiative but it was the corporal who spoke first.

'You see, Pinky – I doubt that is your real name but it will do for now – I am intrigued by you. You are obviously not a tart of the kind who normally comes down here for a quick shag and a lift home. You are a woman who came here for some other purpose and I want to find out what that is before I take you to Headquarters for interrogation. It will look good on my record if I take you there knowing the whole story. So, tell me – what are you doing here?'

Pinky realised that she had made a fatal mistake. This bastard didn't fancy her – he saw her as another notch on his service record! She took another swig of gin before answering.

'You know, Corporal Shit, I've never been lucky in my life – whenever the cards have been dealt, it's always been poor old

Pinky with the crap hand. "Go down to the compound," one of the girls in the bar said. "You can get a lift home for a quick shag.'"

Pinky belched and took another drink of her gin.

'But it's Pinky's luck to find the one corporal who's a bloody queer – here I am, covered in black leather with my tits hanging out and you want to take me to your headquarters for fucking questioning. I don't believe it – sod's law is alive and well!'

'I am not a homosexual – it's illegal – and I don't believe you really are who you say you are. Put your coat back on and we'll go to Headquarters now. You can leave the drink – I have a feeling you won't be needing it for a very long time.'

Pinky did as she was told and followed Corporal Robson into the other room. The three men again stood to attention.

'I'm taking Pinky to Headquarters. One of you get on the phone to them and tell them that we're on our way.'

The corporal put on his outer coat and went towards the door. Pinky noticed that the other three men looked at her. Hunky seemed disappointed and she decided to go to her death in a blaze of glory.

'Sorry, Hunky,' she said and went over to him. 'I didn't keep my promise, did I? This sexy bastard of a corporal wants me all to himself but I'd still like to see your big gun one day.'

Pinky kissed him on the lips and then went out of the door with Corporal Robson, who told her to stand by the hut.

'Don't even think of trying to escape. Stand there and I'll go and get the car but just in case you want to play the heroine, let's add these to your leather gear – I'm told some degenerates in this sick society find the two things have a sexual compatibility.'

The Corporal took a pair of handcuffs from his coat pocket and put them on Pinky. At first he tied her hands behind her back but then changed his mind and cuffed her at the front.

'Thank you, kind sir,' said Pinky. 'Why did you change your mind?'

'With your hands tied behind your back your enormous tits stick out even more than normal and it was disgusting to look at. Now stand there and I'll bring the car around – you'll sit in the back. Don't worry – one of the men will open the gates.'

The Corporal went off in the direction of the vehicles and Shirley waited. Things weren't too bad, she told herself – one on one in the car, she could have a go at him and make sure that they never reached Headquarters, wherever that was. She leaned back against the hut and sighed. She reckoned that she'd given Phil his hour or very nearly but she hadn't seen or heard anything of her fellow conspirators – perhaps they hadn't managed to get through the fence. She heard Hunky and his friends in the hut laughing and she knew it was probably a joke about her. What the hell, she told herself, she'd done her best and she still had a chance in the car with Corporal Shit. She walked towards the barrier and waited.

The first explosion, when the Corporal switched on the ignition in the car, knocked her off her feet and sent her skidding back against the hut. The next, when it came a few seconds later, nearly blew her head off with its noise. Mack, Fred and Hunky came running out of the hut and began to shoot at anything and nothing. The third explosion was nearer the hut than the other two and two of the guards immediately went down in the flames that engulfed them. Shirley heard their screams and saw that one of the men was Hunky – she wanted to go and help him but she knew that it was too late. By now, this end of the compound was an inferno. Both huts were on fire and all the vehicles around were exploding. Shirley ran to the cliffs for protection and would have made it in time if the fourth explosion had not erupted. It blew her sideways and against the end of a tank. She felt her hair and eyebrows burning and scrambled under the vehicle. She found the ground was wet and rolled around thinking it was water but soon realised from the smell that she was bathing in fuel.

She crawled out and looked about her. The whole compound was now on fire and vehicles were exploding every few seconds. She saw two huge tanks on the seaside that still seemed to be intact but there were flames lapping all around them and she didn't give much for their chances for very much longer. As if on cue, one of the tanks suddenly ignited in a big ball of flame, sending sparks hundreds of feet into the night sky. Some of the vehicles must have contained ammunition because they exploded more than the others.

Shirley took stock of her situation – she was handcuffed, covered in oil and fuel and her hair was already burning. In addition, she was locked inside a military compound that soon would be swarming with guards. What the hell was she going to do? The gates were locked and that was the way the guards would come in. Then she had a thought – if Phil and the others hadn't come in by the gates then there must be some other entrance on the cliff side away from the gates! She started to make her way along the side of the cliff but it was slow going.

The handcuffs made keeping her balance difficult and she slipped and slid all over the place. There were fires everywhere and for the fist time that night she was grateful for her boots and leather trousers. The explosions continued but they weren't having the same effect as before because the compound was now ablaze in one enormous conflagration. It seemed to Shirley that the whole coastline was on fire and for the second time that night she thought of her twins.

If this is what they had seen just before their deaths then she pitied them and, now, said a silent prayer. She could hardly see – her mascara had joined with her tears and she rubbed her eyes vigorously.

She looked for Phil's entry point and eventually saw what looked like a chink in the fence. Of course! These were the old steps down to the theatre – Phil would have known about them in the old days when he and Rosie had taken the kids down to the beach. She and Geoff had done exactly the same with their two lovely girls. She reached up and felt along the fence and found that it had been recently cut. She pushed against the piece that had been used by the others as an entry and exit point and then sat down and cried. That bastard Phil King had closed the door behind him!

The fence had been repaired when they'd gone and someone had clamped the hole shut with heavy metal wire. There was no way she was going to be able to make a hole and scramble out this way. Just as she thought her situation couldn't get any worse, she heard the sound of sirens and the gates were bulldozed open. Hundreds of guards and firemen tumbled out of lorries and fire engines which entered the compound. They were too late, of course, to save any of the vehicles in the compound but they could perhaps douse the fires a little. They could certainly fan out and find a woman who was already handcuffed and ask her what she knew about the night's events.

There was one other thing that the authorities would have to do. They would have to get some guards up on to the cliff road to control the crowd that had gathered up there and were celebrating and cheering at the chaotic scene below them. People had obviously been woken by the explosions and had broken the Curfew to see what had been happening.

Shirley could hear the shouts and cheers – it was like bonfire night to some people – and then she heard the automatic rifles of the guards and the shouting and cheering stopped. She was left alone again – her head hurt and the guards who were now commencing a detailed search of the compound were getting closer. They were still a couple of hundred yards away from where she was hiding but she knew it wouldn't be long before she was discovered. She considered her options.

She decided, after just a few seconds, that she didn't have any and stood up. She would walk towards the guards and give herself up. If she put her hands up and showed the cuffs, they might not shoot her on the spot but take her in for questioning. Her decision made, she walked towards the gates and the guards and hoped that either Shirley or Pinky would find a bloody good explanation for her predicament. After a few steps she stopped and went back to the repair in the fence. She crouched down and for the last time that night she decided to solve her problems with a head-on approach. She spoke in a loud whisper.

'Listen, Phil King – you're a bastard! I'm covered in oil and God knows what else. I'm handcuffed and my hair has been burned off. My tits are so cold that you could hang your washing on them but what do you care? You don't give a shit because you had your hands down my knickers this afternoon and that's all you wanted. I'm going to die but that's all right – everybody dies eventually and I have no problems with that – but... But if I ever see you again I'll just ask you one question: why the fuck did you have to close the hole in this fence?'

Shirley sat down and waited for the guards to find her. She realised it wouldn't take them very long.

Eighteen

When Phil and Karen reached the cliff road, they waited for Edward and Billy to join them after repairing the hole in the fence. Eventually, the four of them lay on top of the cliffs and looked down at the tranquil scene below. There was a light on in one of the huts but otherwise there was no sign of life in the compound.

'All we can do now is wait,' said Edward.

Phil King nodded, keeping his eyes on the guard hut and wondering how Shirley was getting on. Somehow he had to go and help her but he knew that Edward was right and they would have to wait and see what happened. Suddenly Billy pointed to the hut that had the lights on – the door had opened and two people came out. It was too far away to see who the people were but after a short conversation one of the people stayed by the barrier and the other walked towards the first line of cars.

'Don't choose one of those, you daft bastard,' said Edward. 'They were too near the huts – Billy and I didn't fix any of them. Go to the next row.'

It was as if the person had heard Edward's instruction because he walked through the first line and made for a car in the next one.

'Here we go. OK, Phil – let's see if your plan is going to work.' Edward smiled and shook hands with his son.

Karen looked at Phil and crossed her fingers. Phil didn't know whether this meant 'Good luck with the plan' or 'Let's hope Shirley is all right' but he hoped it was the latter – the plan didn't seem to matter much to him now!

They heard a car door being closed and then there was a short pause when the whole world seemed to hold its breath.

They felt the first explosion shake the cliffs beneath them and from then it was difficult to keep track of the exact chain of events – everything seemed to happen at once. Men came out of one of the huts shooting but they didn't seem to be aiming at anybody or anything and then the huts caught fire. They saw two of the guards being blown into the air and landing back on the ground engulfed in flames. There were more explosions but now the fires took over and the river of fuel that Phil and Karen had created ran everywhere, burning everything in its path. People began to arrive on the cliff road – shouting, jeering, clapping and pumping their fists in the air. The first of the big storage tanks blew up and everyone tried to find some cover as sparks swept over the cliffs, borne by the sea wind. The second tank went up soon after and the watching crowd went wild.

They heard the sirens and saw a convoy of vehicles sweep into the compound. Guards poured out of the first two or three trucks and began to shoot at the ecstatic crowd on the cliff road who dispersed very quickly. The guards and the firemen at first tried heroically to stem the fires but soon gave up – the compound and everything in it had been destroyed!

A sort of quiet returned and the four conspirators surveyed their handiwork with a mixture of awe and satisfaction. Edward broke the silence.

'Sorry about your friend, Phil – I don't see how anyone could have survived that bloody lot.'

'Do you think she could have got out before it all started?' asked Phil.

'The gates didn't open until those daft bastards turned up trying to impersonate Fireman Sam so I don't see how.'

'I'd hate to think she burned to death in all that,' said Phil. 'It was bad enough watching those guards die like they did – and they were the enemy! I shouldn't have asked her to do it – I should—'

'Shut up a minute, you two,' said Karen. 'I thought I heard something.'

'What?' asked Phil.

'It's time we were moving anyway,' said Edward.

'Shut up – listen. There's someone down by the fence. It sounded like Shirley's voice.'

Phil hadn't heard a thing but he jumped up and grabbed the wire clippers.

'Are you sure, Karen?' he asked.

'I'm not sure it was Shirley but I did hear a voice from down at the bottom of the steps.'

'The guards are coming this way, Phil – you'll never make it. Come on, we need to get home and away from here.' Edward said this with sadness in his voice and he knew he was right but he also knew that Phil wouldn't take any notice of him. 'But if you're determined to go, take Billy with you – he's a big strong lad and you might need some help down there. Karen and I will wait here. Good luck and bring my boy back.'

Phil didn't hear the last of this speech – he was already bounding down the steps with Billy a close second. Billy threw the barbed-wire barrier to one side and they chased down the last ten steps. Shirley was crouched on the other side of the fence and looked in a terrible state – her hair and eyebrows were singed and her face almost black.

'About fucking time! I thought you said you'd come and rescue me in a tank if I was in trouble.'

'The tank got burned. You look awful – are you all right?'

'I'm fine – and thanks for the compliment about my appearance, you bastard. Who's this?'

'This is my friend Billy and we've come to get you out of there.'

'Thanks, Billy. Hurry up – the guards are coming.'

During all this banter, Billy had been recutting the clamps that he and his dad had put on the fence after they escaped. He cut just enough for him to prise back the fencing and make a hole big enough for Shirley to squirm through. Phil grabbed hold of her and pulled her through the last few inches.

'Don't worry about putting the clamps back, Billy – let's get out of here.' Phil turned to go up the steps, dragging Shirley behind him but Billy stayed where he was and began to make sure that the fence was secure again.

'Dad always says, "If a job's worth doing then it's worth doing right". You two go – I'll be OK. Tell my dad I'll see him at home.'

Phil and Shirley were near the top of the steps when they heard the sound of the automatic gunfire. They didn't stop until they got to the cliff road and fell down exhausted by the side of

Karen and Edward. Phil looked at Edward, who was staring at him.

'I don't know, Edward – he told us to go so we went. He said he'd see you at home but that was before the gunfire.'

Edward got to his feet.

'Right, I'd better get off there, then. Don't worry, Billy's a good lad and if he's only injured, he won't tell them anything.'

He looked down at Shirley. 'You're something else, young lady. I don't know what you did down there or how you got out but you are definitely in a class of your own.'

'If anything's happened to your son, Edward, I'll never forgive myself. I hope he's all right. Before you go, though, you haven't got another pair of those wire clippers, have you? I don't fancy walking the streets in handcuffs.'

'Christ!' said Phil, who had only just noticed them. 'What have you got handcuffs on for?'

'I thought I'd even up the odds a little – four to one didn't seem like a fair fight to me! I got arrested, you daft bugger! Thanks, Edward.'

Edward used the other clippers and released the cuffs from Shirley's wrists. He put the pieces in his coat pocket and slowly walked away without another word.

Phil, Karen and Shirley set off in the other direction and headed for Shirley's house. Karen and Shirley walked in front with their arms around each other, with Phil following on behind. Nothing was said until they were safely inside the small cottage and they were sitting at the kitchen table except for Karen, who was running around fetching bowls of water and cloths to see what she could do about Shirley's injuries. Shirley told her story first and then Phil gave his version of the night's events. Karen cut Shirley's hair even shorter than it had been and got rid of most of the burnt parts. She bathed her face and her chest and brought her a sweater to wear. They had tea and then sat in silence for a time. In the end it was Karen who asked the question that the other two were dreading because neither of them had a clue as to what the answer was.

'Well, I thought it was great tonight. Joey would have loved the explosions! So, what do we do next?'

'I know what I'm going to do,' said Shirley. 'I'm going to bed – I'm bloody exhausted. I'm going to have a lovely long sleep and then I'm going to get up in the morning and go to work at the shop at the usual time.'

'I didn't mean that, Shirley,' said Karen. 'I meant what are we going to blow up next? Tonight was great and we really put one over on those bastards.'

'I know exactly what you meant, Karen, and perhaps you're right but I'm in no fit state to think of what comes next at the moment. I need some sleep. I want to find out what has happened to that young boy, Billy, before I throw my hat in the ring again. If you two want to stay here, that's fine by me, but I need some space at the moment so I'll love you and leave you. Goodnight.'

She kissed them both on the cheek before going upstairs. They heard her going into the bedroom and pottering about, and then came silence. This lasted for about three minutes before the sobbing began. They listened as their friend cried her heart out. Karen made a move to go to her but Phil put out his arm and stopped her.

'If she wants either or both of us she'll let us know. Let her grieve – she's been through a hell of a lot tonight. We'll stay; she'll know we're close by if she needs anyone. You sleep on the sofa in the lounge and I'll get my head down in here. It's no use us going back to Victoria Way, anyway – the place is a tip and we'd have to clear up before we could find somewhere to sleep.'

Karen did as she was told and left Phil alone in the kitchen. He was desperately tired and he put his head down on the table and within minutes was asleep. Karen slept, as youngsters do, and thought of nothing. Shirley woke up twice because she thought she was burning to death but luckily went quickly back to sleep. Phil King didn't really sleep at all – his tiredness faded into the background as the guilt took over. He dozed and thought of Billy. He dozed and thought of Edward. He dozed and thought of the woman upstairs. He dozed and wondered whether it had all been worth it. He dozed and finally woke up and made himself another cup of tea.

There was no sound from outside and obviously the people of the town hadn't taken their cue from the blaze and taken to the streets. The destruction of the compound hadn't brought about the overthrow of the authorities. He had no idea what to do next. Perhaps Shirley was right – carry on as normal and find another target – but he knew that was going to be a waste of time. If the town hadn't erupted after what they had done tonight, then it never would. Somehow, the three of them would have to find a way out of this terrible mess and leave the others to fend for themselves. Perhaps it should be five now – Edward and Billy had earned the right to go with them if they wanted to after tonight. Perhaps it would be only four if Billy had been killed or captured. Perhaps it would be seven or six if Leroy and Davie wanted out as well.

But how? The Border was impregnable as far as Phil could tell – or at least the bit that he had seen was. The sea was an even worse bet – they'd need a boat and would have to run the gauntlet of the gunships stationed just off the coast. No, it would have to be overland and that could only mean somewhere away from the border post that Phil visited every morning. Phil would have to find another crossing point, where there weren't any guards and floodlights. But this presented huge problems – he knew he was under surveillance already, at least in the shop, and after last night this might be extended to watching him every minute of every day. He decided to leave it all to later that day after having had a word with Shirley and started to get ready for his trip to meet Amos. He seemed to exist in a world of semi-darkness nowadays – he hardly ever saw real daylight.

He tiptoed upstairs and looked in on Shirley. She was still asleep and the tears seemed to have disappeared. He kissed her lightly on the lips and went downstairs again. Karen was sprawled on the sofa and away with the fairies. He went back into the kitchen and wrote a note to them both, saying that he would see them at the shop at the normal time. As he straightened up he heard a knock at the front door. Oh God, he thought, they can't have traced us already. He went into the hall and heard another knock. He was puzzled and intrigued because it wasn't the kind of loud knock that the guards would have made if they were coming to arrest him. He went to the front door, opened it and sighed with relief.

Leroy and Davie stood on the step covered in the biggest grins that Phil had ever seen. They came in and shook his hand.

'Philip King, you're a star!' said Leroy. 'I presume that was your work down at the compound tonight – what a fucking carnival! Davie and I were in a drinking club under the old Grand Hotel and after the first explosion we raced out to watch the show. Jesus, I've never seen anything like it – if that doesn't wake everybody up in this town then I don't know what will.'

'It hasn't though, has it?' said Phil leading the boys into the kitchen. 'Listen to the streets outside – I wouldn't say that the town had woken up, would you?'

'Everybody's talking about it, Phil,' said Davie. 'In the club, afterwards—'

'That's no fucking use, people talking about the firework display – why weren't they out there stopping the guards and the firemen coming to the rescue? They weren't there because they don't give a shit and now I don't give a shit about them. I want out. Do you know a way? There could be five of us – seven, if you two want to come as well.'

Leroy looked at the floor and then at Davie who nodded.

'We know a way out but we won't come with you – we still believe that this system will have to be crushed from the inside but after tonight I suppose you've earned the right to go if you want to.'

'Don't go,' said Davie. 'We could use all the plans you've got if tonight is anything to go by.'

'No, my mind is made up – you might be right about this mess being cleared up from the inside but that's a young man's game and I learnt tonight that I'm not a young man anymore. All I need to know is that the escape route is safe – or as safe as it can be. I don't want to take my friends on some crazy stunt that ends with us all getting killed.'

'The escape route is as safe as houses,' said Leroy. 'Charles Corcoran used it all the time and never had a problem.'

'Oh, no,' said Phil, starting to laugh. 'You can't be fucking serious? He was on their side – it's not surprising that he never had a problem. You'll have to come up with something better than that – I said *safe*.'

'The route is safe – Charles told us that before he died – because he didn't tell anyone about it. His daddy refused to let him have an escape route because he didn't want him to compromise his cover. He told him to get any messages back through his sister but Charles wanted to prove to his daddy what a clever son he had and he sorted out this route on his own. He told no one about it even though his daddy was desperate to find out how he managed it and Charles refused to tell him because he wanted to appear a superhero in Daddy's eyes. His sister doesn't know about it either and is absolutely pissed off because Daddy started to tell her how wonderful Charles was. The family works totally on competition, all trying to be a bigger bastard than the next – fuck knows what the mother is like!'

'How do you know all this?' asked Phil.

It was Davie, who answered, in his slow Scottish drawl.

'It's surprising what a man will tell you when he thinks he's going to be killed and is hung upside down on a fence post. Especially when he's got a mad Scotsman pressing a knife against his balls.'

'It's not surprising to me,' said Phil. 'I'm still not convinced – give me a day or two to think it over and I'll let you know – is that all right?'

Both men nodded and agreed to call in the shop sometime in the next forty eight hours to find out Phil's decision. They talked for a little while about the compound fire and then Phil told them he had to go to the Border and the lads turned to leave and congratulated him again. The sting in the tale about the escape route came from Leroy as he was leaving.

'There is perhaps one thing you should know about the escape route whilst you're deciding what to do. Charles said that it terminated somewhere on the Corcoran estate but he died before he could tell us how big the estate was or where the route came out.'

Phil closed the door behind them. It occurred to him that nothing in his life nowadays seemed simple or easy!

He reached 108 Victoria Way, went into the backyard and looked at his bike – he had forgotten about the puncture! He hadn't time to fix it – with his crude tools and pieces of paper tape it was a good hour's work and he was late already. It would be a slow, painful journey and the tyre would probably be ruined but he didn't seem to have a choice. He went into the house, found his normal work clothes and changed. He rolled the clothes that he had worn overnight into a bundle and took them with him. He looked around at the house that had once been full of laughter and felt a little sad at the mess it was now in after the 'search' by the guards. What the hell, he thought, I'll be leaving it soon.

He went back into the yard and got his bike. He threw the bundle of clothes into the trailer and set off. Halfway down England Avenue, he stopped, took the clothes from the trailer and went into a burned-out shop. He took a box of matches from his pocket and set the bundle alight. It blazed fiercely and he threw it towards the back of the site.

He carried on with his journey but he was now very late and he had so wanted this to be a 'normal' morning after his activities the night before. He reached the guard post at the end of England Avenue and noticed there were a couple of vehicles parked there – an armoured car and a large van with small windows at the side. Perhaps last night was already having an effect and security was being stepped up. But there was nobody about and he waited by the barrier, as he normally did, for the guard to come and check his papers and let him through.

He was kept waiting for a lot longer than normal but he daren't pass the barrier until he had been checked. He supposed that, because he was so late, they weren't ready for him or thought he wasn't coming. After a while, Phil King began to worry. He heard voices from inside the hut and then the door opened and a guard, whom he'd never seen before, walked slowly over to him. He was carrying an automatic rifle, which was not normal. Although the guards were armed at this barrier, they never brought their guns out of the hut to let Phil through. Phil kept looking at this first man but out of the corner of his eye saw another three similarly armed guards emerge from the hut.

'Mr King, is it?' asked the first guard. 'Mr Philip King of 108 Victoria Way? You're off to the Border to pick up some produce for your shop in England Avenue, is that right?'

'Yes, that's me. I'm sorry I'm a bit late this morning. Is there anything wrong?'

'No, nothing wrong, Mr King – we're just doing a full-scale security check this morning. If you'd like to leave your bike and trailer there and come over to the hut for a minute we can check your papers properly and have you on your way in no time at all.'

Phil left the bike as ordered and followed the guard towards the hut. The three other guards stepped to one side to let them pass and they were just a couple of yards from the door when the first guard stopped and turned round. His voice was icy cold now.

'So you're the bastard who killed Corporal Robbo and our other three mates?'

'What?' said Phil. He didn't finish the question. He doubled up as the butt of the first guard's gun was driven hard into his stomach. It was the second blow to the back of his head that knocked him unconscious. Perhaps that was a blessing since he then wasn't able to feel the numerous kicks that thudded into his ribs and legs.

The three guards picked him up and threw him into the back of the van where he was left on the floor. They locked the rear door, got into the cab and drove off at high speed leaving the first guard to survey the scene. After a moment, the regular guard, who Phil normally saw on his errand, came out of the hut and joined him.

'What should I do about the bike and trailer?' he asked.

'I couldn't give a shit – take it home, throw it away or leave it where it is. That bastard won't be wanting it again.' With that, the first guard jumped into the armoured car and set off in the same direction as the van.

The normal guard gave a wry smile and wandered over to the bike and trailer. They were old and nearly falling apart and he couldn't see that he would ever have a use for them. He noticed the puncture in the front tyre and wheeled the two of them behind the hut to where a ditch ran down from the Border. He pushed them in and saw them half-sink in the watery mud.

Funny, he thought, that Mr King didn't seem a bad sort of chap – a bit quiet at times, but who wasn't these days? He re-entered the hut and began to fill in the paperwork for the arrest. After completing it, it took him all of three minutes to forget Philip King, his bike and his trailer, for ever.

Nineteen

Phil King woke up a few hours later and found that he ached all over. His legs ached, his stomach ached and his ribs felt as though they had caved in. Worse still, his head throbbed to the rhythm of some crazy Afro-Caribbean jazz tune. He was lying face down on a cold floor and he tried to turn over to see where he was. Every little twist of his body caused spasms of pain but he somehow managed to sit up and lean against a wall.

The room was small and square, about nine feet along each wall, and there was nothing in it except him. He presumed it must be a cell of some sort because there was a small window high up in one of the walls and it had bars over it. This was the only source of light in the room – there were no switches or bulbs to be seen on the bare walls and ceiling. The walls, the ceiling and the floor were all bare stone and reminded Phil of the dungeons you saw in mediaeval castles. He saw no point in trying to stand up since there was nothing to see or do. He sat there and waited for the wooden door, set in the wall opposite the window, to open.

It seemed to him that he waited for a very long time.

He was asleep when they came for him and it was the noise of the door creaking open that woke him. Two guards entered the cell and picked him up under the arms – the pain made his body shudder but he noticed that the drumbeat in his head seemed to have had the volume turned down a little. The men frogmarched him out of the room and turned right into a corridor, which was lit by fluorescent tubes hung from the ceiling. Nobody said anything and, after a couple of more turns in the corridors, which all looked exactly the same, they came to a set of stone steps. This took them to something like an anteroom with a desk at one corner behind which sat another stone-faced guard whose voice was the first heard by Phil King since the one at the Border had mentioned something about Corporal Robbo.

'Number Five – they're waiting for him.'

The men who were holding Phil promptly led him down another corridor and stopped outside a door marked with a big, bold brass number '5'. The one on his left knocked and opened the door, pushing Phil inside. The guards didn't enter the room and so Phil was forced to try and stand unaided for the first time – he nearly lost the battle with his aching limbs but just managed to keep his balance. He looked around him and found himself in a light, airy room fitted out as an office.

There was a large window opposite the door which gave a view of rolling fields and hedgerows. The room itself was decorated in cream and contained a desk, a sofa and a few chairs dotted about the walls. There were two other occupants in the room – one of them was, inevitably, Miss Arabella Corcoran/Jeffers who was wearing her simple guard's uniform. The other person was a man who Phil had not seen before.

Tall and wiry, he looked about fifty-years-old and was completely bald. He wore an ordinary lounge suit with a dark blue shirt and a dark blue tie. His thin face was pale and wire-framed glasses perched on the end of his pointed nose. He was standing behind the desk reading some papers but now looked up and stared at Phil over the top of his glasses.

'Welcome, Mr King, pull up a chair. We want to have a chat with you. You know Miss Jeffers, I think. Let me introduce myself – my name is Smith. Come on, don't just stand there – get one of those chairs and we can make a start.'

The voice was high-pitched and, if it had an accent, Phil couldn't detect it. Phil went and got one of the chairs and placed it by the desk, positioning it so that he had a good view of the window. Mr Smith also sat down behind the desk with Miss Jeffers on his left, almost opposite to Phil.

'Good,' said Mr Smith. 'I don't think this should take too long if you cooperate, Mr King. I'll begin by telling you what we know – we know that it was your plan to blow up the military compound last night because you outlined it to the resistance group the other night. We know that you were going to get Edward and Billy Houghton to help you and we know that Billy Houghton was there last night because he was shot dead whilst trying to escape. We know that there were probably one or two others there with you to carry out the plan. That is what we know and this is what we want you to tell us: who was the woman who distracted the guards whilst you and the others were actually setting light to the compound?'

Phil looked at Mr Smith and Miss Jeffers and then looked out of the window.

'Did you hear what I said, Mr King?'

'I heard every word,' answered Phil. 'Can I go now?'

Mr Smith leaned forward, put his elbows on the desk and cupped his hands together.

'I was hoping you were going to be sensible about this but obviously I was wrong. Do you deny that you put forward such a plan at the resistance group meeting?'

'No.'

'Well, there we are – you admit that it was your plan?'

'Yes. Who told you all this?'

'That doesn't concern you.'

'But it does concern me, Mr Smith, because your source, whoever he or she is, hasn't told you the whole story. I went to the meeting and said I had a plan and that I would look into its feasibility over the next seven days and report back at the next meeting. I went and saw Edward Houghton and his son Billy and we discussed the matter and came to no firm conclusion and I began to rethink the whole idea. It was a plan – nothing more, nothing less. It's not my fault if somebody carried it out before I was ready.'

'So you deny any part in last night's demolition of the compound?'

'I do. I'm a bit pissed off about it, really, because it was my plan. But what the hell – a demolition is a demolition. Can I go now?'

It was the lovely Miss Jeffers who spoke next.

'Let's stop this charade, Philip – we know you were there. All we want to know is who the woman was.'

'How do you know I was there?'

'It must have been you. It was your plan.'

'That's not what I asked – how do you *know* I was there?'

'We believe it couldn't have been anybody else and with the Houghtons involved it rather completes the case against you. You have just admitted that you spoke to them about the plan yesterday morning.'

'Was Edward Houghton there?'

'He must have been – he never lets Billy out on his own.'

'So, let me get this straight. You know Billy Houghton was there because you killed him but you're presuming the rest of this pile of shit you've just come out with. Am I right?'

'You are not right, Mr King,' said Mr Smith. 'We have enough evidence to convict you of murder and we will bring charges.'

Phil stood up and eased his aching limbs over to the window. He looked out at the winter landscape and started to laugh. He turned and addressed the lady in the room.

'Bloody hell, Jeffers – where did you find this daft bastard? He must be from another planet because he certainly doesn't live in the town that I've just left. Evidence? Murder charges? Fuck off, Baldy – just kill me now like you did with the other 30,000 people you've got rid of in the last three years. I'm surprised at you, Jeffers – you should find more intelligent people to hold interrogations with.'

Miss Jeffers looked away and waited for Smith to speak, but he declined the opportunity and it was left to her to continue. Phil turned his back on them both and looked out of the window again. Pale winter sunlight was spreading across the fields and the view seemed to give him some comfort.

'Mr Smith is a distinguished member of our legal team and as such tends to see everything in the terms of the law.'

Phil spun round and began to shout at them both.

'There you go again – the law? What the fuck has the law got to do with all this? I'm picked up at the barrier in England Avenue and kicked half to death and then left in a cell to rot until I'm brought up here to answer some fucking stupid questions about something I know nothing about. If all this is lawful, where's my fucking solicitor? I'm not talking anymore until you get my lawyer up here.'

Phil sat down and crossed his arms in defiance. Mr Smith and Miss Jeffers had a whispered conversation between the two of them and then Mr Smith left the room closing the door behind him. Miss Jeffers came round to Phil's side of the desk, pulled up a chair, sat down and lit a cigarette.

'I'm sure we can work this out between us, Philip. Let's calm down and see where we can go from here.'

This intolerably cruel woman had reverted to using her dinner party voice and it made Phil even angrier. He knew that there was no way he was going to get out of this and so decided to go down fighting and with a bit of pride.

'What's your name, Jeffers? You call me Philip – what can I call you?'

'Does that matter?'

'It matters to me. Come on – what do your lovers call you in bed? They surely don't have to call you "Miss Jeffers" – or are you into the dominant woman bit?'

'My name is Penelope but my friends call me Penny.'

'Then I shall call you Penny. Penny? Yes, that's a nice name. Have you got any friends, Penny?'

'Lots – why?'

'I bet you don't tell them what you do for a living – torturing people, killing people. You wouldn't have many friends left, then, Penny.'

'I do neither of those things. I'm an administrator.'

'You're ever so modest, Penny. You're a spy – you told me so yourself. Spies torture and kill people – I've seen them in films.'

'Shall we get back to the reason why you're here, Philip? We want to know who this woman was who took care of the guards. When you've told us that, I'll see what I can do about getting you out of here.'

There you go again, thought Phil, making promises that you've no intention of keeping. How do you do it, Jeffers? Surely it can't all be a desire to please Daddy, can it? You are a sad, sad woman, Jeffers, and you need to break away from Daddy and get a life. You are a beautiful woman, Jeffers – you could have made something of yourself, had a career, a marriage and children instead of being in the centre of this gruesome experiment. You've got blood on you hands, Jeffers, and I doubt if you'll ever be able to wash them clean.

'Did you hear what I said, Philip?'

'I've made a decision,' said Phil coming out of his reverie. 'I don't like the name "Penny" any more – I shall give you a new name that I like and I shall call you by that. There was a girl at my primary school who had the most wonderful name and all the boys were in love with her. She wasn't very nice-looking but we all fell in love with her name. The name stood out in a class of "Cheryls", "Tinas" and "Debbies" and seemed to have the beauty of poetry about it. I used to repeat it over and over again to myself when I was walking home from school. Yes – I shall call you "Arabella".'

Miss Jeffers looked at Phil and paused before she spoke.

'What difference does a name make?'

'It makes all the difference in the world, Arabella. Don't you like your new name? I think it suits you – if your parents had called you "Arabella" instead of "Penelope" you might not have turned out to be the bitch you undoubtedly are. Can I go now?'

'Sit down and try to be serious for a moment.'

'Why the fuck should I be serious, Arabella? What's the point? I'll leave this room and one of your bastard guards will kill me. I'd rather have a laugh before I die, thank you. You can be serious if you want to – it suits you!'

'Listen to me – there is a chance that I could get you out of here. The military are furious about last night and are blaming the civilian authorities. They want revenge and are saying that a firmer hand is needed to stop things like last night. They want to take over in the town instead of working for us and that wouldn't be good news for anybody.'

Phil looked at her in astonishment.

'You're a bloody sad case, Arabella – a "firmer hand"? Have you any idea what living in that town has been like over the last three years? No, you haven't. I think most of the few people who are left would welcome martial law in preference to your civilian regime. I see it all now! This is a fight between the military and you lot as to who assumes power – it's just like Germany in the 1940s when the German army and the Gestapo were at each other's throats all the time. Well, fuck the lot of you – you're all as bad as each other and if you think I'm going to help you in your fight against the military, you can bloody well think again.'

Phil slumped in the chair.

'Helping us might be your only hope of staying alive.'

'You don't get it, do you, Arabella? Why would I want to stay alive? What would be the point? My family has disappeared, my house has been destroyed, I'm in some sort of prison. What have I got to live for? What's the incentive to me for helping you? Don't give me all that shit about my family again because I might be forced to hit you. They're probably dead and if they're not you haven't got a clue where they are. So, what's the alternative inducement – three more years in that rat infested shit-hole of a town? I'd rather be killed by the guards.'

'All the military want to know is the name of the woman who distracted the guards.'

'I don't know about any woman. I wasn't there, remember? How do they know there was a woman?'

'The corporal told one of the guards to telephone through to Headquarters saying that he was bringing a female prisoner in for questioning. The guard was on the phone when the first explosion occurred.'

'She was obviously killed in the blaze.'

'They didn't find her body – only the charred remains of the three guards. The corporal was blown to bits in the first explosion. They think he activated it when he tried to start the car.'

'Well, that's it, then – the corporal was taking her to Headquarters and they were both in the car and she was blown to bits as well. Problem solved.'

'The military don't think so – haven't you got any idea as to who she could be?'

'No, I wasn't there, but the woman may not have been part of the plan – she certainly wasn't part of mine. Women used to go down to the compound from the drinking dens to see if they could get a lift home from the guards for services rendered after their shift was finished. If I were you, I'd look at the old slags who frequent the dens. Can I go now?'

'No, Mr Smith will no doubt want a further word with you – wait here and I'll go and get him.'

She left the room and Phil was alone. The first thing that he had learned from the conversation was that there was still a traitor in the resistance group but he now doubted very much whether he would ever be able to find out who it was. The second thing was that, for some reason that Phil couldn't understand, the military was desperate to find Shirley. Perhaps it was because they felt she was the person mainly responsible for the guards' deaths but that didn't really make sense. He just hoped that Shirley was keeping a low profile and not wandering round the shop showing her scars and burnt eyebrows from the previous night.

Mr Smith re-entered the room and took his place behind the desk. He peered at Phil over his glasses and asked his first question.

'What do you know about these women who frequent the drinking dens, Mr King?'

'Why are you and Jeffers so desperate to find this woman who supposedly distracted the guards?'

'Answer my question, Mr King – what do you know about these women from the drinking dens?'

'Absolutely bugger all – I've never been in one. I tell a lie, I went in one the other night on my way to the resistance group meeting but I don't think I'll be going there again – I wasn't impressed! Now, you answer my question – why are you so desperate to find this woman?'

'We are certain this woman is the key to the whole thing. She will be able to tell us who recruited her and lead us to all the perpetrators of this devilish crime.'

This was crazy, thought Phil, they had just told him that he was the main suspect so why didn't they interrogate him properly and extract the names of all the 'perpetrators of this devilish crime'? Had Shirley seen something she shouldn't have down in the compound? She hadn't mentioned anything, but in the state she was in when they had pulled her through the fence this wasn't surprising. Phil was missing something but couldn't for the life of him see what it was. Mr Smith was not telling him the whole story.

'Why are you so interested in this woman?'

'I've told you—'

'No, you haven't! What did this woman see down there?'

'I doubt if she saw anything that could make any difference to anyone or anything. We're interested in who she spoke to and what she spoke about.'

This, according to Phil, was getting more stupid by the minute. Shirley had spoken to a corporal and three guards – and they were all dead!

'I thought there were just ordinary guards in the compound.'

'Normally that is true but because of sickness in the ranks the corporal on duty that night should not have been there. Corporal Robson was a party to some information that we would not like to become common knowledge.'

'Information about what?' asked Phil.

Robson? Robbo? Corporal Robson; wasn't he the one at the party with the nervous wife, Doreen? Was that why he had been invited to the dinner party, because he did a special job? He was dead, of course – but Doreen might know something. But where the hell would he find Doreen? Phil had no idea where the guards and their families lived but Gerald Fairfax might. The information that Robson had was obviously very important and it might be the key to escaping from the town. All Phil had to do was get out of the prison, go to Gerald's house, ask him where he could find Doreen Robson, go to Doreen and ask her about this 'information'.

'The information is secret and does not concern you but we must ensure that this woman, whoever she is, did not speak to him about it. Corporal Robson was not normally allowed to come into contact with ordinary people and it was most unfortunate that for this one night he was exposed. We need to find this woman.'

The first thing Phil had to do was to get out of this prison!

'Perhaps I could help? Ask around, go to the den where the resistance group meet and see if anyone knows anything?'

Mr Smith looked at Phil quizzically and smiled a thin smile.

'Why on earth should we let you go to find out such things, Mr King? You are our prime suspect.'

'You don't seem to have much choice – who else are you going to get to help you?'

Mr Smith was silent for a moment.

'I'll need to speak to Miss Jeffers,' said Mr Smith and abruptly left the room, leaving Phil alone again.

Was there a way out? Could he somehow wangle a promise of safe passage in return for agreeing to help these obnoxious people find the mystery woman? One thing was certain – if he did, he would have to stay well clear of Shirley! But he still couldn't work out what information Robson could have had that made the authorities so worried.

Smith and Jeffers re-entered the room and resumed their seats. It was Smith who spoke first.

'Miss Jeffers has grave reservations about your plan but I think the situation is so serious that we should release you to see if you can find out anything about this woman.'

'It might take a few days to find out anything,' said Phil, desperately trying to gain some time, which he knew Jeffers would be loath to give him.

'You have twenty-four hours,' she said sternly. 'If you haven't found the woman by then, you'll be back in here as chief suspect.'

'How long have I been in here by the way? How long was I in the cell?'

'It's now five o'clock in the afternoon of the day you were picked up – doesn't time fly when you're having fun?'

Phil refused to accept the bait from the sneering Jeffers.

'So I've only lost a day out of the rest of my life. I suppose that's something,' said Phil. 'Can I go now? Will I get a lift back to the shop or do I have to walk? In that respect, where am I?'

'You are at Military Headquarters just outside the town. We will arrange transport back,' said Mr Smith. 'Make sure you come up with some results or your next interrogation might not be so friendly.'

They both rose and left the room. Phil wandered over to the window and looked out. He didn't recognise the landscape. All of Suffolk appeared the same in winter – rolling fields and a huge grey sky. There were no landmarks, like a church steeple, to give a hint as to where the place was. After a few minutes three guards entered the room, took hold of him and frogmarched him down the corridors back to his cell. He was left there for a short time before the door opened again and a guard came in and blindfolded him. Phil made no effort to resist; he had got what he wanted: at least twenty-four hours of freedom. He felt a prick in his arm and remembered nothing else until he woke up propped up against the wall of his shop in England Avenue.

Twenty

He slowly slid down to the pavement. The drug they had given him was obviously very effective and time-sensitive but his earlier beating ensured that most of his body still ached. He stood up and tried to get his bearings. The aches and pains were easing all the time but there was a throbbing in his ears, which he put down to the drug they had given him. He walked into the shop, which Karen was preparing to close.

'Where's Shirley?' he asked.

'She took the day off – where have you been?'

A huge wave of relief swept over Phil.

'That's the first piece of good news I've heard today. I've been in custody but we've no time to talk now.' Phil grabbed Karen by both arms and was almost shouting at her. 'Listen, go to Shirley's now and tell her to stay indoors. She must not be seen. I've got things to do and I'll come for you both when it's time for us all to get out of here. But Shirley must not leave her house. Tell her I love her – now, go and go quickly! Don't ask any questions – just go!'

Karen ran out of the shop and was gone.

Phil locked up and went round to Victoria Way, hoping to find Leroy and Davie but he was disappointed – there was no one there. He had no time to waste – he would have to find them later and find out about the escape route. He ran out of the house and headed for Churchill Crescent and the house of the judge advocate and her husband, Gerald Fairfax. He ran through the derelict streets and past deserted buildings until he reached the leafy suburbs. The going was harder here because he had to run through overgrown gardens and across streets where some houses still showed lights but eventually he reached the houses on the opposite side of the road from the Fairfaxes' house. He moved slowly until he found the front garden of the house directly opposite the drive where the car had taken him to the dinner party. He lay on his stomach well back in the trees and waited for dusk to turn to night. He spent the time watching the guard at the barrier at the end of Churchill Crescent and noting his movements. There was no traffic and the guard had little or nothing to do – he spent most of the time in his little hut.

After an hour, Phil got to his feet and ran to the half-demolished wall that bordered the garden he was in. After a quick look at the guard post to ensure that the man was inside his hut, he raced across the road and ran down the drive of the Fairfaxes' residence. After about thirty yards, he cut into the trees on his right and found himself in a thick forest. He kept on moving parallel to the drive, which he knew would lead him to the house. The trees were huge old oaks and the ground was littered with fallen branches. Every time Phil stepped on one, it seemed to break with a crack that he thought might wake the whole county. He slowed down and tried to pick his way more carefully. It took a good hour before he noticed that the trees were thinning out – he must be getting close to the house by now – and he moved further to his right. He did not want to set off any alarms and he certainly didn't want to activate those bloody floodlights!

The trees gave way to parkland and he saw the vague shape of the house in front of him and to his left. He returned to the treeline and edged further round to his right. This time he needed the back door – he didn't wish to be announced. It took him another hour to make it round to the rear of the house, where he left the safety of the trees and began to cross the parkland. This brought him to a large patio covered in gravel, which he didn't want to cross because of the noise. He moved to his left and found a concrete path. There seemed to be no one about, although a few lights shone through the back windows of the house. He inched forward along the path and managed to reach the back wall of the house without making a sound. He leaned against it and began to breathe a little easier. Now all he had to do was find a door!

He tried to his left first but reached the corner of the house without finding anything. He retraced his steps and then moved to the right. He ducked under two windows, although they were both dark, and moved on. He was looking for a door and therefore didn't see the sunken steps in front of him – he lost his footing and fell down three or four steps and came to rest against a hard wooden door. He waited for a moment to get his breath back and to see if the noise of his fall had alerted anyone. There was silence and he stood up. He seemed to have broken no bones and he looked at the door. It was obviously an old cellar door and looked as though it had not been opened for years. He scrambled back up the steps and continued his slow progress along the rear wall of the house.

At last he found what he was looking for. The back door to the house was also wooden but he could tell that it was in constant use – the handle shone even in the dark. He stood there knowing that this was the moment when he could turn round and go back home and forget about this whole mad escapade. He only thought for a second and then pushed down hard on the brightly polished handle. The door opened with ease and without a sound and he entered what he found was a utility room filled with washing machines and driers. Wellington boots were stacked in one corner beside a wicker pot containing walking sticks and umbrellas. He inched forward, saw another door and noticed a shaft of light protruding from underneath it. This time he listened to see if he could hear anything on the other side. There was no sound and he gently pushed the door open. He saw a kitchen.

He took a few moments to let his eyes adjust to the light and then walked in. There was nobody else there and there were no signs that the kitchen had been used that night. He moved silently across the large room and found another door. Opening this, he saw that it led on to the hall where he had been greeted on the night of the dinner party. He heard music playing and realised from the geography of the place that it was coming from the library where they had had pre-dinner drinks. It sounded like a string quartet from Haydn but he realised that he hadn't got the time to decide whether it was No. 45 or No. 46 and he went to the door of the library, opened it and marched straight in.

There was only one occupant in the room. Gerald Fairfax was seated in his wheelchair listening to the music. He had his eyes closed and although he was facing the door didn't see who the intruder was.

'Is that you, Mandy? Is it time for my pills already? I got lost in the music.' He opened his eyes as Phil closed the door.

'What the fuck are you doing here?'

Phil held a finger to his lips, telling Gerald to be quiet and walked around the room.

'Is there anyone else in the house tonight, Gerald? Don't lie to me – we've known each other too long for all that and I'm in a hurry.'

'There's me and my companion-cum-maid, Mandy Stewart. Emily is out at some function or other. What the hell do you want?'

'I want to know where I can find Doreen Robson.'

'Who?'

'Doreen Robson – she was here at your dinner party the other night with her husband. He was a corporal. I need to find out where she lives. Do you know?'

Gerald Fairfax began to relax.

'I haven't the faintest idea but sit down and tell me what this is all about. Get us two whiskies from the cabinet – we can have a drink and it'll be like old times.'

Phil King looked at his host and smiled.

'I haven't got time for pleasantries, Gerald. I've got to find Doreen Robson and quickly. Who could tell me where she lives?'

'He can, Mr King – he knows where everybody lives.'

Neither of the men had heard the dining room door open but both now looked round to see Mandy Stewart framed there with a gun in her hand. She walked over to the man in the wheelchair and pointed the gun at him.

'This man can tell you everything, Mr King – he can tell you first about how he's been betraying the resistance group since the day he set it up. He can tell you about how he tells his bloody wife everything that goes on in the group and any other information that comes his way. Don't deny it, Mr Fairfax – I've been listening to the pair of you for the last year or so.'

Gerald Fairfax had gone white – the blood had drained from his face and he slumped in his wheelchair.

'Why, Gerald, why?' asked Phil, who couldn't believe what he had just heard but knew deep down that it was the truth.

Gerald Fairfax regained his composure and sat up straight again. He looked at Phil and Mandy and laughed.

'Two reasons: one, I love my wife and would do anything to help her. Secondly, I agree totally with what she and her friends are trying to do here. This country was a total fuck-up until they took over. Immigrants from all over the world were arriving to take our jobs and housing and the people who were already here were not much better – stupid bloody arseholes who only wanted to watch television and eat fast food. The country needed a change and I think it's for the better, don't you?'

Phil King couldn't stand this load of racist claptrap any longer and hit Gerald across the face with his left hand.

'I'm tired of all this Nazi shite from you and all your friends, Gerald. I don't have the time to listen to it. Where can I find Doreen Robson?'

'How dare you hit me? I'll see you die for that, you bastard.'

'You won't see anybody die, Mr Fairfax, except yourself,' said Mandy Stewart. 'Tell him what he wants to know or I'll put the first bullet in your balls and make it a slow death.' She aimed the gun at Gerald's groin. 'Don't think I won't do it – you people don't seem to realise what you've made us into. I have no family, no life – except waiting on you hand and foot – and no future. Now tell him.'

Gerald Fairfax at last seemed to realise the seriousness of the young woman's voice.

'All the guards live over by the old docks – they've converted the old warehouses into barracks and the married quarters are in the old offices by the gates. But you'll never get in – they are guarded night and day. Why do you want to see this woman anyway?'

'I don't think I feel like telling you any more of my secrets, Gerald. I don't want them getting back to Emily. Any idea of where Corporal Robson and his wife lived? He seemed to have been an important man for a corporal.'

'He probably lived in the "A" block, then – they are the best quarters.'

'Good – one last question before I go and leave you to the mercy of your maid. Why did you send Emily with that fatuous message the other night?'

'What message?'

Phil sighed. You couldn't trust anyone any more – not even the judge advocate. Everyone told lies!

'I'll see you in the hall, Mr King,' said Mandy Stewart. 'This won't take long.'

'Are you sure you want to do this?' asked Phil.

'I've been looking forward to it for years. I'll see you in the hall.'

Phil went into the hall and closed the door behind him. The gunshot was surprisingly quiet when it came but he stood on the marble floor like a player in a game of *Cluedo*. The maid did it in the library!

Mandy Stewart joined him after a couple of minutes and began to explain why she thought she had to do what she had done but Phil didn't have the time to listen. He knew that both of them had to get away from the house as soon as possible. He guided his new partner in crime to the kitchen where she picked up her outside clothes and then they both left by the back door where Phil had come in. It was not until they reached the forest at the front of the house that Phil realised that Mandy Stewart probably needed to talk and he motioned her to sit down under one of the large oak trees. She sat motionless for some time and then began to cry. Her body shook as she sobbed her heart out and Phil waited.

Phil looked at the young woman in front of him and felt like crying himself. What had she said to Gerald? – 'You people don't seem to realise what you have made us into.' She was right – the experiment had turned normal people into monsters who, because they felt they had no future, could persuade themselves that wrong was right and vice versa. Before him sat a young girl who should have been thinking about dating boys – not crying after shooting her employer. When the crying stopped, Mandy Stewart began to talk and Phil King didn't interrupt.

'Oh God, what have I done? I've just killed a man! I can't believe it. I'm sorry, Mr King. I didn't mean to get you involved and I would have done it anyway. Gerald Fairfax was a two-faced racist bastard who deserved to die but I didn't think I would have the courage to do it. Your coming just brought things to a head – I knew he would sit you down and make you think he was on your side but would then tell Emily everything and they would decide what needed to be done. I've seen it happen so many times before – people have come who knew him from the old days when he was a solicitor and asked whether he could help find their missing families. After they'd gone he'd laugh and ring the guards and tell them to make sure they "disappeared" before they caused trouble. I think he's been doing it from the beginning but it's only lately that I've managed to hear a lot more of the conversations in that dreadful house. The worst thing about the Fairfaxes was that they didn't really act that way because they really believed all that racist crap. They did believe but they were more interested in the power that the system brought them rather than the system itself. They felt that they were born to rule and they would go along with any system that allowed them to do just that. Am I making any sense?'

Phil nodded and let Mandy continue.

'They ignored me – I suppose they thought I wasn't worth bothering about. Most of the time they treated me like dogshit and I went along with it because of the job and the accommodation but underneath I was becoming a very angry young woman. I lost all my family in the Chaos and decided to bide my time until tonight when you turned up. When I heard about the compound being blown up, I knew it must have been you because of what you said at the meeting. I'm sorry about telling you all that pack of lies about Gerald at the meeting but by then I didn't know who to trust – I thought you might have been sent to spy on me. When you arrived tonight, I thought it might be part of your plan and so decided to join in. By the way, I tried to make it look like suicide – I wiped the gun and put it in his hand. I don't think it will convince anybody for very long but I did the best I could. I'm sorry – I'm rabbiting on. What are we going to do now?'

'I think you needed to get all that off your chest, Mandy – and, anyway, I needed to get my breath back. What we're going to do now is to get out of this awful, bloody town. But first I need to ask you a couple of questions. Have you any idea why Corporal Robson was invited to the dinner party? It seems he was a pretty important man or at least was party to some very important information. Did you ever hear Emily and Gerald talk about him?'

'Only the once – when they were deciding who to invite to that dinner. Emily said that they would have to invite a guard and as he was the senior one it had better be him. They didn't say anything about what he did. I didn't like him but his wife was nice. I only heard one thing but I don't know whether it means anything. When I was serving drinks in the library I overheard him talking to that dreadful man, Harry Stanton, the politician. I didn't hear much but I remember Stanton saying that Corporal Robson should carry on the good work he was doing with the 'MP's files' so I suppose he might have been some sort of liaison between the military and the politicians.'

Phil thought about this for a moment. He'd once been friendly with a civil servant who'd worked for Customs and Excise and he'd said that every civil servant's nightmare was to get to work to find a file on his desk which was tagged as an 'MP file'. This meant that a member of parliament had written to the department requesting an answer to a particular question. These files were treated as ultra-urgent and had to be expedited as soon as possible. Perhaps there were still politicians out there who were asking awkward questions and it was Robson's job to answer them. It seemed like a clerk's job to Phil but perhaps an MP's question still carried some weight in the country.

'About these married quarters, do you know anything about them? Have you ever been there?'

'Once. I waited outside in the car while Gerald went in to see someone. It's like he said – they're in the old offices just inside the dock gates and they seemed very well guarded. Sorry I can't be of much more help.'

'You've been a very great help, Mandy, and a very brave girl – come on, I'll take you somewhere safe while I try and find two lads who I think might have the key to our getting out of here. You'll be able to meet the rest of my harem.'

'Your what?'

'Don't worry. I'll explain on the way.'

Phil and Mandy stood up and began to make their way through the trees back towards the road. Phil located the drive again to give himself some sense of direction when he heard the sound of a car. It was coming up the drive towards the house and could only mean one thing – the judge advocate was returning home from her function. Very soon the proverbial would hit a very big fan and time was now of the essence. Phil and Mandy had to get away from this place as quickly as possible. They ran as fast as they could, not caring about the noise they made. More than once they both fell over and had to drag themselves to their feet and carry on towards the road.

Churchill Crescent looked as quiet as when Phil had run across it earlier but he knew that it wouldn't remain like that for long. He grabbed Mandy's hand and they raced across the Crescent, diving over the half-demolished wall of the garden opposite. They landed in the lush undergrowth and weeds but were all right apart from a few bruises. They lay there for a minute and took long, deep breaths. It was then they heard the first siren and then another and the sound of a lot of vehicles racing along the road. Phil didn't wait to see where they were going – he knew! He pulled Mandy to her feet and they battled on through the deserted suburbs of the town. There were a lot of vehicles out on the roads now and they had to slow down and take care.

They reached the derelict streets of the town itself and Phil began to breathe more easily. They were nearly at Shirley's house and safe when it happened. The road they were in had been totally demolished and there was very little cover, so when Phil heard the sound of a vehicle he motioned for Mandy to follow him behind one of the few piles of bricks still standing which would afford them some protection. She was too late. An armoured car turned the corner and caught her full in the beam of its searchlight mounted on the bonnet. It screeched to a halt and three guards got out and walked towards her.

To his dying day, Phil King would never know why Mandy Stewart did what she did next. Was it because she felt such remorse for killing Gerald Fairfax? Was it because she wanted to protect Phil King and allow him to continue the fight? Whatever the reason, Mandy Stewart shouted 'Bastards' at the top of her voice and ran towards the side of the road directly opposite Phil's hiding place.

The guards stood for a few moments, looking as though they didn't know what to do next. Then the firing started and Mandy Stewart's body shot into the air and fell on to a pile of rubble, lifeless and still. The guards walked slowly over to her and one of them kicked the corpse.

'Get on the radio, Mickey. It's her – the one they're looking for. She's still wearing her maid's uniform. What the fuck did she run for? I thought they said they only wanted to question her about Fairfax's suicide, stupid cow.'

The guard shouldered his weapon and picked up the body as though it was a sack of coal and carried it back to the armoured car. The guard called Mickey was on the radio.

'They want to know if she was alone, Sergeant. What shall I tell them?'

'Tell them yes – I didn't see anybody else, did you?'

Mickey spoke to the radio again and the guards clambered back into the vehicle. They drove off with Mandy Stewart's body draped unceremoniously over the bonnet.

Phil King had watched the whole nightmare scene without daring to breathe. He now drank in huge gulps of air. He had been lying face down behind the pile of bricks but he now sat with his legs crossed and put his head in his hands. He knew that he couldn't take much more of this. He was, or had been, a newsagent. Death – violent death – was something you read about in newspapers and magazines. He had to get away from this madness, even if it meant his own death. He got slowly to his feet and continued his weary journey. He decided to go to his own house before linking up with Shirley and Karen again because he needed to find Leroy and Davie and get the details of the escape route.

He reached Victoria Way without seeing anybody else and went up to his front door. It was slightly open and he walked straight in, not knowing or caring who or what he would find in the house. There was a light on in the kitchen and he heard the sound of voices – but they were too low for him to recognise any of them. He moved slowly along the hall towards the muffled conversation but somebody must have heard him because the noise stopped abruptly. The house was now as silent as a grave and, apart from the light showing under the kitchen door, just as dark. He hoped that the voices were those of Leroy and Davie – if it was Jeffers and somebody, he didn't think he would be able to control himself after what he had just witnessed outside. He went to the door, turned the handle and pushed it wide open. Not for the first time that night, the scene in the kitchen took his breath away.

Twenty-One

There were six people in total in the small room. Five of them were seated around the table – Shirley, Karen, Leroy, Davie and Edward Houghton. The sixth was lying face down on the floor with his hands and feet tied behind his back and what looked like masking tape over his mouth. Phil did not recognise him but noted that he was wearing the uniform of a guard. The man writhed for a moment until Edward gave him a kick in the ribs with his heavy boot. Nobody said a word but not surprisingly it was Shirley who was the first to move.

She sprang at Phil and hugged him like a woman possessed, covering his face with kisses and tears.

'You gorgeous stupid bloody bastard – I knew you'd come back for us! Where the fuck have you been? Karen said you'd been arrested! I've been worried sick about you. We all have! Come and sit down – do you want a cup of tea? Shut up, Shirley, you stupid bitch. Sit down here and tell me – us – all about it.'

Phil smiled and accepted her offer of a chair. Shirley sat down by him and held his hand. Leroy asked Davie to go and close the front door and make sure it was locked, which he did. Karen put the kettle on and Edward kicked the guard on the floor again for no reason whatsoever. It was Phil who spoke first.

'I'm sorry about Billy, Edward. I feel responsible – he was a good lad.'

'He was one of the best but we all knew what we were getting into. Don't blame yourself – I don't. I blame those bastards who shot him. That's why I came round here – to see if I could help any more. They came round to the garage this morning and tried to knock me around and get me to admit that I was with him. After they told me he was dead, I was so fucking angry that I nearly killed the pair of them with my bare hands. They eventually buggered off and I used the last of the explosive devices that we had left from last night to make sure the garage takes all the bastards with it if they ever come back. I went to the shop and found Karen, who told me to come and wait here.'

'I didn't have time to tell you about Edward's visit when you came back to the shop at closing time,' said Karen. 'I could tell that you were in a hurry then. I opened up the shop this morning because Shirley was still feeling the after-effects of last night and I told her to take the day off. I opened up but, when you didn't arrive with the stuff from the Border, I knew something was terribly wrong and I went back and saw Shirley. She told me to stay at the shop to see if you turned up. She was still suffering and I told her to go back to bed. Edward came sometime this afternoon and I gave him this address – he wanted to see you and when I called here on my way back to Shirley's to tell him that I had seen you and that you were alive she was already here. I think she loves you as well, Phil – the three of us waited here until Leroy and Davie turned up about an hour ago. They brought *that* with them!' She pointed to the guard on the floor.

'We found him outside taking an unhealthy interest in the house,' said Leroy. 'It seemed only natural to let him have a look at the inside as well! Edward's been doing a great job keeping him quiet. You've ignited a fuse in this town, Phil. I know you thought that the attack on the compound hadn't had much effect but believe me, it has. People all over the place are standing up and giving two fingers to the guards – it won't be long before this place blows up.'

'He's right,' said Davie. 'People want to join us and do something.'

'I still want out,' said Phil. 'I want that escape route – I've seen enough in this town tonight to last me a lifetime.'

He told his story from the time of his arrest at the guard post in England Avenue to when Mandy Stewart was shot dead.

'I want to get out but I want to speak to Doreen Robson first to find out if she knows what her husband knew that is so important. Your friend on the floor might be able to help with locating Mrs Robson but I do need to escape from this fucking madness – otherwise I'll go mad myself. I'd like you all to come with me but it's up to you – I don't think I have much chance of escaping but I've got to give it a go.'

'I'm staying,' said Leroy, 'because, as I've said before I think this pile of shite needs to be toppled from the inside. But you can have the guard and details of the escape route. What about you, Davie?'

'I'm staying with you, Leroy – you wouldn't last two minutes without some Scottish muscle behind you.'

'I'm going with Phil,' said Shirley. 'I don't want to lose this man again. I've had a terrible day not knowing where he was.'

'I'm going with my sister,' said Karen and hugged Shirley.

'That just leaves you, Edward. What do you think?' asked Phil. 'Do you want to stay here and fight or run away like us three?'

Edward Houghton thought for a moment before replying.

'There's nothing to keep me in this town. My wife died years ago before all this crap began, thank God. Now Billy's gone too I'll go with you Phil. You can't look after these two lovely ladies on your own and I may be of some help if we need the physical stuff. Also, you'll need someone to carry this pile of shit on the floor if you think he's going to be of some help along the way. But I wouldn't like anybody to think I was running away, as you put it. I think of it as a two-pronged attack – one inside, with Leroy and Davie, and one outside with the rest of us. You never know – we might even get the bastards in a pincer movement and win.'

Phil felt humble and stood to shake Edward's hand.

'One pincer movement coming up, Edward. You look after Karen and I'll try and take care of her sister.'

'It'll be more like me looking after you, Philip King,' said Shirley. 'You're a bloody walking disaster on your own.'

'Agreed,' said Phil. 'Now, let's work out a timetable of action but I have to tell you that I need some sleep before I do anything else. What do you say, Leroy, to going over this fantastic escape route now and then us all getting our heads down for a bit?'

'OK, no problem. We'll take you through the route that Charles told us and I suggest you all listen and learn it so that if anything happens to any of you then the others will know how to proceed. After that, I think we should split up – Davie and I will disappear and Phil, Shirley and Karen should go back to Shirley's place and get some sleep. That leaves Edward and the guard here.

I don't know what you think about this, Edward, but do you think you can cope with him here on your own until tonight?'

'No problem,' said Edward, who promptly kicked the guard again.

'Right,' said Leroy. 'I'll let Davie take you through the route. I'll take the guard into the lounge and make sure he's secure for the night. That will also mean that he won't hear anything that we don't want him to hear just in case Davie and I want to use the route ourselves someday. It's all yours, Davie.'

Leroy got up and dragged the guard out of the room, feet first. Davie Lennox produced a crumpled piece of paper from his pocket and began to talk.

'I've made a drawing of what Charles told us but it's not to scale and it's not very good – but here goes! As you can see from my map, the Border that Phil goes to every day is just the start of the fortifications around this town. The fences go way beyond where he is allowed to go and it looks impossible that anyone could keep hidden for that distance. But Charles looked for the shortest route and found it here at the top of my drawing.

'The docks in this town used to be the busiest and the biggest in Europe. When the authorities cut the town off after the Chaos they cut the docks off as well but found that this brought too many questions from outside. So, they opened the half of the docks that was furthest from the town and the questions stopped. But this left only a border of some five hundred yards between the town and the rest of the world. Charles found a storm drain that went under the closed docks and the Border and came out on the far side. He found that it brought him out to within only a few yards of the fence that separated his family's estate from the newly opened dockyard. He made a hole in the fence, which he closed every time he went through and he was home and dry – well, perhaps not dry since he had had to crawl through a storm drain to get there but you know what I mean.

'The secret to the whole route is the entrance on this side of the Border – it's marked A239 and is in the middle of the roundabout that used to be the busiest in England, just outside the old Gate 1 of the docks. As far as I can tell, you just get into this entrance and head south.'

'What are the chances that I can get out of this storm drain and go and see Doreen Robson once we're under the docks?' asked Phil.

'I knew you were going to ask that,' replied Davie, 'and the answer is that I have no fucking idea. As far as I can tell, Charles didn't stop to have chats with the wives of guards when he was using this route.'

The five of them stared at the drawing for a few minutes and then Davie burned it. The goodbyes and the hugs began between them all.

It wasn't long before Leroy and Davie left the house and Phil set out the timetable for the escape.

'As I said before, I need some sleep even if the rest of you don't, so I propose we leave tonight. But we'll have to have started by half past four at the latest because Jeffers said that I had twenty-four hours to find the woman or I would be back in custody and that was at five o'clock yesterday. I also think we need to go separately or in smaller groups because five of us together, including the guard, will look too suspicious. What about this guard, Edward? Do you think you can manage to get him to the roundabout on your own? Do you know where the roundabout is?'

'I know where it is and I'm pretty certain I can make it there with that bastard – we'll find a bottle of something from somewhere and go down there disguised as a couple of drunks. He won't try anything with my hand round his throat but I can't take him dressed the way he is. Can we dress him in some of your clothes, Phil, and you take the uniform? Perhaps you could wear it under your clothes – it might be useful if, or when, you go and try and see this Robson woman.'

'Good idea, Edward – go and strip him now and I'll try it for size. You can have any of my clothes from upstairs – no matter what happens I'm never going to come back here.'

Edward left the room and for the first time Phil King looked at the new love in his life. Shirley Tate had aged about ten years over the last few hours but she still looked beautiful to him. She and Karen had done a good job with her hair but her eyebrows still looked scorched and her face had given up with trying to hide her stress lines.

'You're the big worry, Shirley – we must make sure that nobody gets a good look at your face. The scorch marks will give you away.'

'You say the nicest things, Mr King – is that one of your usual chat-up lines? You don't look too good yourself, you bastard! I'll put some more make-up on and by half past four it's getting quite dark so I'll be all right. And before you ask or decide to the contrary, I'm coming with you! For a start, I don't know which roundabout we're talking about and wherever you go now, I go!'

'I wasn't being... You know what I mean... They are desperate to find you. Did Robson say anything to you that might give us a clue as to what his job was?'

'Not a bloody thing that I can remember. He was a slimy piece of shit and I wouldn't have trusted him as far as I could throw him but he never said anything about his work. He just wanted my arrest on his service record to aid his career. Does it matter now? I thought the idea was to escape – how could our knowing what Robson did for a living help?'

'I don't know but I'm convinced that he is our passport to freedom. If we get caught we'll need something to bargain with and at the moment we've got absolutely bugger all. It may not be possible to reach Doreen Robson and even if I do she might not be able to help but I'm going to try.'

Edward came back into the room with the guard's uniform draped over his arm. Phil undressed down to his underclothes and, with the sisters giggling and wolf-whistling, put the uniform on. It was big in some places and too small in others but in the dark he might get away with it. He put his own clothes over the top.

'I didn't realise how fat you were, Mr King,' said Shirley. 'You should go on a diet – cut out the carbohydrates.'

'And the sex,' said Karen, who got a quick slap on the leg from her sister.

'God, can you find something to laugh at in everything? This is serious – we may all be dead by this time tomorrow.'

'That's the reason they're laughing, Phil,' said Edward joining in the joke. 'If they didn't laugh they'd cry.'

Phil smiled as well and knew that he was right.

'I'll go to the roundabout on my own,' said Karen. 'I know where it is because I met Charles there when he was coming back from one of his little trips. No one's looking for me so I can just walk down there.'

'Are you sure?' asked Shirley.

'Yes, it's the best way. It means that there will be three groups and no more than two people in each group. But I think that Edward is going to have the most trouble getting there because he'll have the guard to look after so I'll try to keep behind them and give him some help if he needs it. Don't worry, Edward – you won't see me and neither will the authorities. I've had a lot of practice with Leroy and Davie getting around this town unseen.'

'Right,' said Phil. 'Any questions?'

'What do we take with us?' asked Shirley.

'Nothing,' said Phil. 'Or at least nothing that we can't carry in our pockets. We don't know how wide this storm drain is to start with and I can't see what we'll need on our hopefully short journey.'

'I've brought some tools with me – wire cutters, spanners and the like,' said Edward. 'But they'll all fit in my pockets or in the pockets of him next door.'

'Good. I'm worried about your being here with the guard, Edward. What if they come looking for me again?' asked Phil.

'They'll be looking for you, not him and me and, anyway, I propose to be away from here by noon. I can't carry him down to the roundabout in one big journey – I'll do it in short trips, each one bringing me nearer to the roundabout.'

'I'd better stay here, then,' said Karen, 'and then I can leave here just after Edward and watch his back all the way.'

'That would be good. Come on, Karen – let's go and hide the bastard next door and find somewhere to have a sleep. You're a lucky girl.'

'Why's that, Edward?'

'This week you've not only gained a sister but a grandfather as well – I'm too old to be your brother!'

It was goodbye time again and there were hugs and kisses all round. It was agreed that they would all meet at the roundabout outside the old Gate 1 at half past four later that day and Phil and

Shirley left 108 Victoria Way for the last time, hand in hand. By the time they reached Shirley's house the guard had been secreted in the loft of the house they had just left and Karen was asleep on top of Phil's bed.

Edward Houghton went round the house and made sure that both the front and back doors were locked, bolted and barred. He then took a last look at his new 'granddaughter' and went to sleep on the sofa in the front room.

Shirley let Phil into her house and it was only then that they kissed properly.

'What about the shop? Won't they think it suspicious if you don't open?'

'They'll think it more suspicious if I do – I've lost the bike and trailer so I couldn't have gone to the Border anyway and I'm supposed to be out looking for the mysterious Pinky.'

'Thank you for the message you sent with Karen. I love you as well – what the hell are we going to do if we escape and find Rosie and the kids and Geoff waiting for us?'

'File for a double divorce? I haven't got a bloody clue – does it matter? Here is now – let's go and fuck each other senseless and then get some sleep.'

It was two hours later, before they went to sleep, that Phil took up this conversation again.

'You know what you were saying before about our escaping and finding our previous lives waiting for us?'

'Yes,' said Shirley, wondering what was coming next.

'Well, I want to say two things to you about it. Firstly, whatever happens in the rest of my life – whether that's short or long – I shall never forget the joy of falling in love with you over the last few days, weeks or months or however long it's been. I shall never forget the sheer bliss of being in love with you for the few short hours we've had together. I always thought that this kind of thing happened in films or books and I never thought it would happen to me. It was different with Rosie – it was love that began with a kind of affection that became something more – a lot, lot more – as time went on. I loved her but not in the same way as I love you. I'm not explaining myself very well but I wonder if it's possible for a man to love two women at the same time in different ways. I only know that I wouldn't want to have to choose between the two of you. The kids, if they're still alive, would complicate the whole thing. I wouldn't want to do anything that would hurt them. But, my God, I love you!'

Phil turned to Shirley and kissed her long and hard on the lips.

'The word "love" doesn't come anywhere near describing what I feel for you at this precise moment. There should be another word that means "love" multiplied by a thousand or more.'

'You explained yourself very well, Phil. All I can say is that it's the same, exactly the same, for me. Promise me you won't leave me – if we're going to die, I want us to be together.'

'I promise.'

'You said there were two things you wanted to say. What's the second?'

'Ah, yes, back to reality. The other thing was that I wouldn't worry your sweet little head about meeting Rosie and Geoff because I don't think we've got a hope in hell of succeeding in this escape.'

Shirley propped herself up on one elbow and looked at him.

'Why not?'

'Look at the plan – an untried escape route supplied second-hand by a known bastard, which brings us out in the middle of the estate of the bastard who thought up this whole fucking mess. That's the good news – I'm a newsagent who's seen so much in the last few days to last him a lifetime. I'm not James Bond – I'm bloody useless and I'm the leader! Then there's you, who did a great job down at the compound but are still suffering from the effects of that. Karen has just come out of a trauma that struck her dumb for nearly three years! Edward is an old man! The authorities have held this town in a grip of iron for more than three years – there's no way that the four of us have any chance of escaping from them. I just thought you should know how I felt – sorry if I've dented your confidence.'

'I think you're being too hard on yourself and I'm certain you've underestimated your companions. Karen is a hard nut and she won't let you down. Her three years living by her wits, six months of which were with Leroy and Davie, have made her into one hell of a girl. I like Edward – I know he's old but he's not senile and I'd back him in a fight against the guards any day. As for me – I learned something about myself when I was playing Pinky. Whenever I felt afraid I thought about my lovely twin girls and you. As soon as the three of you flashed before my eyes, the fear disappeared. You said that we shouldn't take anything with us and I won't, except for two things – a photograph of my two little girls and the real you. We'll make it and I've no doubt you'll be the one who gets us out – you were born to play James Bond!'

They hugged each other for a long time before drifting off into an untroubled sleep.

The world outside sped by without mishap until three o'clock in the afternoon when they were both awakened by a loud knocking on the front door.

Twenty-Two

Shirley was the first to react but Phil told her to stay where she was – it was her they were looking for! He dressed quickly and went down the stairs. The knocking continued and Phil thought for a moment that they weren't even going to get as far as the roundabout! He opened the door a fraction and let out a sigh of relief. Filling the doorstep was the stout figure of Margaret Hills.

He let her in and closed the door.

'I thought you'd be here, you dirty bastard. Been having a good shag have you? I went round to the shop but found it wasn't open and thought, I know where he'll be. He'll be round at that Shirley's getting his end away. Where is she?'

At that moment, Shirley came down the stairs in her boots and leather trousers and Margaret continued with her rant.

'Oh my God, it's kinky sex now, is it? Black leather – isn't that a bit too young for you, dear? It's certainly too young for this bastard you've been bouncing on for the last few minutes.'

Shirley was about to protest but Margaret put a finger to her lips and pointed to the open kitchen door. Phil and Shirley followed their old schoolteacher in and she shut the door behind them.

'Sorry about that, kids, but it's my experience that the authorities only have directional microphones that can pick up in the halls of people's houses unless they wire the whole house. It's good to see you both again. My congratulations on last night – what a bloody wonderful wake-up call that was. The whole town is talking about it and you wouldn't believe the number of people who want to join the group. Peter Jackson and I will have to hire the Town Hall for the next meeting! You don't need to tell me all about your plans or what you've done – I saw Leroy this morning and he told me everything. Come here, Shirley Tate – I'm sorry about all that crap I said before. Give me a hug before you go.'

The two women hugged each other.

'I thought you believed I was some kind of common whore – I love Phil.'

'Don't be silly – if I thought that I wouldn't be here. Well, good luck to you both. I hope you make it. We are going to try and help – Leroy has organised a march for five o'clock down England Avenue and hopefully that will keep most of the guards occupied when you begin your escape. I'd better go now. If you make it, give them hell!'

The three of them walked into the hall and Margaret resumed her old persona.

'It's disgusting, two people of your age. You seem to think that sex is the be-all and end-all of life these days! What about your customers, Mr King? While you're here having your end away with your fancy woman, we're all starving to death.'

She turned to them, winked and then was gone out of the front door.

Phil and Shirley began to laugh, remembered what Margaret had said about the microphones and ran upstairs. They dressed, with Shirley in the same clothes as Pinky had worn except she replaced the see-through blouse with a roll-necked sweater and Phil with the guard's uniform under his outdoor clothes. Shirley made sure that Phil saw her take the photograph of her twin girls from the dressing table, kiss it and put it in her pocket. Phil took her in his arms and whispered in her ear, 'Good luck, my love. I love you – thank you for everything!'

'I love you – I don't need any luck as long as I have you.'

They walked down the stairs and out of the front door. Shirley didn't look back – she knew that whatever life had in store for her was not in that house. It was mostly in the shape of the man who now gripped her hand so tightly as they crossed the road and made their way to the centre of the town.

There seemed to be more people around on the streets – was this part of the plan by Leroy to help them? They made their way along England Avenue until they reached the cliff road and then turned right along Bulldog Boulevard until they came to the back of the Report Centre. This was perhaps the most difficult part of the route because there were many more guards about in this area than in the centre of the town. But they were lucky – it had started to rain and the guards had retreated to where they could find some shelter.

They made their way slowly towards the roundabout and reached it without any problems at about a quarter past four.

First objective achieved, thought Phil. They sat down on the damp grass behind the treeline but did not speak. All they had to do now was wait for Edward and Karen and their prisoner to arrive and they could proceed. Phil looked at the roundabout and noticed that it was covered in weeds. In the old days it would have been sponsored by a local firm, probably the Dock Company, and it would have been neat and tidy with flowerbeds and the name of the sponsor emblazoned across it in tulips. Now, it had been left to rot – but the weeds would offer some protection even in the dark.

They sat there for half an hour and were getting very wet. Phil motioned to Shirley to follow him and he led her over to the building directly opposite the dock gate. The building had been half-destroyed but some of the walls and a piece of the roof were still intact and they sat on the floor enjoying a bit of shelter from the rain. In the old days this had been a fast food restaurant. Phil wondered how the authorities had squared things with the big chain when the Chaos had happened. Perhaps it had been easy – 'Sorry for the inconvenience but would you like a site in a new shopping centre up north at a reduced rent for fifty years?' That's probably how they did it.

'If we went out for the day with the kids, Rosie and I would promise them that we would stop here on the way back if they were good. It never failed – by the time we got here they were both asleep and we never had to come in. I've always wondered what it was like.'

'Stop torturing yourself, Phil. We need to concentrate on today. Where the fuck are Edward and Karen – they're late.'

'I'm sorry – you're right. Do you think something's happened to them?'

'I don't know but it won't help them – or us – if you keep reminiscing about the "good old days" and Rosie and the kids.'

'You know what I love about you, Shirley Tate, more than anything else?'

'No, what?'

'You're always fucking right.'

They lapsed into silence again and then Phil moved across the floor to where he could get a better view of the roundabout. He could see no movement, only the lights of the old docks beginning to pierce the dusk of the February evening. Inside the dock gate stood the old offices where Doreen Robson lived. There were lights here and there but there didn't seem to be any guards.

There was no noise except for the patter of the raindrops on their ruined building. This seemed to Phil to be a bad omen – they could do with some noise to cover their attempts to get into the storm drain. He moved back to where Shirley was sitting.

'I'm sorry about before.'

'Piss off, Phil – don't you think I'm adding up all the times Geoff and I and the girls came past this place? But I'm getting worried about Edward and Karen – Edward said he was going to do the journey in short stages starting at noon. I thought he'd be here before us.'

'So did I. Perhaps they've hit a problem – how long should we give them before we try and go on our own?'

'Christ, I don't know. I don't want to go without Karen. Anyway, what about the guard helping you to find Mrs Robson?'

'Fuck Mrs Robson – if we have to go on our own we'll go and take our chances without knowing what Robson knew. The only timescale we have is that we have to go tonight so if necessary we can wait until midnight for them. We'd better keep watch – the place over there where I was before gives a good view of the roundabout and all the area. I'll go over there first – you try and get some rest.'

Phil moved back to his vantage point and looked out. Nothing moved. Two hours later it was pitch black, the rain had ceased and there had been no sign of Karen and Edward, or anybody else. Shirley came over and joined him.

'I'll take over – you go and have a rest.'

He grabbed her and kissed her.

'A rest? I don't think so – I feel responsible for them. Please God, let them be safe.'

Shirley took his head and laid it on her breast.

'They knew the risks, darling – it's not your fault. If you want to go now, let's go. It must be eight o'clock. Do you want to go, just the two of us, or shall we wait?'

'We have to wait,' said Phil, his eyes filled with tears. 'I couldn't go with the thought that they might be only two minutes away.'

Shirley let him weep. Eventually he fell asleep, cradled in her arms.

It was perhaps an hour later that she heard movement in the trees behind them. She laid Phil's head carefully on the ground and crept to the other wall of the building. Yes, there was someone in the trees. She looked but could see nothing because of the blackness of the night and then she saw a figure emerge towards the building. It was Edward and he was alone. Shirley called out in a loud whisper.

'Edward, this way.'

Edward Houghton changed direction and came toward her. He reached the building and sank down on the floor. His face was covered in bruises and most of his clothes were soaked in blood. Phil had woken by now and went over to the pair of them.

'Where's Karen?' he asked.

'She's… She's… She's—'

'She's what, Edward?' screamed Phil.

'Shut up, Phil – let him speak,' said Shirley.

Edward Houghton summoned the last of his energy – there was blood in his mouth now – and spoke the last five words of his life.

'She's coming… wait for her.'

Phil King hugged the old man as he died. The son and now the father, both dead. For what? Some political experiment? Someone had to be told about the human cost of this experiment. Someone would have to pay! Phil and Shirley knew that they couldn't bury the body – it was too risky – but a derelict fast-food restaurant didn't seem a fitting final resting place for the brave old man. They carried the body back to the trees and covered it as best they could with leaves and bark. Neither of them spoke out loud but both silently wished the old man well – wherever he was going.

They were creeping back to the building when they heard a noise behind them. Shirley realised that she had no choice and was the first to speak.

'Karen, is that you?'

'Yes, where the bloody hell are you?'

'Make for the building – we'll see you there.'

Phil and Shirley scrambled back to their hiding place and a few moments later Karen joined them.

'God, what a journey! Did Edward make it? That man is one hell of a brave bloke. He can be my grandfather any day!'

Phil explained what had happened with Edward and Karen lapsed into silence for a few moments and then began to tell her story.

'It all started off so well. Edward and I slept OK and the guard was no trouble whatsoever. When we were ready to move at midday, Edward rigged up some sort of harness for the guard so he was handcuffed to Edward's belt under their coats. Edward had his arm round him with his hand over his mouth and I think he'd warned him what might happen to him if there was any trouble. I found an old cider bottle in your backyard, Phil, and filled it with water and the two of them set off down Victoria Way looking and sounding like two drunken old men. They didn't look out of place at all because you see such people everyday when they've spent a night or longer in one of the drinking dens.

'Edward was singing a song about the yeomen of England in a loud bass voice – I bet he's a good singer but I think he put a few wrong notes in there on purpose. I followed them and I was about two hundred yards behind. They kept stopping and sitting on a wall or an old pile of bricks and I thought it was all part of the act until we reached Bulldog Boulevard. The stops were getting more frequent and Edward wasn't singing any more. I decided to move a little closer to them and quickly realised that something was seriously wrong. Edward was having difficulty walking and I decided to go and give him a hand. I was about five yards away when the two of them fell over in the middle of the pavement. I ran to them and saw that Edward was having difficulty breathing – he must have had a heart attack or something very much like it. I screamed at him and asked him what was wrong but he couldn't speak. He was lying on top of the guard who was struggling like mad to release himself. I didn't know what to do. It was mid-afternoon and there were a few people about but nobody came to help. I suppose they thought it was just two drunks having a fight!

'I don't know what I'd have said if anybody had come over – two men handcuffed together writhing about on the floor. Edward must have summoned some strength from somewhere and he managed to get to his knees and that gave me the chance to drag them both into an alley.

'I tried to help Edward and that was my mistake. I forgot about the guard, who by now was kicking like mad at us both. He began to scream for help at the top of his voice, shouting that he was a guard and had been kidnapped. I kicked him a couple of times and he shut up for a minute but his screams had been heard.

'Five or six lads turned into the alley – they were drunk and were obviously looking for a fight. They were carrying bottles of booze and came right up to us. I tried to explain that the guard was a prisoner and that Edward and I were the good guys but they were too pissed to take much notice. They set about the guard and literally kicked him to death. It was awful – they kept saying that the guards were a bunch of wankers and needed to be taught a lesson. Edward was right by the poor sod, of course, and he got a few kicks as well.

'When the lads had finished with the guard they turned towards me. They started to unbuckle their trousers and I wanted to run but I didn't want to leave Edward so I picked up our empty bottle and tried to keep them away. It was stupid, of course – there were too many of them. One of them grabbed me by the arms from behind while another came towards me with a big leery smile on his face. I knew then that I was done for but suddenly there was a loud crash and the grip on my arms loosened. I turned round to see the lad who had been behind me lying on the ground. Edward must have somehow unlocked the handcuffs and was behind him with a broken bottle in his hand. He looked like a raging bull or an elephant on a charge. He tore into those lads and they didn't put up much of a fight – a couple of them had a bit of a go and hit him with a bottle but they didn't stay around too long. Edward was roaring and shouting and waving the bottle about, even after they'd run off. I tried to calm him down, telling him that they'd gone but he kept on going. Eventually, he just fell over and lay there – I thought he was dead but when I went over to him I found he was still breathing. I held him in my arms for what seemed like hours and I knew we were going to be late for the rendezvous with you but there was no way I was going to leave my granddad there after what he'd just done for me.

'It grew dark and Edward opened his eyes. He could hardly speak and I knew he was in a bad way but he managed to tell me that he was going to carry on to the roundabout and that I should follow him just like before in case he had another attack. I stood him up, he kissed me on the forehead, whispered "my lovely granddaughter" to me and walked or, more rightly, stumbled off. That was the last I saw of him. God knows how he made it all the way to here on his own – he must have had the strength of five men!

'I'm late because I stayed behind in the alley and buried the body of the guard as best I could. I thought it might give us a little more time. I'm sorry Edward is dead – he died because he wanted to protect me. I didn't know him – I only met him a couple of days ago – but I'll always think of him as my granddad.'

Phil and Shirley were unable to speak and the silence enveloped all three of them. Nobody spoke for a few minutes and then it was Karen who whispered the first words.

'I know you want to get off and make a start, Phil, but would you mind if Shirley took me over to where you left Edward's body for a couple of minutes. I won't be long – I just want to say goodbye properly.'

'Jesus, Karen, take all the time you want. He deserves that much. Go with her Shirley – I'll wait here until you both get back.'

The sisters crawled away and left Phil to his thoughts. How many more deaths was he going to be responsible for? He wept silently and then sobbed out loud. He couldn't take much more. He knew he was on the edge. All he had wanted to do was to escape from the madness in which he was living but it seemed it was impossible to escape it. The madness followed his every step.

What if something happened to Karen or Shirley now? He dried his eyes and realised he had no choice – he had to carry on and see what happened. But someone had to pay for this carnage! Someone had to be brought to book for this wholesale slaughter of innocent lives.

Shirley and Karen reached the spot where Phil and Shirley had buried Edward and Karen bent down and removed the few leaves that covered his face. She leant down and looked at the old man. Her tears fell in a torrent and landed on his closed eyes and then she bent down and kissed him on the lips.

'Goodbye, Granddad – thank you,' she said quietly and then replaced the leaves carefully. She stood up and embraced Shirley.

Her sister had no words for the occasion – they had all been said – and they made their way back to Phil's hiding place. They found him standing up with a determined look on his face.

'Right,' he said, 'let's get going – I've decided to give myself half an hour – no longer – to find the Robson woman if I can see a way out of the drain inside the dock gates. Are we ready? Come on, let's find the fucking entrance to this storm drain.'

With that he was off in the direction of the roundabout and the girls followed behind him. They ran across the road and clambered up the side. The rain had eased but everywhere was still soaking wet and so were they after a few moments of crawling around the place looking for a manhole cover, which bore the number A239. It was Shirley who found it and called out to the other two.

'Over here, it's over here. Fuck, it's heavy – I can't move it.'

Phil and Karen joined her and all three tried to lift it. It didn't budge an inch.

'Didn't Edward say that he would have some tools in his pocket for just this kind of thing?' asked Phil. 'Did you empty his pockets, Karen?'

'I never thought,' replied the girl.

'Neither did I,' said Phil. 'I'll go back and check his coat.'

'No you fucking won't,' said Shirley. 'I'll go. You're not leaving this girl's side again after what she's been through today.'

Shirley got up and ran back to the derelict restaurant and was gone into the black of the night. Phil and Karen didn't say a word

– they just held hands. Shirley was back within five minutes.

'You were right about your granddad, Karen – what a man! I found wire cutters, pliers, a spanner and this.' Shirley held up a crowbar. 'It was in his big inside pocket – I don't think I could have walked here with that in my pocket without having a heart attack! I gave him another kiss from all three of us and put some more leaves on him.'

Karen smiled while Shirley handed the crowbar to Phil.

'Go on, 007 – do your stuff. This is what we brought you along for.'

Phil inserted the crowbar into one of the holes in the cover and put his weight against it. The cover moved upwards an inch or two and the girls got their hands underneath it. Phil dropped the crowbar and the three of them managed to push the cover to one side. They stared down into the inky blackness and saw nothing except the top of a metal ladder which led down the shaft.

'How the fuck are we going to see anything down there?' asked Phil. 'It's hopeless – we should have stolen a torch and brought it. Why didn't I think of that?'

'Because you're a useless pillock,' said Shirley with a smile. 'But Edward did.'

She took a rubber torch from her pocket and shone it down the shaft. The ladder went down about twenty feet and stopped a few feet above a brick floor.

'Thank God for Edward,' said Phil, and he began to climb down the ladder.

'Should we close this cover after us?' asked Shirley.

'I can't see the point,' answered Phil, 'but if you can pull it over a bit it might stop someone seeing the torchlight when we're down there.'

They went down the shaft – Phil first, then Karen, with Shirley bringing up the rear. Shirley pulled the cover over as much as she could but she couldn't close it. Karen held the torch – it had been her granddad's – and the three of them were soon standing at the bottom of the shaft in a surprisingly large space surrounded by brick walls. There were two exits. One of them seemed to lead back into the town and the other was in the direction of the docks. Phil took the torch and motioned the two women to follow him down the latter. The drain was high enough at this point to allow them to walk upright. Despite the quick shower of rain they'd had earlier, the drain was dry and Phil surmised it was only used when the other drains in the town couldn't cope with a surplus of water. It was dry but there was a smell of decay coming off the walls. They had gone about fifty yards along their tunnel before Shirley spoke.

'I forgot to tell you, Mr Bond, if there's any fucking rats down here I'm off back up to the surface – I can't stand the bloody things. I have nightmares about them ever since we were forced to read *1984* at school.'

'Shut up, Shirley,' said Phil, 'this is a storm drain, not a sewer – there are no rats down here, I think!'

'Oh, thanks a bunch, lover. "You think"? Don't you know?'

'No. Be quiet for a minute – I'm trying to count.'

'Great, I'll be quiet then. The great love of your life has just told you that she has a fucking big problem but you'd rather count. Count what, may I ask?'

'The number of times he's made love to you in the last forty-eight hours,' interrupted Karen.

'He hasn't got that many fingers,' said Shirley before they both collapsed into a giggling fit.

'Quiet, the pair of you,' said Phil stopping and turning to face them both. 'Listen, I've been counting my steps since we left the roundabout. There's another shaft above us and I think it will come out inside the dock gates and pretty near the married quarters. I'm going to have a go and see if I can find Doreen Robson. If I'm not back within thirty minutes go on without me. No, Shirley – don't say it. Somehow, you have to get Karen out of this fucking nightmare. I love you both but this is something I've got to try – if I succeed it might mean the difference between success and failure in this escape of ours.'

Phil began to take off his outer clothes to reveal the guard's uniform. He kissed both of the women who had put their trust in him and told them again to wait no longer than thirty minutes.

He climbed up the ladder in the shaft and put his shoulder against the cover. It obviously wasn't as heavy as the one on the roundabout because it moved easily and for a moment he was looking at the night sky with all its stars on view. He climbed out and saw that he was in the shadow of the first building inside the dock gate. He replaced the cover over the shaft and went to the end of the building where he had seen a door from his vantage point in the restaurant. There was a list on the right-hand wall of the doorway. He saw that the top line read 'Robson – Flat A1'. He had been important – the best flat in the best block! He pushed the door but found that it was locked and then noticed a button alongside the writing 'Flat A1'. He pressed it and heard a buzz and then a voice.

'Hello?'

'Mrs Robson, my name's Phil King. We met at the Fairfaxes' dinner party. I wonder if I could have a quick word with you.'

'How the hell did you get here? What do you want? My husband's dead. What do you want?'

'I want to talk to you for about ten minutes – that's all! Please let me in. I'll explain everything to you.'

'I don't know why you want to talk to me. I know nothing but I remember that you were kind to me at the dinner. I'll let you in – push the door when you hear the buzzer. I'm on the first floor, directly opposite the stairs.'

The buzzer sounded and Phil went in through the door. He found Flat A1 and knocked softly on the door. Doreen Robson opened the door and he walked in. The woman had changed since the dinner party. She was dressed in a chocolate-coloured dress that left little to the imagination as to what kind of figure she had, which to Phil's eyes was quite tasteful. Doreen Robson was also drunk. She had a glass in her hand and swayed as she made her way to the cream sofa. She sat down and patted the seat next to her. Phil sat down next to her and she turned to him.

'OK, Mr Phil – how can I help you?' asked the very different and very drunk Doreen Robson.

Almost exactly twenty-five feet vertically beneath the cream sofa sat two women who were having a laugh. As Edward had said, that's how you kept the fear away.

'He's a brave man, that Philip King,' said Karen.

'Nobody braver,' replied her sister. 'He's got nerves of steel and the thighs to match.'

'Is that right? How long is thirty minutes?'

'Fuck knows – I haven't got a watch.'

'We'll have to wait here for him then.'

'Might as well – he usually turns up. Usually late and full of apologies, but he means well.'

The two sisters sat and reminisced for an hour and a half. They stood up when they heard a noise from above and switched on the torch. Phil King came sliding down the ladder, grabbed his clothes and ran down the storm drain.

'I'm sorry I'm late. Come on we need to get out of here – follow me. Where's that fucking torch? Shine it down here. Let's go!'

The sisters looked at each other and laughed. All three of them ran down the drain and none of them heard the sound of rushing water.

Twenty-Three

They ran until they had to stop to catch their breaths.

'What did the lovely Mrs Robson have to say?' asked Shirley.

'Not much – but enough,' said Phil. 'She was pissed.'

'She's just had her husband blown into a thousand bits – it's one way to cope with your grief, I suppose.'

'She wasn't pissed because she was grief-stricken over her husband's death. Quite the opposite – she was celebrating. She hated him and she's glad he's dead. It seems he was a bit of a bastard before all this started but after the Chaos he made her life a misery. He was only interested in his career and made his wife a very poor second in the list of the priorities in his life. He sucked up to everyone in authority and expected Doreen to do the same. Of course nobody took the slightest bit of notice of him – he was a shit corporal and that's probably were he would have stayed. His dreams of becoming an officer were doomed to failure before they even began and it made him bitter and frustrated.

'About eighteen months ago they gave him a new job and told him that he was very important, which suited him down to the ground. He was given his own office and told to do the new job in secret – nobody else was involved. According to Doreen, he did the job very well but, although he was a bastard, he wasn't stupid. He soon realised that the job could have been done by anybody who could file papers and write a few letters.

'The good corporal was on duty that night at the compound because that was where his office was. If you remember, Shirley, there were two huts down by the gate – one for the guards and another one that was all locked up. That hut was Robson's office and his own private little empire. Nobody went into that hut except him. He did his work there – nine to five, Monday to Friday – and, so Doreen says, didn't speak to anyone else down there, ever. That's why the guards you spoke to called him Corporal Shit – they thought he was a jumped-up twerp who thought himself superior to the ordinary guards.'

'But why were the authorities so anxious to trace me? What did Robson do?' asked Shirley.

Phil didn't answer the question. At last he had heard the noise in the storm drain behind them.

'What's that noise?' he asked.

Shirley and Karen listened as well.

'It sounds like a car or a lorry or something,' said Karen, 'but whatever it is, it's a long way away. I think it's coming from—'

'That's not the noise of an engine,' said Phil.

He listened again and put his ear to one of the walls. He turned and looked at the girls with panic written all over his face.

'That's the sound of rushing water and it's coming our way. Come on we've got to find one of those shafts and get up the ladder.'

They started to run as the sound of the water got louder.

Karen was the first to fall. She screamed as she scraped her face and arms on the cold, hard brick floor. Shirley turned round, ran back and helped her up. Phil stopped and waited for them to rejoin him.

'What are we going to do, Phil? Where are those fucking shafts? We haven't passed one for ages.'

'Christ knows. There's another thing as well – this drain is getting smaller. I'm having to duck my head in a few places.'

They ran on and both Shirley and Phil took their turns at falling down and picking themselves up and continuing.

The sound had now become a roar. All the time the drain seemed to be contracting until all three of them were running in a crouched position.

Phil carried on and now noticed that he was splashing through water. Where was the next shaft? It flashed across his mind that if somebody was trying to drown them then they couldn't have picked a better spot – the drain was now down to half its previous size and there were no maintenance shafts here! He was now wading through knee-high water and his progress had slowed considerably. He looked behind to see the girls helping each other as best they could but he knew that his job was to find one of those shafts.

At last he saw it, twenty yards ahead.

'Shirley, Karen – I've found the fucking shaft. Only a few more yards. Come on – we'll be safe if we can get up the ladder.'

Shirley shouted something back which sounded a bit like 'About fucking time,' but Phil couldn't hear properly because of the roar of the water.

He reached the shaft and shone the torch up. For a split second his life flashed before his eyes. The ladder in this shaft didn't come right down to the floor – it started at least ten feet above ground level. The girls joined him and looked up as well.

'Philip King,' said Shirley. 'If we ever get out of this mess don't start looking forward to a happy and prosperous new life because I'm going to fucking strangle you with my bare hands at the first opportunity.'

'Don't worry, we can make it. Stand on my shoulders – you'll be able to reach the ladder and then you can pull Karen up.'

Shirley did as she was told and easily made the ladder but only after giving Phil a kick on the side of the head.

'She's not angry with you about the ladder, Phil,' said Karen as she climbed up on to Phil's shoulders.

'No? You could have fooled me.'

'No, it was the rat. One swam through her legs back there and she's terrified of them.'

Karen also made it to the ladder and so only Phil was left standing up to his waist in foul-smelling water with nobody's shoulders to climb on to. He tried jumping to see if he could reach the ladder but his sodden clothes and the weight of the water made it an impossible task.

Shirley was screaming from halfway up the ladder.

'Jump, you bastard. You can't drown. I want the fucking pleasure of killing you myself!'

'I can't reach it. You two go on up – I'll take my chances down here – go on. Good luck.'

It was debatable whether either Karen or Shirley heard this last shout from Phil because the noise had reached a crescendo. The water roared into the shaft and Phil went under the surface and nearly died there and then in the putrid sewage that had engulfed him.

Shirley saw him go under and cried out.

'Phil, don't leave me! Phil, I can't go on without you – what would be the fucking point? Phil—' Her screams died under a surge of tears and it was Karen who answered her.

'Climb the ladder, Shirley – let's get out of this place. See if you can move the cover at the top. Shirley, climb the ladder – let's move! Shirley, I'm begging you – climb the ladder. What about me? Shirley, we need to save ourselves if we can.'

Shirley climbed and threw off the cover at the top of the shaft with her shoulder – it was obviously a lot thinner than the one where they had climbed into the drain. She pulled Karen up behind her and the two of them lay exhausted on the ground. Shirley moved across until she could see down the shaft but all she could hear was the noise of the water. There was no sign of Phil.

Phil had gone under the water and for a moment had lost his bearings. The force of the water had disorientated him and he didn't know which way was up and which way was down but then he remembered a film that he had seen where people were drowning and they had made it to the surface because they had followed the air bubbles – they always went up! There was hardly any visibility in the water but he managed to see one of the air bubbles from his breathing and he followed it. He made it to the surface in the shaft, took a deep breath and looked around him. The surface of the water had risen to such an extent that he was able to grasp the bottom of the ladder and haul himself up the first few steps. He stopped and took another deep breath.

'Fuck me,' he said quietly to himself, 'that was close,' and began to climb the ladder. He heard a voice from above him.

'Get your arse up here, Philip King, and make it quick – I thought you were dead.'

It was Shirley's voice and Phil had never been so glad to hear such words of endearment in all his life. He scrambled over the lip of the manhole cover and fell into her arms. They nearly crushed each other with the intensity of their embrace before Karen joined them and wrapped her arms around both of them. They stayed like that for quite a few minutes until the three of them separated and lay on their backs looking up at the stars.

'Do you think somebody did that on purpose?' asked Karen. 'I mean, did somebody turn the water on deliberately and try to drown us?'

'Listen,' said Phil, 'do you hear anything?'

'No.'

'Well, that answers your question – the water's stopped. Whoever turned it on reckoned that we would be dead by now and, if we hadn't made it to that shaft in time, we would have been!'

'So what do we do now?'

'I'll go down and check that all the water has gone – they probably divert it into the docks – and then we can continue along our escape route.'

'But they might flood the drain again,' said Karen. 'What happens if we don't find another shaft at the right time?'

'That's a chance we'll have to take but they might not have enough water to do it again. We'll be OK – you two wait here and I'll go and see what it's like down there.'

Shirley had been listening to the conversation but had not, as yet, said anything. She now decided to make a firm statement.

'Good luck to you both but I'm not going down there again.'

'What?' asked Phil.

'I can't go down there again – I'm sorry but I can't. I was terrified down there, what with the rats and the noise of the water. I was scared bloody shitless and I'm not going down there again. I'm sorry, but I'd rather take my chances here above ground.'

Phil looked around for the first time. They were in a dock area but there was no one about and it looked as though the machinery and the cranes hadn't been used in a long time. They were probably in the docks nearest the town – that had been closed down – and that meant that they would still have to negotiate the docks which had been reopened. Did they work a night shift these days? He couldn't hear any noise but that didn't mean anything because he didn't know how far away they were from the working docks. Even if they made it overground and reached the Border – how would they get across and where would they come out? There were too many unknowns in that strategy – they would have to go back down the storm drain and Shirley would have to go with them!

Phil began to explain why they had to go back down into the drain.

'That's a non-starter, Shirley. We've got to go back down – it's our only hope. We'll never find our way out up here.'

Shirley looked at Phil and Karen. She didn't want to let them down – not after all they'd been through together. She knew in her heart of hearts that Phil was right but she couldn't go back down there. She'd rather die where she was than go through all that again!

'I can't, Phil – I know it sounds fucking stupid after what I did at the compound but I can't! You two go down and get out of this place but I'm not. I'll go back and give myself up to the guards, which will probably give the two of you a bit of extra time. I just can't go down to that tunnel again.'

'You have to, Shirley – I'm not going to leave you here, you stupid sod. Come on, I'll look after you. Karen, tell her that she's got to come with us.'

'He's right, Shirley – it's our only chance and I'm not leaving you here alone. If the water has gone there should be no problem. We'll help you. Come on.'

'I'm not going – can't the pair of you understand? I'm finished. I don't want to go on. I can't go on and I'm fucking certain that I'm not going on through that tunnel. Go, the pair of you – leave me!'

Phil stood and grabbed Shirley's hands. He dragged her to her feet and put his arms round her.

'I'm not leaving you anywhere and if you don't want to go down to the drain again, I'll get you out up here. Karen, what do you think? Shall we take our chances up here and give it a go or do you want to try the drain on your own?'

'I'm not going anywhere on my own – if you two are going to have a try up here then I'm with you but I think we'd be better off in the drain. At least down there, nobody will be able to see us.'

'I agree,' said Phil, 'but Shirley has made her mind up so it seems we have no choice.'

'Agreed,' said Karen. 'Which way do we go?'

'That's the problem,' said Phil. 'I don't know.'

'Which way was the tunnel heading?'

'That way,' said Phil, pointing away from the town. 'I suppose we should follow that line and see where we come out. Here, hang on to Shirley for a minute while I go and check the direction of the tunnel – it would be bloody stupid if I had got the wrong direction and we ended up on England Avenue!'

Phil walked over to the top of the shaft after making sure that Karen had hold of Shirley. He had only taken three steps when he heard the sound of an automatic rifle and, turning round, saw Shirley and Karen fall. He raced back to them.

'She's been shot. They've shot her!' screamed Shirley. 'The bastards have shot her! Oh, no – oh, please God, no – she's fucking dead. They've killed her! Karen, Karen – speak to me. They've shot her in the back. You fucking bastards! Phil... Phil... She's dead.'

Shirley was right – Karen Markham was dead and her bright green eyes would sparkle no more. Phil King pushed the two of them to the ground. He took one look at Karen and knew that he couldn't help her. He dragged Shirley away and pushed her down the shaft to the drain. He followed, pulling the cover back, before he descended the ladder. There were only two of them left and they sat at the bottom of the shaft and cried their hearts out.

Twenty-Four

The two tormented people sat there for a long time without saying a word. A few rats scuttled past down the tunnel but Shirley didn't seem to notice or care. Phil didn't know what to say or think any more.

'I killed her, didn't I?'

'What?'

'I killed her. If we hadn't stayed up there and had that debate about whether or not we should come down to the drain again she would still be alive.'

'You didn't kill her – that bastard with the automatic rifle killed her. I killed her, bringing her on this stupid fucking escape attempt. The authorities killed her.'

'I killed her.'

'Don't think that way, Shirley – you didn't kill her.'

'I killed her. She was my sister and I killed her. I killed her because of my fear of fucking rats and the sound of fucking water. Funny, isn't it? The fear's gone! I'll take them all on: rats, water, the bastard with the automatic rifle, the authorities, whoever! It doesn't matter. That girl must not have died in vain. Are you listening to me, Philip King?'

'I'm listening.'

'Good, right, let's get going. I want to get out of this town and find the bastards responsible for all this shite and then I want to get an automatic rifle and kill them all. Don't let me down now, Philip King – it never seemed to be personal before but it is now. Move your arse, let's go!'

Phil rose to his feet and started on down the tunnel.

'It would have been nice to have had a kiss or a hug to show that you loved me before we set off but never mind – I'll make do with "move your arse, Philip King".'

'We've no time for kisses and hugs – it's serious now. I don't want to lose the fucking anger I'm feeling at the moment. I'll give you a kiss later, if Geoff says I can.'

'Geoff's dead. So are Rosie and my two kids.'

'Who told you that?'

'Doreen Robson. They're all dead – every last one of them.'

They stopped and looked at each other. They were all they had left. The two of them were alone with each other. There was no one else to worry about or to worry about them. Shirley stepped towards him but they didn't know what to do. Was it a time for celebration because they had each other or was it a time for remorse because of the loved ones they had lost?

'Don't tell me the details – I don't want to know,' said Shirley, lost in her memories. 'It's just another reason to get even with these bastards.'

'You're right, as usual. Come on, let's see what we can do about getting out of here in the first place. Do you really want to shoot all the bastards who thought this up?'

'No, I want them to suffer first. I want them to beg for fucking mercy before I finish them off. Karen's death was the turning point for me. She didn't deserve that! Who does?'

'Nobody,' agreed Phil, who was now reduced to crawling along the tunnel, which had become little more than a pipe.

The going became harder and Phil wondered how the fat Charles Corcoran had ever managed to negotiate his way through this small space. He knew in an instant that he hadn't and that this was another trap – somehow Shirley and he would have to find a way out of the tunnel before it reached its end. Otherwise, they might find a welcoming committee waiting for them!

But there were no vertical shafts leading off the pipe and Phil wondered how he was going to tell Shirley that they would have to go back!

They crawled on for a few more yards before Phil stopped and peered round at Shirley.

'How are you doing?'

'I'm OK but this is getting to be bloody hard work – how much further do you think we've got to go?'

'I've no idea and I'm not sure we're going in the right direction. Charles Corcoran was a fat slob and he would have had a hell of a job crawling through here – I'm beginning to think that he didn't come this way at all!'

'Well I haven't seen any turn-offs – this must be the right way, or is this a polite way of saying that we'll have to turn round and go back? Keep going. I don't want to go back.'

'Your wish is my command,' said Phil and pushed on.

They were soaked and cold and the going had become hard work but just as Phil was losing hope, he sensed that the pipe was broadening a little. After about fifty yards he found that he could raise himself up to a crouching position and another hundred yards saw him stand for the first time since they had re-entered the tunnel. Shirley joined him and they jumped up and down together to get the circulation back into their arms and legs. They didn't pause for long but the journey was much easier now that they could walk.

'How big are these fucking docks?' asked Shirley. 'We'll be in Essex soon! We seem to have been walking and crawling for miles!'

'Bloody big,' said Phil. 'Ships from all over the world used to come in here. Huge bloody ships with their containers came in, discharged their cargo, loaded up and then sailed again in about twelve hours.'

'I didn't want a lesson in the trade patterns of western Europe, thank you! I wondered if you knew how much fucking further we had to go.'

'Why don't you ask me a question I know the answer to?'

'How did Geoff die?'

Phil King stopped in his tracks. He knew that the question had been coming and he knew that he would have to answer it. He put his arms around Shirley and held her tight.

'He was shot dead by a firing squad on the same day that they took him into custody. He wasn't tortured or even questioned – they just took down his name and address and took him outside and shot him. I don't know any more details and I certainly don't know the answer to the next question you want to ask – "why?".'

'I'm glad he didn't suffer much. I know they shot him but I'm glad he wasn't tortured and everything. Poor Geoff – why didn't they just tell me all that instead of letting me hope for three years? They are bastards! What about Rosie and the kids?'

'They're dead.'

'How? Or don't you want to talk about it?'

'I don't even want to fucking think about it but I'll have to one day – it might as well be now! All three of them died on the Saturday, soon after they left the house. I presume that Rosie saw or heard the news about the town being closed because of the plague and bundled the kids into the car and took off. I don't blame her for not coming round to the shop to find me – the roads were clogged with traffic and the kids were the important ones. She probably tried to ring me but I could have been on the phone to someone trying to find out what was happening. What the hell – it doesn't matter what happened now. Rosie, Robin and Deborah never made it. They died in somewhere called Centre 3. Have you ever heard of it?'

'No.'

'Neither have I – but I'll tell you this: they didn't die alone.'

'What do you mean? How do you know that?'

'Hundreds, thousands, of people died in Centre 3 during the first few days of the Chaos.'

'How did they die – were they shot as well?'

'I don't know, Shirley – does it matter?'

'No, I suppose not. This fucking mess is far worse than we ever thought, isn't it?'

'Far, far worse. I don't know all of it but the little I do know tells me that we are dealing with a very dangerous group of people. Do you want to go on? We can turn back if you want and see if we can make it back to the town.'

'Fuck off, Phil – we're going on. We can't go back. What is there to go back to? Give me a kiss and then we'll move.'

They kissed each other hard and long, as if it was for the last time.

'I love you, Philip King. Whatever happens to us, thank you for the last few days. They know we're here, don't they? We're trapped, aren't we?'

'We probably are. If they didn't know where we were before, they did after the shooting of Karen! Ah, bollocks to them all! Come on, Shirley Tate – let's go out in a blaze of glory. Fuck 'em!'

'That's what I wanted to hear. You're right – fuck 'em all!'

With that battle cry ringing in their ears, the two of them separated and carried on down the tunnel. The drain was now as large as it had been in the beginning and their progress was swift and fairly uneventful. They met a couple of rats along the way but Shirley took great pleasure in kicking and stamping on them and they met no other problems. There was no sound of water and every time they stopped for a breather they listened to see if they could hear anybody following them – they could hear nothing. It was after another ten minutes of fast walking that they encountered the real problem.

'Shit,' said Phil. 'What the bloody hell do we do now?'

Shirley joined him and saw the problem for herself. They were in a circular chamber, which wasn't a problem in itself – it was quite a nice feeling to escape from the tunnel and have the ability to walk round as normal. The problem was that there were three exits from the chamber – one to the left, one to the right and one straight on. They all looked the same and there was no evidence that any of them had been used more than the others.

'Any suggestions, Mrs Tate?'

'Easy – no problem, Mr King. The left one would take us under the docks and I don't want to see any more fucking water for as long as I live – so that's definitely a no-no. The middle one is probably the one that bastard Corcoran used because he would want to go via the quickest route. Since I think we are both agreed that he was a two-faced bastard, if we went down that way we would be met by his fellow bastards. That tunnel is again discarded. Therefore we will proceed by way of the tunnel on our right, which would give us the best possible chance of escape. Agreed?'

'That was a load of old bollocks! You haven't got a clue either, have you?'

'No, but it sounded good. Can you do any better?'

'The one to the right would take us back towards the town so we can discount that one immediately. The centre one is the one they think we'd choose so that's a no-no. The left one is perfect for our purposes – we could surface in one of the dock basins, board a ship bound for the Pacific and be sunning ourselves on a desert island within a couple of weeks.'

'Are you taking the piss?'

'Yes.'

'So what are we going to do?'

'We're going down the one to the right.'

'That's the one I said we should take.'

'I know. Come on, let's go – it'll be interesting to see if you're right.'

'What if I'm wrong?'

'I doubt that I'll ever get the chance to punish you for making a bad decision.'

'What's the punishment?'

'Shut up, we have to get a move on. I don't want to come out on the surface in the daylight and it must be nearly dawn now.'

They pressed on and at times Phil switched the torch off to conserve the batteries. The tunnel was large and they made good progress. They reached the shaft after about fifteen minutes.

The ladder was again ten feet off the ground and so Shirley climbed onto Phil's shoulders and began to ascend. She stopped halfway and whispered, 'There's a hell of a lot of noise up here – do you want me to go and have a look?'

'Yes, see if you can have a look outside – just lift the cover a bit and see what's going on.'

In less than a minute, Shirley was back down at his side.

'We're in the middle of the working docks – there are hundreds of people and forklift trucks all over the place. We'd never be able to get out from there – and the whole place is floodlit.'

'OK,' said Phil. 'We'll have to go on to the next shaft. How are you feeling?'

'I'm all right but I could do with a sit-down and something to eat and drink. Let me know if you see a Little Chef anywhere in this bloody tunnel!'

For the first time in a long time, Phil laughed. This woman would do for him! He just hoped and prayed that he could get her out of this mess in one piece!

They investigated the next three shafts in the same way and every time Shirley's report was the same – busy docks! The fourth shaft was different: Shirley reported that they were not under the docks any more – the surface was scrubland – but she could still hear the sound of the docks when she opened the cover at the top of the shaft. They decided that it might be wise to carry on and get as far away from the docks as possible.

The sixth shaft was the same but the noise from the docks was now barely audible. Shirley was feeling weak but she realised the importance of distancing themselves from the town and they carried on down the tunnel.

Phil noticed that Shirley was having difficulty climbing the ladder at the next shaft and realised that this was the end of the road as far as the tunnel was concerned. Whatever was on the surface, they had to get out and have a rest!

'It seems perfect, Phil,' said the voice from above him. 'It's thick woodland and there doesn't seem to be anybody about. How are you going to get up the ladder?'

'God knows – but I'll find a way. Get yourself out of here and find somewhere to hide.'

Phil looked around for something to stand on but there was nothing. He looked up at the bottom of the ladder, which seemed a mile away from him. He couldn't fail now. They were nearly there! Then he remembered something. The last time he had attempted to jump up to the bottom of the ladder he had been up to his waist in water. Perhaps he could make it without that weight dragging down his lower body? He took a deep breath, jumped and very nearly made it. His right hand had been about an inch short! He tried again and managed to hold the bottom rung for a couple of seconds before he lost his grip and fell down to the floor of the shaft. He knew then that he hadn't got many more attempts left in him – he was as tired as Shirley. He sat and waited. He thought of the woman waiting for him at the top. He had to make it to the surface!

He took a long time to get his mind together and to recover his strength and then jumped. His right hand closed around the bottom rung and this time he held on! He didn't believe he had the strength to pull himself up until he had his feet placed squarely on the bottom rung and paused to get his breath back.

He climbed the ladder and looked out at the top of the shaft. Shirley had been right – it did seem perfect. They were in a thickly wooded area with lots of undergrowth and ground plants. The trees were tall and thick and there didn't appear to be anyone else about. He clambered out and replaced the cover over the top of the shaft. He stood up and looked around him. Yes, it was perfect but there was one small problem – he couldn't see Shirley anywhere!

The shaft had come out in a small clearing but there was no sign of the woman he now loved with every bone in his body. He moved to his right and reached the treeline at the edge of the clearing. He moved in a circle of about twenty yards from the top of the shaft but saw no sign of her. He was making a noise, with all the dead leaves and branches on the ground but that didn't seem to matter to him – where was Shirley? He increased the radius of his search circle and then he saw her.

She was lying on her back with her arms crossed over her chest. He walked over to her, thinking that she was dead and dropped to his knees. He took her head in his arms and sobbed. This wasn't right, he thought to himself, not Shirley! No... No... Not Shirley. Not Shirley, please God... not Shirley!

'Where the fucking hell have you been? I want to go to sleep – give me a cuddle.'

Phil didn't know whether to laugh or cry now. He certainly was not going to be angry!

'I had a bit of trouble coming up the stairs, darling. Go to sleep, my love. I'm here now – I'll give you a cuddle.'

Phil lay down next to this remarkable woman and pulled his coat over both of them. He cuddled her and waited until she fell asleep in his arms. He saw the dawn arrive and then fell asleep himself. It was perhaps the only time in the last three years that nobody else in the world knew where they were or what they were doing. They slept for a long time and it was nearly midday when Shirley stirred. She gave Phil a punch in the ribs.

'Stop snoring, you lazy bastard. Where are we?'

Phil wiped the sleep from his eyes and looked around.

'We're in the woods, m'lady.'

Shirley woke up fully, leaned across and gave Phil a kiss.

'We made it. I knew you could do it! You're my hero, Mr King.'

'I don't want to spoil the party but there is a problem that you may have overlooked. We don't know where we are and we don't know which way to go.'

'I know that but... you'll find the way out. I love you and I've every confidence in you, you gorgeous, lovely, sexy hunk of a man. Listen, shall we do it here under the trees?'

Phil laughed again and Shirley joined in. They didn't do it under the trees – they came to the realisation very quickly that they needed food more than sex! Phil checked the direction of the tunnel they had just left and they set off in that direction hand in hand through the woods.

The weather was being kind to them – it was a bright day and the sun shone. Perhaps spring had arrived early! In any other circumstances it would have been a good day for a brisk country walk but Phil and Shirley were hungry and, although they had slept for a few hours, they were still tired from the previous night's exertions. The forest was quiet and they saw no one as they made their way briskly across its floor.

After about a mile or so, the trees began to thin out and Phil suspected that they were coming to the edge of the forest. He told Shirley that they had better slow down. They walked on and soon they encountered a different landscape. The trees disappeared and they were in open country with ploughed fields and hedgerows. Phil stopped and looked around.

'Any ideas? Do you recognise anything? It all looks the same to me.'

'No,' said Shirley, 'but I suggest we keep to the hedges because we'll be seen from miles away in the fields. Hang on a minute – what's that over there?'

'Where?'

'On the right, in the distance – do you see it? It looks like smoke.'

Phil looked and saw what Shirley was pointing at – a thin wisp of smoke rose lazily into the bright winter sky.

'It might be the town,' said Phil. 'There's always fires breaking out in the derelict buildings.'

'Don't be bloody stupid – we're miles away from the town now. I vote we go and have a look. It might be a farm or a cottage.

I need something to eat, Phil – at least let's go over there and find out where the smoke's coming from.'

'OK,' said Phil. 'Let's go, but don't get too excited – it might be nothing.'

'No, I have a good feeling about this – I reckon that smoke is from a log fire in a large Suffolk farmhouse stuffed full of food. The farmer and his wife are kind people who feed us and let us stay for three weeks to get our strength back. They also have a strong young son who fancies me and they lend us their Land Rover and we drive away to a new life together.'

'You and the son?'

'I haven't decided yet – it depends whether he's better looking than you. Yes, I've decided – me and the son!'

'You're right about one thing.'

'What's that?'

'You need some food. You're hallucinating!'

They used the hedges as cover and made their way towards the smoke. It appeared to be coming from some sort of hollow in the ground and they couldn't see anything else except the smoke until they were quite close and perched on a small rise. Shirley had been right about the smoke not coming from the town but she had been wrong about the large Suffolk farmhouse.

In a little valley stood a small half-derelict cottage. The smoke was coming from a smouldering bonfire by one of the side walls. There was a small vegetable patch and an empty chicken run. Old bits of metal and cars were strewn around the site and at one end there was a huge barn which had no roof. The barn was empty apart from a huge pile of rusty milk churns stacked in one corner. There were a few wooden outbuildings in various stages of decay. If this had been a farm, it looked as if it had fallen into disuse some years ago.

There was no sign of life and only the smoke from the bonfire disturbed the scene.

'What do you think?' asked Phil. 'There doesn't seem to be anywhere else for miles around.'

'Let's give it a go – if I don't eat something soon I'm going to collapse.'

'OK then. I'll go down and have a look – you stay here until I say it's safe for you to come down.'

'"No" is the simple answer to that plan. We go together or not at all. What if something happens to you down there? What would I do – go and try and find somewhere else? Come on, let's go and meet the kind Suffolk farmer and his wife.'

They rose and began to walk down the slope towards the cottage. They reached the door and had still seen nothing and no one moving. Phil knocked lightly on the door and took hold of Shirley's hand. They waited. Phil knocked again a little louder this time.

'Perhaps they're out at the shops,' he said, trying to relieve the tension.

'Perhaps they're dead,' said Shirley.

'Somebody must be about – the fire's still smouldering.'

'Perhaps they burned to death on the fire.'

'Quiet – someone's coming.'

They could hear the sound of footsteps approaching the door and Shirley gripped Phil's hand as tight as she could. The door stayed closed and then they heard a woman's voice.

'Who are you? What do you want?'

'We're from the town. We wondered if you could let us have some food – we haven't eaten for about twenty-four hours. We don't want any trouble.'

There was a long pause before the woman spoke again.

'I don't believe you. Nobody comes here from the town. Clear off.'

'We are from the town,' said Shirley. 'We escaped and we're starving. We won't harm you – all we want is some food, please!'

'Nobody escapes from the town and we've been told that if they ever do we mustn't help them. Go away – my husband is here and he's got a gun.'

'Well, thanks for all your help,' said Phil. 'We'll go, and good luck to both you and your husband – it's nice to know a good Suffolk welcome is still on offer around the county.'

They turned and began to walk away from the door until Shirley stopped and shouted at the top of her voice.

'You miserable fucking cow! You can stick your food up your tight-fisted arse.'

'Come on, Shirley,' said Phil. 'It's no use – she's as afraid as we are. We'll have to find somewhere else.'

'You wouldn't believe people could be so cruel – let's bash the door down and knock the shit out of her.'

'Let's not – you heard her say that her husband was with her and that he had a gun.'

It was at this moment that the door opened. Shirley and Phil both looked to see who was there but no one appeared. Then an old woman came, stood on the step with her arms folded and spoke to them.

'My husband says that he wants to hear your voice again.'

'What does he want me to say?' asked Shirley.

'Not you – him,' said the woman, pointing at Phil.

'I'm sorry if we frightened you – as I said, we mean you no harm.'

The woman looked behind her as if she was listening to someone standing further inside the cottage and then looked back at the frightened couple of people just outside her door. She moved to one side and a man appeared beside her. The woman hadn't been bluffing – the man was holding a shotgun, which was pointed directly at Phil and Shirley.

Twenty-Five

The man with the gun looked at the two escapees and then at the land around his cottage. Suddenly his face broke into a smile.

'It's him, Mary – I thought I recognised the voice. Bloody hell – I wondered where you'd disappeared to. I never thought I'd see you again, and certainly not here. Come in, you daft bastard, and bring your lady friend. Well, well – I never thought I'd see the day.'

Shirley looked at Phil, who was standing there in shock.

'Do you two know each other?'

'In a way, yes.'

'Who is he?'

'His name is Amos and I've been meeting him every day for the last three years. He's the man I get the vegetables from at the Border. Bloody hell, Shirley – I think we might have struck lucky at last!'

Phil and Shirley followed Amos and Mary into the cottage and, after the introductions had been made, they all sat down around a huge oak table, which dominated the kitchen. There was a log fire but it wasn't lit and Phil noticed that the room was crammed with furniture. Although the table was the biggest thing in the room, there were sofas, chairs and dressers all vying for the small space that was left. He also noticed that the furniture was of good quality – it looked as though everything of value had been packed into this one room.

'We need to talk,' said Amos, 'but you'll no doubt want something to eat first and you both look as if you could do with a sleep. We'll talk later. Mary, get the pan on and give these two young people some of your best hotpot – I know there was some left over from last night's tea. As for sleep, I hope you two know each other quite well because we've only got the two bedrooms. You can have the one on the right at the top of the stairs.'

Mary went over to the stove, which was on the wall opposite

the fireplace, and began to get the meal ready. Shirley went and joined her.

'I'm sorry for what I said outside, Mary. We were desperate – I couldn't face the prospect of trying to find somewhere else. I'm sorry.'

Mary turned to look at her.

'Amos sometimes gets to know things that happen in the town – if only half of them are true then I think I got off pretty lightly. But I will say this: I do object to being called a cow – they're such stupid beasts!'

'I take it back and I'm sorry.'

'We'll say no more about it. Now, do you want to have a wash before you eat? We can't run to a bath – we have to have a few hours' notice for that – but there's a bathroom through that door if you want to have a quick swill.'

'I'll get a bath ready for after the meal,' said Amos who had obviously heard the conversation. 'There'll only be one tubfull so I hope you're not bashful.'

He went out of the room and soon there were sounds of a generator being cranked up and various pieces of plumbing starting to clank and hiss. Shirley stood at Mary's side still.

'Is there something else?' asked Mary.

'You wouldn't have any shampoo, would you? You wouldn't believe what I've had to swim through in the last twelve hours!'

'For God's sake!' exclaimed Phil. 'We came here for something to eat, Shirley – not a bloody beauty and therapy session.'

'I'm sorry – I just feel so dirty. I'm sorry, Mary. I'll just go and have a wash.'

Shirley wandered out to the bathroom.

'There's an old bottle of shampoo in the cupboard under the sink,' shouted Mary. 'Take no notice of him. You wash your hair and you'll feel a thousand times better – I always do. He's a man and doesn't understand.'

Mary busied herself with the cooking and Phil sat at the table on his own. Was this the lucky break that they needed to help them to escape? Amos and Mary seemed genuine enough and, with a good meal inside them and after a sleep, perhaps they might be able to get away from the town.

Amos came back into the room with some clothes over his arm.

'I've found these for the pair of you – I suggest you put them on after your bath and then Mary and I will have a go at washing and drying your own clothes while you are asleep. Come on, let's eat. Where's Shirley?'

'Would you believe it? Washing her hair!' said Phil.

'Yes, I'd believe it!' said Amos.

Mary produced a large pot of steaming stew and set it in the middle of the table. There was a basket of crusty, stale bread and a thick slice of cheese on a wooden platter. Mary started to dole out the stew on to the four plates and Phil began to eat. The stew was thin but hot and tasty. For the first time in his life, he forgot about table manners and ate like a pig at a trough. He was halfway through his meal when Shirley came back into the kitchen. She might not have looked a thousand times better but she had certainly recaptured some of her sparkle! Her blonde hair had regained its shine and she sat down at the table.

'Good God,' said Phil. 'I think I'll go and wash my hair.'

'It doesn't work for men,' said Mary. 'Finish your stew!'

The meal continued in silence mainly because Phil and Shirley were eating so fast that they didn't have time to talk! When it was over, it was Amos who spoke.

'Right, get those smelly clothes off and I'll run your bath. It'll be the same water for you both so you'll have to decide who gets in first. Then put those old clothes of ours on and get yourselves up to bed. We never have any visitors here so you'll be quite safe. As I said before, we need to talk, but that can wait 'till morning.'

Phil and Shirley followed Amos's instructions and two hours later were lying side by side in a huge antique bed in one of the bedrooms of the old cottage.

'This is too good to be true,' said Shirley.

'I know,' said Phil, 'that's why I don't believe it.'

'Do you think it's another trap?'

'God knows – Amos and Mary seem OK but—'

'But what?'

'It's too convenient, isn't it? We escape, we're lost and then we find the one man I know from outside of the town. I've never had luck like that before!'

Shirley thought for a moment and then turned to the man beside her.

'Do you think we should make a run for it?'

'Run where? We don't even know where we are but we can't be too far from the Border because Amos goes there every day. I don't know what to do, Shirley. What do you think?'

'I think we should make mad, passionate love to each other – just in case it's the last time. Then we should fall asleep and see what tomorrow brings. I'm through with running away.'

An hour later they fell asleep in each other's arms. They were too tired to dream. Nothing disturbed them and it was eight o'clock the next morning when Phil went downstairs to find the cottage deserted apart from the two of them.

There was no sign of Mary and Amos anywhere. Phil and Shirley's clothes lay around the stove and the dying embers of a fire that had obviously been burning the night before. All the dishes had been cleared away and were stacked neatly at one end of the table – washed and dried. He went back upstairs and looked in the other bedroom. There was nobody there and the bed didn't look as if it had been slept in. Phil went into the bedroom where Shirley was still asleep. He shook her shoulder and she woke.

'They've gone.'

'Who's gone?'

'Amos and Mary – the place is deserted apart from us.'

Shirley sat bolt upright and looked at Phil.

'They can't have – they must be around here somewhere. Have you looked outside?'

'No.'

'There you are, then – they must be out in the yard or the fields or something. Go and look!'

Phil went downstairs and dressed in his own clothes. He went outside and searched the yard and the barn and all the outbuildings. He went to the top of the rise, from where he and Shirley had first seen the cottage and scanned the surrounding fields. There was not another living thing within miles of the cottage.

When he got back to the cottage, Shirley was dressed apart from her trousers.

'There's nobody here.'

'Have you seen my leather trousers anywhere?'

'What?'

'My lucky leather trousers – they're missing. Have you seen them?'

'No, I haven't. Does it matter? Amos and Mary have disappeared.'

'Of course it matters – ever since I started wearing those pants, I've been lucky. I'm not going anywhere without them.'

'Fucking hell,' said Phil, 'I've heard it all now. Have you been listening to what I've been saying?'

'I've heard every word you've said. Amos and Mary have gone so we'll have to get out of here and proceed on our own. That's OK but I want my leather trousers.'

Phil sank into one of the sofas. He didn't know what to say.

Shirley rummaged around the room for a few minutes.

'Ah, here they are. Mary put them in the bin – she must have thought they were so scuffed that I wouldn't want them any more. How wrong can you be?'

Shirley pulled on the trousers and smiled at Phil.

'Have we got time for a cup of tea before we move out?'

'Why not? If we can waste time looking for a pair of leather trousers, we might as well have a cup of tea before we go!'

They drank their tea in silence. It was when they were stuffing their pockets with food they thought they might need for their journey that they heard the sound of a vehicle. They slid to the floor and Phil crawled over to the window. He looked out and then went back to Shirley.

'It's a military Land Rover.'

'Oh, shite! What do we do?'

'You go and find somewhere to hide and I'll keep an eye on it – and see if you can find Amos's gun.'

Shirley crawled away in the direction of the stairs and Phil went back to the window. He looked out and saw that the Land Rover had pulled up at the entrance to the yard. Nobody got out and it was a couple of minutes before he saw the driver's door open. Out stepped a guard who turned and went round to the rear of the vehicle. The Land Rover now obscured Phil's view of him but it sounded as if he was having a conversation with someone, but they were too far away for Phil to hear what was being said. He heard a noise behind him and turned to see Shirley crawling towards him with the shotgun in her hand.

'Have you ever used one of these?' she asked, giving the gun to Phil.

'Never. Is it loaded?'

'I don't bloody know but if it isn't we've got problems because I couldn't find any bullets.'

'Cartridges.'

'Pardon?'

'You fire cartridges from a shotgun, not bullets.'

'I'm glad you told me that – that might prove very helpful in the next two minutes of my life! You can be a patronising pig at times, Philip King. Anyway – whatever they're called – we haven't got any. What's happening outside?'

'A guard got out of the Land Rover and he's talking to some-one but I can't see who it is because they're round the back. I thought I told you to go and hide.'

'You did but I'm back now so I might as well stay. Let me have a look.'

Phil moved over and Shirley peered out of the window. There was still no sign of the driver and whoever he was talking to. Phil broke open the gun, saw that it was loaded and cocked it again. He started to sweat – apart from air rifles at various funfair stalls, he had never fired a gun in his life. He wasn't sure that if it came to a head he could do so now! Suddenly, the guard came round the Land Rover again and got into the driver's seat. He turned the engine on, moved forward slowly and then accelerated away from the cottage in a wide circle, creating a huge cloud of dust.

One man had been left behind – obviously to guard the place, thought Phil. Two of them, one of him – perhaps there was a chance, after all, for them to escape again.

He stood up and gripped the shotgun tightly.

'I'm going to the front door. Let me know if our friend out there comes towards the cottage. Perhaps, I can shoot him without having to open the door. I'm not sure I could look at him and then kill him.'

246

Phil went and stood just inside the door while Shirley kept looking out of the window and saw the dust cloud evaporating.

'He's walking towards us but very slowly. Get ready! No, he's stopped by the vegetable patch. Right, here he comes.'

The sweat ran down Phil's back in rivers. His hands were clammy as he pointed the shotgun at the middle of the door. He glanced at Shirley who was still looking out of the window.

'OK, he'll be outside the door in about five seconds. I wouldn't kill him, though.'

'Why not?' croaked Phil, his voice having gone as well.

'It's Amos.'

Phil lowered the gun and let it fall to the floor. He looked at Shirley who was sucking her thumb and smiling at him.

'Shirley Tate, I will never, ever forgive you for what you've just put me through.'

'I'm sure you will,' said Shirley, putting her arms round his neck and kissing him lightly on the lips. 'I bet you forgive me the next time we're in bed together.'

'You are one hell of a crazy woman. I'll have to sit down – my legs are like jelly after all that.'

'My kisses usually have that effect on men.'

'It's not you – it was the Land Rover and the guard and that gun.' Phil saw that Shirley was laughing and began to laugh with her, and that's how Amos found them when he walked into the kitchen.

'Good, I'm glad to see you're up and about. Put the kettle on will you, Phil? I must have a cup of tea before I tell you all the news. Did you both sleep well?'

'Very well,' said Shirley, 'but we were a bit worried when we came down to find that both you and Mary were gone.'

'Well, I thought it best if I went to the Border as usual, so as not to arouse suspicion. I usually walk to the end of the lane where I get picked up by the Land Rover and that's what I did this morning. The lane is a mile long so you wouldn't have heard them pick me up. I did all my work up at the farm and the Border and then, as usual, they gave me a lift back. Sometimes they drop me at the end of the lane but if it's raining or I'm feeling a bit tired they bring me all the way up to the cottage. This morning I told them they could drop me off here because my old leg was playing me up. I thought that way they wouldn't have any suspicions as to whether I was trying to hide you two here. My only worry as I came up the lane was that the lovely Shirley would be on the doorstep waving to me and telling me that my breakfast was ready.'

Phil and Shirley were looking at each other in alarm.

'Oh, yes – they asked if I had seen you. They seem a bit anxious to get hold of you, if you ask me. I told them that I hadn't seen anybody at my place for at least two years and they seemed satisfied.'

'What were you talking to the driver about at the back of the Land Rover?' asked Phil.

Shirley brought Amos his tea and he took a long time, adding sugar, stirring it and taking a sip, before answering.

'Look, young Phil – we don't know each other very well. I know we've been meeting every day for three years but we don't know much about each other. But, I've taken to you – I don't know why but I have. I like you, and your good lady here. Well, people who know me will tell you that if I like a person, that's it! I never let them down. I'm old now but I still have the same values as I did when I was a young man. Trust means a lot to me but it's a two-way thing. I'm not explaining myself very well because I'm an old Suffolk bumpkin but I can tell by the tone of your question that you think I might be playing some sort of double game here. I'm not! I was talking to the guard about the weather and the prospects for the harvest this year like I normally do. Before he was drafted in to do his military service, that young lad lived on a farm in Essex and we talk about farming – that's what farmers do! Mary would tell you that is all I did when I had other farmers to talk to! My point is, you're free to go if you think you're in danger here. You can have the food that I see you've both stuffed into your pockets and neither I, nor Mary, will tell a living soul that you've been here. But if you want to stay for a few hours or days even, until the search is called off, then you'll have to show some trust towards Mary and me.'

Phil stood up and walked round to where Amos was sitting. He held out his hand which Amos took.

'I've forgotten how to trust people in the last three years, Amos. I've been lied to so many times by so many people that it's going to be hard for me to get the habit back. I'm sorry I doubted you – forgive me, please. We only took the food because we thought you and Mary had gone off and left us and we would have to continue without your help. Where is she by the way?'

'She's at work. She'll be back by lunchtime.'

'Where does she work?'

'She cleans, up at the Big House – Nacton Manor.'

'Who lives there?'

'Sir Reginald and Lady Corcoran. It's not far – this is all their land round here.'

'Have they lived there long?' asked Phil.

'No, they bought it after all the trouble. We never did find out what happened to Lord and Lady Nacton – one day they were there and the next they were gone. The house and the land had been in their family for generations and then Corcoran came and all the trouble started. Land was compulsorily bought by the military and then bought back by Corcoran. You may not believe it but four years ago I was one of the richest men in Suffolk. Mary and I owned a farm – we had 200 acres of prime arable land and a dairy herd of a hundred cows. We'd worked bloody hard, the pair of us, for what we had but they took it all away. No compensation. At first I tried to get some explanations, but I gave up about twelve months ago – they just kept writing a load of legal bollocks to me. This used to be my cowman's cottage – we were evicted from our lovely farmhouse. It nearly broke Mary's heart. They said we could live here if we wanted and we came because we had nowhere else to go. We've no children so I'm not too worried about the money side of it but the unfairness of it still makes me angry.'

Amos looked down at the table.

'Have you ever met Sir Reginald?'

'No, and I don't bloody want to.'

'How did Mary get the job at the Manor?'

'They asked all the old staff to stay on and in our situation we couldn't afford to turn down the money – not that he pays very much! Mary has been working there for thirty years, off and on.

In the old days, Lord and Lady Nacton opened the house and grounds to the public for about nine months of the year. Mary was a guide for the organised tours. She didn't get paid – it gave her something to do for three mornings a week and she loved it! When Corcoran came, he offered her a job as a cleaner and, as I said, she took it because we needed the money.'

'She knows the house pretty well, then?' asked Shirley.

'She knows every nook and cranny, every priest's hole, every entrance, every exit and every secret staircase. She'll bore you to bloody death if you ask her about Nacton Manor. But listen, I've got some news for you. The town has erupted – there was a march down the main street the night before last and the guards and the marchers had a rare old battle. Lots of fights and looting – Archer's the tailors was completely destroyed and some place called the Report Centre was burned to the ground. The lad from Essex, whom I was telling you about, said the guards in the town were now on Code 7 Alert, which is the highest.'

Phil and Shirley reached for each other's hand and smiled.

'I think that may have been some friends of ours who were trying to cover our escape. Did your lad know of any casualties?'

'No but there must have been some,' replied Amos. 'The guards had guns and tanks – what did your friends have?'

'Nothing,' said Phil.

The three of them were silent for a few moments. Shirley thought of Margaret Hills, and Phil of Leroy Preston, Davie Lennox and Peter Jackson. Amos was turning his mind to how he could help these two young people to escape. The silence was interrupted by the door opening.

Mary stood in the kitchen, looking at the three of them. For the first time, Phil took a long hard look at her. Her short grey hair framed a face that had once been beautiful. She had bright blue eyes that had not faded with age and gave a hint of the beauty she had once been. But as she stood in the doorway, Phil noticed her mouth was set tight. This was a woman who had something serious to say!

'Amos, they've got to go – now! They're going berserk at the Manor trying to find these two. They called all the staff together this morning and told us that if any of us were caught helping or harbouring them we would be shot.'

'What did you tell them?' asked Amos.

'I didn't tell them anything.'

'Good – that gives us all time to work out what we're going to do. What's for lunch?'

Twenty-Six

Lunch – another stew – was a quiet affair. It was only after the meal that the talking began. Phil told his and Shirley's stories first. He told Amos and Mary everything from the Saturday when the Chaos started until they had seen the smoke the previous day. He left nothing out, apart from the details of his talk with Doreen Robson. Amos and Mary sat and listened without interrupting. It was Mary who spoke first.

'Amos, I'm ashamed of you. How could you think of throwing these two people out after what they've been through? Now get your brain in gear and work out a plan of escape for them both.'

Amos smiled wryly.

'I've been doing some thinking and—'

'It's not your husband's brain we need, Mary,' interrupted Phil. 'It's your memory.'

'My memory? What are you talking about?'

'We want to escape,' said Shirley, 'of course we do; but we want to try and put a stop to this mess once and for all. To do that, we need to confront Sir Reginald Corcoran and your husband says that you know more about his house than anyone else on earth. Will you help us get in there without being seen?'

'You're mad!' said Mary. 'Have you any idea of how difficult that would be?'

'No – but you would,' replied Shirley. 'We promise never to tell anyone where we got the information from – we could say that we had taken one of the tours in the old days when the Nactons opened the house to the public.'

'Whether you decide to help us or not, Mary,' said Phil, 'we are leaving tonight as soon as it's dark. We won't put you and Amos in any more danger; we're well fed and rested so there's no reason for us to delay our departure any longer than that.'

Mary looked at Phil and Shirley and then at her husband.

'Tell them they're mad, Amos. They shouldn't do this – tell

them to leave and get as far away as possible from here. It's too dangerous to go to the Manor.'

'I think they've made up their minds, my dear. If you help them they might have a faint chance of getting away with it – if you don't... well... they have no chance at all.'

'But the place is guarded day and night by guards with dogs who patrol the perimeter fence.'

'How far is the perimeter fence from the house?' asked Phil.

'About half a mile.'

'What about inside the fence – how many guards are there in that half a mile and the house itself?'

'None,' answered Mary.

Phil and Shirley smiled and Amos looked surprised.

'You can wipe that smile off your faces, you two. When I said "none" I meant that there were no military guards in there. Sir Reginald is determined to make life at the house as normal as possible and that would be impracticable with soldiers walking about all over the place. In the day there are about a hundred people working there – cleaners, cooks, valets, secretaries and office staff and the like – and at night there's a skeleton staff of about twenty. Nobody's ever made it through the perimeter fence and with all those people around I think the family feels completely safe. The point is that the night staff is not made up of locals, like those in the day. Sir Reginald brought all of them with him and I reckon that at least half of them are bodyguards and I wouldn't bet against some, if not all of them, being armed.'

'So,' said Shirley, 'all we have to do is get through the perimeter fence – which no one's done before – overpower the twenty armed bodyguards and then go and see Sir Reggie. I thought you said that it was going to be difficult, Mary!'

'I forgot to mention the alarm system,' said Mary. 'The house is alarmed with the latest technology and is wired straight through to Military Headquarters. I suppose if it's set off there would be hundreds of troops down there within about ten minutes.'

'Hm,' said Phil. 'Isn't there any good news, Mary?'

'Well, I can't help you with getting through the perimeter fence. I've only ever seen it when I pass through the gates in the morning to and from work. It's high, I can tell you that – about thirty feet – but I don't know whether it's electrified or not and I don't know anything about the guards and their patrols.'

'Never mind the fence,' interrupted Amos. 'I've got an idea about that. What about the house and the alarm system?'

'I know of a way into the house that has not been alarmed because only about three of us old locals know about it. It brings you into the old wine cellar and I know it isn't alarmed because I was down in the cellar doing some cleaning a couple of months ago and I had a look at the door; it hasn't been touched for years. I can also tell you everything you want to know about the interior of the house – secret staircases and priest's holes and such like – but I don't know what the night staff actually do or when, so you'll have to take care of them yourselves.'

'What do you think, Shirley – do you still want to give it a go or shall we try and get away from the whole bloody mess?'

'My head says we should leave now and head for the Outer Hebrides and try to disappear but my heart tells me we should go and confront this monster. He needs to be told about Geoff and the twins, and Rosie and your kids, and Karen and Edward, and Mandy – the list goes on! I want to spend the rest of my life with you – whether that's twenty-four hours or twenty-four years – but I remember something you said a couple of days ago. You said you were ashamed of sitting on your arse for three years and allowing all this to happen. I'm with you on that – I was a wife and a mother who did fuck all for three years after these bastards had killed my husband and my two lovely daughters. I don't think I could live for another twenty-four years knowing I could have done something but didn't.'

Phil was the first to speak after a long pause.

'Right – that's settled, then. We'd better split up – Shirley, you go with Mary and try to memorise everything about this bloody house and I'll get Amos to tell me about how we can get over this fence.'

'Under,' said Amos, 'not over – I suggest we try and get you under the bloody thing and I think I know just the place.'

'Oh, no,' said Shirley, 'not another fucking tunnel.'

'I'm afraid so, my dear, but I promise it won't be as long as the one you told us about earlier.'

'It had better not be or I might start packing now for a trip to that Scottish island.'

'Come on, Shirley,' said Mary, 'let's go into my bedroom. Amos has his old desk in there and I can start drawing you some maps of the house.'

The women left and Phil and Amos got together round the kitchen table.

'Now, young Phil, the first thing you have to realise is that all Corcoran's land was once nearly all my land, which I farmed for fifty years. I know every blade of grass, every furrow and every tree on it and every other bloody thing about it. I still walk the land even since Corcoran came. They don't mind – they think it's just daft old Amos remembering the good old days.

'Anyway, when they put their bloody fence up, they made sure that it was in open country so that it could be guarded easily but there's one place where that was impossible. The east side of the house is surrounded by forest and I suppose Corcoran didn't want to cut it all down because he thought it would be nice to have a genuine forest as part of his garden. So, the fence goes through that forest and some of it is pretty thick stuff, even in winter. I was down there the other day and there's an old dried-up riverbed, which the fence crosses. The riverbanks are bloody steep at that point so the fence has to bend a long way down to continue on its way. I wasn't interested in the fence when I was there – I was looking for a badger's sett that I saw a couple of months ago. Well, I didn't think about the fence being electrified, I put my shoulder against it to get a better look at the sett and I nearly pushed it over – it had hardly been buried in the ground at all! I think it would only take five minutes to dig a tunnel under there – even if the bloody thing is alarmed, it won't matter because you won't touch it.'

'What about the guards?' asked Phil.

'I don't know about them but it's a long way inside the forest – they probably never even go there.'

'OK – seems good enough to me. Now, you'll have to show me how to find this place.'

'No need – I'm coming with you.'

'Oh, no you're not, Amos – you've done more than enough for us already.'

'I'm coming with you and that's final – no argument! You'd

never find the spot in the dark whereas I could find it blindfolded. Also, you'll be using my spade. Where are you going to leave it after you've got through – somewhere those bastards can find it and trace it back to me? You fill in your side of the fence with your hands and I'll cover the hole at this side and even if the guards do come along later they won't know you've been through.'

That made sense to Phil – it might give them a couple of extra hours inside the fence without anyone knowing.

'There's also another reason,' said Amos.

'What's that?'

'I've sat on my arse for three years as well – I haven't enjoyed it. I'm old and I can't do much in the way of fighting back but I'm going to do what I can. Tonight might be my chance to start and I think I'm going to enjoy it.'

Meanwhile, in the bedroom, Shirley was being treated to a verbatim guided tour of Nacton House – the family home of the Earl of Nacton and his descendants for generations. Mary was well into her subject, in which she was an expert, and Shirley found a lot of it interesting but she knew that she must hurry her guide so they could proceed to the part which would be of help to her and Phil in the coming hours.

'You're very good, Mary, and I'd love to hear more about when the King came to stay in the original house in the early seventeenth century but... and I don't want to be rude... but time's getting on and I need to find out about the layout of the house.'

'God, you should have said something before – I'd forgotten what all this was about! I'd prattle on all day if nobody stopped me – now, where's a piece of paper and a pencil and let's get down to it! You've disappointed me, young Shirley – after hearing the way you talk since you came here, I'm wondering why you didn't say, "cut out the shite, Mary" earlier in your guided tour.'

Both women laughed as people do when they have found a kindred spirit and then got down to business.

'The original house was started in 1567 by a man called Robert Smythson who was one of the master masons employed by Sir John Thynne, who was the architect and the builder of Longleat

House in Wiltshire. Smythson incorporated a lot of Thynne's ideas but of course the house was on a much smaller scale and we've never been able to find out who he was building the house for. In the event, it was bought by the Earl of Nacton in 1580 and has been in the family ever since, until Corcoran bought it three years ago. Well, we presume he bought it – perhaps he just appropriated it like our farm! The house, like Longleat, faces south-east, in defiance of the common rule of the time that houses should face the opposite way. The Elizabethans detested the south wind: Shakespeare made Caliban curse Prospero in *The Tempest* with the words: "A south-west blow on ye, and blister ye all o'er".'

'Mary,' interrupted Shirley, 'you'll have to cut out the shite – we could be here for weeks at this rate!'

'Oh – I'm sorry! Right – last bit of history, which is relevant. Thynne and Smythson also ignored the tradition that the main rooms should face inwards towards a courtyard. Despite all the rebuilding over the years at Nacton Manor, this idea has been kept. So always remember that the main rooms all face outwards from the house – the inner rooms are used by the servants and the lowest of the low like me! I'll show you on this little map I've drawn.'

Mary placed her map in front of Shirley and for the next hour went through where all the stairs, cupboards, empty rooms, kitchens, wine cellars, drawing rooms, morning rooms, reception rooms, banqueting rooms, unused rooms and offices were. The woman's knowledge of the place was mind-boggling and Shirley soon realised that she wouldn't be able to commit all the information to memory, even if she stayed for a fortnight! But she also noticed something that was good news – at least half of the house wasn't used at all and another quarter was given over to offices. If she could try to remember the relevant parts, she might have a chance!

'Right, Mary – this is what I'm going to do. I'm going to copy out your map but I'm only going to fill in the bits we might need. Then, I'm going to try and do it again from memory and we'll see how they compare. OK? Then I want you to burn your map so nothing can be traced back to you.'

'Good idea,' said Mary. 'I'll go and put the kettle on and we can all have a cup of tea.'

Mary left the bedroom, went downstairs to join the men and Shirley started work.

'How are you two getting on?' asked Amos as Mary came into the kitchen.

'We've nearly finished – Shirley is just trying to commit it all to memory. How about you?'

'We've finished and we are all ready to go,' replied her husband.

'We?'

'I'm going with them to the fence. Don't say anything – I'm going and that's that. You stay here and I'll be back in an hour or so. I've sat on my arse too long and done nothing – I'm going to help these two youngsters. If you don't bloody like it, you can bloody well lump it!'

'At last, you've come to your senses. I would have been bloody annoyed if you hadn't offered to go with them. If I was twenty years younger, I'd take them into the house myself!'

Amos looked at Phil.

'Women!'

'I know what you mean,' said Phil.

The tea was made and they waited for Shirley. She arrived a few minutes later and passed the maps to Mary.

'That one was done as a copy of yours and that one was done from memory – you'd better check them and we can correct all the mistakes before Phil and I end up in an office which needs a password to let us out!'

Mary checked the maps in turn and only had to make two amendments on the last one.

'Did you do this last one from memory?'

'Yes.'

'Then, you never know – you might have a chance! You made two mistakes – this set of stairs from the kitchen only goes up one flight, not two, and this dressing room in the family's private quarters is connected to both bedrooms, not just the one on the right. You have a fine woman to help you, Phil – look after her.'

'I trained her very well,' answered Phil.

258

'Cut out the shite, Phil,' said Mary and the two women collapsed into hoots of laughter. Shirley was thinking of her recently lost friend, Karen, whilst taking comfort from her newly found friend, Mary. She guessed that Mary was worried about her husband joining these two insane people, while she herself was simply afraid.

It was Amos who broke the air of conviviality that had enveloped the kitchen.

'What about weapons – what have you got with you?'

'Nothing,' said Phil.

'You'll have to take something – what about the shotgun?'

'The last time I thought I was going to have to use that I nearly died myself! I don't want to kill anyone, Amos – I want people to accept the blame for their stupid fucking experiment and put everything back as it was. Anyway, it's your gun and it could be traced back to you – I don't want you on my conscience as well.'

'I've got a pistol that can't be traced back to me. I won it in a poker game at a hotel about twelve years ago. It was after the Suffolk Show up at Ipswich and a few of us were too drunk to drive home. We started playing cards and this silly bastard from Stowmarket kept on playing after his money ran out. I won the last hand, he couldn't pay his share of the pot and he asked to see me in private. We went to his room and he offered me his gun as full payment. I didn't know how much it was worth but I didn't want any trouble so I accepted. I was too pissed to ask him why he was carrying a loaded gun around Ipswich! It's been in my briefcase ever since – if you want it, you can have it.'

'Don't ask me, this time, Phil,' said Shirley. 'This is your decision and yours alone.'

Phil thought for a while and considered the alternatives. Almost immediately, he dismissed them all and said he would take the gun. Amos went upstairs and came down with what looked like a gun that Phil had seen cowboys carrying in western films.

'I haven't fired it but it's fully loaded so you've got six bullets. Do you want to try it outside to make sure it works?'

'I think I'd rather live in hope, Amos, and we could do without the arrival of a lorry-load of guards to find out what all the shooting is about.'

Mary burned her map and the one that Shirley had copied from it and handed the one done from memory to the younger woman. Shirley studied it again for a few moments and then put it in her trouser pocket.

'I see you retrieved your trousers from the dustbin,' said Mary. 'I thought you might like to change into a pair of mine – those look a bit scuffed now.'

'No thanks, these will do fine – they've brought me safely through "fire" and "water". It's "earth" tonight down your husband's tunnel. God knows when we'll meet "air" – perhaps we'll escape in a plane!'

The four of them busied themselves with preparations for the night's adventure. Amos explained the workings of the old gun to Phil – where the safety catch was and how it fired – and said that it was a myth that you could shoot someone with the intent to wound them.

'Point the bugger at their chest and pull the trigger. Don't start trying to hit them in the arm – by the time you've taken aim they'll have shot at you and you'll probably be dead!'

'I hope I don't have to use it, Amos,' said Phil, 'but, if I do I'll try to remember what you've said.'

Mary and Shirley went over the layout of the house once again without the aid of the map.

'Remember – that old entrance is on the north corner of the east wing and Amos is sending you in on the east side of the house so you won't have too far to go to find the door. The family apartments are on the front of the house so you might be able to make your way along the wall of the East Wing without being seen. The rooms facing out are all offices along there and they'll all be shut down by the time you get there. The old wine cellar will bring you out into the old kitchen – neither of them is used any more – so the first trouble you might come across is when you emerge into the corridor that links the old kitchen with the new offices. Good luck, my dear – you'll need it! Oh and one last thing: if you do get to meet Sir Reginald, don't call him "Reggie" like you did earlier. He hates it and it sends him into a rage that you wouldn't believe – he becomes a different person.'

'I'll remember that but he'd better not call me "Shirl" because I hate that as well!'

The weather was being kind to them – it was dry and the winter night came early to that part of Suffolk. There was no moon and here in the country there were no street lights to pierce the darkness. By six o'clock, they were ready.

Shirley kissed Mary on the cheek and thanked her for all her kindness to them and then she did the same to Amos because she thought there might not be time down by the fence. Phil shook the hands of both his hosts but couldn't find any words which would adequately describe his feelings for them. Amos said goodbye to Mary, said he would be back in about three hours and then they were off into the pitch-black night.

Amos picked up a spade from the yard and handed it to Phil to carry and led the way up to the lane. They walked along the muddy track until they came to a gate in the field on their left. Amos opened it and beckoned them through. Shirley shut the gate behind her, trying not to make any noise.

From that moment their journey was conducted entirely over fields and pastures. They kept to the sides of the hedgerows and, after about half an hour of walking, Phil knew that Amos had been right about one thing – they would never have found their way on their own! Phil was completely lost. They seemed to have doubled back on themselves about three times – he wouldn't have been at all surprised if, after the next corner, he found himself back in Victoria Way! He looked behind him to see if Shirley was all right and keeping up. She shrugged her shoulders – she was lost as well!

Ten minutes later, Amos stopped for the first time and waited for them to catch him up.

'I've brought us to here because I didn't want us to spend too much time in the forest – the leaves and branches on the ground make an unholy row and we don't want that! But we're near the fence now so take care!'

They entered the forest and tried to make as little noise as possible. They had gone about three hundred yards when they heard a noise. All three of them lay flat on the ground and listened. The noise was coming from their right – the opposite direction from where Amos had said the fence was. They waited, hardly daring to breathe. The noise got louder. Phil felt for the gun in his pocket. Amos saw the movement and shook his head.

The noise stopped and Amos looked around. He got to his feet and Phil and Shirley joined him.

'It must have been a fox or something. It certainly wasn't a guard – he'd have made a lot more noise than that. Come on, it's not far now.'

They walked on, taking greater care where they stepped, but it wasn't very far before Amos stopped them and pointed. There was the dried-up riverbed and, after negotiating the steep banks, they were soon standing at least twelve feet below the surface of the forest. After another few yards they saw the fence, which towered over everything apart from a few of the larger trees. As Mary had said, it was at least thirty feet high and impossible to climb without a set of ladders. Amos led them on until they came to the foot of the fence.

Phil began to dig. The earth was soft and, after ten minutes, he had dug a hole about two feet square down to a depth of three feet. He then began to dig sideways below the surface and under the fence. He took his coat off and got into a rhythm of working. Shirley and Amos stood and watched. In no time at all it seemed he was looking at them from the other side of the fence. It wasn't a tunnel as such that he had dug – just a small hole that went right under the huge obstacle in their path! Shirley hugged Amos for one last time and squirmed her way through the tunnel to join Phil on the other side.

Phil pushed the spade through the hole and Amos began to fill in his side. Shirley and Phil used their hands to try and disguise the hole on the inside. Their efforts would easily be seen in daylight but difficult to spot in the dark.

Phil and Shirley stood with their arms around each other and waved goodbye to Amos. The three people knew that this would probably be the last time they would see each other. Phil remembered the last time that he had seen Amos in such circumstances, with a fence between them. It was at the Border at dawn but this time there was a difference – Amos was smiling!

Twenty-Seven

Phil and Shirley turned away and made their way along the riverbed – Amos had suggested that they went right to its end. When they emerged they would be able to see Nacton Manor.

After a few minutes, Shirley asked Phil to stop.

'Why did you accept the gun? I was surprised.'

'So was I. But I've been thinking about it and now I'm glad I said yes. There are four bullets for anyone who gets in our way. I don't know whether I'll be able to shoot them but I'm going to have a damned good try!'

'That leaves two. What are they for?'

'You and me. If the worst comes to the worst, perhaps the only consolation we will have is that we can choose when, where and how we die.'

Shirley nodded. They didn't speak again until they reached the end of the riverbed. The old river didn't seem to go anywhere – it just came to a stop and presumably disappeared underground somewhere. They climbed a grassy bank and were able to look down at Nacton Manor.

The house had no 'back' to it. There was the south-facing front and an east wing and a west wing. The northern aspect was completely open to the surrounding countryside. The inner courtyard was gravelled, with an impressive fountain in the centre, but if all went to plan Phil and Shirley would have no need to go anywhere near that. They could see lights in the back of the west wing, which was the one furthest from them, but the facing east wing showed no lights at all. The magnificent-looking front of the house had lights on on the first floor. A car was parked by the front door.

There didn't seem to be any activity outside the house, which was only about four hundred yards away from them. The silence was eerie because of its totality. There was not a sound to be heard – even the birds seemed to have stopped singing.

'What do you think?' asked Shirley in a whisper.

'It looks just the way Mary said it would. No guards and no lights on the outside of the east wing. I say we make a run for it and head for halfway down that wing. Are you up for it?'

Shirley nodded to show she understood and they clambered out of the riverbed and began to run. They didn't care about the noise they made as they sprinted through the last few yards of forest. They were soon running on grass and downhill. Shirley slipped twice and Phil stopped to help her. Neither of them was really fit and their hearts were soon pumping as fast as their legs but they kept going and they eventually made it to the gravel that surrounded the whole house. They stopped and lay on the ground and then Phil motioned that they should get to the shelter of the house.

They tiptoed across the gravel and sat with their backs against the wall of the east wing of Nacton Manor. They sat, holding hands, in silence until their breathing returned to something which could be described as normal.

'So far so good,' said Phil.

'Too fucking good to be true, if you ask me.'

'What do you mean?'

'I can't believe this,' said Shirley. 'This is the house of the most hated man on God's Earth and yet we've managed to sit by his house. Christ, Phil, I'm a middle-aged mother of two and I don't think the SAS has been on the phone to you lately asking where your application is. There's something funny going on here and I don't like it. We're amateurs, Phil – how the hell did we get this far?'

'Luck?'

'Bollocks! Do you remember before all this started, when we had televisions and the like?'

'Yes. What's your point?'

'Every politician and head of state was always surrounded by hundreds of bodyguards and people like you and I couldn't get anywhere near them. Surely the protection would be even heavier since we now live in some sort of fascist state?'

'You heard what Mary said – Sir Reginald doesn't like having his family life disturbed by a heavy military presence.'

'That's crap as well and you know it! In his position what's the first thing you protect at all costs? Your family!'

'Perhaps the twenty people inside make him feel secure enough. What do you want to do – go back?'

'No – we're here now and we'll have to go on but I have a terrible feeling we're missing something. Call it woman's intuition if you like but, if we get into the house, I think we should be watching our backs all the time.'

Phil had every intention of watching their backs even before Shirley's little outburst but now he put his amateur, non-SAS mind on red-alert. He had learned to trust his companion's intuitions.

They made their way slowly along the wall until they reached the corner at the rear of the east wing. Phil looked round the corner and confirmed that there was no one in sight. They went round and came to the short flight of steps that led to the door that Mary had said was not connected to the alarm system.

Shirley pushed past Phil and descended the steps first. The door at the bottom was certainly old and Shirley turned the handle. The door opened easily and she stepped inside. Phil followed and shut the door behind him. There was no sound of any alarm going off. Shirley had the torch and she shone it around the room. It was just as Mary had said – an old wine cellar with lots of racks but no bottles. They made their way across the room, which was covered in cobwebs – Mary hadn't cleaned it very well – and came to another door. Dousing the torch, Shirley opened this one as well to reveal another abandoned room.

This one was obviously an old kitchen with work surfaces and butcher's blocks dotted around. A spiral staircase, at the far end, led up to another door. This room was full of cobwebs as well. They went up the staircase and Shirley turned off the torch and put it back in her pocket.

'According to the map, and Mary, from here on in is where it gets scary. We're on the ground floor now and this door leads to a corridor where all the offices are. There should be nobody working there but we'll need to be quiet. We turn left and the corridor will take us to the front of the house where Sir Reginald lives. Are you ready?'

'No. Move aside – I'm going first. Will there be any lights on?'

'There should be. Mary said there was a night light system all through the house.'

'Right then, here we go. Stay close.'

'I'll be so close, you'll think you've grown a second arse!'

They smiled at each other before Phil opened the door an inch. He looked out into the long corridor. Mary was right again.

Every five yards a dull light set into the right-hand wall gave enough light to see by. There was no one in sight.

Phil opened the door so that they could both squeeze through and they set off. All the doors were firmly closed. The house appeared deserted and it was not until they had gone about halfway that they heard a noise. It was a man's voice and was coming from one of the offices on their left.

'Look… I must go now… I'm late already… I'll see you at the Club tomorrow about one… All right… I'll get it sorted.'

The man was on the telephone but was leaving. Phil grabbed Shirley's hand, took a deep breath and yanked open the first door on his right that he came to.

'All right… Bye, Jeremy.'

There was no light at all in the room behind the door Phil and Shirley had entered and they stood holding each other, hardly daring to breathe. They heard the sound of a telephone being slammed down and then a door being opened and closed. A man's footsteps echoed down the corridor but away from them, towards the front of the house. Was it his car parked at the front?

Was the family now alone with its faithful bodyguards? Shirley switched on the torch and they saw that they were in a linen store. Racks full of tablecloths, napkins, pillowcases, sheets and towels lined the walls. They still didn't dare to move and it was only when they heard the distant sound of a car revving up and driving away that they relaxed.

'Jesus,' whispered Shirley, 'I can't take much more of this – I nearly wet myself then! Let's find him, shoot the bastard and bugger off!'

'We're nearly there, Shirl – we can't give up now.'

'What did you just call me?'

'Shirl.'

'Well, don't. I hate it – my name is Shirley. Right?'

'Sorry, Shirley. I'll remember in future.'

'That might not be too hard – I predict you've got a future life expectancy of about three minutes!'

'Oh God! Listen – do you want to go back?'

Shirley brushed away a tear and held Phil close.

'Don't take any notice of me – I'm terrified but we'll see this thing through to the end. Come on, Jeremy's friend has gone. Let's find Reggie.'

They slid out into the corridor again and found it as deserted as before. They continued until they emerged into a hallway. This was no corridor but a beautifully decorated passageway with paintings on the walls. They had reached the front of the house! Sculptures and bronzes were displayed on antique tables along the sides and a deep-piled red carpet ran along the centre of a mahogany parquet floor. The scenery may have changed but there were still no doors open. They walked along the carpet but took no notice of the works of art around them.

Suddenly they heard a soft humming noise. Phil looked around to see where it was coming from. Nothing seemed to have changed in the hallway – perhaps the noise was coming from behind one of the doors. Then he looked at the end of the hallway. A metal grille was slowly descending from the ceiling to the floor where they had entered from the office corridor. He turned frantically and saw the same sort of grille coming down at the far end of the hallway. He started to run back the way they had come.

'Run, Shirley – we're going to be trapped!'

They ran as fast as they could and Phil could have slid under the grille before it reached the floor but Shirley was three or four yards behind him and she would never have made it. Phil realised that if he had gone under they would have been on opposite sides of the barrier. He pulled up short and Shirley crashed into him. They fell in a heap against the grille which was now firmly embedded in the parquet floor.

'You could have made it, you daft sod,' said Shirley. 'I'm sorry I was so slow but it took me a couple of seconds to realise what was happening.'

'Forget it – I'm not so sure I would have made it anyway. Well, what happens now? Come on, stand up and make yourself look respectable – we might as well look our best for whatever fate awaits us.'

They stood and waited for no more than twenty seconds before they heard a disembodied voice speaking to them through an invisible loudspeaker.

'Welcome, Mr King and Mrs Tate. There is no chance of escape from where you are so please do not try anything. If you have any weapons concealed on your persons, please lay them on the floor now and move ten yards away along the hallway.'

Mr King and Mrs Tate did as they were told. Phil took the gun that Amos had given him out of his pocket and laid it on the carpet by the grille. They walked along the hallway and stood and waited for their next set of instructions.

'Thank you. Continue along the hallway and open the second door on your right. Wait in that room until I come to collect you.'

The room was a small sitting room with easy chairs and a coffee table. There were a few cheap prints of hunting scenes on the walls and a vase of plastic flowers on the mantlepiece but no other ornaments or photographs. The room was dowdy compared to the hallway.

Shirley sensed that Phil was not impressed.

'Remember Mary said that the inside rooms were for the servants.' She took the map she had made out of her pocket and had a quick look. 'This is a staff restroom – that's why it's furnished like 108 Victoria Way!'

'It's not that bad – but it's a bit of a disappointment after the hallway. You were right, weren't you, about this being a trap. I'm sorry – we should have gone to the Outer Hebrides.'

'We made the decision together to come here. Funnily enough, I've no regrets – I want to meet the devious bastard who thought all this up.'

'We may not.'

'Oh, I think we will. He wouldn't have let us get this close unless he wanted to meet us. He's probably as curious about us as we are about him!'

They sat down in a couple of the chairs and waited… and

waited… and waited. It was probably an hour before there was a polite knock on the door.

'Er… Come in,' shouted Phil, thinking that this seemed a very civilised imprisonment.

The door opened and a man entered Staff Restroom Number 7.

He was tall, clean-shaven, dark-haired, broad-shouldered and immaculately dressed in a dinner suit. He wore a white shirt, claret bow tie and highly polished black patent-leather shoes completed the ensemble. His face alone gave the game away – this was a man who knew how to look after himself! A flattened nose was above a mouth surrounded by very fat lips. His eyes were steely blue and cold. When he began to speak Phil recognised the accentless voice as the same as they had heard in the hallway.

'My name is Mr Pierce and I am here to conduct you to Sir Reginald Corcoran. He wishes you to join him in the Grand Salon for coffee. The family has finished dinner and is taking coffee there. However, I regret that you will need to be searched before I take you there.'

'You're not putting your dirty little hands all over me, Mr Pierce,' said Shirley.

'That will not be necessary, Mrs Tate – a female colleague of mine will be here in a moment to search you.'

On cue, the ugliest woman that Shirley had ever seen walked into the room. Fat, old and sweaty, the woman looked as though she had been in a traffic accident! Shirley knew she was being unkind but what did it matter any more?

'I take it all back, Mr Pierce – I think I'd rather have you than Dracula's mother here.'

Phil laughed and caught her mood.

'Let's swap – I've always liked ugly women.'

'Cheeky bastard,' said Shirley. 'Whoops darling – be careful with those fingers of yours. I wouldn't secrete anything there – it's too precious. But I doubt if you know that! Do you think this is Mrs Pierce, Phil?'

'Not a chance – I hope not anyway – because if she is he must be blind and we could have escaped when he came in!'

Mr Pierce and his colleague gave no intimation that they had heard this banter and went about their work of searching the prisoners in a very professional way. When they were satisfied that Phil and Shirley had no weapons, or anything else, hidden about their persons, 'Dracula's mother' left the room and closed the door behind her. Mr Pierce spoke again.

'Sir Reginald has ordered that you be handcuffed together by the wrist and the ankle as he doesn't wish to put his family in danger but he would like you to partake of coffee if you so desire. If you could put your left leg forward, Mr King, and then I can secure it to the right leg of Mrs Tate. Now your left wrist, Mr King – thank you – and your right, Mrs Tate. Good – thank you for your cooperation. Please wait here and I will go and ensure that Sir Reginald is ready for you.'

Mr Pierce exited the room and Phil and Shirley collapsed into howls of laughter.

'The last time I was like this,' said Phil, 'was when I was doing the three-legged race at Robin's sports day. "Would you like to partake of coffee, Mr King?"; "Thank you, Sir Reginald, I would. I'm glad I've got one hand free to hold my fucking cup but I would be grateful if you'd pour the fucking milk for me since my other hand seems to be incapacitated at the moment."'

'"Well, I would get up, Sir Reginald, and help myself to an after-dinner mint but it would mean my pulling my lover's fucking left leg off so I'll decline this time – but thanks for the offer!"'

'What on earth are these people like? They must think it's all some sort of computer game.'

'They're deranged,' said Shirley. 'They're all round the fucking twist.'

'Are you afraid?'

'Of what?'

'Anything, everything – what's going to happen?'

'No, I'm ready for anything – and everything – now!'

'You were terrified an hour ago.'

'That was before they shackled you to me and thus made sure that if we are going to live, we'll both live – and if we die... well, let's not think about that. I tell you what, why don't we give old Piercey a fright? You never know, he might even have a heart attack! We're chained together. Come on, lover – put your handcuff behind my neck and have your way with me. We've never done it in chains!'

Phil King sat there and looked at the woman beside him. What a life they could have had! He put his handcuffed arm behind her neck and kissed her with a passion that he didn't think he was capable of.

'I love you, Shirley Tate.'

'I love you, Philip King.'

They were interrupted by another polite knock on the door, but this time Mr Pierce didn't wait for an answer and walked straight in.

'Sir Reginald will see you now – please follow me.'

'You're a pain in the arse, Mr Pierce' said Shirley. 'I'm going to speak to Sir Reginald about you! You are very courteous and considerate but your timing is atrocious!'

Phil and Shirley followed Mr Pierce out into the ornate hallway and he led them away from the end where they had come in. They had difficulty at first walking with any kind of rhythm because of their ankles being tied together but they mastered it and came to a stop alongside Mr Pierce opposite a door in the left-hand wall.

Mr Pierce knocked and opened the door, ushering Phil and Shirley into the most beautifully decorated room that either of them had ever seen. The walls were crimson and adorned with large ancestral portraits. Ornate armchairs, upholstered in red silk, were grouped around an enormous low coffee table, the top of which was inlaid with ivory. Red velvet curtains covered four enormous windows. The ceiling was decorated with blue medallions and from it hung three huge chandeliers which lit the room to show it in all its glory. At one end was a fireplace in white marble and at the other a gallery overlooked the sumptuous scene.

Mr Pierce announced their arrival like an old-fashioned butler.

'Mr Philip King and Mrs Shirley Tate. I have taken the liberty of sending most of the staff to their quarters but three of us will be outside in the hallway if you need us and the grilles have been reset. The eagle is in the pavilion as usual.'

Mr Pierce exited and closed the door behind him. Phil took his eyes away from the grandeur around him and looked at the other occupants of the room. There were five – a man stood by the fireplace with his elbow resting on the mantelshelf whilst the other four were sat round the table. The man by the fire was unknown to him, as was a strikingly beautiful woman sitting nearest to him but he knew the other three people very well indeed.

Arabella Corcoran was dressed, as she had been for the dinner party at the Fairfaxes, in a simple black dress, which showed off her feminine charms. Next to her sat Amos, in a dinner suit with a brandy glass in one hand and a large cigar in the other. Mary, looking radiant in a dark-blue evening dress, sat opposite the other three, sipping coffee from a small china cup.

'Welcome to Nacton Manor,' said the man by the fire. 'I'm so glad we're able to meet at last. My name is Sir Reginald Corcoran.

'Some of the people here I think you know but I'm a stickler for formal introductions, so I'll do the honours. I suppose I'd better introduce our visitors first – Mr Philip King and Mrs Shirley Tate. This is my wife, Lady Miranda Corcoran.'

The beautiful lady, who was wearing a dark green, silk trouser suit, bowed her head to Phil and Shirley who nodded, not knowing what else to do. Phil thought 'bizarre' might describe what was going on but realised the word didn't come anywhere near portraying this utterly ludicrous pantomime!

Sir Reginald continued.

'This is my daughter, Arabella, whom I think you know, Philip, but she has never had the pleasure of meeting Mrs Tate until tonight.'

'I've heard a lot about you, Shirley – may I call you Shirley?'

'No,' replied Shirley, who could think of nothing else to say.

'Last, but by no means least, we come to the two people whom you have got to know very well over the last two days – Amos and Mary. However, as I said, I like the little formalities in life and thus I shall give you their full names and titles. The man you know as Amos is none other than the Right Honourable Arthur Michael Oliver Stephen Fitzlander – the nineteenth Earl of Nacton and 147th in line as heir to the throne of England! His wife, Mary, who is in fact the sister of my own lovely wife, should have the full title of Lady Mary Davina Constance Nacton.'

.

Twenty-Eight

Sir Reginald Corcoran was of average height and build – in fact everything about him was average. Phil didn't know what he was expecting the great man to look like but this wasn't it. He looked elegant in his tailored dinner suit but the man hadn't the figure to go with the elegance. He had a beer belly that protruded over the top of his cummerbund and his bandy legs must have given his tailor an enormous amount of trouble during the fittings for the suit. His face was a perfect circle and showed a thin mouth, a long, pointed nose and a pair of blue eyes that seemed to work independently of each other. He was a man who had gained his position because of either family connections or a superior intellect to those around him – he certainly had not attained it because of his looks! Perhaps the one thing that was striking about him was his blonde hair, which he wore long – it cascaded down over the collar of his dinner jacket like a waterfall.

'Please sit down and help yourselves to coffee,' said Sir Reginald, 'and then we can talk.'

Phil and Shirley were still in shock after learning of the true identities of Amos and Mary and remained where they were.

'I don't want any of your coffee,' said Phil. 'I'm tired of all your games – let Mr Pierce take us away, lock us up and shoot us.'

'Don't be a sore loser, Philip,' said Arabella. 'Come and have some coffee. We have been noting your progress in the escape attempt – you both did very well, by the way – but we would still like to learn a few things from you.'

'I don't want to play any more. We lost, you won – checkmate! Let's all go home.'

'Come, come, dear boy,' said Lord Nacton, who had lost his Suffolk accent and now spoke like a peer of the realm. 'We really would like to have a little chat and find out where we can improve the security around the town and the Manor.'

'You want me to sit down and help you see where you can

make improvements to security – is that right?' Phil shook his head in disbelief.

'You can either do it here in these fabulous surroundings and amongst agreeable company or we will hand you over to the military and they will extract the information from you by whichever means are necessary.' Arabella had reverted to her 'Miss Jeffers' persona with a brusque tone to match.

'Agreeable company? I don't see any of that – except the woman standing beside me. As for the rest of you – well, it's a toss-up as to who is the biggest bastard! Lovable old Amos over there, who gives long speeches about trust and then lies through his aristocratic teeth for two days had better not come too near me because he might find that cigar in a different orifice to his mouth!

'The only words to describe his fellow actor Lady Mary would be "lying bitch". You, Jeffers, lie and cheat your way through life for a living and then treat it as one big joke. Your father has so much blood on his hands that we can probably put him in the same category as Pol Pot and Adolf Hitler! I don't know your mother but considering who she's got round her as family role models, I don't give much for her chances of having led a blameless life! I'd rather spend the night being tortured by the guards than sit around drinking coffee with a bunch of ghouls like you!'

'It's not entirely your decision, though, is it?' said Sir Reginald. 'We haven't heard from Mrs Tate yet what she thinks.'

Shirley looked around her and then whispered something in Phil's ear. Phil nodded his agreement and at last Shirley Tate spoke at length for the first time since entering the room.

'What do I think? Well, Sir Reginald Corcoran, I think you have a lovely house. You and your good lady wife should be very proud of it. I was thinking of having my outside toilet done in this very shade of red, Lady Corcoran, but decided against it in the end. I went for the modern look of unpainted railway sleepers – they're all the rage now, you know. I love the ancestral portraits as well – they add so much gravitas to a room such as this. I presume they are all originals. I only have prints at home but they do hide the holes in the walls so elegantly. Do you have holes in your walls, Lady Corcoran, made by stray tank shells?'

'I don't think I understood your answer, Mrs Tate,' said Sir Reginald. 'Do you want to stay here and talk to us or go with Mr King and take your chances with the guards?'

'We're both staying here, Sir Reginald. My partner and I have agreed, we don't really want to speak to you but I am desperate for a cup of coffee. Come on, Phil, pick up your left leg – let's "partake" of a cup or two.'

They struggled over to a pair of chairs by the table and sat down, knowing that they had agreed they would have no chance if they went with the guards. Here? Never say never! Lady Corcoran poured the coffee from a silver Georgian pot into two small cups. Phil took a sip and found it was hardly even warm.

Shirley took a huge gulp, half stood and spat the contents of her mouth all over Lady Nacton. She caught her full in the face and the coffee ran in rivulets down on to her beautiful dress. Mary shrieked and extracted a white silk handkerchief from her left sleeve.

'You stupid, filthy, disgusting bitch!' shouted Mary, as she tried to wipe away the stains from her dress and dry her face.

'You deserved that for the way you lied the last two days and I was determined to show you what I felt about you! Right, Sir Reginald, my little outburst is over – you may begin your questioning. My partner and I are all ears.'

'I demand an apology, Reginald,' said Mary. 'The woman is mad.'

'Calm down, Mary – it was only lukewarm coffee. Our talk with these two could prove very helpful – sit down and compose yourself.'

'One thing before we start,' said Phil. 'I'd like to know how you knew we'd go to the cottage and why Amos and Mary were waiting for us.'

'I don't see any harm in telling them that, Reginald,' said Amos. 'It's not as though they're going to be able to tell anybody, are they?'

Phil and Shirley both realised the significance of that comment! This was the end – after the coffee and the talk there was only death.

'I suppose so. You tell the story, old Amos,' said Sir Reginald with a laugh in his voice. 'You do the accent so well – doesn't he, Mr King?'

Phil grunted and Shirley smiled.

'There was nothing really sinister about it,' began Lord Nacton in his normal voice. 'When the town was sealed off, we knew that Reginald would want somewhere to live and use as his headquarters, and Mary and I were getting old and the estate is a hell of a big thing to run. We all came to an agreement – quite amicably – that they would move in here and we would go and live in my old estate manager's house. Then the decision was taken to bulldoze all the properties on the estate, except that one, which would make it much easier to guard. There was no problem about the workers – they could be sent to live in the surrounding villages and bussed in everyday. So that was what was done but unfortunately the guard charged with the job of demolishing the properties got his geography wrong. He knocked down the estate manager's house as well and all we were left with was that old gamekeeper's cottage. There was hell to pay, of course – I think the guard was shot – but Mary and I went down to have a look and decided to give it a go. Grandeur palls after you've lived in it for seventy years, Mr King, and Mary and I have been very happy down there. We take most of our meals up here, at the Manor, and we still see our old friends when they come to call on Reginald.

'When we had word that you had actually managed to escape from the docks, we asked Reginald for permission to play the roles we did when you arrived. We didn't know you would turn up at the cottage – you could have just carried on with your escape attempt – but we thought you would be tired and hungry and you might just call in to see if anybody would help you. I thought we were very convincing, although I say it myself, and it was good fun!'

'I still don't understand how you were "Amos" at the Border for three years,' said Phil.

'Another bit of fun, old boy. I didn't want to go down to the cottage and vegetate. I've always been an early riser and when they wanted someone to go and impersonate an old Suffolk peasant, I volunteered. I didn't grow any of the rubbish I supplied to you – that was all the crap that the military didn't want. They'd load it on to the trailer and pick me up at the end of the lane and drop me back either there or somewhere on the estate from where I could walk home. It kept me fit and I enjoyed it, except when it was really cold and then I'd come straight up here to the Manor and get Cook to do me a full English breakfast.'

'I'm glad you enjoyed yourself,' said Phil. 'I suppose you must have got an enormous amount of fun out it – taking the piss out of me for three years!'

'Oh, Phil,' said Shirley, 'don't be so ungracious. The old fart was only carrying on doing what he and his kind have been doing for centuries. He didn't know any better – he was taught to treat the common people like shit at school!'

'I resent that remark, young lady. It was a bit of fun!'

'My husband has never done any harm to anyone,' interrupted Mary. 'It was a lark!'

'Sir Reginald, I thought you had some questions to ask Phil and me. I think we should proceed, don't you? There is one proviso, though – if that cow Lady Nacton opens her big mouth just once more it won't be coffee she gets in her ugly face, it'll be the fucking cup!'

'Mrs Tate, please moderate your language – there are ladies present,' said Sir Reginald.

Phil King started to laugh and couldn't stop.

'Have I said something funny, Mr King?'

Phil wiped the tears from his eyes with his sleeve.

'No, it wasn't funny – but it was pretty bloody stupid, even for you. Go on ask your questions.'

It was Arabella who spoke first.

'When you were in the storm drain, how near were you to drowning when we turned the water on?'

'I'll answer that one, Phil,' said Shirley. 'I don't think black suits your colouring, dear – I would go more towards a cream if I were you. Yes, a cream with a slight pattern on it – vomit, I think it's called. It's going to be very popular this year during the season. Now, the question – how near to drowning were we? We never had the slightest problem in the drain, dear, did we, Philip?'

'No.'

'There you are – next question, please.'

'I don't believe you,' said Arabella.

'I don't really give a monkey's fuck whether you believe me or not, my dear.'

Shirley's voice was getting posher and posher as she spoke and Phil realised she was trying to score points, make these people angry and give them both some time to see if there was a way out. The trouble was that Phil had no ideas about a possible escape. They were chained together, there were three guards outside in the hallway and 'the eagle was in the pavilion as usual' – whatever that meant! He needed time to think.

'Can we have some more coffee, Sir Reginald?' asked Phil. 'This appears to be cold.'

'Certainly. I'll call Pierce.' Sir Reginald pulled on a rope by the side of the fireplace and Mr Pierce appeared in less than three seconds, his right hand inside his jacket pocket. At least we now know where Pierce keeps his gun, thought Phil. The coffee was brought and poured and Sir Reginald asked the next question.

'Why did you leave the body of Karen Markham in the dock area – why didn't you take it with you back down the storm drain?'

Phil sensed Shirley beside him preparing to explode.

'I'll answer that one, Sir Reginald – if you don't mind.' Phil paused and just hoped that Shirley would quickly regain her composure. 'There are three reasons for our action on that occasion. Firstly, it was Karen's dying wish that she be left to die under God's glorious night sky. She was an outdoor girl – did you know that? She was outside on the day her brother died when he was shot dead by one of your tanks. He was nine years old but he'd had a good life! He died outside, as well – in her arms! Secondly, we didn't like to move the body because we knew you would have to do forensic tests and have an autopsy in order to help you catch the killer. Thirdly, we were scared shitless. I notice your wife hasn't spoken yet, Sir Reginald – I wonder if I might ask her whether she's ever been as frightened as we were the other night.'

'No, you may not ask my wife anything. You should go to bed, my dear. I don't think you should listen to the rest of this discussion.'

'I'm staying.' Lady Corcoran was younger than her husband, but not by much. He was probably in his early sixties and she in her late fifties but she was a very beautiful woman still. She outshone her older sister and even her daughter looked a little plain beside her. She sat back in her chair and like the others waited for the next question to be asked.

It was Arabella again.

'I'm curious to know why you made the attempt to escape now. Why didn't you try in the previous three years?'

'Bureaucracy,' said Shirley.

'What do you mean "bureaucracy"?' asked Sir Reginald. 'You don't have to have your papers stamped to try to escape.'

'No, not yet anyway, Sir Reginald, but you have to ask stupid questions to stupid officials and wait a very long time for even stupider answers to come back when you are trying to find out what happened to your loved ones. At one point, Phil and I were contemplating going to the Citizens Advice Bureau to see if they could help but then we remembered that you burned that down in the first week. We tried a solicitor, Gerald Fairfax, but he turned out to be a twat so we just kept knocking on doors and getting the same unhelpful replies from those very stupid officials of yours. It took us three years to realise we would have to come and ask you yourself what had happened to Geoff, Rosie, Robin and Deborah. So here we are! But, before you try and answer, there's no need to worry yourself about the fate of my twin girls. I saw them die! I couldn't bury them of course because there was nothing left to bury but I trust they are at peace.'

There was an uneasy silence in the room before Lord Nacton spoke.

'There are bound to be some casualties in a war, my dear – it's inevitable. Even Sir Reginald and Lady Corcoran have suffered the loss of their only son – it's not been easy for any of us.'

'You are an obnoxious, stupid, unfeeling bastard, Amos,' said Phil. 'Charles Corcoran was in his twenties and knew exactly what he was doing, playing at spying so he could impress his daddy. He got caught and suffered the consequences of his actions. Shirley's twins were seven years old! They'd just learned to ride their new bikes! They burned to fucking death in their own house, where kids are always told they should feel safe. They weren't "casualties of war", you daft sod – they were innocent children!'

Lady Corcoran began to cry, but Phil couldn't work out whether it was for the loss of Charles or a reaction to the story of Shirley's tragedy.

'Oh, shut up, Mummy,' said Arabella. 'Lots of people have died during the experiment but not as many as people would have you believe. Charles was a fool and he was careless.'

Lady Corcoran regained her composure and wiped away her tears.

'That's a nice phrase,' said Shirley. '"Shut up, Mummy" – I'd liked to have had someone to say that to me in the years to come.'

Phil sensed that Shirley was getting upset at this point and decided to change the subject, but Arabella spoke again and did his work for him.

'I think it's pointless going on with this, Daddy. They're not going to tell us anything of use. I think we should call Pierce and send them to their fate.'

'Will there be a trial?' asked Phil.

'There's no need. You're both guilty of escaping from the town – that's an offence punishable by death. Don't worry – it'll be quick and painless.'

'We're pleased to hear that, Arabella. Aren't we, Shirley?'

'We're both very grateful, Miss Corcoran – I hope yours is slow and full of fucking pain when it comes.'

'However,' said Phil, 'before that happens, I have a question for you, Sir Reginald – a sort of last request from the condemned man. I've never had a satisfactory answer to the question. General Turner, Emily Fairfax and her husband, and your son and daughter have all told me little snippets but I still don't understand. I'm told you were the man who organised this "experiment" so I'm hoping you can give me the definitive answer to my question. You see, I understand "when?" and "where?" and "how?". I understand who the subjects of the experiment were and who the perpetrators were. But I still don't understand why. I can't work out why you started it and I certainly can't see why you're continuing. So, just let me die a happy man – or at least a man not haunted by this nagging question. Why?'

Sir Reginald puffed out his chest and stood up straight. This was a man who had been asked to lecture on his favourite topic and he wasn't going to let the opportunity pass. He collected his thoughts while he strolled back and forth across the front of the fireplace and then he turned, looked straight at Phil and began.

'The answer is very simple, Mr King. I can even give it to you in one word – although I will elaborate to help you understand.'

I bet you will, thought Phil, but that was part of his plan – to give him time to think of a way out of his and Shirley's worsening position.

'The answer is: money.'

Twenty-Nine

'This experiment is worth millions, if not billions, of pounds to this country. Let me explain that statement to you. All governments in the world, and it doesn't matter where they are in the political rainbow, have an agenda – a set of policies that they want to put into practice. Communists, fascists, conservatives, socialists and liberals all publish their manifestos before an election – if they have one – and hope their electorate will vote for them on the basis of those policies. We all know that's not strictly true because people vote for personalities as much as policies and they work out who they can trust and who they can't, but politicians still cling to the old view that it's policies that matter.

'So, before an election, they try to work out what will appeal to the people and put it in their manifesto. They get the party workers to go round, knock on doors and ask the people what they would vote for. We also know that not everything that's in a manifesto becomes law because the party, any party, finds, when or if they achieve power, that a particular policy is too costly to implement or, more often than not, they find that the party workers got the mood of the country wrong. These policies are lost under mountains of paperwork and never see the light of day again!

'But what about the policies that are brought into effect that were never in a party's manifesto? Where was the research done for them? I'll give you an excellent example. In 1997, when the first New Labour government came to power – the very next morning after the election result was known – the new Chancellor of the Exchequer, Gordon Brown, said that he was going to transfer the power to set interest rates to the Bank of England. The Treasury would set the overall guidelines but it would be up to the Bank to set the actual rates. Now, where did this policy come from? It certainly wasn't in New Labour's manifesto and the party workers had never mentioned it on all the doorsteps they had visited. How did New Labour know that the people would accept this change? And why did they implement the new policy so soon after the election?

'They brought the policy in quickly because they knew that it would show the party to be dynamic and ready for change. As regards whether the people would accept the change, they knew that the electorate couldn't have cared less! All the man in the street was interested in was whether he could afford his mortgage – who set the interest rate was of no consequence to him whatsoever! The policy was implemented and nobody uttered a word of protest. But where did Gordon Brown and Tony Blair get the information from that, right from the start, the people would accept the change? Was it a gamble that paid off handsomely or was it part of a well thought-out plan?

'It was no gamble! Gordon Brown spent the previous two years visiting the countries that already used the system and looked at their statistics and surveys and found to his delight that they all said the same thing. The system worked well – if the system was a success then the Chancellor would be congratulated on his foresight and if it went wrong then the Bank of England could be blamed. No wonder he jumped at the chance to implement the policy at the earliest opportunity!

'But his visits came at a price! Don't get me wrong – no money was passed under the table in brown paper bags – but in the next few years this information would have had to be paid for. It may have been in the form of export credits; an arms deal; a diplomatic scandal hushed up; a loan to a foreign businessman to help him set up in the UK; an alliance against another country or even something as simple as arranging an audience with the Queen. But our government paid for the information it had received and before we came to power we knew that foreign governments would pay us in the same way if only we could ascertain what it was they needed to know.

'The Right Alliance sent out a working party to talk to governments around the world to find out what it was they needed. I was a member of that group and we went to over thirty countries before we found what we were looking for. I remember the day very well – it was sunny and warm and we were talking to a Spanish politician in a location overlooking the Mediterranean. We talked about what governments knew and didn't know about their peoples. I remember the man's name was Raoul – I never knew his last name or if I did I've forgotten it – but he was the one who put the idea into my head.

'He said that a government, any government, needed to know the depths of privation that their people would be willing to withstand before they rebelled en masse. He said that he was not talking about taxes or short-term food shortages and things like that but murder, mayhem, martial law and chaos over a long period of time. He also said that there couldn't be any levels of deprivation like there was in Nazi Germany, with one set of people lording it over another set of people – i.e. Aryans and Jews – everyone had to be in the same boat! In addition, the people must know that what was being done was in the name of the elected government of the country – it was no use having them think they were freedom fighters! Raoul said the Russians and Chinese had probably tried to do something along these lines in their hard line communist days – but the systems were too large and nobody had bothered to find out whether they worked and if not, why not? He said that governments would pay the earth to get the results of a properly controlled experiment.

'So, there you have it. We came back from Spain and talked to 555 and they readily agreed to help us set the whole thing up. I offered the town as a venue because I could see the possibilities of closing the whole place off. The offer was accepted and I think we've done very well – the whole place is carefully monitored on a day to day basis and in two years' time we will be able to present the results of our five-year experiment.

'There are already 132 governments around the world who have shown an interest in seeing our findings and I have no doubt that our Prime Minister will ensure that we get paid handsomely for all the trouble we've gone to. Does that answer your question of why, Mr King?'

Phil King didn't know whether to laugh, cry or just try to kick the supercilious Sir Reginald in the balls. Was that it? Was that why Rosie and the kids had died – so the government could earn some foreign currency?

'Yes, it does,' said Phil. 'It makes me madder than I've ever been before in my life but it does answer the question!'

'Good – I'm glad you understood.'

It was while Phil was nearly retching with his anger that he thought of a possible way out. He leaned over to Shirley and whispered in her ear, 'Ask to go for a pee but make sure the female guard doesn't come back with you. We'll play it by ear after that, OK?'

Shirley nodded and then spoke.

'Sir Reginald, I'm very sorry, but I'm sure your wife will understand. I must go for a pee – all that coffee, you know? Could you call Mr Pierce and get him to unshackle me?'

'I don't think that would be a wise move, Daddy,' said Arabella. 'They're much safer when they're tied together.'

'I'm not going for a piss tied to him – I mean, I like him and we have been intimate in the last couple of weeks but I don't do water sports, Arabella. Is that your fetish, dear? I should have guessed! Hurry up, Sir Reginald, I'm bursting – call Mr Pierce before I give your daughter a thrill by peeing all over your lovely Persian rug!'

'You're disgusting,' replied Arabella, as her father pulled the rope to summon Pierce.

Pierce appeared after only two seconds this time.

'Unshackle them, Mr Pierce – Mrs Tate wants to go to the toilet. Make sure there is a female guard with her at all times.'

Mr Pierce did as ordered, grabbed Shirley's arm and frogmarched her out of the room.

Shirley rubbed her arms and legs to get the circulation in her body going again after sitting down for so long and then her heart sank. The fat and unfit female guard must have gone to bed and Mr Pierce passed her into the custody of a fit-looking young blonde woman who placed a grip like iron on her arm. They walked together down the hallway and stopped in front of an unmarked door. The guard took a large key from her pocket and unlocked the door, leaving the key in the lock. Shirley had never seen a ladies toilet like this in her life! All the fittings were in pink marble and the taps were gold. Fresh flowers adorned the tables and chairs which were dotted round the room and there were bottles of water and crystal glasses for those who were thirsty.

On the far wall were seven cubicles, each with the door open. The toilet bowls were also in pink with the old-fashioned cistern high on the wall and each had a gold chain! Now what? thought Shirley. The walls of each cubicle seemed to be made of solid wood and the doors reached from the floor to very near the ceiling.

The guard motioned to Shirley that she should do what she needed to do and Shirley went into the middle one of the seven cubicles. She locked the door and sat down still fully clothed.

'There's no paper,' she shouted and unlocked the door.

The guard's hand came round the door with a roll of toilet paper in it and Shirley took the one chance she would probably get.

She grabbed the guard's wrist and pulled with all the strength she could muster. The guard came into the cubicle and Shirley swung her round and slammed the woman into the back wall. The woman's head hit the pink marble with a sickening crack and she slumped unconscious to the floor.

Shirley didn't bother to look whether she was still breathing or not – she hadn't time! She unhooked the chain from the cistern and fastened it tight round the woman's neck. She dragged the body to the door, slid the bolt across and hooked the chain to it. She found the toilet roll and began stuffing as much as she could into the guard's mouth. She hadn't got anything to tie the woman's hands but she reckoned she'd have enough problems if she ever came round!

Shirley Tate then did the hardest piece of exercise she'd ever done in her life: she stood on the toilet bowl, pulled herself up to the top of the cubicle and crawled along, first to the left and then back to the right, closing all the other doors and locking them, which she could just manage to do without getting down into each cubicle. Having finished, she dropped to the floor, exhausted, and took a long drink out of one of the water bottles. Hoping she had immobilised one of the guards and given her and Phil some time, she looked at herself in one of the large ornate mirrors.

'That was for the twins,' she said and winked at her reflection.

She walked into the hallway and stood in front of the door – Mr Pierce was twenty yards away in the direction they had come. Shirley carefully locked the door behind her back; put the key in her pocket and walked towards Mr Pierce.

'She said she wanted one as well – she said she won't be long.'

Mr Pierce nodded and ushered her back into the Grand Salon.

'Welcome back, Mrs Tate,' said Sir Reginald. 'You've not missed anything of importance. Mr King and I were discussing some of the details of the occupation of the town – I'm afraid he regards them as rather harsher than was necessary but we have agreed to disagree, if you know what I mean.'

Shirley leaned over to Phil and whispered, 'One down, two to go – but I don't think we've got much time. I didn't see the other guard!'

Phil King stood up, walked over to the fireplace looking as though he was deep in thought.

'I suppose that's it, then – you call Mr Pierce and Shirley and I go to face the firing squad like a good little girl and boy! Pity really; I was going to put a theory of mine to you that I think you might have enjoyed. Well, never mind – another day, perhaps?'

Phil sprang and was behind the chair of Lady Corcoran in an instant. He grabbed her neck with both his arms and held on tight.

'But we're not going without a fight – if you go anywhere near that rope, Reggie, to call Pierce, I'll break your wife's pretty little neck. And don't think I won't – I've nothing to lose now. Shirley, get something to tie them up with.'

'Like what?'

'I don't know – use the cords off the curtains or something. Tie Reggie in a chair first.'

Shirley went to work and began running around like a madwoman, pulling lengths of cords off curtains and drapes. She tied Sir Reginald in a chair and then went to work on the others while all the time Phil was holding Lady Corcoran. In a way he felt sorry for her because out of the five people here she had done the least to harm them, but his and Shirley's situation was desperate.

288

'You're mad,' said Lord Nacton. 'There's no way you can get out of this room even – let alone the house! We've treated the pair of you civilly – you're only making it worse for yourselves.'

'How can it be any worse, you daft old sod?'

'Well... What I mean is... Reginald tell them – they haven't got a chance.'

Sir Reginald Corcoran was not listening to any of this – he was staring at his wife, who was being half-choked by Phil's grip.

'Let go of my wife, Mr King, please! She's not a well woman at the best of times and I fear you could harm her if you continue.'

'You tell your daughter to stop pissing about while Shirley's trying to tie her up and I'll relax the grip.'

'Arabella, think of Mummy – stop it. If we stay calm, I'm sure we can all come out of this alive.'

'It's so degrading, Daddy. I shall never live this down if anyone gets to hear of it – and to be tied up by this whore!'

Shirley readjusted the rope around Arabella and pulled it as tight as she could. Arabella winced with pain.

'You're in no position to start calling me names, young lady. Shut your fat mouth and think of your mummy!'

Eventually, all five of them were tied to their chairs and Phil scratched his head – he hadn't got a clue as to what to do next!

'Well, young man – what happens now?' It was Lady Corcoran who had spoken, after recovering from a coughing fit that had happened when Phil released her. 'As soon as Mr Pierce finds out that something is wrong, he'll be in here and you two will be dead. How are you going to escape from this room? You'll have to be quick but Mr Pierce is in the hallway and there are no other exits. What are you going to do?'

'Mummy,' said Arabella, 'shut up – you sound as if you want to help them.'

'Do I? Good – because that is exactly what I want to do. I've never liked your experiment, Reginald, and after what Mary told me at dinner tonight about what these two young people have been through I now detest the bloody thing! I know you say that only 500 have been killed but that is 500 too many. Did you listen to their stories? It's an abomination that such things could go on in this country. I'm changing sides – I'm with them!'

'You stupid woman!' shouted Arabella.

'Stupid I may be, but thank God I'm not a cruel bitch like you. There is another reason for my change of mind as well as being against the experiment. I want to be on the same side as Mrs Tate, who is the first woman to get the better of you. I will always love you, Arabella, because you are my daughter and I bore you for nine months and gave birth to you, but I don't like you and haven't done for a good few years. You are a cruel, heartless… er, what's the word I'm looking for, Mrs Tate?'

'Cow.'

'Thank you – you are a cruel, heartless cow and when this is all over tonight – whatever happens – I don't want to see you again, ever!'

'Well said, Lady Corcoran,' shouted Phil, 'but I'm going to leave you tied to the chair because we've heard it all before and whoever has said it has been lying. But what the hell do we do now?'

'Miranda,' said Sir Reginald, 'you should have told me you felt like this.'

'What good would it have done? All you and your daughter think about is your bloody experiment.'

'Shut up all of you,' said Phil. 'I'm trying to think.'

'Too late for that now, old boy—' said Lord Nacton but he was stopped in mid-sentence by the glare he got from Phil.

But the situation was taken out of their hands in the next second as Mr Pierce burst into the room brandishing a gun. Quickly, he took in the scene and aimed the gun at Phil.

'The female guard is dead, Sir Reginald – we've just found her body in the women's toilet.'

All eyes turned towards Shirley.

'Don't look at me – she was having a pee when I left.'

Nobody was convinced.

'What do you want me to do, Sir Reginald?' asked Pierce.

'Untie me first and if either of the prisoners moves shoot them both!'

Pierce went over to Sir Reginald and Phil noticed for the first time that he was holding the old cowboy gun that Amos had given him. Obviously, Mr Pierce fancied himself as John Wayne or

Clint Eastwood! Now was the time, whilst Pierce was trying to untie the cord around Sir Reginald's chair, thought Phil, and he flung himself at the butler-cum-bodyguard.

The element of surprise helped but he was no match for the younger man, who threw off the tackle in an instant, leaving Phil crouched on his knees on the floor. Pierce brought the gun round and aimed straight at Phil's forehead.

'You can't!' screamed Shirley.

'No, Reginald – not in here,' shouted Lady Corcoran.

The other people in the room seemed too shocked and they just sat and watched. Sir Reginald, still trussed in his chair, gave a thin smile and said in a very quiet voice, 'Kill him.'

Phil looked up at Shirley and they exchanged glances before Phil looked back at the barrel of the old Colt .45 and closed his eyes.

There was an enormous explosion and everyone started to scream and shout. Phil realised he was still alive and looked around. There was blood everywhere – on Sir Reginald and on one of the portraits hanging to the side of the fireplace. Pierce was on the floor, moaning, with half his right arm blown off. Arabella was screaming the loudest – perhaps she hadn't seen violence at such close quarters before – and Shirley slapped her face to shut her up. Phil knelt down and had a look at Mr Pierce. The gun must have exploded and it had caught him in the arm and the face. He was a sorry sight and wasn't making a sound. Blood was gurgling in his mouth and he died as Phil tried to lift his head.

'Bloody hell!' said Lord Nacton.

'You can say that again, Amos – one hell of a prize in a poker game, wasn't it? Come on, Shirley, let's find the other guard.' He reached into Pierce's pocket, extracted the man's real gun and slipped it into his own.

'You won't have to go far, Mr King, to find the other guard,' said Sir Reginald with a sneer in his voice.

Phil and Shirley followed his eyes up to the gallery and saw a guard with an automatic rifle surveying the scene.

'Shit,' said Phil.

'I couldn't have put it better myself, Mr King,' echoed Shirley.

Thirty

The man stood motionless and said nothing. He looked at Pierce on the floor and then cast his eyes around the room. There were five people tied in their chairs and a man and a woman standing behind them. He knew he could kill them all with one burst but it was nearly impossible to be selective in your target with such a gun. Mr Pierce would have known what to do but it looked as though Mr Pierce wasn't going to be much of a help to anyone anymore. He waited for instructions from someone – anyone!

Slowly, Phil went and stood behind Sir Reginald's chair.

'You've got a problem, young man, haven't you?' said Phil. 'I saw those guns in action during the Chaos and if you shoot me, you'll almost certainly kill your boss as well. So what are you going to do? Shirley, get behind Arabella.'

Shirley followed his instruction and the guard tensed a little more.

'Shoot them, you bloody fool!' screamed Sir Reginald but the guard remained still.

'He's right, Sir Reginald – if I shoot, I might hit some or all of you. What should I do?'

'Throw your gun down here and stay where you are,' commanded Phil.

'Don't even think of carrying out an instruction from one of these two bastards. Shoot them, now!'

The guard hesitated and that gave Phil his chance. Slipping his hand into his pocket and gripping the gun he had taken from Mr Pierce earlier, he ducked down behind Sir Reginald's chair and took the gun out of his pocket. He hadn't got a clue how it worked but just hoped that Pierce was the kind of man who walked around on duty with the safety catch off!

He moved to the side of the chair, aimed the gun at the gallery and began to pull the trigger. Again there were screams and shouts but not from the guard – he had toppled over the rail on the gallery and landed with a thud on the floor of the room. Phil could tell from ten yards away that he was dead but he walked over and made sure. He turned round, faced the others and then threw Pierce's gun at one of the chandeliers, breaking it into tiny shards of crystal.

'You bastards, all of you! Look what you've made me become – a fucking murderer. You and your fucking experiment. I hope you all rot in hell.'

Shirley went to him and put her arms around him but even she couldn't stop the sobs that wracked his body.

'Come on,' she said, 'we've got to get out now. Forget what happened – let's go and see if we can find that Scottish island.'

'You won't escape,' said Lord Nacton. 'The other guards will have been wakened by that shot and they'll be here in a minute. Your only option is to untie us and surrender.'

Phil pushed Shirley away from him and went over and put his face right into that of the 147th heir to the throne of England.

'Amos, I'm getting fucking sick and tired of your stupid bloody comments. If the other guards were going to come, they would have been here after matey shot his right arm off, so I think we can safely assume they are too far away to have heard the last shot. Therefore I reckon Shirley and I have a few minutes to tell you lot a few home truths. Let's start with a question to you, Reggie. When you gave the analogy about Gordon Brown and the Bank of England, what would have happened if he'd been told a load of old bollocks by the countries that already had the system in place? Suppose they'd falsified their figures and statistics to prove that the people would accept the change whereas in reality the people were all pissed off about the whole thing. What would have happened to the export credits, the favours and the audiences with Her Majesty?'

'They wouldn't have happened, I suppose,' said Sir Reginald, going red in the face.

'No, they wouldn't and I bet our Chancellor and the government of the day would have let it be known to other countries who it was that had given them this load of shit. Am I right?'

'I suppose so – but what's your point?'

'My point, Sir Reginald bloody Corcoran, is that that's what you are doing with the figures from your fucking experiment. You're falsifying the statistics, Reggie, and one day someone is going to tell the rest of the world.'

'We're doing no such thing. We keep a careful record of everything that goes on in the town and everyone will be able to inspect all the figures when it's all over.'

'I didn't accuse you of not keeping records, Reggie – I accused you of falsifying them.'

'Why would we do that? It doesn't make sense.'

'It would make sense if you knew that by publishing the real figures no other government in the world would be at all interested in your experiment or its results. They'd know that the cost would be too high to implement such a policy in their own countries. Let me turn to you, Lady Corcoran. A minute ago, you said that 500 people had died in the town – where did you get that figure from?'

'It's the figure quoted in all the papers and my husband gave the figure of 502 when he answered a question in Parliament. Mostly from the plague – about 450, I think – and the rest in civil disturbances.'

'You're an innocent, gullible woman, Mrs Corcoran. There was no plague – that was a spurious lie, invented by your husband and 555 to get the experiment started. But that's not important now – what we need to look at is the mathematics involved; let's see if you can help me with regards to that. Three and a half years ago the town boasted 35,000 people – at least that was what the last census said, which had been done two years previously. I would say that the town now, today, has no more than 3,000 people living there and that is probably an overestimate. So the population has gone down from 35,000 to 3,000 in three years. That makes a difference of 32,000 people and if we take off the 500 who have died, according to your husband, we're left with a missing 31,500 people! Where have they gone? They haven't come to live in your house and they don't all lodge with Amos. Where are they?'

'That's easy, Mr King – they've all been rehoused and resettled in different parts of the country.'

'Do you know where these people are? Have you visited any

of them? Has anybody visited them?'

'They were promised anonymity, Mr King – they didn't want their neighbours to know that they came from a town that had the plague.'

'Were they given new names and new identities?'

'I presume so – why is this so important to you? Do you want to search for your wife and children? I'm sure my husband could find the new name and address for you – they're all in the records.'

'Shut up, Miranda – you don't know what you're saying. Look here, you two, you'd best be on your way if you want to escape. It'll be light soon.' Sir Reginald's face was now a deep red colour and he was sweating profusely.

'What's the matter, Reginald? You look as if you're having a heart attack.'

'There's nothing the matter with me. I'm all right – I just want these two to go.'

Phil leaned a little closer to Lady Corcoran and spoke in a soft voice.

'Do you know why he wants us to go, Miranda? He's not worried that he might have a heart attack – he's worried you might kill him yourself when I tell you what I know.'

'What on earth could you possibly know, Mr King, that would make me want to kill my husband?'

'It would be a waste of time for me to go looking for my family. They're all dead. They died in somewhere called Centre 3 on the first Saturday, when the town was closed off from the outside world. It's no use Shirley looking for her husband – he was shot dead by a firing squad two hours after he was arrested. In fact, Lady Corcoran, it would be futile to look for any of the 31,500 people who have gone missing from the town – they are all dead! The "new identities" are a sham. Your husband and his cronies realised pretty early on that they wouldn't be able to let anyone out of the town alive and they didn't! This is the simple truth about your husband's experiment – at its best, it is mass murder to prove a political point. At its worst, it is a form of genocide so that your husband's government can earn some extra money!'

'How do you know all this?' asked the sobbing Lady Corcoran.

'I spoke to the widow of the man whose job it was to make up the false records. All the official records were destroyed when the military compound was blown up the other night but Corporal Robson was a bit of a bastard, with his eye on the main chance. He wanted to see who would come out on top after the experiment and he made copies of all the false records – I suppose he would have used them for blackmail or to save his own skin, as evidence in a court of law. When I first heard about Corporal Robson, I thought he was something to do with Members of Parliament – answering their queries and such – but I made a mistake when thinking about what the letters "MP" stood for. They also stand for "Missing Persons" and that was Robson's job. He sat in his sad little hut in the compound, and, hour after hour and day after day, gave the 31,500 murdered people fictitious new identities. His widow said he used telephone directories and voters' lists to mix and match names and addresses. The records were meticulous and detailed but they were all false – a load of old bollocks!'

'Is this true, Reginald?' asked Mary.

'Good God, man – what have you been doing?' asked Lord Nacton. 'I never agreed to any of this – you killed them all?'

Phil realised they hadn't known – he could tell by the looks on their faces. Playing their parts, as old Amos and Mary, had been fun but this had never been in the script! He was also sure that Lady Corcoran didn't know about her husband's secret, but it was her daughter, Arabella, who spoke next.

'What does it matter? No one will ever know. I'll have his widow brought in for questioning tomorrow and we'll find these duplicate records. Don't worry, Daddy – it'll be all right.'

'You're too late, Arabella,' said Phil, 'the records have already gone and so has the widow, Doreen Robson. The guards have internet access in their quarters and Doreen Robson e-mailed the records to every newspaper in the world the other night – I suspect at least one of them might be doing some checking of names and addresses by now! Doreen said she was going to leave as soon as she had finished speaking to me – her late husband's colleagues were very sympathetic and had offered to drive her to the station.'

It was Lady Corcoran who spoke next.

'Mr King – go now. Take Mrs Tate with you and leave us to our shame. I don't think we can be of much help but you may have a chance under the cover of darkness.'

'Not much of a chance without some insurance,' said Phil. 'We'll take your daughter and your husband with us, just in case we meet any guards.'

'You're welcome to the pair of them – at least it will get them out of my sight.'

Phil and Shirley undid the cords on the chairs of their two hostages and then retied them in a standing position. They gagged them both and found more cord to tie their hands behind their backs. Phil retrieved the gun from where it had fallen after he smashed the chandelier and Shirley picked up the automatic rifle by the guard's body.

'Do you know how to use that?' asked Phil.

'I got my AK47 badge in the Brownies.'

'Love you.'

'Love you too, Mr Bond.'

'Let's do it, Pinky.'

'Let's, for Karen and Edward and Billy and all the rest of them.'

They went out into the hallway, pushing Sir Reginald and Arabella before them in case any other guards had woken. There was nobody there and they slowly started to walk towards the front of the house.

'Phil, when you said "let's do it" back there – what did you actually mean? Do what?'

'Escape!'

'How? Wouldn't it be better if we went back the way we came in? At least we know we can get out that way. I don't see the point of coming along here. We might meet some more guards – and even if we don't, which door are we going to use?'

'We're going to use the front door,' said Phil. 'I'm fed up with sewers, storm drains and dried-up riverbeds. We've nothing to be ashamed of so we don't need to crawl away like a couple of criminals. We'll leave with our heads held high!'

'You've gone fucking mad,' said Shirley. 'Let's go back – we might have a chance out the back way – this is suicide!'

'I know,' replied Phil. He took the time to shove Sir Reginald against the wall and then turned to face the woman he loved. 'We have no other choice, Shirley. Wherever we go they'll find us – what kind of life would we have, looking over our shoulders all the time? Look, if you want to go back and try to escape through the old wine cellar, go – take Arabella – but I'm going this way.'

'Don't be so bloody stupid! What if I did mange to escape that way? What would be the point without you? I'm not spending the rest of my life with fucking Arabella. I've told you before – I go where you go. The front door it is.'

Shirley led the way down the hallway, keeping Arabella in front of her. When they reached the corner, where the hallway turned along the front of the house, they stopped and Shirley peered round. The hallway became twice as wide but otherwise it continued as before, except there were no rooms on their left. The hallway had huge windows, which overlooked the start of the grounds and the ornamental gardens. There were no curtains and Phil and Shirley could see the beginning of the Suffolk dawn as the sun struggled into the eastern sky.

They walked in the silence of the great old house. Arabella and Sir Reginald didn't put up much resistance to being pushed along and, the one time that she did, Shirley gave Arabella a smack across the face and told her to behave herself.

Sir Reginald looked like a beaten man and shuffled along the hallway with his head down. He gave Phil no trouble whatsoever and all four of them soon reached the exact centre of the front hallway. Phil and Shirley stood in wonder at the scene before them.

The entrance hall soared above them with two white marble staircases leading to the upper floors. There were more paintings here but the most impressive items were a collection of marble busts. Set on plinths, raising them to shoulder height, the sculptures were of old Roman Emperors. Phil wandered round the black and white tiled floor looking at the various great men of the past. He took the gag out of Sir Reginald's mouth.

'Their empire didn't last, Reggie, and their foundations had a bit more substance than yours! I pity you because you think what you're doing matters – it doesn't! In a thousand years, or less, nobody will remember the name of Sir Reginald Corcoran – I'm glad about that! We've got to leave you now. Don't worry, I'm not going to kill you – I'll leave that job to your friends and family. Do you want to say anything before we go? But keep your voice down – I'd hate to deprive your friends and family of the pleasure.'

'You'll never get away – we'll hunt you down. And don't pity me! I have no regrets – the experiment will be seen to be a great success. People must be controlled—'

Phil replaced the gag – he couldn't bear to listen to any more of this madman's ramblings!

'Anything you want to say, Shirley, before we go out in a blaze of glory?'

Shirley looked at Sir Reginald and Arabella and shook her head.

'I've nothing to say to these two pair of bastards but I would like to ask a question to you.'

'Go on, ask away,' said Phil.

'Can I give them both a fucking good kicking before we leave?'

'Why?'

'It'll make me feel better. They've not suffered enough for what they've done. They still live in this wonderful house and will probably go on living here for years to come. Where's the justice going to come from? They'll talk their way out of it all. You know they will – people like them always do!'

Sir Reginald and Arabella were staring at her with fear in their eyes. Arabella was trying to speak but she was still gagged.

'All right, young lady,' said Shirley. 'I'll take the gag off and you can have your say but, like Phil said, whispers are the name of the game!'

'That's not justice, you stupid, bloody woman – that's revenge. Daddy and I have done nothing wrong – we were carrying out the express wishes of the parliament of this country. You can't just kick us to death!'

'Why not?' asked Shirley. 'Give me one good reason why I shouldn't, because I can give you three good reasons why I should! Their names were Geoff, Penny and Polly!'

'Their deaths were unfortunate but we've all suffered—'

Shirley replaced the gag and looked at Phil.

'Unfortunate – did you hear that? Fucking unfortunate – does that mean fucking unlucky?'

She grabbed Arabella by the throat and squeezed tight.

'Leave it, Shirley,' said Phil. 'They're not worth bothering about. Come on, it's time we weren't here.'

Shirley relaxed her grip and Arabella began to breathe again. The two unnecessary hostages were told to sit on the floor and Shirley and Phil threw their guns down the hallway. The sun had now risen and an insipid daylight filled the entrance. Phil walked to the front doors and pulled them open. It was cold outside and the inrushing clean air refreshed him. He looked around the entrance hall, took Shirley in his arms and held her tight when suddenly a thought came into his head from seemingly nowhere.

Thirty-One

When Sir John Thynne built Longleat House in Wiltshire, one of the startling innovations he introduced was a series of small square rooms on the roof to serve as 'banketting houses'. In the sixteenth century, 'banquet' meant 'dessert' and, after dinner, Sir John and his guests would stroll up to the roof for a final glass of wine, to watch the sun go down behind the Mendip Hills.

His apprentice designer and architect, Robert Smythson, was so taken with the idea of these rooftop pavilions that when he came to build Nacton Manor, he insisted that the house had something similar and two such rooms were built on the roof of the Suffolk house. The pavilions were never used for after-dinner drinks as intended but some of the Nacton family had used them over the years for growing plants and the 15th Earl had used one as an observatory. They were still in good repair and the one on the corner of the west wing had been used constantly during the last three years as an observation post.

During daylight hours it was manned continually by guards from the house, who could see for miles in any direction and warn their colleagues in enough time if trouble was seen to be approaching the house or its inner gardens.

At night, the guards gave way to a solitary man, who was still a mystery after three years. He slept during the day and ate his meals alone. No one could remember his speaking a word during those three years and his colleagues now regarded him as just part of the furniture of the house. Every night he sat in the west pavilion and guarded Nacton Manor.

There was a subtle difference, though, between this man and the daytime guards. Whereas they were ordered to relay any problems to their superior downstairs, he told no one what he saw.

He had orders to shoot dead anyone within a hundred yards of the House. He was a trained marksman – the best – and he worked for 555.

His name was Jeremiah Baldeagle.

Mr Pierce had been right – the eagle was in the pavilion, as usual.

Clear River Bald Eagle (which was his birth name) was born in 1975 in South Dakota and could trace his lineage right back to Sitting Bull, the great chief of the Sioux nation. He was one of seven children and he had been hungry from the moment he started to breathe outside his mother's womb. His father, like many of his generation, was a drunk and hardly figured at all in his son's upbringing. His mother wanted the best for all her children and that meant their leaving the family home as soon as possible. When he was eight years old, Clear River was sent to a Baptist school a hundred miles from his family home and taken in by the well-intentioned religious fanatics that ran Wellington Baptist College. They gave him the name of Jeremiah and taught him to read the Bible every day, and very little else.

When it was time for him to leave the college at the age of fifteen, he couldn't remember where his home was – he had never been back there and no one had visited him and so it seemed sensible to join the army. He was a big strong lad and was always fighting, usually to avenge some derogatory remark from his fellow soldiers about 'Indians' and the Sioux in particular. He made little progress up the career ladder and was only a corporal when he left at the age of thirty. He entered the job market with only two attributes: an encyclopaedic knowledge of what is said in the Bible, without knowing what any of it meant, and the ability to hit anything with a sniper's rifle up to a range of 1,000 yards. He was perfect for recruitment to 555 and he joined that organisation two weeks after he abandoned the military life.

He knew absolutely nothing about the organisation he worked for. They had looked after him from the first day of his recruitment and he had repaid them handsomely. He had forgotten how many people he had killed all over the world but it never troubled him and he lived at peace with himself. The organisation took charge of all his travel and accommodation requirements and if he wanted a woman it supplied one of those as well. The accommodation was always five-star and the travel first-class. His gun was always waiting for him on arrival, together with the instructions of when and where an assassination should take place. He had never missed.

Four years before, he had been in Venice and shot dead an Italian banker as he had been leaving St Mark's Square. The mission had been a complete success but 555 started to hear rumours from its many contacts around the world that people were beginning to talk about an American Indian who travelled the world acting as a contract killer. 555 didn't want to lose the asset it had and so decided to put him into cold storage for a while. Jeremiah was sent to Nacton Manor as its last line of defence and for the past three years had sat in his pavilion every night ready to shoot any intruders.

Jeremiah didn't mind – it was all the same to him. He was well fed and during the day he had time to reread his Bible.

He had only used the rifle, which stood at his side now, ready for action – he cleaned it every day – once before. Three men had approached the house from the north-west, carrying some things on their shoulders but as soon as they crossed the notional line of one hundred yards from the house, he had shot all three of them dead. He had heard talk the next day from the guards who came to the pavilion to relieve him that the men had been poachers but he didn't know what the word meant and never thought about the incident again.

Jeremiah Baldeagle scanned the grounds of the house as the dawn arrived and picked up his rifle.

Two people, a man and a woman, were making their way along the main drive. They were walking away from the house, which was strange, and they were holding hands, but to Jeremiah orders were orders. The man and woman were within one hundred yards of the house and it wasn't his job to make decisions.

He aimed the rifle at the back of the woman's head and gently pulled the trigger. She fell like a stone and never moved again.

Jeremiah waited for the man's reaction. The man began to shout and curse and wave his arms about and then sank to his knees beside the woman. He took her in his arms and cradled her head. He was still screaming.

Jeremiah took aim again and put a bullet into the side of his neck. The man slumped forward and fell beside the woman. The man reached out with his arm, took the woman's hand in his and lay still.

Jeremiah replaced the gun against the wall, sat back in his chair and waited for the three guards to arrive to replace him. When they did, he returned to his bedroom in the west wing, read a few verses of his Bible and slept for eight hours.

Epilogue

Sergeant Bill Harris and Private Charlie Rowlands were just beginning their shift at Military Headquarters on that February morning when they were summoned to the Colonel's office. The men were cooks and were looking forward to the end of their time at HQ. Their six months were nearly up and they couldn't wait to rejoin their regular units in other parts of the country. This place in Suffolk was a pain in the arse – no leave, no straying off base, no time off whatsoever.

They entered the Colonel's office, thinking that he must have some important visitors coming for lunch and wanted to change the menu but it was not food the Colonel wished to talk about.

The Colonel was small and dumpy and he tried to sit on his padded chair behind his desk as much as possible so any visitors wouldn't notice his lack of stature. This morning was different – he was standing by the window of the room when the two cooks marched in and saluted.

'At ease, men. I'm afraid we have a slight problem and a shortage of manpower. As you probably know, every available man is on duty in the town trying to bring the latest round of civilian unrest under control, and so I have to ask you two men to do a little job for me. It would appear that two terrorists managed to enter Nacton Manor last night and cause something of a problem. There was no loss of life to any of the inhabitants of the house – thank God – and the terrorists were shot dead when they tried to escape but there's a bit of clearing up to do. You need not worry yourselves about the house itself – that will all be taken care of by the resident staff – but the two bodies are lying on the drive near to the house. I want you two men to go and pick them up and bring them back here for identification and whatever else is necessary. All right?'

'There is a slight problem, sir,' said Sergeant Harris.

'What's that?'

'There's no transport, sir. After the compound was blown up the other night, trucks and jeeps have been in short supply to say the least, and the few that are still road-worthy are all out in the town at the moment dealing with the disturbances.'

'Isn't there anything you could use?'

'Well, there's the old open truck that's used to take old Amos to the Border every day but it's full of rotten vegetables because Amos didn't turn up today.'

'That'll do – they're only the dead bodies of a couple of terrorists. Use that and get a move on. I don't want anyone at the house having to look at such things.'

Both men saluted, turned and marched smartly out of the office. The truck was behind the cook-house door and the two men got in, with Charlie Rowlands behind the wheel. He started it up and slammed it into first gear.

It wasn't a long journey but both men were grateful to be out of HQ for the first time since they had been posted there.

They lit a cigarette each and looked at the Suffolk countryside.

'Do you reckon it's them two that we've had all the leaflets about in the last few days, Serge?'

'Fuck knows. No, it can't be them two. They said that they had escaped from the town – how the hell could they have made it out here from the town? Our lads would have picked them up before they got anywhere near the Manor.'

'I suppose so,' said Charlie. 'Still the leaflet said they were dangerous and resourceful – whatever the fuck that means.'

'It means they were cunning bastards, Charlie – like all terrorists. But they're dead now so who gives a shit? Anyway, our lads had full descriptions of them so they would have spotted them.'

The truck came to a halt at the main gate of the Manor and Sergeant Harris explained to the guard their business. He waved them through and they made their way down the mile-long drive that separated the Manor from the road.

They eventually went round a bend and got their first view of the historic old house.

'Fucking hell!' said Charlie.

'A bit like your mum's house, is it, Charlie?'

'My mum wouldn't be seen dead in an old place like that – she loves her new council flat.'

'They could make that place into a few council flats, couldn't they? Steady now, slow down – I think I can see what we've come for just ahead of us. Pull on to the grass by the side of them and reverse so we can drive straight out. But make sure you get close because I don't fancy carrying the bloody things too far!'

Charlie obeyed the orders from his sergeant and brought the truck to rest a few feet from the bodies. They got out and went round the back to have a look.

'Jesus,' said Bill Harris. 'I thought that smell was from the dead bodies but it's them fucking vegetables in the back of the truck.'

'It doesn't seem right to throw their bodies on top of that lot – no matter what they've done.'

'Fuck off, Charlie – they're terrorists. A load of stinking vegetables is probably more than they deserve to carry them to their graves. Come on, let's get the bastards on board and get out of here.'

It didn't take long for the two men to throw the bodies on top of the putrid pile of cabbages and turnips.

They got back into the cab and lit another cigarette each to try and get rid of the smell.

'Fucking strange,' said Charlie.

'What is?'

'Terrorists dressed up as though they were going to a ball or something. She was a bloody good-looking woman in that black dress and he was wearing a dinner suit that didn't look cheap.'

Sergeant Harris thought for a moment and wondered what Charlie was going on about.

'It could have been them two from the town,' said Charlie.

'Why?'

'Our lads would never have picked them up. The descriptions in the leaflets were all wrong.'

'What do you mean?' asked Sergeant Harris, getting bored with the conversation.

'Well, the leaflet said that the woman had blonde hair and the man had dark hair. Those daft bastards at HQ got it the wrong way round! Our lads didn't have the right descriptions so they could have got through from the town to here.'

'What are you talking about, Charlie?'

'The two we just threw on the truck; the woman had black hair – matched her dress actually – and the man had a full head of blonde hair down to his shoulders. I reckon it was the two who escaped from the town.'

'Just drive the fucking truck, Charlie,' said Sergeant Harris.

Printed in the United Kingdom by
Lightning Source UK Ltd., Milton Keynes
140739UK00001B/15/P